See No

Book One Of

The Society Series

By

Ivy Fox

COPYRIGHT

See No Evil – The Society
Copyright © 2020 Ivy Fox

Editing by Heather Clark
Cover photo courtesy of Michelle Lancaster –
www.michellelancaster.com / @lanefotograf
Cover model – Lochie Carey
Cover design, formatting, and edit courtesy of
https://www.facebook.com/pg/X.Factory.Designs

For more information, visit:

https://www.facebook.com/IvyFoxAuthor

https://ivyfoxauthor.wixsite.com/ivyfox

ISBN: 9798638371333

TABLE OF CONTENTS

DEDICATION

To the strong women who every day make their neck of the woods their bitch... You got this.

See No Evil Playlist

The Society

Listen to the full playlist on Spotify (search: See No Evil - The Society Book One)

"Seven Devils" by Florence + The Machine

"Paint it, Black" by Ciara

"Monsters" by Ruelle

"One Way or Another" by Until The Ribbon Breaks

"Paranoid" by Post Malone

"Royals" by Lorde

"So Thick" by Whipped Cream featuring Baby Goth

"Sweet But Psycho" by Parker Jenkins

"My Blood" by Twenty One Pilots

"Candy" by Guccihighwaters

"Birthday Cake" by Rihanna

"Horns" by Bryce Fox

"No One" by Mothica

"All The Time" by Jeremih, Lil Wayne and Natasha Mosley

"I Wanna Be Yours" by Arctic Monkeys

"Monster" by Meg Myers

"Soldier" by Fleurie

"Fuck It I Love You" by Lana Del Rey

"Kill Our Way to Heaven" by Michl

"Sweet Dreams" by Emily Browning

"Everybody Wants to Rule The World" by Lorde

Epigraph

"It is a man's own mind, not his enemy or foe, that lures him to evil ways."

— Gautama Buddha

PROLOGUE

The sun beats down on my back, scorching its way through the rich, dark fabric of my clothes, the unyielding heat turning this day even more relentless. No one bothered telling the North Carolina sun that it's still May, and this heatwave that is so intent on lashing out on us is uncalled for. Even though it's technically still spring, there isn't a hint of a breeze in the air to give us any comfort. Just the blazing sun overhead, making this despicable affair that much more insufferable.

The somber crowd curses the rising temperature, shifting from left to right in their restlessness and sweat. Some go as far as using umbrellas to provide some shade in the hopes it will cool them down, while others just suffer the sun's punishment and stew in their discomfort in silence.

My nose twitches in disgust, but it has little to do with the stench of body odor in the air and more to do with the scene in front of me. My revulsion to this charade is potent, yet my sorrowful frown is stitched in place, mimicking everyone else's expression to a fault.

Fucking fakes, the lot of them. With their false tears and wet, stained handkerchiefs.

However, it's not the mourning crowd that has my blood boiling. It's the men standing side-by-side in front of the polished caskets who deserve my utter contempt. I look at all four of them, appearing forlorn in their grief as if they weren't the the reason why we had to bury two of Asheville's most esteemed inhabitants today. Their fabricated act is impeccable, making everyone here join in their misery. It sickens me how well they play their part in this abhorring sham, pretending to be heartbroken rather than admitting it's because of them that these two bodies are meeting their final resting place.

The preacher continues with his rant, while the mourners' soft, lamenting wails give his words that extra pitch of melancholy. I feel my nose flair in loathing, and I have to bite my inner cheek to prevent me from scoffing at the ridiculous words being uttered by the clergyman.

"For as much as it hath pleased Almighty God, it is of his great mercy to take unto himself the soul of our dear brother and sweet sister here departed. We, therefore, commit their bodies to the ground as our Lord intended. Earth to earth, ashes to ashes, dust to dust."

Earth to earth, ashes to ashes, dust to dust.

Right.

Some of us aren't made of the same substance. Some of us were born and molded in lies, betrayals, and hate. My eyes lock, yet again, on the subjects of my disdain, knowing they are proof that we are not all born equal, nor should we leave this earth in the same way we entered it. And if the Almighty is too busy to deal with their pesky souls, then a vengeful, earthbound hand should guarantee their fate.

I clench my fist beside me as I watch them.

They think they've gotten away with it.

That no one is aware of their scheming ways.

But I know.

I know it all.

Not just what occurred on that fatal night, but also how their lives are nothing but well-fabricated tales that portray an immaculate exterior and conceal the corruption within. They think they rule the world, but their time is over. One by one, I'll tear them apart and make them pay for their arrogance.

I repress the sinister smile that begs to tug at my lips, knowing exactly who I'll play with first. My choice might be obvious, but it still gives me a sick satisfaction by starting off with the weakest link in their twisted quartet. The one who thinks himself invincible, with no vulnerabilities for anyone to exploit—Finn Walker.

I discreetly observe him running his fingers through his wavy blond hair, looking like the quarterback god he is, even though at this moment he is miles away from any football field. Not one tear falls down his passive face, yet his deep-blue eyes are pensively locked to the two coffins in front of him. To everyone gathered around, they'd think he has nerves of steel under such depressing circumstances. They don't realize that the trail of sweat trickling down Finn's neck isn't from the blazing heat, but from an emotion no one would ever dream of him having—fear.

He should be afraid.

Very afraid.

They all should be.

My examining eye leaves Finn's stoic pretense only to land on the six-foot-three, toned, shrewd frame of the friend at his side—Easton Price. In his preferred black gear, he looks like the majestic, dark prince he believes himself to be, but lacks the usual bored expression on his face. Today, he's just a blank canvas, hoping no one can see past his facade and read the turmoil running through his wretched soul.

But I see you. Don't I?

You can't hide from me, Easton.

None of you can.

Right next to him, dressed to the nines, as if he's just stepped out of his house for a Vogue photo shoot, stands the most vicious of the group—Colt Turner. I see, however, that instead of the relaxed swagger he's known for, his spine is ramrod straight, and his shoulders are stiff as a board. His cocky grin—the one that always seems to make him look so regal as if he owned the fucking place—is wiped off his face, too.

Good.

That grin should have never crested his lips, to begin with. He might have had a silver spoon in his mouth since the day he was born, but at this moment he looks like he's being force-fed something too bitter and rancid to swallow down. It's making him twist and contort his face into something ugly, just like his damned soul.

Not looking so fucking royal now, are you, Colt?

What happened? Did your conscience finally get the best of you?

Do you even have one?

He's standing there, trying so hard to hide his true self, but I know exactly what type of filth runs through his veins. Just like the rest of them, he's a waste of space.

But you're not even the worst of them, are you, Colt?

Nah. Not even by a long shot.

That place on the podium goes to his cousin, and Asheville's golden boy—Lincoln Hamilton. He's the real wolf in sheep's clothing. He looks like a damned choir boy when, in reality, he's just as hideous as we all are. Yet here he is, solemn and teary-eyed, as we all stand back and watch his parents being laid to rest. The fucker is the reason they are now worm food, yet he has the audacity to look torn.

But unlike the others, that isn't a ploy, is it Lincoln?

He is torn up inside for what he's done, for what he allowed to happen right inside his own home. Through whispers in the night and plans cunningly crafted in the shadows, he convinced himself and his fucking lackeys that no one would ever be the wiser of their crime.

And that makes you the most arrogant asshole of them all.

I know exactly what happened. He might think he can fool the whole world, but he'll never fool me. He never has.

I know the real you, Lincoln. The dark and ugly part of you.

I know all his fears and aspirations. I know his secret desires and forbidden cravings. His Adonis looks and well-mannered, serpent tongue might deceive everyone he comes in contact with, but I never fell for his charms. And because of that, I'll leave him for last.

You will be the one I will toy with the most. I'll take pleasure in watching you squirm.

You stole something from me, and yet, you still want more.

But I won't let that happen.

The day blood ran through his hands, he made himself vulnerable and weak. I'll exploit that weakness to its fullest extent, making sure that my sweet vengeance is the only thing coming his way.

Do they honestly believe this is over? Do they really think that by burying the proof of their wrongdoings and their ruthlessness, no one will come after them?

You're so fucking wrong.

You will all pay dearly for it.

I'll make sure of it.

I'll give them enough time to develop a false sense of security. Just enough to ensure they'll never expect the threat lurking in the corner. Then I'm going to enjoy every flinch, every cringe, and all the times they'll nervously watch over their shoulders, wondering if that's when I'll strike. I won't just make their poor existence a nightmare, but I'll make sure that everything they do from here on out will be for my own personal gain. Stack the cards in my favor for once.

Benjamin Franklin was right after all—three can keep a secret if two of them are dead.

If it were only Lincoln left standing, then maybe I would have shown mercy to the friends at his side. Maybe. But he dragged them into this mess, so I'm more than happy to hand out their punishment to each one of them individually.

They should have done a better job of concealing their crime, but most of all, they should have recognized one irrevocable truth—secrets don't stay buried for long. I always knew their insolence was going to be their downfall. They should have watched their backs, but because they haven't, they will now be looking behind it every second of every day until I finally end them. Once and for all.

This isn't just your victims' funeral.

It's also yours.

You fucked up, and because I'm just like you, I won't be taking any prisoners either.

Before the end comes, they'll be wishing we never crossed paths. They'll curse the day they met me and tried to take what's mine. Now I'll make them all pay for what they've done.

Trust me. It's not going to be pretty. I promise you that.

The mournful crowd begins to disperse, selfishly interrupting my contemplation and bringing my thoughts back to the current matter at hand. All the pretty words have been said, and every last useless goodbye has been uttered, it seems. Now that this deplorable scene has finally come to an end, I decide to move my first pawn into place and start my glorious chess game.

I slowly make my way over to the one man who will become my biggest triumph once I bring him to his knees. I tenderly place my hand over his shoulder, making him spin his head toward me. Lincoln stares into my eyes and relaxes the minute he recognizes a friend at his side. I offer him my own reassuring smile, squeezing his shoulder as he covers my hand with his own, grateful for my offered solace.

Such a pretentious fool.

This is one of your biggest flaws, Lincoln. I never once saw you as a friend, only as a threat. To me, you've always been my sworn enemy, but you were just too self-centered to notice. Now the joke is on you because I'm the one who is going to shoot first. I'll make you bleed. Bleed just like you made them.

So, enjoy your summer, boys.

You won't know what hit you once I'm done.

They've all signed their death warrants unknowingly. And the best part will be to witness their shocked faces when they see it was me who pulled the trigger and carried out their sentences.

Such a pity they'll never even see the threat coming.

And too bad for them, *I'm* already here.

CHAPTER 1

FINN

I park my Porsche in front of the opulent mansion, but instead of getting out of the car and rushing in as I've done for most of my life, I stay frozen still in my seat, gripping the steering wheel while trying hard to ignore the tightening of my chest.

It astounds me how a place that once held so much joy now fills me with dread. I've spent Christmases and New Years here. I played football on this very lawn while waiting for Thanksgiving dinners to be served, and during the madness of Fourth of July cookouts. I've stayed over more times than I can count, making me more like family than anything else. But for the life of me, this is the last place I want to be at.

I mean, it's only natural, right?

I'm not a monster for not wanting to step foot inside the home that used to hold most of my favorite childhood recollections when none can compare to the last horrid memory it gave me.

But I guess what they say is true—a criminal always returns to the scene of the crime whether he wants to or not.

I shake my head, trying to avoid these thoughts that have been tormenting me for the past three months. Instead, I pick up my phone and pretend to fiddle on it just in case Lincoln can see me parked here from inside his house. Although, common sense tells me that Lincoln Hamilton has more pressing demons to face then waste his time gawking through a window at the scenery of his driveway. Still, I keep up my moronic pretense, hoping to gain some time for me just to man the fuck up and knock on my best friend's door.

"Shit!" I mumble, aggravated for being such a fucking pussy.

But, fuck, it's not like this shit comes with an instruction manual on what's the best protocol to use with your accomplices. I haven't seen Lincoln all summer, so who knows what fucking mess I'm going to encounter. Last night when he sent me a text, asking me to be here at first light, every fiber of my being wanted to pretend I didn't see it, just so I could have another day without having to face him or the repercussions of what transpired here.

I don't do feelings right.

I never have.

Touchy-feely shit is just not my thing, so I'm not exactly ecstatic for putting myself in a situation where I have to be someone's support system. I mean, I suck at it. I'm not *that* guy. I might look all approachable and shit, with my light eyes and messy blond hair giving me that homecoming-king vibe, but five minutes in my presence, and everyone knows I'm a fucking insensitive prick.

I don't hide it either.

Why would I?

I have no one to impress but myself.

But when life gets real, and I'm expected to talk about feelings and shit, I almost break out in hives. I don't do heavy. The only weight I can deal with is clashing against the adversaries on the football field. Or better yet, when I have a hundred-pound jersey chaser on my lap, getting me off after a win. That's as heavy as I'm willing to go.

Call me shallow.

Call me crass.

I don't give a fuck.

But this is different. This is a whole other level of a clusterfuck. Worst of all, this is Linc, my best friend since we were in diapers, for crying out loud. I know the asshole needs me, needs all of us. Not only for support but also to keep our fucking mouths shut or face the consequences. And no way is that even an option. I'm too fucking pretty to go to jail. I'd be a hot commodity in the big house. Not exactly the kind of assplay I'm down with. Not judging or anything, but I like firm, hairless, peach asses in my grip, not the other way around.

"Shit!" I grunt again under my breath, this time throwing my phone on the passenger seat.

What if Linc wants to talk? What if he expects to hash out what happened that night? What if he's having second thoughts and wants to go to the police?

"SHIT! SHIT! SHIT!"

I punch my steering wheel twice with my clenched fists, my frustration getting the better of me. This is so fucked up. Our lives did a one-eighty with just a mere snap of a finger. Because of one lousy night, our futures are now left hanging by a thread. I spent all summer in fucking denial, just so I didn't imagine all the ways this one macabre incident could end up ruining and uprooting our lives so completely.

So mercilessly.

But it already did. It happened, and as much as I try to ignore it, there is no way around what we've done. And as a result, my best friend became an orphan.

Hmm.

Can you still be considered an orphan at twenty-two? I mean, technically he's a grown-ass man. The orphan title always reminds me of those old movies Grandma had playing on her TV when I was a kid. Especially the one with the curly, red-haired girl that, for some reason, always felt the need to break out in song when she was getting herself in all sorts of trouble. What was her name? It's on the tip of my tongue. What was it?

Fuck it.

It doesn't matter anyway. Lincoln is the one with no parents now. We buried them right at the end of our junior year. Going back to Richfield tomorrow and trying to finish college with that boulder on our shoulders is not going to be fun. Not one bit.

A pound on the hood of the car makes me jolt in my seat, throwing me back to the here and now. My heart drums hectically in alarm and only settles when familiar, devious, gray eyes stare back at me from the front of my car.

"You break it, you pay for it, motherfucker!" I yell at Easton, who just shrugs nonchalantly, unleashing his best cocky-ass smirk, as if I were one of his late-night booty calls, ready to be fucked on his doorstep.

I'd roll my eyes at the asshole if I weren't already so wound up from being here. I watch him lean back against the side of my car while lighting a cigarette, as if it were the coolest thing in the world, and not the cancerous instrument that is shortening his lifespan.

It's a filthy habit. And I'm not saying this just because I'm one of those jocks that believe their body is a temple or some nonsense like that, but because my intellect is very aware of all the lethal chemicals my friend insists on puffing into his lungs. Between the nicotine, tar, formaldehyde, and arsenic, Easton willingly inhales a cocktail of poison on a daily basis. And as much as I get on his case about it, he just blows me off as quickly as he does the toxic smoke from his lips.

Sensing my accusing glare, Easton smugly blows a string of puffy gray rings in the air. I must admit the bastard looks like a dark James Dean when he does that sweet trick like its second nature to him. Always looking bored with the mundane, and unapologetically closed off to the world and its lectures, a person would think that nothing gets under Easton's skin. Only the four of us know that's a fucking lie.

"Are you going to stay in your car all day long or what?" he asks, his eyes up to the heavens, watching the smoke disappear into thin air.

I hate it that he's capable of picking up on my hesitation without even looking at me. That's another thing about Easton Price—he reads people like most do magazines. He doesn't have to read the small print below each picture to know exactly what's going on. A quick glance your way, and he can pinpoint all your flaws and imperfections. A trait I usually envy, but right now, it's pissing me the hell off.

"Just need to send a text to my father," I lie, picking up my phone from the side seat and tapping away on the screen as if the text I'm pretending to send was so damn fucking important.

"No, you don't," he quips back unceremoniously, taking another long haul of his cancer stick.

His tone is even and sure. And like with everything else Easton does, he takes his time enunciating each word. It's almost as if the world decided to stop just to revolve around his inner clock, and everyone else would be wise to follow suit.

He's always been the dark horse in our little band of brothers. Sure, he comes from money as we all do, but if you didn't know his ripped-up jeans cost a few hundred, you'd think he bought them at a second-hand store. He probably would have—just to piss his stepfather off—if he wasn't a vain fuck.

East might like the rebel aura he puts out into the world, but he likes to look good even more. Girls at Richfield aren't known for fucking homeless-looking douches, but they will drop their panties in a hot minute when they realize you share the same surname with the bank their daddies deposit their weekly salaries in. Richard Price is Easton's real-life version of Daddy Warbucks. A truth that East resents but doesn't shy away from reaping the benefits of, either.

"Annie! That's the ginger's name!" I yell, slapping my forehead with the sudden realization.

"God, you're such a weird freak. Get out of the car, Finn. Stop stalling."

Instead of defending myself or sticking to my lie, I do as he demands and finally get out of the car. I keep my shades on because the blazing August sun is brutal on my light-blue eyes, even at this early hour. But mostly, I keep them because I can't deal with Easton's crap. They say the eyes are the windows to the soul, and in this moment, I'm not comfortable in letting any fucker see how tormented mine is. Not even East.

I walk over and lean next to him against the hood, turning my back to the large estate behind us that, at one time, felt like a second home to me.

"Didn't know you'd be here," I say, instead of the warm greeting that a friend would expect to receive after so many months apart.

"Well, that answers the question of whether you missed me at all this summer," he goads, knowing full well I'm not the kind of guy who goes all sentimental over anyone, even if the circumstances we've found ourselves in might call for it.

Easton lets out a soft laugh and nudges my shoulder with his, and it's enough to placate my nerves a smidge.

"Fuck off, you dick. I texted, didn't I? Not like we're dating or anything." I tease him, getting another low chuckle out of my best friend.

"Who are you kidding? Even if we were, you'd be too busy two-timing me with every short skirt Florida had to offer," he retorts amusingly, letting out one last puffy ring above our heads, before stomping the cigarette butt with his foot.

I laugh at the ridiculous comment, especially considering I was too busy over the summer to waste my time or even care about getting laid. But Easton doesn't have to know that.

"You jealous?" I cock my brow mockingly.

"Little bit. Summer in Asheville sucked balls. You could have lightened it up."

"When have I ever lightened anything up? I'm not particularly funny," I reply lightheartedly, trying to deflect the conversation from the reason why his vacation was a total buzzkill.

Easton could have gone anywhere in the world he wanted. He could have wasted his summer days lying on a Polynesian beach drinking mai tais or sipping sangria off the coast of Spain. He could have gone just about anywhere that tickled his fancy, but he stayed put just to make sure shit didn't hit the fan. He can be a dick like the rest of them, but he's loyal to a fault. And in our world, loyalty is a rare commodity.

"Anyway, that's always been more Colt's domain. He's the one who's the life of the party, not me," I add, desperate to move away from the topic I see playing around in his silver eyes.

"Yeah, well, that fucker went bumming through Europe all summer, so I couldn't count on him for any diversion. And while you at least texted, that asshole completely forgot he had a life back here. Not one fucking call or message," Easton announces, looking pissed our friend could shrug shit off so easily.

I understand why Easton might feel bitter at Colt's apathy, but that's just the way he's built. He's just as loyal as Easton is, even though he does act all aloof sometimes. Without question, I know where his loyalties lie—especially when it concerns his cousin Lincoln.

However, Colt has one quality we all lack. A virtue I wish we all could tap into. I might not be equipped to handle feelings right, but Colt can turn them off completely with a switch of a button. He can walk into a room and brighten it up with life and laughter, or he can just as easily walk away and not give two shits about you. He can make a person feel like they are walking on air, but if you're not careful, he can cast the cruelest of shadows that makes you shiver in his contempt. Trust me. No one wants to be around Colt when he's being a heartless dick. I might be an insensitive fucker, but Colt Turner can be arctic when he wants to be. Vindictive and sadistic in every imaginable way.

"Can you blame him?" I cross my arms over my chest, thinking Colt might just be the smartest out of all of us.

"No, not really. I guess it's just easier for some people to move past shit than it is for others," Easton explains, slumping his shoulders a bit, revealing the weight he's been carrying for the last few months.

"I don't think anyone is capable of moving past what we've done. Only try to keep it away from our minds as best we can," I admit, bowing my head and kicking the air at my feet.

"Is that what you did?" Easton questions, his whole body turning toward me.

I lift my head and take off my shades because I sense the asshole wants to have one of those touchy-feely moments I despise. I'm not such a dick that I won't at least give him, straight to his face, the honesty he deserves.

"Honestly? I tried to. But some shit is too hard to sweep under the rug and just pretend the big pile of crap isn't there. Know what I mean?"

"Tell me about it," he huffs out exasperated, running his hands through his unruly, jet-black hair.

"Have you seen him?" I finally ask, hoping Easton will be able to prepare me for the worst.

"You mean Linc?"

"Yeah."

"A bit. He didn't get out much, so I kind of had to come over and see if the fucker didn't blow his brains out like his daddy," he replies bitterly, but the ill joke falls flat on the concrete.

"That's not funny, asshole," I censure accusingly.

"It wasn't supposed to be. Just calling it like it is." He shrugs somberly, making the rocks that were lying on my chest fall to the pit of my stomach, thinking of how Lincoln may be worse than I imagined.

"That bad, huh?"

"It was in the beginning. It was fucking excruciating to watch him fall apart the way he did. But he's gotten better. Or at least he's trying. Kennedy helped."

"Bet she did." I sigh out, relieved.

Kennedy Ryland is probably the only person on God's green earth that could pull Lincoln from any dark hole he dug himself in. She's his beacon of light. Always has been, always will be.

"You know it's not like that, Finn. Her fiancé wouldn't like hearing you hinting that shit, either. Or her brother Jefferson. And don't even get me started on her fucking daddy. Don't let any of those fuckers hear you insinuate crap like that. Linc has his plate full enough as it is," Easton reprimands me immediately as if I announced to the world that Lincoln has it bad for the engaged girl who has been his best friend since he was five.

"Dude, chill, will you? I'm not an idiot. But come on, that engagement is bullshit, and you know it. Both the dean and her brother must know that the wedding is never going to happen. I mean, Kennedy Ryland getting hitched to Thomas Maxwell? What a fucking joke. I'd bet my left nut that Tommyboy is probably just as much into Linc as Kennedy is. You know she's just his fucking beard, and sooner or later, she'll come to her senses and call the whole thing off."

"Well, she hasn't yet, now has she?" Easton retorts.

"That's because Lincoln hasn't made his move. Friend-zoning her was the stupidest thing that fucker ever did," I blurt out unapologetically.

In hindsight, however, Linc keeping Kennedy at arm's length probably wasn't the worst thing he's ever done. If he kept her any closer, then she'd have the same blood on her hands as we have on ours.

Easton looks up at the sky, probably thinking the same thing I am, and the pregnant pause that ensues is killer to my nerves.

"One thing is for sure—Senator Maxwell won't be too happy to find out that his pride and joy likes sucking cock as much as his mistresses. Tommyboy should just fess up and get it over with instead of putting on this dog and pony show for his old man's benefit," I mumble, cracking my knuckles to fill the deafening silence.

"He's just doing what everyone expects of him. So is Kennedy," Easton defends, even though I know there's no love lost between him and the senator's son.

"Yeah, well, a lot of shit is expected of us, too. When does it become too much to deliver, huh? When do we reach a point that it's just better to wave the white flag and surrender?" I relent, my nerves finally getting the best of me.

"You don't, Finn. You just trudge on the best way you can. Surrendering is never an option. Only winning is," he deadpans, his gray eyes turning a shade darker, showing that he means business.

Easton's demeanor is also a reminder that thoughts, such as the ones I'm having, should stay far away from my head. It actually slaps some sense into me since the words he decided to throw are the ones he's heard spill from my lips countless times.

Yeah, surrendering really isn't an option. Not for us, at least.

"Is that the type of shit you've been struggling with all summer?" he asks point-blank. I give him a stiff nod, admitting my moments of weakness. "Well, it ends today. No more second-guessing and no more bullshit about waving the white flag. It's not only your ass on the line. Remember that."

I swallow dryly, but I stiffen my spine for him to see his words got through to me.

"You're right. I guess I've just been thinking too hard."

"Well, stop. I can see the fumes from here, and trust me, nothing good will come out of any one of us overthinking shit. Just let sleeping dogs lie," he rebukes steadfastly.

"Fine," I mumble, hating how I've somehow made Easton see me as being weak.

"And anyway, if push comes to shove and we do have to think things through, leave that shit for the pros, will you?" he says, pointing his thumbs to himself with a smug grin on his face.

I flip him the bird because he's being a cocky shit, as usual, which is enough for the tension between us to simmer down somewhat.

"It's good to see you, man. I honestly thought I wouldn't get the chance to hang out with you and the guys before returning to Richfield tomorrow," I admit, squeezing his shoulder.

"Linc sent me a text last night asking me to come over. If I knew you'd be coming, I might have blown him off," he taunts, widening his trademark grin.

This time I elbow the fucker in the stomach, making him yelp like a little pussy. His laughter outshines his discomfort from the gut punch, which leaves me feeling a bit better for being here.

"Yeah, Lincoln sent me a text, too. Do you think Colt's going to show up?" I ask, turning around to face the massive house that looks so eerily empty. I guess it's to be expected now, seeing as only one person inhabits it.

"Don't know, but I doubt it. You know Colt prefers to spend his Sunday mornings between the thighs of whoever he hooked up with the night before."

"I never did understand the fucker. He does the longest hit 'em and quit 'em I've ever seen," I joke playfully.

If I'm the crude asshole in this group, and Easton is the cool, collected prick, well, Colt is definitely the Romeo in our quartet. Guy gets more tail than anyone I have ever met. And the thing is, he doesn't even have to be sleazy about it. Women just flock to him like moths to a flame, and even after he gives them their walking papers, they still get starry-eyed when they see him again. It's the weirdest fucking thing since I know what a cold-blooded bastard he is.

"And that, my friend, is why the ladies love him and hate you. He gives them what they want while you only get what *you* want." Easton laughs, while my scowl deepens.

"You say that like it's a bad thing or something?" My question gets another howl from the friend beside me, increasing my confusion. "What?" I exclaim, not getting what's so funny.

So I'm a no-strings-attached kind of guy. What's wrong with that? I don't make any false promises, so I'm not a complete asshat. I make sure the girls I mess with have just as much fun as I do. I'm just not the kind of guy that cuddles afterward or spends the night faking interest in anything they have to say. I really don't see what the big deal is. I'm upfront right from the bat. Doesn't that deserve some recognition?

"Shit, what did I tell you about thinking too hard? You're giving yourself wrinkles, dude. Just stop. But if you're really interested in knowing the difference between you and Colt, just ask any girl you've been out with what they think of you, and then compare it to Colt's lays. You'll see that their answers are night and day," Easton jokes, finding my sex-life far too amusing for my liking.

"I don't give a fuck. So they hate me afterward—big fucking deal. Everyone knows I don't have time for chicks in my life," I defend stiffly.

"Just one-night stands with girls whose names you can't even remember during them, much less afterward," Easton mumbles under his breath.

"You know what? I take back what I said. I could have gone another day or two without seeing your know-it-all face. And, again, I don't see the problem in one-night stands that don't evolve further than that. We're in our twenties, asshole. In our fucking prime. Why should I waste more than one night with a girl if it's not going to go anywhere? Makes no sense to me." I shrug.

"One day, someone is going to knock on your doorstep, and you'll eat those words," Easton quips back with all the certainty in the world.

"I don't see that happening anytime soon, so it's a moot point. Actually, this whole conversation is a waste of my time."

"What's a waste of time?" a deep, husky voice asks behind us.

We both turn around and see the devil himself, waltzing toward us with messy bed hair, as if he just ended a fuckfest marathon. Knowing Colt, he probably did.

He's donning a bright smile on his face, and his green eyes are glistening in the sun. I have to admit, I really missed the cocky asshole, too. I have no idea how he does it, but Colt always looks right as rain—like he walks around on rainbows and shit. If I didn't know he has the mean streak of a snake, I'd swear the guy was too fucking chipper to have all his screws on tight.

Colt fist-bumps Easton first, and then me, before taking the spot on my other side, leaning his head back on the roof of my car, so the sun kisses his already tanned face.

"Are you assholes going to stand out there all day long?" a voice calls out, making us all turn to face the house at our backs, and my eyes instantly lock on the friend I had been dreading to see for the past three months.

The breath I had apparently been holding in leaves me the minute I register that Lincoln still looks like Linc.

All three of us leave our spots, walking toward the house. The closer I get to him, the clearer it becomes to me that he is far from looking like someone who's carrying the biggest fucked-up secret. There's no frown, nor deep lines under his eyes. No sunken cheeks from lack of eating, nor pale, clammy skin from sleep deprivation due to horror-filled nightmares. He looks like a totally different person than the one I left behind before going on vacation.

As I inspect every inch of him, I can't pinpoint one single trace of damage on his face. Instead of the frail friend I expected to find, I'm astounded to see he looks even better than before. I see he bulked up over the summer, and if my eyes aren't deceiving me, he's also got some mad ink peeking out from under his short sleeve.

He looks good.

Too good.

If most of Asheville didn't attend his parents' funeral last May, then they probably wouldn't suspect the guy in front of me as having gone through such an ordeal and loss.

Hmm.

Loss? Is loss really the right word to be used when all four of us took part in their unexpected demise? I mean, the Hamiltons weren't exactly like a set of keys that you can just misplace or lose. You just don't *lose* two people like that. Nope. Loss is the wrong fucking word in this scenario. They weren't lost. They were killed. And everyone in Asheville believes it was a robbery gone wrong. If anyone ever discovered the truth, then the only thing that could be lost here is our freedom.

"We're here, asshole. What the fuck was so important that couldn't wait? Remy Peterson was pissed as hell when I had to leave her bed this morning," Colt singsongs, wiggling his eyebrows at his cousin.

"Just come inside the house. We need to talk," Lincoln says a bit too harshly, and just like that, my hackles rise up again.

Linc's sunny disposition is long gone. The forlorn mood I expected to find is suddenly imprinted on every feature of his face, and I, for one, hate seeing it there. But that's not even what alarms me the most. My steps falter when his fabricated grin returns once more, shining away, as if we all didn't just see that this new and improved Lincoln is nothing but a mask he's put in place.

The question, though, is why does he believe he needs it in the first place?

"What's going on, Lincoln?" Easton asks anxiously, never one to use kid gloves when facing a problem.

If I knew what Lincoln's response would be to his question, then I would have pleaded with Easton not to open his trap, just so I could have a bit more time to prepare myself better for the fuckery ahead. Because the words that pass through Lincoln's lips are my very worst nightmare coming to fruition.

"Someone knows."

CHAPTER 2

FINN

"What do you mean, someone knows?" Easton belts out menacingly as if he were about to murder someone.

That might be a poorly chosen turn of phrase, all things considered, but I think we've already established that all four of us are capable of such devious acts. It wouldn't come as a surprise if one of us found a liking to it. If I were a betting man, my money would be on either Colt or Easton, so no shock there that East is the one to hurl the first angry outburst, thirsty for blood.

Lincoln looks out past the three of us, and being the paranoid asshole that I am, I follow his stare and check if anyone is close enough to eavesdrop on our conversation. But behind us, there isn't anything but the vast Oakley woods, completely unguarded and vacant of all human life for miles on end. This solitude is one of the reasons we were able to get away with the shit we did that night.

"Not out here. Let's go inside," Lincoln orders, feeding further into my paranoia.

We do as he says and follow Lincoln, who thankfully bypasses the main living areas and rushes to the second floor, taking two stairs at a time. I don't even stop for a minute to see if the rest of the guys are following or not, but by the loud stampede of feet behind me, I know Colt and Easton are not too far behind.

Lincoln heads to his room, and the minute all four of us are safely inside, he closes the door, giving us complete privacy for whatever new clusterfuck he's going to lay on us.

"You're freaking me out, cuz. What the fuck is going on?" Colt exclaims harshly, his cool, relaxed demeanor nowhere in sight.

"This isn't exactly the reunion I was hoping for," Lincoln murmurs under his breath, running his fingers through his dark-blond locks.

It's only now that I realize he let his hair grow longer, too. Just one of the many changes he's made over the summer. He looks more like one of those pro surfers bumming around on an exotic beach somewhere waiting for the perfect wave, rather than the legitimate heir to the Richfield fortune—a reality that only came into fruition with the burial of his parents a few months ago.

"Yeah, well, the last time we were all under this roof, things didn't turn out that great either," I grumble, gaining Easton's disappointed glare and Colt's evil eye.

But it's not their reaction that gets under my skin. Lincoln just looks at me with an empathetic gaze and a somber frown, making me feel like shit for opening my big mouth.

"Sorry. I'm being a dick," I add, feeling like the worst fucking friend ever.

40

"When were you ever not one?" Lincoln tries to tease with a shy smile, easing my discomfort somewhat, and gaining a few agreeing, nervous chuckles from my two other friends.

However, when Lincoln's eyes drop to the floor and he leans against his mahogany desk, seeming to gather the fortitude he needs to start explaining what he began to say outside, my nerves increase tenfold.

"What's wrong, Linc?" I hate hearing the tremor in my voice, but as Lincoln's expression grows darker, my panic becomes unavoidable.

"Yeah, cuz. This suspenseful shit is kind of doing a number on me, too. What do you mean *someone knows*?" Colt questions, taking two steps toward his distressed cousin, placing an encouraging hand on Lincoln's shoulder to get him to start talking.

"You guys ever hear about a club called The Society?" Lincoln asks on a grave whisper, making my mind start to run rampant at the unexpected question.

"The fuck are you on about?" I retort abrasively, annoyed for being completely lost in this conversation.

"Just hold your fucking horses, Finn, for one goddamn second. Let Linc finish," Colt reprimands, his piercing green eyes throwing daggers at my impatience.

Instead of pacing the floor as I want, I take a seat on the bed next to a dead-silent Easton, hoping it will settle my nerves. He looks like he's gotten his shit back together, while I'm sitting here diving deeper into my freak-out.

"Go on, Linc. Why did you bring up The Society?" Colt questions calmly.

"So, you have heard of it?" Lincoln queries back, interested in how the question didn't confuse or mind-boggled Colt as much as me.

"Sure." Colt shrugs unaffected. "Frankly, I'm surprised you haven't. It's just an urban myth around campus. I'm sure every Ivy League school in the country has one. You know the kind—secret societies forged in the shadows, where rich college guys do shady shit to get in and think that being a member will somehow set them for life. Every college has some version of it, so it's not a big reach that Richfield has its own twisted adaptation."

"What do you mean twisted?" Easton chimes in curiously beside me, his brow cocked up high.

Having all eyes on him, Colt steps away from his cousin to lean against the door, his arms crossed at his chest.

"Myth says that every firstborn son is promised to the establishment to keep the bloodlines pure. They claim the members become the ones who rule this country with iron fists, and if you get in, the sky's the limit. They'll do whatever underhanded thing necessary to keep their power. Still, The Society makes sure it stays within the same families, only opening exceptions from time to time to those deemed worthy. Basically, it's a boy's club that promises a 'get out of jail free card' for the wealthy and privileged to use and abuse," Colt explains with an amused tone behind each word, clearly showing his disbelief in such a load of crap.

"Is that it? You want to get into some secret society to make sure we don't get caught?" I interrupt, getting yet another scowl from Colt. "The fuck is your problem?" I bluntly ask, tired of his patronizing glare.

"My problem is that you're a gullible idiot. There's no such thing, asswipe. As I said, it's an urban legend, which means it doesn't exist, asshole," he scolds as if I were an errant child.

"Well, excuse me for asking," I snap, giving him the finger, pissed off at his holier-than-thou attitude.

"I don't think it's a legend," Lincoln interjects before Colt has time for a comeback, pulling our full attention back to him.

"It is, Linc," Colt replies soothingly, obviously thinking his cousin may have lost all rationality over the summer if he spent it looking up fairytales and urban legends.

Shit, I'm surprised it took him that long to lose his mind. I've been a fucking wreck since it happened, and they weren't even my parents. I can only imagine what Lincoln must be dealing with.

"If such a thing existed, don't you think we would be in it by now? I mean, look at us. Who better to recruit into such a hush-hush society—ruled by one-percenters—than us?" Colt jokes, trying to sway our solemn friend away from his madness.

"Actually, I'm going to play devil's advocate on this one. None of us are the firstborns in our families, so *technically* we wouldn't be invited to join," Easton interrupts, giving his own non-committal smirk to Colt's cold-fronted stare. "Just stating facts." Easton shrugs, leaning back on the bed, his elbows keeping his torso up.

"You're not helping, East," Colt chides, his eyes yelling at him to shut the fuck up. Colt then turns over to Lincoln with a more sympathetic appearance, and hoping to bring his cousin to his senses, he tries to mitigate and says, "Listen to me, Linc. There is no such thing. The Society is just a story that college kids talk about in dark corners of libraries or drunk at frat parties, trying to add some excitement to campus life. Nothing more, nothing less."

Unfortunately for all of us, Linc's expression continues to be steadfast, bringing an uneasy chill to creep up my bones.

"Why? Why are you asking about The Society?" Colt queries unnervingly once again, his tone beginning to show some loss of his self-assured confidence.

"Because I think we just got our recruitment papers," Lincoln proclaims, throwing an envelope that was tucked in his back pocket onto the bed.

All four of us look silently at the black envelope, sitting neatly on the mattress between Easton and me as if it were a bomb ready to explode.

"What the fuck is this?" Easton questions as he bravely picks it up, while I try to scoot my body as far as I can away from the cursed thing without dropping off the bed entirely.

As East examines the envelope, back and front, the first thing I notice is the unusual, red seal attached to the black paper. I can't make out the design for sure, but if I had to guess, it looks like some sort of elaborate pentagram. The other thing that immediately captures my attention is how the seal has been broken, hinting that Lincoln already knows the contents of the envelope.

"Read it," Lincoln orders coldly, and Colt, looking a little bit worse for wear, takes the necessary steps to join us on the bed so he can assess the contents with his own eyes.

Easton takes one more look at our troubled friend, who continues to keep his distance from the wretched thing. Linc's vigilantly cautious demeanor is so unlike him, it even has Easton opening the envelope with care, worried it might contain a tripwire that could go off with the slightest miscalculated touch. Ever so carefully, East pulls out a folded, black stationery paper from the wax-sealed envelope. As he unfolds it, I catch a glimpse of gold lettering and the same familiar, red seal stamped at the bottom of the page.

Easton clears his throat before starting to read each word out loud. As his voice begins to crack with each sentence, so does my spirit. My mouth runs dry, and the fist that has been clutching my heart since this horrific nightmare began gives it another infernal squeeze, letting me know the worst is yet to come.

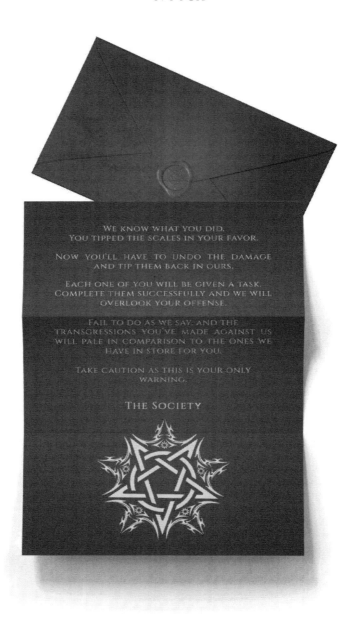

WE KNOW WHAT YOU DID.
YOU TIPPED THE SCALES IN YOUR FAVOR.

NOW YOU'LL HAVE TO UNDO THE DAMAGE
AND TIP THEM BACK IN OURS.

EACH ONE OF YOU WILL BE GIVEN A TASK.
COMPLETE THEM SUCCESSFULLY AND WE WILL
OVERLOOK YOUR OFFENSE.

FAIL TO DO AS WE SAY, AND THE
TRANSGRESSIONS YOU'VE MADE AGAINST US
WILL PALE IN COMPARISON TO THE ONES WE
HAVE IN STORE FOR YOU.

TAKE CAUTION AS THIS IS YOUR ONLY
WARNING.

THE SOCIETY

"This has got to be some sort of macabre joke," Colt chokes out, ripping the letter from Easton's trembling hands so he can have a read through of his own.

"I don't find it particularly funny," I snap back, getting up from my seat, franticly pacing the varnished wood floor as I usually do when I find myself too overwhelmed.

I've never been one to keep still when shit hits the fan. My body's default mechanism is always to keep moving, so my mind can take its time to process the information to avoid a full meltdown. And right now, my feet can't keep up with all the wheels turning in my head.

"It's not a joke. Whoever sent this letter knows what happened that night," Easton adds, his face stoic and unfeeling, already coming to terms with the notion that, somehow, *someone* out there knows what happened in this house last spring.

"That's absurd. We were the only ones here! How could anyone have found out?" Colt tries to reason, but when he starts grabbing at the ends of his hair, showing his aggravation, it's a telltale sign he's no longer as certain that this so-called society is nothing but an old wives' tale. "Linc, when did you get this?" Colt interrogates, clutching the envelope in his grip, and rereading each damning word for the third time.

"Last night. Right before I texted all of you."

Colt nods on autopilot, while his green eyes scrutinize every sentence as if he'll find some missed clue as to who sent it.

"Okay. I don't want any of us doing something stupid. This," Colt says after a long silent pause, holding up the evil paper in his hands, "could just be someone fucking with us. No one knows shit. As long as we keep our mouths shut and pretend everything is fine, nothing will come from this."

"You sure about that, Colt? What if whoever is behind this letter sends another one and doesn't like the fact that we haven't followed their instructions? You sure you're okay with everyone finding out what we've done, especially from someone who might not be as forgiving with the details of that night?"

"No one will find out, Easton!" Colt yells, demonstrating how rattled he is.

I swallow dryly as I watch my two best friends butt heads. I dread that the collision of the fire and ice coursing through their veins could be worse than whatever The Society might have planned for us.

"Hey, assholes! This is not the time for you two to start your shit. We've got bigger fish to fry," I chastise, bringing the two hotheads to heal.

It feels unfamiliar that I am the voice of reason. Usually, this type of stuff is Lincoln's area of expertise. He's always been the glue that kept our band of brothers together. The one friend we could count on who would pacify our tempers, keep us sane through our messed-up lives. However Linc's mind is miles away, not even registering that his two best friends are ready to go at each other's throats because of the unknown threat that may, or may not, be headed our way.

"Linc, this is your show, man. Whatever you want us to do, we're behind you one hundred percent. It's your call. How do you want to play this?" I add insistently, hoping that my plea is enough to slice through his apathetic state.

All our eyes fall on the friend who has more to lose than the rest of us combined, praying that his head is cool enough to get us out of this mess.

Again.

"For the time being, we can't do much but wait," he states pensively.

"Wait?" I exclaim flabbergasted, not liking that plan at all. "I'd rather we find these fuckers and punch some sense into them. They have no idea who they are fucking with."

Fuck waiting. I'm more of an offense kind of guy. Show me the target, and I'm like a bull in the ring. Waiting for the shoe to drop is why I've been a fucking mess lately. I'd rather do something than sit on my ass, waiting for the next shitstorm to implode.

"I think they do, Finn. And violence isn't the answer. For now, at least," Lincoln replies, his frame suddenly turning rigid with an impenetrable, steel wall beginning to take form and rise around him.

Lincoln's ocean-blue eyes resemble a storm of ungodly retribution. Looking at his demeanor, I'm no longer fearful of the person who believes himself to be the puppet master but troubled by the man who actually is. How far is Lincoln willing to go to keep our secret intact? From where I'm standing, his haughty glower screams that nothing is off the table.

"If this society is legit, then we can assume they outnumber us," Lincoln continues sternly. "Which means they might have enough power to back up their threat. I say we play it by ear. See what they ask, and on the back end, we investigate everything on The Society. We'll have to discover

49

who they are and what dirty little secrets they have. We all know everyone has a skeleton or two hidden in their closet. We find out theirs, and then we'll try to come to a compromise, exchanging their dirty little secret for ours."

"And what if that doesn't work? What if we can't even find out who is behind this, let alone what shit they've done in the past? Or let's say we do. Let's say we get the names of every last fucker in The Society, and we tell them we got dirt on them, too. What's to stop them from coming after us anyway?" Easton asks, concerned that Lincoln's plan may not hold water to it.

Our grim brother just shakes his head and replies, "That won't happen. They don't want us, East. If they did, they would have outed all of us by now. No. We're not their end game. We're just the means they believe they can use to get whatever they want."

"Are you sure?" I croak out, hoping Lincoln's logic is on the money.

"Positive. They want something, so we'll play along and pretend to give it to them," he says, throwing us a sinister smile.

It makes me cringe, seeing it on his face. It reminds me too much of another smile I saw that horrific night. A grin that comes to me in my nightmares, taunting me how none of us will ever truly escape our fate. We sealed it that night with the pact we made out of blood, and this ominous letter might just be the beginning of our demise.

"What if what they want from us is a reenactment of what we did last spring?" Colt asks, making the shivers down my back more profound.

I don't dare look away from Lincoln's face, hoping the compassionate friend I grew up with still lives and breathes inside him.

"Then they've drawn a line we aren't willing to cross. And if that's the case, we'll wait for them to show their hand. I don't think they'll go to the authorities. I'm positive it won't come to that. Blackmailers never want justice. They are only in it to gain something in return."

My lungs breathe a little easier, relieved that Lincoln still has his soul intact. But as his last words begin to take root inside me, it dawns on me exactly what this little letter means.

"So that's it, huh? We're being blackmailed."

I know I'm stating the obvious, but saying the words out loud just cements the idea. It makes it easier for me to confront and deal with it better.

"Afraid so," Lincoln adds coolly, erasing any doubt that there could be something more to this than just good old-fashioned blackmail.

"Fuck!" Easton shouts, falling to the bed while cursing the sky above him.

Colt gets up, leaving the whole bed for Easton to have his meltdown, and walks over to the window to scour the eerily remote scenery.

"You okay with this, Colt?" Lincoln asks his cousin, walking to stand beside him, as both take in the dark, green backdrop of Oakley woods.

"You want the truth? I'm not okay with anything as of late. But if you want us to play along, then that's what we'll do. At least for now," he hushes at his side, and this time, it's Lincoln who places his hand on his cousin's shoulder, offering a light, consoling squeeze.

"Fuck it!" Easton exclaims, jumping off the bed. "I'm in too. Whatever it takes, Linc. We got you."

"Finn?" Lincoln swings his head over his shoulder my way, waiting to see where I stand in all of this.

Is there really a choice? No, there isn't. It's not only Linc's life at stake. We're all in this. If one of us goes down, we all go.

"Yeah, I'm in."

"Good." He gives me a grateful, tight nod, but he knows as well as I do that my hands are tied like his.

"These assholes think they have us over a barrel, but they fucked up. They have no idea what kind of devastation we can bring," Colt states, trying to uplift our spirits.

However, it does nothing for me. It only makes me feel even more uneasy.

The Society might not have an idea of what depths we are willing to go, but we sure do. We are capable of doing the most heinous things if one of our lives is on the line. We proved our loyalty, and now I guess it's being put to the test again.

The rest of the morning is spent talking about how we are all going to handle this. Lincoln and Colt hatch out a plan to get their hands on anything related to The Society, leaving Easton and me to handle the commands they throw our way. Like good little soldiers, we wait on orders from their general, which is fine by me. I'd rather be doing something on the front lines than stuck in some dusty old library reading shit that will make my head spin.

I'm just not sure what that will be, though. I don't do well with surprises, so I'd rather know what to expect than be taken off-guard.

When I finally get home a few hours later and see a black envelope with my name on it sitting on top of the lobby desk, I realize that The Society is as impatient as I am to get this show on the road. And lucky me, I'm the first one they decided to set their sights on.

Fuck them.

They want to play? That's fine with me.

I'm used to playing dirty anyway.

CHAPTER 3

FINN

Some people never learn where their rightful place in the world is. It's up to us to remind them. We made sure you knew yours.

Now it's your turn to prove your worth, and erase a certain pebble in our shoe. Or should we say a stone?

Stone Bennett is our target, and therefore, yours.

The enemy of my enemy is my friend, after all.

Befriend her first, to destroy her later. We'll be watching.

THE SOCIETY

I fiddle with the envelope in my hand, while Easton drives us to God knows where. The minute I saw the fucking thing in the foyer, amongst the forgotten junk mail, I immediately grabbed it and called Easton, ordering him to haul his ass over to my house.

I have no idea when the letter arrived, but I'm hoping that no one in my family saw it before I got my hands on the deplorable thing. Thankfully, my mother has been consumed with my baby nephews and nieces that she pays little mind to anything else, much less mail. And unless the letter comes from Chapel Hill, my father isn't interested in it either.

Still, it was careless of The Society to send the correspondence to my house. For all I know, my own black, sealed envelope could have come on the same day Lincoln received his.

With the numerous people passing by in our foyer, someone might have gotten curious enough to see what it contained. It was reckless of our blackmailers to do such a thing.

I get them sending it to Lincoln's house since his place is basically an empty mausoleum. But my house? It's always full of people.

My two older brothers live close by with their respective families and come over for almost every meal, bringing their wives and small children in tow. This makes my house a revolving door of hectic activity, filled with grubby little hands and siblings who are always in each other's business.

I mean, who sends letters nowadays when an email will suffice? I guess fucking secret societies prefer to do their dirty work the old-fashioned way. It does make it harder to track down who the assholes are, that's for sure. And even though there is a risk involved in them contacting me this way, the actual danger falls solely on my shoulders—meaning I'm the one who will need to be on the lookout twenty-four-seven, since I'm the one with everything to lose, not them.

Once Easton got to my place and took his sweet time reading the unwelcomed letter, he called up some people, and in a matter of minutes, he knew everything there was to know about Stone Bennett. I have to admit that I've never heard the name before in my life. But Easton has a lot of shady friends with even shadier acquaintances, who were all too willing to give us details about the girl.

The first thing we learned is that she's a Southie, and knowing my target is some girl who lives in the wrong part of town, didn't settle my anxiety any. With a name like Stone, who knows what I'll be facing. Most likely, it's some junkie or thief that got her hands on the wrong asshole's wallet, and now they want me to teach her a lesson.

When Easton told me to be ready to go on a little outing tonight, I never thought for once that he'd bring me to such a hole in the wall. I don't know why I'm surprised, though. I should have expected as much.

The minute he parks his truck, and I see exactly where we are, I have half a mind to tell him to turn around and take our asses back home. How am I ever going to befriend some chick who works in a fucking biker bar? The eyesore is located on the edge of town, right in the middle of a notoriously dangerous neighborhood—the type that everyone pretends doesn't exist, and turns their nose up in a stink until they are faced with one.

When people think of Asheville, they instantly imagine big plantation houses or mansions that would put the White House to shame. A place where the elite lives, enjoying their accumulated fortune under the North Carolina blue skies, warm weather, and southern hospitality. They wouldn't be wrong either, but where there is wealth, there is a whole lot of poverty hidden away, too. And in this very moment, Easton and I are smacked right at the center of such a destitute place.

Every house in this neighborhood looks like it's on its last leg—uncared for and forgotten, much like its Southie inhabitants. Still, even the poorest of souls deserve a drink, even if only to forget their miserable sorrows. Judging by the number of bikes parked out front, this disease-ridden watering hole seems to be everyone's bar of choice.

The huge, red neon light blinking the words 'Big Jim's Bar' accompanied by a silhouette of a woman riding a chopper with her breasts out, shows just how classy the inside will be. Easton, of course, doesn't hesitate and strolls into the bar like he's in his element. I can't help but hate the fucker a little bit for looking like this place doesn't unnerve him in the least. I'm not as cool. My lead feet have barely taken three steps inside the place, and I already want to hightail it out of here.

I'm not trying to be a conceited prick or anything, but fuck, doesn't anyone know how to use a fucking mop or a dust cloth? No way am I drinking out of one of those glasses. Might give me an STD, tuberculosis, or some shit like that.

Easton looks around the dimly lit bar and points to an empty table next to some guys playing pool at the back. I'm not bothered by the noise they're making since it muffles the commotion coming from the other end of the bar, where a makeshift stage hosts a wet T-shirt contest as tonight's entertainment.

There is an array of women being doused with buckets of cold water, leaving them drenched to the bone. I wouldn't mind it too much if most of the women on stage didn't look like they are my momma's age. Definitely past their prime. Yet they don't look one bit embarrassed about their saggy boobs and muffin tops being on display. Judging by the howling and wolf calls coming from upfront, the male clientele doesn't care either.

One goes as far as pulling the flimsy wet material down a redhead's breast and sucking on her nipple like it's there for his pure enjoyment. His buddies beside him all whoop at the bare boob being fondled, while the woman grabs her groper's head closer to her bosom so he can milk her for all she's worth. I'm more repulsed by the spectacle than the foul smell of poor hygiene in this place.

Head held high, I follow behind Easton because the prideful bastard that I am doesn't want anyone to see any weakness in me, even if being in a place like this has me feeling like bugs are crawling up my back. It's dirty, loud, and too damn revolting to stomach.

"Fuck," I grunt as I feel a crunch come from whatever insect I just annihilated with my shoe.

I look at the grimy floor and see the remains of a cockroach while its pals speed away from their impending death, once again making my nose flare-up in disgust.

Again, not being a dick or anything, but come on!

Cockroaches? Really?

I don't care if this place is in the worst part of town. Some shit should never dwell where people eat and drink, for God's sake. If I found cockroaches running around in any establishment on my side of town, they sure as fuck would get an earful from me. But this place is on a whole other level of repulsion. It stinks of urine and puke all at once, and by the looks of the couple on stage who are two seconds away from fucking, it's about to stink of jizz, too. I'm not sure if I should use my nose or my mouth to breathe while I'm in this dump. Suffocation feels like a good alternative at this point.

But my lungs not getting enough oxygen isn't even the worst part of being in this joint. I stand out like a sore thumb, which makes my presence at Big Jim's even more unbearable. Not that I have an issue with being the center of attention. I'm used to it, just never for the wrong reasons. While Easton looks like he's just another customer looking for a good time and a cold beer, I look like I'm about to do a fucking audit on this poor excuse of an establishment, which, by the way, would fail miserably. Just saying.

It's not that I'm dressed like a boring, tired-looking inspector, or even a prick with more money than sense. I mean, I didn't go overboard with my get-up or anything. Only black slacks and a white shirt, nothing flashy.

When Easton said this Stone girl worked in a bar on the south side of town, I didn't expect fancy, so I didn't dress for it. But never did I once expect this shithole. Even if I came in here with just an old pair of jeans and a T-shirt, I would still stick out like a sore thumb. I look like a crisp dollar bill, while everyone else looks like they're still scraping for change.

"Jesus. Take a seat, Finn. Your uptight scowl is giving me a migraine. Just relax," Easton barks out with a laugh, making fun of my discomfort.

"Let's just get this shit over with," I groan, aggravated by some leather-wearing patrons over at the bar counter looking at me funny.

Why couldn't this boogeyman society have given this job to Easton instead? I mean, he fits right in. But me? I'm going to have a fucking hard time trying to get close to a girl who works in such a pigsty. No way am I spending my nights here just to fulfill some half-brained order from our blackmailers.

Fuck that!

"Relax, Finn. This is going to be a piece of cake." Easton winks at me as if I weren't the one who The Society sunk its fangs into first.

"Just tell me again what you got on this Stone girl," I counter back, preferring to distract myself from my surroundings by getting down to business.

The sooner I get this over and done with, the faster I can go back to living my life. Not that it's been a bunch of laughs lately, but anything is preferable to this putrid environment.

"Well, aside from working here most nights, my sources say she's a local, too. Lived on the south side most of her life. But don't let that fool you. She's not like one of those skanks looking for their next sugar daddy. Your girl managed to crawl her way out of the sewer somehow. She even attends Richfield like us."

"First things first—she's not *my* girl, she's a target," I reprimand, making it clear to him that whatever happens— whatever I *need* to make happen—will be done strictly out of a cold heart and a calculating mind. No compassion. No mercy. Just like on the field, I play to win, and no one likes winning more than me. However, this bit of information that Easton just shared does work in my favor. "Let me guess. She's a scholarship kid, huh? Happy to know the girl's got some gray matter working for her," I add, thinking maybe I can find an excuse to meet up with her at school rather than this dump.

"That she does. Top of most of her classes, from what I've heard. However, that tidbit wasn't the first thing my buddies told me about her."

"Oh yeah? So, what did your so-called buddies tell you?" I goad back, making childish bunny ears over the word buddies.

Aside from me, Lincoln, and Colt, Easton doesn't have friends. He has a lot of assholes who owe him favors, but friends, not a single one. Hey, again, not judging. None of us exactly have sparkling personalities—I'm a dick, Easton is a conceited prick, and Colt is a moody fucker. The only one that something nice can be said about is Lincoln. But that's just because he's genuinely a good guy underneath it all. Sure, he might ruffle some feathers here or there, but he's not nearly as much of a douche as the rest of us. Or at least up until last summer, he wasn't.

Then everything changed.

Lincoln has to live with the blood on his hands, and I'm not sure if he's equipped to deal with that shit without turning into someone who none of us will recognize. I sure as fuck didn't think I could handle it. Yet here I am, doing my best to clean the fucked-up night away with more underhanded scheming. Guess we take after The Society more than they would have liked.

"So? What did they say?" I ask again after Easton takes forever to spill what he's obviously dying to.

"They told me she hates us Northside fuckers, and that's a direct quote, my friend." He laughs into his fist, loving that my task is already doomed from the start.

"Fan-fucking-tastic." I roll my eyes, letting out a frustrated growl.

Isn't that just the icing on the cake? I somehow have to get in this girl's good graces, and she already hates me on mere principle alone. Just fucking great.

"So she has a chip on her shoulder. Nothing you can't thaw out, right, Romeo?" He wiggles his brows sarcastically.

The asshole knows I suck with chicks. So much so, he's always on my case because of it. So of course he's loving the fact that I'm going to have to make nice with one, and by the looks of it, she's going to give me a run for my money. I haven't even laid eyes on the girl yet, and I already resent her.

"You got anything else?" I ask Easton, as his eyes scrounge through the bar instead of paying me any mind. I snap my fingers in front of his face, and he slaps my hand away. "I asked if you have anything else on this chick that I can use?"

"What? And do all your homework for you?" he challenges with a smirk.

"No one has ever done my homework, asshole, and you know it."

I might be a jock, but I'm not a fucking moron. Actually, if I had it my way, football would be the last thing I would be doing with my time. But thanks to my father, the thing I want to do most will never be in my grasp. Not if I don't want to lose my whole family just for following my dreams. My father would rip me in half if I told him what I really wanted to do with my life.

The thing is, I really couldn't give two shits if he laid it out on me with his disappointment. I don't even care that he'd take my inheritance away from me. Fuck the money. The only reason why I don't confront him is that my father is a vindictive prick. He'd forbid my brothers—and worst of all, my momma—to ever set eyes on me again, just because I went against his football wishes and Super Bowl ring dreams.

It's not like I didn't see firsthand while growing up what happens when you defy my father. One of my older brothers foolishly tried once. Beau must have been drunk with bravery the day he told the old man he wanted to teach instead of playing football. My father kicked him out of our house so fast he never even saw the foot up his ass showing him the way out.

The only reason Beau was even allowed back in was that my momma came up with a compromise both Beau and my father could live with by getting him a job coaching ball at the local high school. This way Beau could still teach—in a manner of speaking—and Dad could still brag that all of his sons have football in their blood. And even though that argument took place eons ago, to this day, our father sometimes glowers at Beau across the dinner table, as if still tasting my brother's defiance on the tip of his tongue.

Shit, if he ever found out how I truly spent my summer in Florida, I would be shunned in a heartbeat. However, it's something I've come to terms with. I'll do what everyone expects of me and go pro next year. The only reason why I haven't been drafted yet is that I made it clear I want to finish college beforehand. Big teams don't usually like that very much since it increases my chances of getting hurt on the field, which would make me useless to them.

My father was of the same mindset too, but thank fuck my momma wasn't. She put her foot down on that one. 'Degree first, football second, Hank. And if you push the boy more on this one, expect to spend your nights sleeping in the guest room,' she had warned. And even though my father is the man of the house and his word is law, he knows better than to piss off my momma when she's made up her mind about something.

In any event, it only bought me some extra time. Whether my heart is in it or not, I'll eventually end up doing what they want. My father will be happy, Momma will be happy, and I'll have them both out of my hair and not catch shit for doing my own thing as a hobby. I guess that will have to be enough. No one ever said you were born to be a hundred percent happy, right? You do what you have to and grab whatever joy you can in the little moments afforded to you.

I crack my knuckles, my wayward thoughts sullying my mood further. But thankfully, I don't have time to dwell on things I can't change, since Easton nudges me on the shoulder, grabbing my attention back to my current fucked-up predicament.

"There she is. That's your girl," he announces eagerly.

I'm about to correct, yet again, his absurd comment, but my coherent thoughts leave me when my eyes lock on the girl I've been destined to ruin.

Standing bored while taking the order from the table in front of us, she is exactly what I suspected a Southie-born girl to look like—only so much more. Her bluish-black hair is purposely wrapped in a messy bun to proudly showcase her numerous earrings on both lobes and the barbell piercing on her brow. The way she's playing with her tongue as she writes down her patron's order, tells me she's got more piercings hidden on her body—the only thing she's probably hiding since most of everything else is on display.

She's got on a short, ripped-up top with a cut so deep at the front that you can't help but stare at the red lace holding up two impressive, creamy breasts. The black shorts she's got on barely covers her ass, but I think that's intentional, so everyone can appreciate the red and black phoenix tattooed on her thick thigh.

All of her is too much. Too loud, and definitely too in your face. She's nothing like the thin-twig debutant girls I've grown accustomed to. Not in the slightest. She's all luscious curves, huge tits, and an even bigger ass. It's like she was force-fed southern-fried cooking all her life while listening to Metallica—big, loud, and mean. Yep, that is the perfect description of Stone Bennett.

Even though she's probably around five-foot-five, compared to my six-foot-four, she looks like she'd be able to swallow me in and spit me out with a fucking smile on her face. She's not some wallflower that blossomed in the Southside dirt. She's a force of nature who made that roughneck of the woods her bitch.

I'm so fucking screwed.

"She's cute," Easton has the audacity to say after taking stock of all of her features.

"You have got to be shitting me?" I bark out, outraged.

"What? She is. Actually, she's more than cute. She's fucking hot." He smirks, going for another once-over of all her tempting curves.

I'm tempted to smack him upside the head for his constant staring at her thick thighs and small waist, but I play the indifference card instead.

"If I were looking for Marilyn Manson's bride to be, then yeah, I'm sure she'd fit the bill."

Easton stops his flagrant ogling of Stone, snapping his head toward me, his annoyed frown taking center stage on his face.

"Stop being such a prejudiced douche, Finn. Even you can appreciate her level of hotness."

"I'm not being judgmental or anything. I just don't like being with a girl who looks like she might cut my balls off rather than suck them," I grumble, tapping my foot repeatedly on the floor to show my disgruntlement.

"Well, make sure her tongue doesn't have any sharp objects then," he teases me, cocking a brow and waving the girl in question over to our table. "However, you should be so lucky to have that mouth anywhere near your junk, you dick," he hushes beneath his breath, all the while smiling over at Stone as she heads in our direction.

I stew in my own misery when she waltzes over with that same bored expression married to her lips, but not to her stunning, emerald eyes. As she comes closer, I can't help the unnerving feeling that I like the color of her eyes way too much. They are the only light thing about her. Soft, green meadows that resemble cool, spring days. The ones we hardly ever enjoy down south, unique and invigorating.

Tattoos, thick thighs, and pretty eyes.

A lethal combination that ensures I'm fucked.

"Are you boys lost?" she asks right off the bat, not even taking those stellar eyes off her notepad to look at us.

"Excuse me?" I grunt.

"I said, are you lost? Your kind usually don't show up around these parts," she spews, this time making direct eye contact with me, not one bit intimidated by the pissed-off glower I'm giving her.

"*Our kind?*" I cross my arms over my chest. "And what exactly would our kind be?" I challenge.

She huffs out, looking even more bored with this conversation than before. She taps her pencil on the notepad, taking me in from head to toe as if making an inventory of all my flaws. I try to keep as rigidly still as I can, even though her scrutinizing glare is making me anxious.

Being the captain of the Richfield football team, I'm used to getting attention from the opposite sex. Having girls look you up and down like you're either their next meal or their ticket out of here seems to be part of the job description. But Stone's piercing emeralds don't have that flicker of lust in her eyes, nor greed. Quite the contrary. They look like I'm just as nasty as the cockroaches running around in this bar.

"Cat got your tongue?" I provoke. "Just what did you mean about our kind, little girl?"

She lets out a scoff and bites the tip of her pencil, throwing a flash of silver inside her mouth, confirming my suspicion the girl has more hardware on her.

"Oh, you know. Spoiled, rich, pretty boys who think 'fun' is throwing a ball and getting beat up by sweaty guys twice their size," she mocks, directing her offensive remark at me, seeing as Easton is not the athletic type. The only sport he's into is fucking, so that doesn't count.

"Twice my size?! Take a good, hard look at me. I doubt you've met many men as big as me," I defend with a snarl.

"Or with the same inflated ego, I'm sure. So, what do you want? I got better shit to do than spend my time here talking to you, quarterback."

Before I have time to come up with a proper comeback, Easton steals my limelight and orders two beers. She wiggles her brow at me once again before turning around, shaking that damn fine ass in my face as she sashays over to the bar.

"How the fuck am I going to befriend *that*?" I belt out, making sure the bane of my existence is out of earshot.

"There are plenty of ways you could do it. You don't need to be her BFF, Finn. All you have to do is be on her radar long enough to do whatever The Society wants. And from the looks of it, it won't be too hard either." He snickers.

"Oh, no? And how do you propose I do that, Einstein?"

He leans back on his chair, his eyes following Stone behind the bar counter as she fetches our order.

"Easy. Seduce her."

"You have got to be kidding." I choke, my eyes bugging out of my head at his proposal.

"Nope. You want easy, right? Then use your Walker charm, if you can find it, to get into her bed. And make sure to stay there long enough to get your next order from The Society. Shouldn't be too hard for ya, right champ?" he jokes, patting me on the back to antagonize me further.

"I hate you. You know that, right?"

"Yeah, I know." He laughs. "But jokes aside, all I'm saying is, if you want to get close to Stone, then you have to do it in a way she sees coming. She already thinks you're a cocky asshole, so live up to the hype and take what you want."

"And you really think a girl like that will believe I want in her pants?" I rebuke back bitterly.

"Fuck, yes. Every last fucker in here does, so why would she suspect you to be any different?" he replies nonchalantly.

I look around the place and see that, in fact, every guy here is either blatantly checking her out or doing it discreetly enough that their dates don't catch on. But let's be real here. If a guy brings you to a shithole like this on date night, do you really expect him to be a charmer?

As much as I hate to admit it, Easton is right. Stone is probably used to guys hitting on her all the time. Even the redhead at the end of the bar—who is now on her knees giving head to the guy who had been sucking on her tit a few minutes ago—isn't getting the same attention Stone is just by walking around the bar doing her damn job. She really is a fucking knockout under all that ink and attitude. Maybe even because of it.

Okay. I can do this. I'd be taking one for the team, right? Say what you will about me, but I've always been a team player. Even when my heart is not in it, I give it my all. I always have. And this time, losing isn't an option, since the repercussions of me failing The Society's first assignment might be the end of us.

If sleeping with Stone Bennett is how I get them off my back, then that's what I'll have to do.

I mean, how hard can it be to seduce the devil's spawn anyway?

CHAPTER 4

STONE

Can this night get any shittier?

First, Big Jim tells me I'll have to lock up tonight since Janet called in sick, turning my six-hour shift into a nine-hour one, which will definitely show tomorrow morning on my first day back at school. There won't be enough concealer under the sun to mask the bags under my eyes. And secondly, Janet bailing couldn't have happened on a worse night. If I didn't know any better, I'd swear the bitch did it on purpose. Anytime my boss announces there will be a contest to win a few bucks, the desperate and needy of Asheville crawl out of the woodwork for a few Benjamins, while the vultures flood our doors, thirsty to watch the deplorable show go down.

Tonight's poor excuse for a contest is an old favorite of my employer's, as well as every last pervert within a twenty-mile radius. The wet T-shirt night at Big Jim's Bar is not like the ones broadcasted on TV or spring break music videos. Instead of girls gone wild, it's more like moms without shame.

A prime example of this is Wanda and her old man doing it doggy style for everyone's eyes to behold, while her seven-year-old kid is probably sound asleep at her grandma's place again. Poor kid should be thankful her folks didn't bring her in tow this time. Watching her parents get wasted and do live porno would scar her for life. But if I'm being real, she's probably seen worse.

Most of the kids who grow up around here are used to shit like this anyway. I sure as hell saw my share of fucked-up things growing up. I really wish I could say this sort of crap was a one-off here at the bar, but it's not. Shit like this happens most nights. I guess you just become immune to the filth after a while.

It's also a side effect of living on this end of town. We expect the grime and the dirt. It's the shiny and new that raises our hackles. Case in point—Finn Walker and Easton Price sitting at a table casing the joint like they are planning some sort of heist. It's oddly funny considering Easton's stepdaddy owns one of the world's most prestigious banks there is. He could probably buy this bar with his lunch money, so why Big Jim's would suddenly grab his fancy is beyond me.

However, Easton doesn't get on my nerves as much as the friend frowning at his side. Easton wasn't born into money like Finn was. His momma just managed to marry into it. Rumor has it that before Price put a ring on Easton's momma's finger, she was turning down beds and cleaning toilets at some swanky hotel, living in a one-room, rat-infested apartment up North with her kid. At least Easton knows what it's like to live in squalor.

Finn Walker, however, wouldn't know the first thing about sacrifice, let alone worrying about where his next meal is coming from. I mean, look at him! Not only is he drop-dead gorgeous, with his wavy blond locks and piercing blue eyes, but he's as big as a tank. That boy hasn't missed a meal in his whole life. Sure, it's probably steel muscle from all the workouts he has to do to keep in shape for football, but damn! He puts most of the guys sitting here to shame.

Worst thing is, he's a cocky asshole, and he knows it. Just by the way he gloated about his size, he's proud of it too, making him as vain and shallow as I suspected him of being. He's just like any other jock with a pea-sized brain that thinks muscles will get him far in life. I can't help but be a little bit resentful of guys like him because, in Finn's case, that's all he really needs to make it in this world.

While I bust my ass and study like crazy, trying to get out of the Southside, Finn Walker only needs to get buff in a private gym and take a few blows to the head to have his future guaranteed. And it's not like he even needs the hassle, either. Both his parents come from a long line of southern aristocracy. Christ, I'm sure you can probably trace his ancestors as far back as the Mayflower. Their wealth is unimaginable, so pretty boy Finn Walker slumming it in my part of town has my spidey sense tingling. Guys like him don't come down here without a good reason.

Just what the hell are those two up to?

I place five beers on a tray, ready to head back and give these losers their booze, leaving the two college boys for last. When I finally get to their table, Finn's scowl is still ingrained on his face. Even though he's trying to mask it as indifference, his ego is obviously wounded by my harmless teasing. I'd laugh if I didn't think it was so pathetic a man of his size being unable to take a little criticism.

"I think we started off on the wrong foot," his smooth-talking friend begins, deepening his learned southern twang like he's one of us.

"Did we, now?" I cock my hip to the side, wondering what fine line Easton Price is going to spin.

If he thinks he'll get anything out of me, he's dead wrong. The 'rebel without a cause' persona Easton Price lives by doesn't get my motor running in the least. His dark attitude is all for show and less than original. I know bad guys. I was raised by one, so Easton is shit out of luck if he thinks he can sweet-talk me into buying whatever he's selling.

His blue-eyed friend would stand a better chance, even though everything the elitist jock represents annoys the fuck out of me. With all his faults, Finn might have a few traits that I could see myself using. Especially with school starting, there's a little itch he could certainly help me scratch. I'd gladly climb up that massive tree and find out if all of him is as huge as he likes to advertise. Yep. A hate-fuck would definitely hold me out for the semester. But with my luck, Finn is likely just as overrated as all the other Northside pricks. All talk and no game.

"You're Stone, right? Finn and I were just talking about how we've seen you around campus before," Easton continues, feeding me a bullshit lie.

Like hell, they have.

Guys like them don't pay attention to anything or anyone but their own reflection. I'd never be on their radar, so Easton suddenly knowing my name is all the warning I need to know they are definitely up to no good. I'm not sure what their intentions are, but I certainly need to make it clear I want no part of it. I have better things to do than waste my time with two entitled Northsiders looking to cause trouble on my side of town.

Screw that and screw them.

"And?" I quip back, unamused, hoping my resting bitch face is enough to dampen whatever game they've got going.

"*And* my friend here is trying to be polite. How about you cut him some slack, huh?" Finn counters, the annoyed scowl on his brow deepening by the second.

"Oh, that's so cute, you sticking up for your boyfriend. Is that why you boys came here? To hide your love affair away from your mammas and pappas? Chin up boys. It's the twenty-first century. No one gives a rat's ass if you like cock or not. Own that shit. I do," I reply sarcastically, giving them a little wink and blowing a kiss to Finn to annoy him further.

I sway my way back to the bar, the tiny adrenaline from toying with those idiots putting a smile on my face. It will probably be the only amusement I'll get tonight. But too quickly is my fun tarnished when Finn-fucking-Walker jumps over the bar counter like a stealthy cat, and corners me against the wall of liquor shelves behind us as if he owned the damned place.

"You are something else, you know that, little girl?" he growls, his chest heaving against mine.

Standing up to his full height, Finn really is a sight to behold. Unfortunately, I'm unable to appreciate all of him at the moment. My neck is craned so far back that the strain of it is actually painful. He's twice my size, both in height and in width, but if he thinks he intimidates me, he's got another thing coming. I've dealt with far worse than pretty boy here.

"Stone, you okay? Do you need me to pull that motherfucker out of there?" Lamar asks, promptly leaving his post at the door and walking toward the bar, ready to earn his bouncer paycheck.

There are a few curious eyes on us, but none of them are too concerned for my welfare. That's because they know I can handle shit just fine on my own.

I hold out my hand, halting Lamar's next step, and with resolve stitched into my expression, I state evenly, "I've got this one, Lamar. I'm good."

Finn lets out a little arrogant scoff but doesn't break eye contact with me for a second. From my peripheral vision, I watch Lamar go back to his post, all the while keeping one eye on us, just in case I have to tap out and let him deal with the heathen of a man before me.

Never going to happen. Like I said, I got this.

Most of the privileged brats who attend Richfield are all bark and no bite, and Finn is no different. The minute someone stands up to him, he'll shrivel back into his little shell, running away with his tail between his legs and licking his wounds because a girl from the Southside got the best of him. He has an ego as inflated as his hatred of being challenged. Sad thing is, I've dealt with this brand of intimidation before—bullies relying on their size and not their brains to terrorize the weak. Someone should have warned him that I might be small, but I've got a damn big mouth ready to sling bricks and stones where it'll do the most damage.

"Okay, *pretty boy.* You got my attention. Now what are you going to do with it?" I taunt, not one bit threatened by his size or his imposing form.

Finn's brows push together on his forehead, revealing his confusion. His perplexed glare isn't as irritating as

76

witnessing him lose a bit of the angry steam that was fueling his drive.

So disappointing.

He's already unraveling, and all I had to do was to give him a little nickname. I watch his Adam's apple bob, his eyes still fixed on mine, and I have to give him props for not taking advantage of peeking down my shirt. Most guys here have gone to far greater lengths to see the goods, so I commend Finn on his restraint at least.

"Cat got your tongue, *pretty boy*?" I tease him again with his own line, biting my lower lip, triggered by the flicker of the furious fire in his eye ready to lash out.

"You talk too much," he finally grunts and my smile only grows wider at the poor excuse of a comeback he came up with.

"Oh yeah? And how do you propose to shut me up?" I provoke, unimpressed, but before I have time to chastise him any further, he takes the wind out of my sails when he grabs the back of my head and presses his lips forcefully on mine.

Every other time an asshole dared to put his hands on me without my say so, he'd have been kneed in his family jewels so fast he'd need surgery to see his dick again. But my knee-jerk reaction is nowhere in sight because Finn's warm lips come as a surprise to me in more ways than one.

His plump, rich mouth dominates my own, his tongue teasing my lower lip in a way that leaves me helpless not to open up and let him take whatever he wants. But Finn doesn't take my red-carpet invitation as I expected. Instead, he leaves me frustrated, using his teeth to scrape at my lower lip and then extinguish the tiny ache by sucking on it with his full, luscious mouth. His kiss is a combination of both brutish dominance and alarming tenderness. His lips promise wicked, dirty adventures, while his tongue toys with me, hinting that I'm not ready for everything he's capable of giving.

Well, I'll be damned. The boy does have some moves, after all.

If this is Finn at his tamest, then I shiver in anticipation at what he's like at his wildest. When I feel the tip of my toes starting to lift me of their own accord—just so I can lean into his kiss more fully—he pulls away, ending one of the hottest kisses I've had all year.

Maybe even ever.

The smoldering look he gives me is enough to build a small fire in my core, leaving me needy for more. I'd rather die than let on he's affected me so much, so I instantly school my features as best I can to feign annoyance. It's awfully hard to maintain the charade since Finn seizes the moment by running his thumb over my lower lip, making my tongue ache to come out and play with it. And since shame is not part of my vocabulary, I give in to temptation and wrap my lips around his digit, his throbbing cock immediately responding to the gesture by the way it's poking at my midsection. With his eyes fixed on mine, Finn lets out a suppressed moan when I finally let his imprisoned thumb out of my hot cage with a loud pop. I'm pretty sure the term 'panty-melting stare' was coined from sexy smolders like the one Finn has plastered all over his face.

"See you around, Stone," he rasps huskily, biting his lip as if restraining himself from stealing another kiss from me.

"I doubt it, pretty boy," I retort, licking my lips to make sure I leave him just as hot and frazzled as he left me.

The corner of his mouth deviously tugs upward as he leans his head down, low enough that I can feel his warm breath tickle my neck. My face is still cool and collected, but the shiver that runs down my spine is unavoidable. I'm sure the bastard knows he got to me.

"Oh, you'll see much more of me, little girl. Count on it," he threatens, biting my lobe so deliciously, my lids shut just so I can relish this one touch.

When sense finally sets in and I open my eyes, Finn is already at the door with his buddy Easton trailing right behind him. The cocky sidekick even has the nerve to throw me a conspiring wink.

Northside bastards.

Hmm. I wonder what that was all about. Finn Walker and Easton Price walking through the doors of Big Jim's is not something you see every day. No. Those guys are definitely up to something. It can't be to score drugs since they are both way too clean-cut for that. It isn't to score chicks either since guys like them have to swat girls away. It's sickening. I see it all the time at Richfield. Most of the girls enrolled there aren't slaving away to get a college degree like me. They're on a mission to lock down some Northside jerk with a huge inheritance that will set them up for life. And Finn and Easton are two of the most sought out candidates on campus, right behind their best friends, Colt Turner and Lincoln Hamilton—the Richfield cousins.

Yep, if you want to hit the jackpot on the husband lottery, then those are the two guys every girl in North Carolina is foaming at the mouth to nab, especially Lincoln. Whereas Colt has to share his inheritance five ways between him and his four sisters, Lincoln has his all to himself. He's the last Hamilton member standing, seeing as his older brother died when he was just a freshman at Richfield, and his folks were murdered last May. I applaud the brave woman who is willing to go after Lincoln Hamilton. I, for one, can't say I want in on whatever bad luck has struck his side of the Richfield family.

But I do sympathize with the guy. I sincerely do. I know exactly how it feels to be born under a bad moon. No amount of prayer or rock salt can change your bad juju. But unlike Lincoln, I'm going to break the cursed cycle I was born into. I'll get from under this rock and breathe fresh air far away from Asheville soon enough. I've worked too hard to stop now. Distractions like Finn Walker and his buddies aren't going to help get me there, either.

So they came to my neck of the woods tonight. Who fucking cares? Not my problem and not my concern. I'll archive that sexy kiss the quarterback landed on me into the filing cabinet in my head under the label of 'things best forgotten'.

I trace my thumb over my lips for just a measly second, recalling pretty boy's kiss one last time. Sure it was possessive and dominating, but it was also sweet and tender. And I don't do sweet. Sweet leads to feelings, and I definitely don't do those.

So, I guess that's that.

Finn got his jollies kissing a Southie, and I got what will most likely be my last kiss for the rest of my senior year. With school starting tomorrow, all I want to think about is acing every class, instead of hot-as-fuck quarterbacks who can kiss the panties off a nun. Let him have fun with the pretty Barbie doll look-alikes that drool all over him because of his games. If he thinks he'll be able to play with me or my time as easily as he does with those football groupies, he's sorely mistaken.

I'm no man's toy.

I shouldn't worry too much about it, though.

I doubt I'll ever see Finn Walker again.

CHAPTER 5

FINN

I wait patiently by the stairs, knowing Stone will have to come this way sooner or later to get to her next class. It's been five days since East and I went to that shitty bar she works at, and I was really starting to think the only way I could see her again was if I went back there. Although we're being blackmailed—and all that nonsense—I'd really rather not step foot in that dump again if I can help it.

Thankfully, one of Easton's so-called buddies came through and got her schedule for me. I have to say, it was fucking impressive. It wasn't the fact that Easton's guy was able to get hold of a student's personal info that fascinated me. I know damn well you can get anything if you're willing to pay the right price. No, that wasn't what grabbed my attention.

What impressed me was Stone's college courses. Being a scholarship kid, I knew the girl had to have some serious brains on her, but I never expected to such an extent. Stone has some heavy workload on her hands with two majors—one in pre-law and the other in political science. And if Easton's intel is on point, she has been kicking ass and taking names in all her classes since her freshman year.

Even though I know nothing about Stone, the piece of paper holding her daily hustle tells me that not only is she as smart as a whip, but she also has the fierce drive and discipline to work her butt off, striving to be the best in everything.

Stone's ambition and commitment is something I understand wholeheartedly, so I can't help but respect the smart-mouthed girl for her take-no-prisoners attitude. Even though our backgrounds are as far from each other as two could possibly be, I guess the hunger to be the best is one thing we have in common.

On and off the field, I give my very all in everything I do. Sure, my heart might not be in playing ball anymore, but that doesn't mean I have the luxury to half-ass it. Not only does my team depend on me to get us into the national playoffs, but so do all the fans that come out every weekend to cheer us on, screaming from the top of their lungs in elation every time I score a touchdown.

For me, being second best is the same thing as losing. One thing that being Hank Walker's son has taught me is that losing is never an option. Even if I were at the Olympics playing any sport other than football and only brought home the silver medal, I'm sure my father would throw it in the trash and bitch-slap me so fast it would make my head spin.

Second place doesn't cut it in our family, and neither do slackers. Your disgraces are a direct reflection of the Walker name. If you suck, so do the people around you who enabled that defeated mentality. I guess when you hear that type of talk all your life, you do everything in your power not to bring your family dishonor or lose the faith your fans and teammates have put on your shoulders.

It's a fucking burden, but it's my reality just the same. My type of desperate drive comes from some pretty dark places sometimes. Places that will have you doing whatever is necessary so as not to visit often.

I know by heart what my motivations are. I just don't know Stone's. However, I hardly think you have to be a rocket scientist to figure them out. The shithole she works at and the part of town she lives in is kind of a dead giveaway as to what her reasons are behind her fearless gumption. The girl wants out of the hellhole she was born into and will claw her way out with gritted teeth and sharp nails if she needs to. You have to admire that. But somewhere along the way, Stone must have pissed off the wrong fucking people.

If she hadn't, then she wouldn't be on The Society's radar.

They haven't made any further contact after their first letters to Lincoln and me, so I'm still not sure exactly what they want with Stone. However, it's clear she's *persona non grata*, enough for them to put me on her scent. If they are as organized and ruthless as legend claims, then they've done their due diligence and know damn well I won't quit until the job is done, whatever that may be. That's just who I am, whether I'm comfortable with it or not.

Whatever I have to do, I just hope it doesn't have too much of a blowback on Stone. Not that I care about the girl, mind you. I mean, how could I when I don't even know her? It's just, after I've had a few days to think about it, I can't say it sits well with me to intentionally mess with a girl who has her shit together and wants a better life than the one afforded her.

Yep. The girl definitely made an impression.

Can't say I did the same for her, though, since she had no qualms in demonstrating exactly what she thought of me—or as she so eloquently put it, *my kind*. To Stone, I'm nothing but another spoiled, rich asshole from the north end of Asheville, who has nothing better to offer the world than to throw a fucking ball.

I guess we all have our prejudices and misconceptions of people just from which side of the fence they're born on. I have to admit, I've been guilty of being just as judgmental as she was. However, the minute I took one look at her schedule and realized I'm probably going to fuck up this girl's life somehow, the idea of it made me a little nauseous.

But a sick stomach can't compare with living behind iron bars for the rest of my life.

So there's that. No matter how shitty this situation is, it can get a whole lot worse. If I have to protect myself and my friends, and ensure our freedom by doing some shady shit to the Southie, then so be it.

Sorry, Stone. Guess you're on the losing team.

I'm still deep in my own twisted reverie when I catch a raven ponytail with bluish tips bouncing off in the distance across the courtyard. But she turns a corner, heading in a completely different direction than what I was expecting.

Shit!!! Where the hell is she going?

I rush my step, leaping over a stone bench and weaving around the innocent students in my mad dash across the quad. I'm sure none of them expected to see me pull a runner so early on a Friday morning while on their way to class, but that's exactly the show they're getting. I'm pulling all the stops just so I can get my ass over to Stone before I lose sight of her for good.

I hear my name being called out by a group of girls curled up together with their iced coffees—or whatever girly drinks are in at the moment—clutched to their hands. Absentmindedly I throw them a wave, causing a fit of giggles to rise from them in the process. I'm not sure if it's the perks of being me that has most girls acting like they don't have all their brain cells, or if chicks nowadays are, in fact, just shallow creatures who swoon over any asshole who can score a touchdown.

He's not even here, and I can already hear Easton teasing the fuck out of me for being so judgmental when it comes to the opposite sex. If it's not for fucking, I don't really see the appeal of hanging out with a chick. I haven't found one who has anything in common with me or is even halfway cool enough to be tempted to spend time with them, unless it involves being stark naked and fucking like bunnies.

Not that I've recently had the pleasure—or even the will—to get my dick wet. Since shit hit the fan in the worst way imaginable last semester, my sex drive took a nasty-ass spill and hasn't made a reappearance yet. If Viagra is the little blue tablet a guy takes to get his Johnson working, then a dash of murder is the bitter pill you swallow to kill off the libido for good.

But my sex life—or the lack thereof—is not my number one priority. It is the foul-mouthed Southie who unknowingly gave me the slip.

I'm still dodging around every obstacle in my way, just so I can catch up with Stone, when I realize that she's not heading to the ethics class like her schedule dictates, but rather strolling toward the parking lot on the far side of campus as if she had all the time in the world.

The fuck?!

Is she blowing off her classes already? On the first week back to school, no less? I thought Stone had more sense than that. Or am I missing something? Maybe Easton's guy slipped us a bogus schedule. Is the girl I had been enthralled by just a figment of the imagination of some douche looking to make a quick buck out of us? I haven't even talked to Stone yet, and she's already managed to piss me the hell off by crushing my expectations of the driven girl I imagined her to be.

I'm still fuming by the time I reach the parking lot. I'm only a few feet away when she opens the door to a beat-up blue truck, which looks older than dirt and twice as mean. It's more like a metal death-box rather than means of acceptable transportation. To each his own, I suppose. However, her poor choice in vehicles is not even the worst thing in my line of sight at the moment.

Stone must be trying to find something hidden in that death trap of hers. And she's having a hell of a time reaching whatever it is because the vexing girl begins to bend half her body into the front seat of the truck. She does it in such a way that her checkered skirt rises enough for me to see a little bit of the underlining of her smooth, tanned ass cheeks. Not to mention the clear view of the large, stellar phoenix tattoo inked on the outside of her upper thigh.

Stone is a short little thing, so when she jumps up a bit to give herself a better vantage point to grab whatever the fuck she's insistent on getting, her skirt continues to inch a little bit higher—enough for a sliver of the sexy, black-laced panties to play peek-a-boo with every pair of male eyes, who are fortunate enough to be in the front row seat to an otherwise private show.

Fuck my life.

To add insult to injury, my cock thinks that now is an ideal time to stir awake, notifying me it's fed up with its hibernation. Fucker wants to play and has fixed its sight on those pretty, black panties of hers, wanting to wipe its mushroom head on it.

'Settle the fuck down. That ass isn't for you,' I reprimand my dick.

'And why the fuck not? I mean, it's right there, begging for us to make an introduction!'

I roll my eyes, shifting my half-mast self to a more comfortable position inside my jeans. Even though Easton's course of action for befriending Stone was to get her in the sack as The Society ordered, I don't think that will bode well for me. A girl like Stone must have some maniac, armed-to-the-teeth boyfriend who wouldn't think twice in slashing my throat if I even thought about screwing his girl. At least that's what I would do in his shoes if the roles were reversed. When my cock twitches again, I tell it as much, to keep the fucker in check.

'Because an ass that fine usually has an owner, dickwad.'

How come you kissed her last Sunday night if she was already taken? You weren't so worried about her having a man then, now were ya, buddy? Did you really think I wouldn't notice you got some lip action, huh? I'm not dead, you know? Just needed some time off to get my shit together. You know how it is. So, thank you for making it worth my while to finally make an appearance. Good on you for bringing me this tasty treat and waking me the fuck up. Now go over there and let me get some.'

'No.'

'And why the hell not?' my cock whines, sounding like a five-year-old.

'Because that one right there is trouble.'

'But we like trouble.'

'Since the fuck when?' I shout inwardly.

'Since it looks that INSANELY HOT, moron!'

This is why men shouldn't make decisions when the little head down there is in the driver's seat, instead of the one on top of their shoulders. The fuckers don't ever think five seconds beyond cumming, which is always a recipe for disaster. Though I might have looked spaced out there for a minute while having an internal debate with my dick, I look around the parking lot and see that I'm not alone in my discomfort. I count at least five other guys slowly adjusting their stiffies as they get out of their cars, obviously suffering from a similar predicament. It's safe to say that I'm not the only one with an uncontrollable hard-on summoned by the little tattooed-slash-pierced she-devil.

Doesn't she care she's giving spank bank material to every guy in close proximity?

Apparently the answer to that question is a hard 'no' because, when Stone finally resurfaces from her scavenger hunt and straightens up back to her vertical self, my eyes instantly fix on the two-sizes-too-small, white T-shirt she has on, which leaves even less to the imagination. Just another perfect example of how this girl doesn't give a flying fuck with what she's throwing out into the world. Her round, firm breasts stretch out the soft material in a way that is most likely illegal in most states. Covering her two remarkable C cups are the words 'Bite me,' and by God, a bold request like that is impossible to go unnoticed by any hot-blooded male. Her rack begs for attention, demands to be teased and groped, nice and slow. Makes a guy wish he could sink his teeth over those diamond-shaped studs until they are wet and puckered to perfection.

'Now you're getting it,' my cock rasps excitedly.

His little stirring just reminds me that getting off is not on the agenda, no matter how much his insistent ass keeps whispering it in my ear. The slouching pout my dick makes doesn't even register with me because, at this precise moment, an unamused Stone Bennett is staring directly at me with a displeased scowl stitched on her pretty little face.

And this, right here, is when I freeze.

What the fuck am I supposed to do now?

Initially, I had planned to intercept Stone on her way to class by accidentally bumping into her like it was a serendipitous event or some shit like that. Then find a way to insert myself in her life without being obvious about it. Maybe casually ask her out for a cup of coffee or invite her to one of my games, something along those lines. My approach needed to look inconspicuous, innocent, and totally natural.

Not this shit!

Instead of the meet-cute I had orchestrated, I look like a fucking stalker. I'm standing just a smidge away from her with a pissed-off expression on my face and a trickle of sweat on my brow from the unexpected sprint I had to make to get my ass over to her.

With an acrimonious glower dominating her light, emerald eyes, Stone crosses her arms over the same cleavage I had pictured my dick being in between not even two seconds ago, waiting impatiently for me to say something.

Think, Finn. Think.

Open your mouth and say something!

This is where Easton is right on the money when he ridicules me so. I don't know how to talk to girls. It's like they're an entirely different species to me. I've never had the need for it, either. Most of the time, the girls who approach me do all the talking for me. They know my reputation and what exactly I'm about. I'm a one-time thing. They mount on, and I get off. No small talk really needed.

I'm not like East, who can say something witty and sarcastic at the drop of a hat to break the ice with perfect strangers. I don't have Colt's panty-melting smile or his cockiness that women naturally seem mesmerized by. And I sure as hell am no Lincoln Hamilton, whose name alone is enough to open a dialogue and gain genuine interest.

I'm just me—blunt, always in his head, occasionally crude, me.

And right now, being me doesn't seem like it's going to cut it.

"You lost again, pretty boy?" Stone asks, finally slicing through the deafening silence, with a cock to her brow and a teasing smirk on her lips.

"Why aren't you in class?" I hear myself grunt at her, rather than using her little taunt to my advantage and starting a normal conversation with her.

"Excuse me? What concern is that of yours?"

"Just answer the fucking question, Stone. Why the fuck aren't you in class?"

She slants her eyes and tries to bypass me without answering. But before she's able to escape, I hover over her, making her eat back her steps until she's leaning against her ugly-ass truck with nowhere to go. Only this time, no one can see her short skirt and her tempting boobs with my bulky frame covering her like a big-ass shadow.

"You know, for a big guy, you sure don't have a lot stocked up in that huge head of yours. You're seconds away from my knee slamming into your junk if you don't step out of my personal space," she states sweetly, deepening her southern twang to make her sound all respectable-like.

The amused glint in her eye tells me she's anything but, and would love nothing more than to kick me in the nutsack and have me fall down into the fetal position at her feet. I don't know why, but instead of heeding her warning, I lean in closer until my face is a breath away from hers, close enough to feel her heart pounding against mine.

"Don't act cute, little girl. Why did you ditch?"

She rolls her eyes and lets out an exaggerated long exhale.

"I didn't ditch, asshole. My ethics professor decided to play a no-show today. He sent everyone in my class an email this morning telling us as much. Happy now?" she explains, waving her hand between us and forcing me to step aside.

But I'm not done.

"Do you always come to school wearing a getup like what you've got on? Are you allergic to clothes that actually fit you, or something?"

She bats her eyes at me, placing her middle finger across her succulent, red-painted lips, and blows me a kiss.

"Fuck you, quarterback. Don't like what you see, then don't look," she counters coolly, before pushing my chest away to gain her precious space back.

She's not strong enough to actually move me from my rooted spot, but I take three steps back just the same.

"It's been real, pretty boy. But let's not make this a common occurrence, yeah?" she singsongs, swaying her hips left to right with her middle finger still up in the air as her parting wave.

I let out a scoff, but my eyes linger on her juicy ass just a few minutes longer.

Okay, so maybe I didn't do much better at befriending her today than I did last Sunday night, but it could have gone a whole lot worse. Any other girl would have freaked if I showed up out of the blue and got all up in her face. However, I highly doubt a girl like Stone Bennett scares off easily. The girl is a looker and certainly has to deal with handsy assholes all the time. I'm sure she would have pepper-sprayed my ass if she thought I was a real creeper.

So, even though it didn't go the way I planned, I'll consider today's interaction with her a win.

I just hope The Society sees it the same way.

CHAPTER 6

STONE

This cannot be happening.

What the hell is Finn Walker's damage?

Argh!

I suck in my teeth as I resentfully slow my ascent up the stairs leading to my psychology class—a class I'm already five minutes late to, I might add.

Mr. Quarterback himself has decided, today of all days, to make the bold move of standing guard right at the door to get my undivided attention. His calculated position makes it that I have to bypass his imposing frame if I want to get inside the classroom, which means I can't ignore his beautiful, sculpted face as I've painstakingly tried to do for the past few weeks. Unless a meteor suddenly falls from the sky onto the big Northside jerk's head and knocks him out cold, I have no choice but to confront the gorgeous beast of a man head-on.

Damn it.

Finn has been pulling this type of crap on me for weeks now. No matter where I go on campus, there he is waiting for me with his eyes locked on my every move, jaw tight and permanent scowl in place, only releasing an aggravated grunt or two when I occasionally acknowledge his presence by flipping him off. The deep-seated black look he always has on display every time he forces these exasperating collisions almost has me believing he hates the very sight of me. But for whatever ludicrous reason, Finn can't find it in himself to stay away, ending up tormenting me instead, with those clear, blue eyes fixed in his usual smoldering glare.

I seriously don't get why the hell I've suddenly become so goddamned fascinating to Richfield's pride and joy star quarterback. His stalking behavior is all sorts of confusing, and frankly, messing with my head more than I would like it to be.

I mean, why me?

What's so fucking thrilling about chasing my ass around campus when half the female population of this school would be on their knees in a hot minute if he so much as snapped his fingers in their direction? He and I both know that I'm not necessarily his type. I mean, let's be real, we are total opposites of each other. He's the captain of the football team while I'm the girl who has never even so much as seen a game in her whole life.

He's all-American perfection.

I'm the poster child for this country's rejects.

He's old Asheville money and privilege.

I'm the Southie eyesore that people steer clear from.

He's caviar dreams and champagne wishes.

I'm the trailer trash his momma probably warned him about.

I doubt it can get any further apart on the social spectrum than the two of us.

So what's his deal?

Unless Finn somehow filled his quota on debutant vajayjays and wants to take a ride on the wild side by slumming it up with a Southie for a change, I'm stumped as to what he wants from me. Especially because he's gone to a lot of trouble to know where I am at all times. Guys like Finn don't make that type of effort for just anyone. He's the type of asshole who expects girls to chase him, not the other way around.

So what gives?

And how the hell did he get his hands on my class schedule in the first place? It's the only explanation I have for him to suddenly have a GPS tracker on me, showing him exactly where I am at any given moment. During all my years at college, I've probably only seen Finn Walker a handful of times. Now, out of the blue, he just happens to pop up and run into me three to four times a day.

Yeah, I'm not buying it. Finn isn't that lucky. Pretty boy makes his own luck, of that I'm certain. I'd bet my poor excuse for a paycheck that the entitled jock got his hands on my class schedule, either by pulling some strings or shelling out some cash for it. No matter how he got it, I feel like Finn is my constant shadow now, one I can't seem to escape from.

Worst of all, he is totally unapologetic about his stalking tendencies. He makes no effort to hide himself from me, nor does he act like it's a total coincidence. It's happened more times than I can count, and honestly, I'm getting sick and tired of this cat and mouse game of his.

"Fuck off," I announce as a way of greeting when I take the final step that puts me face to face with my new nemesis. Or I should say face-to-chest since Finn is fucking huge compared to my small frame.

"Good morning to you too, Stone. You're late." He smirks arrogantly, proving once again the fucker knows my ins and outs around Richfield.

But the cocky grin on his face starts to slip as his eyes begin to roam my body. I stand just a little bit straighter so he can have his fill, getting a sick satisfaction when I watch his scowl deepen, and his brows pinch together in aggravation.

Ever since Finn let out of the bag that my choice in clothing was not to his taste, I take an extra bit of care to be my usual savage self. Today, I've got on my favorite black, ripped jeans that hug my curves like a second skin, and my black army boots with silver skulls drawn on its side by yours truly. My boots are probably my favorite piece out of the whole ensemble, but it's my frayed Sex Pistol's top that has Finn flustered and jaw ticking.

"What? See something you don't like?" I tease when his focus lingers a bit too long on my cleavage.

Pretty boy Finn hates it when Mary Kate and Ashley are proudly on display, popping out from my top a little too much for his liking. Sure, I could probably tone it down by using a different bra to keep the ladies contained, but then what would be the fun in that? His scowl is so deep that I'm sure he's going to get premature wrinkles if he doesn't relax. I stand victorious as I watch him poke his tongue into the left side of his inner cheek, inhaling a long irritated breath before he lets out his peeved reply.

"You think you're cute, don't you?"

"You tell me," I quip back innocently, mockingly batting my eyes at him for good measure.

He releases a sharp exhale up into the air and begins to run his fingers through his wavy golden locks.

Like that will help him deal with my perky breasts all up in his face.

Little does he know that with this innocent force of habit for keeping his temper in check, he's no longer the only one to be pissed off.

Yep, now it's my turn to stew in discomfort.

He keeps combing his hair back absentmindedly, while I try not to stare at the strands that must feel like heaven to touch. Smooth silk teases his fingertips, making me just a tad envious he can play with his dark-golden mane any time he likes, and we mere mortals can only sit back and watch.

While Finn remains distracted eyeing the heavens—trying to have a moment with whatever deity he thinks will hear his disgruntled prayer for my hardcore wardrobe—I take the opportunity to do my own ogling of his majestic form. Today he's wearing a sleeveless, navy blue Tommy Hilfiger shirt that makes his light, sapphire eyes pop.

Finn remains obsessed with my clothing size, but he has no reservations about his own clothes, which are tight enough that I can actually count how many abs he's got going under the soft material—it's eight by the way. Eight gloriously defined, mouthwatering abdominal muscles that must have taken years to perfect. But it's his muscular arms that really pull the drool out of me. His shirt was made to highlight his bulging biceps, appearing as thick as tree trunks. He could easily pick a girl up and put her over his shoulder without breaking a sweat, real caveman-like *(insert drool emoji here)*.

Damn.

I lick my lips as my eyes continue to crawl down his long, refined frame. The universe surely is a cruel bitch for putting such a flawless specimen walking around campus when it knows damn well that most of us don't have the time or luxury to spend daydreaming about such perfection.

My eyes stop at Finn's waist, noticing how he's got low-rise jeans on. The way he continues to play with his hair allows his shirt to rise up slightly, giving me just a little hint of the tantalizing V he keeps hidden underneath.

Sweet baby Jesus! Finn might have been annoying the fuck out of me recently, but damn is he pretty to look at.

So pretty.

I school my resting bitch face as best I can, pretending to be unfazed and bored with his mere presence, before I clear my throat to bring Finn's attention back to me.

"Move, quarterback. Some of us have classes to get to."

His plump upper lip tugs at its side, before he waves his hand as if pulling out the red carpet for me. I try hard not to roll my eyes while I take the opportunity to bypass him, even though he's only given me a narrow opening in between his steel-hard body and the cold, brick wall. As inconspicuously as possible, I take in a long breath, hoping the oxygen will be enough for the short walk through. No way am I going to take a whiff of Finn's cologne again if I can help it.

When he accosted me at my truck a few weeks ago, the rich, warm, woodsy scent clung to me for hours, making it hard to concentrate on any of my lectures for the day. I ended up spending precious class time lost in my own head, picturing naked, sweaty bodies, entwined together by an open fire in the middle of some dark woods, consumed by the frenzy of their lovemaking. I swear, some of the fantasies were so hot that I almost skipped lunch just so I could go to my dorm room and use my favorite battery-operated toy to relieve the ache that Finn's enticing fragrance provoked. Talk about powerful sensory stimulation overload. Pretty boy's pheromones pack quite a punch, and I, for one, do not want to be knocked out again. My hormones couldn't take it, nor could my attention span.

I'm just about to take my second step through when the jerk places a hand on the wall, blocking my passage. I instantly turn to flee from the other side, but his forearm is now pressed against that side, too, rendering my exit strategy obsolete. I crane my neck back to look up at the big gorilla, not so silently killing him in my mind with the daggers flying from my eyes.

"You're starting to piss me off, Finn," I tell him through gritted teeth.

"Ah, so you do know my name," he goads, his sweet, minty breath tickling my nose, and his autumn-night scent seeping into my skin, teasing me that he'll be the lead role of tonight's fantasies.

Damn it all to hell.

Instead of the back-and-forth banter I know he's lusting for, I jam my knee up as hard as I can, hoping the impact to his nuts will have him crying like a baby. To my dismay, Finn is too fast for me. He grabs my knee without even flinching, parting my legs until he's fitted perfectly in between them. Thank God I'm wearing jeans because the heat of our cores colliding has me squirming like a virgin on her wedding day.

"You don't have a boyfriend," he rasps, his translucent eyes transfixed with mine.

"Is that a question?"

"No. I know you don't."

No surprise there. He's stalked my ass long enough to know I don't have time to eat, much less date.

"Lucky for you, since this is quite a compromising position you've put me," I retort sarcastically, pointing out how he has me pinned to the wall like he's about to ravish me, fucking me good and hard right here for everyone to see.

Shit.

Guess I'll have to stock up on batteries with that little scenario stuck in my head now.

He lets out a little smirk but doesn't move an inch. I remain trapped between the two walls—both the cold one at my back and the hot one scorching my front. I know exactly which one I'd rather been leaning against, but I do my best not to cave into the temptation.

"You know this could be classified as harassment," I warn, flicking my tongue ring at him, feigning indifference to the tight quarters he has us in.

No way in hell will I let on that his close proximity is making Mary Kate and Ashley stand to attention. Luckily, his eyes are no longer enchanted with the twins. Nope, those sapphire blues are studying my face, as if memorizing every inch of it.

"You can get me off you anytime you want. Just say the word."

His light eyes dance when I place my hands on his chest, but I make no effort to push him away.

"Tell me something. Did I put my name down for some sort of stalker raffle?" I ask instead, grateful his chest is no longer chafing against my sensitive breasts.

"Something like that," he grunts.

I watch, confused, as the playful glint in his eye takes a back seat to an emotion I can't quite put my finger on. It's almost as if the little joke I just made saddened him. No, sad is the wrong word for it. It looks more like concern. Worry, deep-rooted worry. Seriously, this guy is mindboggling—hot as sin yes, but still damned frustrating to read.

"God, you're weird. You know that, right?"

"You're not the first person to think so, Stone. My best friends tell me that shit all the time."

He lets out a timid chuckle, and wouldn't you know it—that little hint of boyish shyness has my core splashing away like fucking Niagara Falls.

"They do, huh? And what do your so-called friends think about you chasing a Southie around campus like a lost puppy?"

"I'm no lost puppy, little girl, but I have been known to bite." He winks at me.

"That makes two of us," I warn, snapping my teeth to give him the visual of how I could tear him, limb from limb, if given the chance.

"Fuck. I bet you do, don't you?" he lets out gruffly, his sultry gaze dropping to my lips.

I wish I could tell my body to take a chill pill, but my feverish skin enjoys his hungry eyes on me. A little too much if you ask me. The fluttery sensation in my body intensifies when Finn leans in, his lips inches away from my left ear.

"I think we should hang out," he rasps, dragging his teeth along the seam of his lower lip.

"Hang out or *hook up*?" I counter, running a finger down his chest, which is immediately rewarded with a little shiver running down his spine.

"Whatever interests you the most," he taunts mischievously.

I turn my head just enough for our lips to be a hair's breadth away from each other.

"Never. Going. To. Happen. Pretty boy," I point out, so close to his mouth that he can almost taste my rejection on his luscious lips. "Go find yourself a blow-up doll you can have fun with. There are plenty of plastic ones walking around Richfield for your amusement."

I push him off me and run in haste to my classroom, not looking back at the stunned, hot-as-hell jock that must be picking up his jaw from the ground.

Professor Harper slants her eyes at my tardy entrance but doesn't call me out on it. Thank God. My eyes spot a few vacant seats at the far back of the classroom, and even though I probably won't hear a word of today's lecture from all the way up there, I don't scan the room further for a more appealing seating. I don't want to piss Professor Harper off further by disrupting her class any more than I have to.

The minute my ass finds its seat, I let out a little gasp when another student unexpectedly sits right beside me with a loud thud. I turn to see who it is, and my lips thin in contempt—royal blue eyes stare me down, telling me they aren't done with my ass just yet, no matter where I run off to.

Great. Just fucking great.

Like I need the extra distraction today. I swear, if Finn Walker doesn't get the hint, I'll probably murder him. Or fuck his brains out. If I'm honest, it's looking fifty-fifty either way right about now.

CHAPTER 7

FINN

My leg bounces up and down while I impatiently watch Stone take down her class notes, pretending I'm not even here. I know it was a bold move chasing after her the way I did, but to be honest, desperate times call for desperate measures.

Following her into the classroom can go either one of two ways—she will finally acknowledge my existence and hear me out, or she'll march down to the sheriff's department and get a restraining order on my ass as soon as this class finishes.

Can I honestly blame her if she does the latter?

The way I've been carrying on is downright psychotic. If the shoe were on the other foot, I wouldn't handle it with such sarcastic humor as hers. I thought I could keep wearing her down until she caved, but unfortunately, today I got another incentive to up my game when it came to Stone.

Apparently, The Society isn't thrilled with the snail's pace I've been taking to win the brash girl over. This morning, I almost choked on my protein-powder shake when Mom handed me another black envelope with its trademark red seal. Luckily for me, she didn't ask too many questions, but I saw she was intrigued enough to keep lingering around in the kitchen, waiting to see if I'd open it in front of her.

Fat chance that was going to happen.

Instead, I just threw her what I hope looked like a genuine, innocent smile and told her I was late for morning practice. I then gave her a quick peck on the cheek and hauled ass out of there.

When I got to the safety of my car, I ripped open the wretched thing. I thought I was going to hurl my breakfast up in my lap and have to go back inside to change. I got the fuckers' message loud and clear, even though it took me a few times to fully register it in my panicked mind. In bold, golden lettering, their threat pierced my heart, making me realize that all the fun and games were now officially off the table. Things were about to get real if I didn't change my tactics. And fast.

CRUSHING A PEBBLE INTO SAND
SHOULDN'T BE SO HARD.

YOU JUST HAVE TO KNOW
HOW MUCH PRESSURE TO APPLY.

TIME IS A LUXURY YOU DON'T HAVE.

FIND A WAY TO BE THE SOUTHIE GIRL'S DREAM,

OR FORCE OUR HAND
TO UNLEASH YOUR NIGHTMARE.

CHOOSE WISELY.

THE SOCIETY

These bastards, whoever they are, demand quick results, and so far, I haven't been able to give them any. To The Society, chasing Stone's fine ass around campus doesn't count for shit. They want me to befriend her, become part of her life. However, the way I've been going about it hasn't satisfied them in the least.

Fuckers.

I startle in my seat when a gentle hand grips my bouncing knee, halting it to a stop. I turn to the girl who looks halfway pissed, but surprisingly, halfway impressed, too.

Hmm.

"If you're going to stay throughout the class, at least be quiet about it. Don't distract me, Finn. I need to concentrate. Got it?"

I give her a tight nod and keep rigid still, taking an odd breath here and there, hoping that taking oxygen into my lungs doesn't count as a distraction.

Stone never calls me Finn. Only when she is dead-serious, or at her wits' end.

If I'm supposed to win brownie points with her, then keeping quiet and not fidgeting in my seat is the least I can do.

Since my mind will no doubt go back to that cursed letter, which is currently burning a hole through my car's glove compartment, I need to try keeping my thoughts occupied with something else.

My eyes start scanning the small auditorium and see some familiar faces that I wasn't expecting to encounter so early this morning. Sitting in the third row are Colt and the Ryland twins, who are on their laptops taking down their own detailed notes of today's lecture. Kennedy and Jefferson Ryland, with their golden-blond heads curled down, type up a storm, looking naturally in sync with each other. Even if it wasn't public knowledge the two shared a womb, their mannerisms would be a dead giveaway of their familial bond.

Colt, however, doesn't seem as dedicated to the class. Even from way up here, I can see his screen full of pictures of barely-clad sorority girls soaping up cars from the back-to-school car wash they had over the weekend. The event was supposed to raise money for some Greek-row party to celebrate the first games of the season. But let's be honest, it was just a lousy excuse for those girls to appease their snobby, debutant moms who look down on anyone wearing a skirt above knee length. They couldn't care less about any sport, aside from the one that justified them using skimpy bikinis showcasing their summer-tanned bodies and, of course, all the beer they were going to buy from its profits. I predict most of the girls on Colt's screen will have their stomachs pumped this Saturday. Those tight bodies won't look so hot with puke all over them.

Say what you will about Stone, but I doubt I would ever see her make such a fool of herself. The girl might wear clothes that harden every dick within a twenty-mile radius, but she owns that shit. And working at that dump of a bar every night, she's probably seen enough falling-down drunks to ever want to be one.

Not wanting to dwell on the fiasco of this weekend's boozefest, I continue with my perusal throughout the room, only to have Easton turn in his seat and lock eyes with me, apparently having felt my lingering stare in his direction.

"The fuck are you doing?" Easton mouths across the room, brow furrowed in confusion.

"The fuck does it look like?" I mouth back, discreetly tilting my head to the girl at my side.

When his dark glance picks up on the Southie sitting right next to me, who has her nose inside her notebook, he finally gets the hint. He picks up his phone, and I grab mine, knowing the curious asshole will want to talk this shit out.

Sirsmokesalot: *Feeling a bit desperate, r we? U know girls hate that shit, right?*

Me: *Fuck off!!!!!!*

Sirsmokesalot: *I'm serious, asswipe. Crashing her Psychology class is a dumb move. You're gonna piss her off. She's not exactly the friendly type.*

Me: *Have any other bright ideas?*

Sirsmokesalot: *Yeah, like I'm going to help u get laid.*

Me: *Fucker* >:(

Sirsmokesalot: *#NotEvenSorry* :)

Me: *You know it's all our asses on the line, right, Sherlock?*

Sirsmokesalot: *And there you go spoiling my fun* :(

Me: *Fuck your fun* :p

Me: …

Me: *Got another one today.*

Sirsmokesalot: *A letter??????*

Me: *No moron, a hard-on. YES, A LETTER!!!*

Sirsmokesalot: *Shit. What did it say?*

Me: *Not now. I'll show you and the guys over lunch.*

Sirsmokesalot: *The gist, motherfucker.*

Me: *Fine, dipshit. Basically it's just a not-so-gentle reminder that I'm running out of time with u know who.*

Sirsmokesalot: *Fuck.*

Sirsmokesalot: *…*

Sirsmokesalot: *Finn?*

Me: *Yeah?*

Sirsmokesalot: *Stop fucking around and get the girl.*

Me: *I'm trying!*

Sirsmokesalot: *Try harder!!!*

Dick!

It's easy for him to make demands when I'm the one in the hot seat. But as much as I want to deny it, East is right. I do have to try harder. I just don't know how. I mean, how much more in her face can I get? It's not like there is an online instruction manual that I can look up to learn how to woo a girl. Can a girl like Stone even be wooed? And why the hell am I saying woo, all of a sudden?

Shit.

I'm losing it big time. This last letter fucked me up real good.

I'm not sure how much time passes by as I try to come up with ways to get in Stone's good graces. But all too soon, I see students around us beginning to jump up from their seats, officially announcing the end of the class.

As Stone starts putting her stuff away, I just sit there looking like a chump, feeling even more flustered for not coming up with a strategy that will keep The Society off our backs.

"Move, quarterback. I need to get to my next class," she snaps at me, but it doesn't have her usual teasing tone.

Unfortunately, Stone just sounds as frustrated as I feel. Yep, I think I totally fucked this up. Not that it was going well to begin with, but I must have poked the beast one too many times. It's likely that she's now planning on how to take a huge chunk out of me as payback.

"You're pissed, huh?" I ask, staring at my feet, not wanting to face the she-demon head-on.

I hear her let out a long, exaggerated exhale, dropping her book bag back onto her seat.

"Okay, Finn. What do you want? Out with it," she orders instead of answering my question, placing her hands on her hips to demonstrate she's over my shit.

"I told you. Just want to hang out." I shrug, my feet kicking the seat in front of me.

Because if we don't, eventually my best friends and I are likely to see daylight only through iron bars for the rest of our lives. So give a guy a break, will you?

"You said that already," she spews, not one bit thrilled at the idea.

Fuck my life.

We are so screwed. I don't know how to do this. How the fuck am I supposed to win over a girl like Stone when I can't even talk right? I'm a twenty-two-year-old football god at Richfield, yet here I am, all tongue-tied and shit. Seriously, sometimes being me sucks balls. This is just too damn hard. I'll just have to talk to the guys and see if we can go about this some other way without The Society following through on their threat. I mean, maybe Colt or Easton could take over from me. Not that I like that idea any better. Having either one of those assholes hit on Stone doesn't sit right with me. Actually, just the idea of it pisses me off.

Shit. I'm all messed up.

What the fuck am I going to do?

My mind is still a battleground when I feel strong, deft fingers pull at the strands of my hair, tilting my head back to look into piercing, emerald eyes.

"You really do suck at this, don't you, pretty boy?" Stone coos with a softness in her green plains that I've never seen before.

Damn it, she's beautiful.

Sure, Stone might look like she would rather shiv you than kiss you, but that doesn't take away from her natural beauty. She surely is a sight to behold. And here I am, thinking of ways to be in her life just so I can fuck it up when The Society demands it.

Fan-fucking-tastic.

She takes a beat to stare into my eyes, and I force myself to keep them wide open, all the while hoping she doesn't read the truth behind all the lies they are silently feeding her.

Do you see how ugly I am inside, Stone?

What I've done?

What I will need to do because of it?

"You do that a lot, don't you? Get lost in that head of yours? I wonder what goes on in there," she hushes curiously, running her fingers through my wild locks, massaging my scalp to perfection.

Her tender touch feels fucking incredible. And wouldn't you know it—my stiff shoulders start to relax, as does the rest of my body. Well, most of it. My cock didn't get the memo advising that this isn't some kind of foreplay, so when it swells in my jeans, I'm not the least bit surprised.

I lick my dry lips, trying to put some moisture back into them while attempting to summon something to say that won't put me on The Society's naughty list.

"You're right on both accounts," I shyly confess instead, making those light green meadows soften even further.

"Yeah, I gathered as much."

Her genuine smile splits her face wide open, and my focus shifts from her stunning eyes to her succulent lips. When her teeth peek out to drag them over her lower lip, my half-mast cock turns into steel.

"Stop looking at me like that," she rasps, her glorious chest beginning to heave up and down.

"Why? I think you like it when I stare. Besides, I think I've become quite good at it," I counter, bravely placing my hands on her hips, dominantly pulling her toward me.

"God, I hate you," she mumbles as I pin her between my spread legs, so close that the heat of her core chars my aching shaft.

"I don't care."

"I'm not going to fuck you when the next class is minutes away from walking into the room," she warns huskily.

"Not asking for a fuck. Your lips will do just fine," I taunt, running my thumb under her shirt, grazing her hipbone. The girl has skin as smooth as silk, and having only this little sliver to play with is pure torture.

"I'm not going to blow you either, quarterback."

I can't help but chuckle at that. Mind you, I'd love nothing more but to have those red-painted lips smearing my ten inches, coating it nice and slow with her lipstick until a crimson ring is permanently tattooed on the fucker. However, I'll settle for something tamer, something sweeter.

"You're going to kiss me, Stone."

"You're giving orders now?" she teases with one brow cocked up high.

"I can just take it if I wanted to."

"I'd like to see you try."

"Ah, little girl, you really shouldn't have said that," I exclaim with a smug smirk, before lifting her off the ground and cradling her in my lap in one fell swoop.

My hand slowly traces her outer rib, right next to one tantalizing breast, until I reach her exposed neck. When her breath stills, I cradle it at its nape and go in for the kill. And in case I had forgotten that night at the bar when she first came into my life, Stone reminds me just how lethal her fucking kiss is. Her lips open up for me like rosebuds on a spring morning, and this time I don't think twice before plunging my wet tongue into her mouth to meet hers. Soft and pliant, she welcomes me in, as one hand rakes my hair while the other claws at my shoulder. The touch of pain, mingled with her sweetness, only fuels me further, as I eat up her moans, getting lost in our feverish kiss.

Damn it.

For a girl who said screwing was off the table, she isn't shy in letting me fuck her mouth. She tastes like trouble sprinkled with sugar, and at this precise moment I have a reckless sweet tooth dying to be satisfied.

I caress the base of her throat with the pad of my thumb as I nibble on her lower lip, toying with it until her sighs sing around me. My tongue dives into her hot mouth again, and begins to stroke its counterpart, caressing against her slightly cooler piercing. If the sleek metal feels this good playing with my tongue, I wonder what neat tricks it could do to my dick. Jesus, just kissing her has me hard as a rock. I can't even imagine if she took me into her mouth. I'd lose my load just by having her on her knees to use and abuse, let alone feeling that hard, silver ball tease my head.

God, what a fucking visual.

Before I know what I'm doing, my hands have taken over. One is still lightly squeezing the Southie's neck in lust while the other is skimming over her jean-clad pussy, delighting itself on how she's unashamedly rubbing her core against it. My ears pick up voices coming from outside the classroom, and I curse into her mouth, hating the fact I'll have to cut this short. If I could have just two more minutes, I'd see firsthand how Stone falls apart. That's the only endgame I have in mind.

Fuck The Society.

Having Stone under me for my own personal satisfaction just became my number one priority.

I feel her squirm under my touch, as her cheeks turn pink and droplets of sweat form on her brow. She's so fucking close. I'm so hungry to watch her stumble over the precipice that I don't even care if we get caught.

"You have thirty seconds to cum, Stone. Show me just how bad you want it," I growl, biting her lower lip with such force, her eyes roll to the back of her head.

Stone wiggles in my grip, rubbing her pussy even more vehemently against my hand, so I add extra pressure to where her swollen clit is under her clothes. Since I'm working on the clock and don't have time to unbutton her jeans, I'll have to get her off some other way.

My eager fingers won't be enough to get her over the edge, so I break away from her mouth and pull her flimsy, wide-neck T-shirt under one of her breasts with my teeth, exposing her black-laced bra that does a poor job of hiding her pebbled nipple. If I had more time, I'd strip her bare and have her two tits in my face so I could get lost in them for hours. But since time *is* of the essence, I close my mouth over one heavy breast, sucking on her puckered bud through the netted material. My teeth nip around its haloed edge until a loud cry rips out from her throat, her body shaking and quivering in my hold.

Holy shit! That may be the most gorgeous fucking sight I have ever seen.

Stone's short-lived orgasm feels bittersweet to me, so I go for one more kiss, just to lessen the current ache we're both experiencing. However, I should have known that going to the source of such decadence would only amp up our desire. Resentfully, I pull away, her altered breathing coming in quick gasps, to simmer down her trembling body. I fix her top and place a gentle kiss on her slick temple before gripping her chin so I'm all she sees.

"I'm going to pick you up tonight after you've finished your shift at the dump you call a bar. No backtalk, Stone. This is non-negotiable. Understood?"

Her hooded eyes linger on me for a spell, but she doesn't refuse me. Instead, she gives me a bratty wink, tormenting my dick further. I place her back on her unsteady feet, taking her book bag with me to show that I'll be walking her to the next class, whether she likes it or not.

From here on out, we play the game by my rules. Her sassy mouth is not going to get in my way.

"So I guess that's it, then. We're officially going to *hang out*?" She wiggles her brows at me.

Ah, Stone, we're going to do much more than that.

Just wait and see.

CHAPTER 8

FINN

My palms tap away on the steering wheel in sync with my bouncing knee, my restlessness and anxiety showing their telltale signs of being in uncharted waters, something that I'm not exactly thrilled about.

I should have probably waited for Stone inside the bar. It would have been the gentlemanly thing to do, especially considering she came on my lap just this morning. It's not like I didn't try to be chivalrous and shit. I mean, I did go inside. The thing is, when I looked around the dump, filled to the brim with guys eye-fucking her, there was no way I was going to handle it well. Besides, the lingering smell of puke and cum had my ass wanting to hightail it out of there anyway.

So I did the cowardly thing and just texted that I was outside waiting for her in my car. Good thing too, since last time I was here it was in Easton's truck, instead of my precious baby like tonight.

Easton could replace his truck easily enough if some Southie fucker decided to take it for a spin. My Porsche, however, is a whole other story. My father would crack my skull in if he found out it was stolen because I decided to slum it out in the worst part of town on a Friday night. Yeah, that conversation wouldn't go down so well with my old man.

'You're being a conceited, pompous prick,' I hear Easton's voice bellow in my ear. Not that he's here to give me his opinion on the matter, but it's a safe assumption that's what the asshole would say if he were. And maybe he's right. Just because some criminals live on the other side of the tracks doesn't mean that everyone here is a felon. I mean, look at Stone. She's hardworking, keeps her nose clean, and she's a Southie through and through. If I think about it, the Northside has plenty of bad apples, even though we play it off like our shit doesn't stink. Take me, for example, no one would ever think I was involved in a fucking double homicide, but here we are.

Here we fucking are.

I stare at my phone for the umpteenth time and see it's well past midnight. Stone said her shift ended at midnight on the dot—like a misfit Cinderella of sorts—so what is taking so long for her to get her fine ass out of that pigsty and into the leather seat of my car?

Hmm.

She's probably freshening up and making herself beautiful for our first date.

I feel a pull of my lip curve upward with the thought of her taking all this time just to look good for me, but that idiotic notion is quickly crushed into smithereens. When I hear her voice holler goodnight to some drunkards slouching on the wall outside of the bar, I establish she looks exactly the same as she did when I saw her inside earlier.

Not that she doesn't look good. Fuck, in those short shorts, it's impossible for her not to. But still…

I don't know why I'm disappointed, though. Maybe I thought she was going to put on a sexy-ass dress for me or something. I roll my eyes at myself in annoyance, because I should know better. Stone isn't the type of girl who wears girly-girl things for a guy. And she sure as shit isn't the kind of girl who goes out of her way to look pretty for someone she barely knows; maybe not even for someone she does. She dresses for her own goddamned self, so thinking I could ever influence her fierceness in any way, is just downright stupid. This date hasn't even started yet, and I'm already acting like the world's biggest douche.

"Nice ride," she says with a sarcastic, over-the-top whistle, before slamming the car door like a garden gate.

"Thanks," I mumble.

"So? Where are we going?"

"Hmm. I thought you'd have an idea." I shrug.

"You're kidding me, right?" She snaps her neck to me in outrage.

"Hey, its midnight. No. Hold up. It's actually a quarter to one." I poke at the time on my phone screen for good measure. "Not many places I can take you, sweetheart."

Furious with my reply, Stone looms her open palm right over my face, and I sink in my seat, ready for the tongue lashing she's going to give me.

"First things first, don't *ever* call me sweetheart again without expecting me to kick your junk in return. Secondly, this *hanging out* thing was your brilliant idea. The least you could have done was think of a place to take me, asshole," she lashes out, unamused with my lack of plans.

She's right. I know this is all for show, but I should have had a game plan for tonight. I mean, something that will be fun for her while putting up with my sorry ass. Lord knows, when all this goes to shit, she'll be left with a bad aftertaste thinking about the time she spent with me. The least I could do is make a genuine effort for her to be entertained. Maybe even give Stone some good memories to remember me by, since I'm positive she'll have plenty of bad ones in the near future.

Not that I care about that.

Stone is a mark. A hot, sexy-as-sin mark, but a mark just the same. Still, it wouldn't kill me to show up as she deserves, now would it?

I lean my head on the headrest and stare into her pissed-off silhouette.

"I'm sorry, Stone. You're right to be mad. But I told you this morning that I'm not good at these things. It's not like I do this all the time. Just be patient with me while I try to work out the kinks, okay?"

I watch her fury lose a little bit of its steam, her cute nose scrunching in contemplation. She turns her whole body in my direction, those soft, red lips creating the most beautiful frown that could ever have graced her face.

"What do you mean? Like date?" Her brows pinch together suspiciously.

"Yeah, date. It's not like I'm known for taking girls to the movies or fancy dinners. If you want me to be honest with you, the last time I took a girl out was probably to my high school prom. And I did that shit just because it was expected."

She tilts her head, scrutinizing my every feature, as well as each honest-to-God word that just spilled from my lips. Once she comes to terms that I'm telling her the gospel's truth, she slumps back into her seat with her eyes fixed on the hood of the car.

"You curse too much," she finally says after an infernal, pregnant pause.

"Sorry," I mumble in defeat, turning my own body forward in my seat.

"No, Finn. Don't apologize for who you are. I was just making an observation."

"Oh."

I poke my tongue to my inner cheek as the awful silence returns. She's clasping her hands over her bare knees, while I crack my knuckles, hating she's decided not to say anything else, obviously waiting for me to be the one to take the lead.

Fuck it. Here goes nothing.

"It's from being with guys all the time. The cursing, I mean. You know... football banter, locker room talk, and all that nonsense. Plus it doesn't help I'm also the youngest of three boys. There has always been a lot of cursing at my house. It's all the testosterone, I guess."

"I bet your momma loves that," she chimes in, and a flicker of hope springs free when I see her lip twitch in amusement.

"No, Ma'am. I wouldn't dare cuss in front of my momma. Not if I didn't want to get slapped upside the head for it. Or worse, have her clean my mouth with a bar of soap. I've seen her do it, too. My brother Calvin was burping soap suds for weeks after blurting out 'shit' in front of her, and he was already married at the time."

The melodic laugh that ensues from the girl next to me makes my heart skip a few beats. It's the first time I've ever heard Stone laugh, and surprisingly enough, it gives her such a youthful glow that it takes me by surprise a little. I don't know if it's her hard, mean exterior or the piercings and tattoos, but her laugh reminds me that she's just a girl, barely in her twenties, on the brink of starting her life. There's still so much innocence the world hasn't taken away from her yet—something that can only be perceived by her carefree laughter.

Fuck.

I hope I don't change that. It would be a travesty to tarnish something that pure and untouched.

"Okay, so we've established you don't date. I get it. I'm not much for it either. But I do like to have fun, though. So tell me, pretty boy, do you want to salvage the night and have some fun?"

She cranes her head my way with sultry mischief in her eyes, and because that one look could probably get her anything out of me, I repeatedly nod like the fool that I am.

"Good," she exclaims, slapping my knee. "Stay here. I'll be right back."

Before I have time even to utter a word, she's already out the door, sashaying her fine ass back to the bar from cockroach hell. Thankfully, I don't have to wait too long for her return. Not even five minutes later, she's back with a wide grin on her face and a plastic bag in each hand. She slams the door again, making me cringe in my seat. But I don't dare say anything of it since it looks like the night is finally going in my favor.

"What do you have there?" I nudge her bags, hearing the clink of bottles brushing together.

"Finn, meet Jack and Jose—my two favorite men. A crappy date is never as bad when I've got these guys to fall back on." She pokes her pierced tongue at me with a sassy wink.

"Glad to see you have a plan B." I chuckle.

"You think this is plan B? Aw, you're cute when you're naive. This is plan A, baby. You are just here as my side entertainment."

I laugh harder because the girl sure is cocky as fuck. And wouldn't you know it, I kind of dig that about her.

I take a minute to think to myself where we can go to break the seal on the bottles. There is only one place I can think of that feels right to me. I've never really taken anyone there, but somehow, the idea of Stone seeing it excites me.

"I know where I want to take you."

"Do you, now? Just came to you, did it?"

"Yep." I chuckle, turning on the ignition. "Keep those two bad boys in check. We can get our drink on when we arrive, not before."

"Oh, don't you worry your pretty little head about that, darlin'. I've got these two well taken care of," she retorts playfully with the whole southern twang on her drawl.

Once I get us on the road, she starts to fiddle with the car radio to find some tunes to her liking. Although, she didn't so much as ask me if I wouldn't mind putting on music. I've come to realize that Stone just does what she wants, when she wants it, and damn who doesn't like it. It's oddly refreshing.

Most girls are always trying to impress me by pretending to be what they think I *want* them to be, but Stone doesn't give a crap about impressing me one way or the other. In fact, I'd bet my trust fund she's like that with everybody. She's just who she is. Take it or leave it. I guess we have that in common. Well, for the most part anyway.

"So, pretty boy, do you want to give me any hints on where you're taking me?"

"You'll see." I grin, tapping my fingers on the wheel in sync with the drums of the rock song she picked.

"You're not going to take me into the woods and murder me or something, are you?"

"What kind of fucking question is that?!" I belt out, taking my eyes off the road to gawk at her.

Stone just giggles at my stupefied expression and pushes my face forward, so I don't crash us into a ditch.

"Don't get so sensitive on me, quarterback. A girl has to be careful when getting into a car with strangers," she teases unashamedly.

"This morning, I had your pussy grinding on my hand so hard that you came all over it. I think we're well past the 'strangers' stage, don't you?"

"Touché."

She turns her head away for a second, facing the side window, but I can still see the faint blush coloring her cheeks from the reflection.

"I'm not taking you to any woods. So settle your pretty ass down," I tease.

"So, you're not going to put me on some stone altar and use me as a sacrifice to the football gods or something? Because if you are, I hate to tell you that those rituals only work with virgins, and—spoiler alert—I lost my V-card when I was fifteen. You came a little late for that rodeo, pretty boy."

"Fifteen, huh? Pretty young, don't you think?"

"Is it? I never really thought about it." She shrugs pensively. "When did you lose yours?"

"Fourteen."

"That's even earlier than me. Kind of hypocritical, don't you think?" she counters, crossing her arms under her ample breasts, pushing them up in the process. It's distracting as fuck. "Hey, quarterback," she snaps her fingers in my face. "Eyes on the road and less on the girls. Just answer the damn question. Why is it young for me to lose my virginity at fifteen and not young for you at fourteen?"

"I didn't say that it wasn't."

"So, what *are* you saying? Do you wish you lost your virginity later, is that it?"

"God, no. My right hand needed a break by then," I joke.

"But you think *I* should have? Waited, I mean?"

"Didn't say that either," I quip back.

"It's because I'm a girl, right? That double standard bullshit annoys the hell out of me." She huffs.

"Don't put words in my mouth, Stone. It was just an observation, not a political statement."

"Then why did you say it was young?"

"I don't know." I shrug self-consciously. "I always figured a girl's first time needed to mean something to them. I'm not saying having sex at fifteen is young, but having a deep enough connection with someone to even want to do it in the first place feels kind of young to me. Does that make sense?"

"Not every girl needs a fairy tale," she murmurs.

"So, you weren't in love with the guy who popped your cherry?"

"Nope," she explains, popping the 'P' in the end, crossing her arms again.

"Then, why do it?" I ask, genuinely curious.

"The same reason you lost yours. It felt good."

"Huh."

I keep tapping my thumb on the steering wheel as I take her explanation to heart. Every time she opens her mouth, I become further in awe of the in-your-face attitude she has. How can Stone be so fearless—even at fifteen—that she didn't buy into the bullshit of her first time being with someone she loved? Instead, she did the deed just because she was horny, which is freaking astounding. It must be fucking liberating to be her—being able to do whatever she wants, just because she wants it. I have to say that I'm a little envious.

I'm still trying to make sense of such an extraordinary creature, when she playfully knocks on the top of my head, startling my wayward thoughts.

"What's going on in that brain of yours?" she taunts. "Think I'm a slut now, don't you?" she adds humorously, not one bit flustered by what my opinion of her may be after her little confession.

"Not in a million years, Stone. I was just thinking how, even at fifteen, you were freer than most."

She tilts her head back and lets out such a deep, rich laugh that it twists up my insides.

The fuck is that all about?

"I'm not free, quarterback. I've got too many bills to prove how wrong you are. I'm chained and bound to student debt and a whole other list of expenses just to get by. I'm hardly the poster child for American freedom."

"That's just semantics. Your future is going to be out of this world, Stone. Money problems will be the last thing you'll ever worry about. But having your free spirit… that's something money can't buy."

She slants her grin to the side, the little hint of a blush reaching her cheeks again before she squeezes my knee to get my attention.

"For someone who doesn't date much, you sure are a smooth talker when you want to be."

Now it's my turn to cackle.

"That's Easton or Colt's area of expertise. Trust me. I have no game whatsoever."

"You could have fooled me," I hear her mumble under her breath, side-eyeing me under her long, dark lashes.

I clear my throat because there is suddenly a huge-ass lump inside just from the way she's taking stock of my every feature. I wipe my clammy hands on my jean-clad thighs, and inwardly order myself to get it together.

Be cool, Finn.

Don't blow your wad just because a pretty girl is staring at you.

Discreetly I take a little peek at her and exhale a relieved breath when I establish her eyes are back on the road and no longer sizing me up.

"We're almost there. Another twenty minutes or so," I choke out, trying to fill the silence.

"Right. This mysterious place you picked out for us to get wasted and fuck. I can't wait to see it."

I cough into my fist, my eyes bulging out of their sockets.

"Who said anything about sex?" I blurt.

"So, you just want to do what? Talk?" she coos mockingly.

"And why the hell not?! We're having fun doing it now, aren't we?"

She bends her head back and starts to laugh uncontrollably.

"Oh God, pretty boy. You are way too easy to rile up. I swear if you hadn't already told me otherwise, I'd think you were still a virgin."

"Very funny. Haha," I rebuke sarcastically. "Can we just quit with all the sex talk already?"

From my peripheral, I watch how she pretends to zip her lips and throw away the key.

"Thank you," I mumble.

"Oh, don't thank me yet. Just so you know, if we can't talk about sex, then that means the act itself is off the table. You'll have to find something else to entertain me with tonight."

"There are plenty of things we can do that don't involve sex." I push my chin out at her reproachfully.

"So you've said. Apparently, we can *talk*," she teases, doing bunny ears between the word.

"Don't forget, we can also drink." I eye the bottles on the floor at her feet.

"Oh, trust me, I didn't forget." She wiggles her brows in my direction.

"You know, you're a real brat when you want to be."

"So I've been told. It's part of my charm," she huffs out dramatically, flipping her blue-tipped, onyx hair off her shoulder.

"Hmm, and here I thought it was all the hardware and colorful tattoos that made you stand out from the crowd."

"Are you dissing my ink now, quarterback?"

"I wouldn't dream of it. However, I am curious—is there any part of your body that hasn't been branded yet?"

"Wouldn't you like to find out?" She winks.

Yes.

Yes, I fucking would.

However, I'm the idiot who just told her all he wanted from tonight was to talk and drink. The next few hours are going to be killer on my nerves and self-restraint, that's for damn sure.

I look down at my junk, feeling his angry stare back at me, as he shakes his head left to right, not at all pleased with how I don't have his back. I just cockblocked my own goddamned self, and he's livid.

And the award for the biggest moron in all of Asheville goes to… Yep, you guessed it—Finn-fucking-Walker.

'If you don't get me some of that almighty hotness, we can't be friends anymore,' he whines, throwing a tantrum.

And as much as I want to chastise my dick for only thinking about himself, on this matter, I'm inclined to agree with him.

What the fuck was I thinking?

CHAPTER 9

STONE

"I have to say this isn't exactly the kind of place I thought you'd take me to," I announce in awe, appreciative of the amazing view I'm enveloped in.

The gazebo's strong-looking granite pillars surrounding me look much like any you'd find in North Carolina. However, these pavilion structures are usually on some rich folk's property, not right in the majestic Blue Ridge Mountains. They look to have been abandoned for decades, and in need of some TLC. But to me, they're just as exquisite as they must have been in their prime.

The clandestine gazebo faces the lights of Asheville's city center, making the town look grander than what it realistically is. The glowing illumination from far way gives the view a nostalgic feel, like being trapped in another time where those same lights once shone.

I've got to hand it to pretty-boy Finn. He did good in bringing me up here. Real good.

"Does this place have a story?" I ask, curious about the history behind such a secluded landmark.

"Doesn't every building in the south?" He shrugs as he reaches into the car to grab something behind the seats.

"Not everyone lives in a home which was built in the eighteen hundreds. Some of us live in places with wheels on them."

"You live in a trailer?" he asks, standing straight and looking appalled on my behalf.

"Take it down a notch, quarterback. I can feel your judgment from way over here," I quip back with a bite to each word.

Luckily for Finn, my temper is mollified when he looks instantly ashamed of his knee-jerk prejudice, his eyes staring at his feet rather than meeting mine.

"Sorry. That made me sound like an asshole, didn't it?"

"Don't sweat it." I shrug. "I already know you're an asshole, so I can't be surprised when you act like one, now can I?" I raise my brow his way mockingly.

He rolls his tongue over his teeth, the mischievous glint in his eye that I've become addicted to returning in full force.

"Always the fucking brat. One of these days, your mouth is going to get you in trouble, little girl."

"I'm counting on it," I taunt to piss him off, even though at this point, our back-and-forth banter feels more like our own brand of flirting than taking jabs at each other.

To keep me occupied and away from such idiotic notions, I walk over to one of the bags filled with alcohol and pick up my man Jose Cuervo. When I turn around, Finn is already making himself comfortable on one of the two sports towels he has unrolled side-by-side over the lavish green earth. With my hands on my hips, I let out an exasperated sigh and holler at the fool.

"Why are you all the way over there?" I ask, standing in the very center of the monumental gazebo.

"Because it's the best seat in the house. I don't want to miss the view," he explains, and I eye-roll him so hard, my eyeballs are in danger of popping out.

Seriously, how many hits to the head do football players need to take before they realize the damage they're subjecting themselves to? Case in point is Mr. Star Quarterback himself sitting pretty on the open field, facing into the darkness.

"The view is right over there, Einstein," I shout, pointing in the direction of the town's lights.

"No, it isn't," he replies buoyantly, lying down on the towel with one arm under his head and the other pointing at the sky. "That's the view I don't want to miss."

I take the two stairs down from the white monument and look up to see what he's going on about. And when I do, my jaw falls to the ground in astonishment.

"Oh my God, Finn. It's beautiful," I hush, utterly amazed, taking small steps his way with a bottle in hand.

In all my twenty-one years of life, I don't think I have ever seen so many stars. The whole sky looks like dark-blue fabric stretched as far as the eye can see, punctured through with a pin, making beams of glorious, white light descend all the way down on us.

It's breathtaking. Just breathtaking.

Still speechless, I take a seat by his side and crane my neck, just so I don't miss one bit of the spectacular sight.

"Pretty amazing, huh?" he asks, amused with my sudden muteness.

"I don't think that's the right word for it. At least not the one I'd pick to do it justice."

"What word would you use, then?"

"Transcendent," I mutter softly, still trapped within the surreal scenery.

As Finn's silence lingers a bit too long, I turn to look down at him and see a wide, boyish smile shining on his face, which is almost just as stunning as the stars above us. He must sense my gaze on him because one minute he's consumed with the specks of light over our heads, and the next he's looking into my eyes.

"You're missing the view," he whispers, his tongue licking his suddenly dry lips.

I don't think I am, pretty boy. The view looks mighty fine from where I'm sitting.

I watch his Adam's apple bob away, his gaze still transfixed on mine, and my pulse begins to accelerate just by watching his own blue eyes light to life. Thankfully, he breaks the spell and begins to shake his head, pushing back whatever sultry thought had popped into that mind of his. Just when I'm thinking I'm out of the woods, he disarms me, yet again, by throwing one of his genuine, shy smiles my way, which seems to always make my knees weak. Not that I'll ever let on to the fact that those suckers have become my kryptonite. It will be a cold day in hell before I admit that Finn Walker has any effect on me whatsoever.

"Come here, you little brat," he orders playfully, before pulling me down to lie right beside him.

His bicep serves as a pillow to keep my head off the cold ground, so I don't know if I should be thankful he's being thoughtful or pissed that his burly tree-trunk for an arm is trapped under me and I can't do anything about it.

"Relax, Stone. Just take it all in," he breathes in my ear, and the gooseflesh my body is suddenly conflicted with, has nothing to do with the chill of the night around us, and everything to do with Finn's strapping body scorching the left side of my petite frame.

Instead of making him aware of the cruel torture he's putting me under, I do as he says and just lie there, admiring every inch of the marvel above us. Just when I'm becoming semi-relaxed, Finn breaks the silence with his husky, low voice, the very one that always gets my lady parts all tingly and stupid.

"I'm happy you're able to see the beauty in this. Not many people do."

I turn to my side, propping my elbow on the towel as my palm keeps my head in place, so I can look down at him.

"I have to confess, you surprised me tonight, and that doesn't happen very often," I admit.

He picks up a lock of my hair and begins to play with it, entwining the blue-colored strands around his fingers.

"That's a shame. A girl like you deserves to be surprised more often."

"I'd rather not have many pop up on me if I can help it. Most of the surprises I've endured in my life are either headaches or heartaches. I prefer the mundane and predictable, thank you very much."

"Huh," he huffs out, sounding surprised himself with my little confession.

"What?"

"Nothing. It's just, the word 'predictable' is something I would never tie in the same sentence with you," he explains, still playing with my hair as if it were his to touch.

Wish I could have another go at his too, but if I start touching him, I'm not sure I'll be able to play with his hair only. You can't expect to have a tempting slice of devil's food cake flaunted in a hungry girl's face without her taking a big bite out of it. No one has that level of restraint. Especially if the said girl has been on a self-imposed diet for way too long. And when I say diet, I mean sex. And Finn here is sex on a stick, just waving it in my face and taunting me to have a lick.

"Well, I never took you for a stargazer, either. Guess we both learned something new about each other tonight," I say, instead of what is really running through my mind.

"We did, didn't we?" He smiles widely, making the idiotic organ inside my chest do cartwheels.

Settle down, bitch. He's just a cute boy with a nice smile, not the damn Powerball winning ticket.

Before I do something stupid, like kiss Finn for the second time today, I pull myself up and grab the bottle of Tequila, making sure my hair is no longer at his disposal.

"Sit up, quarterback. We're going to play a game."

"What game?" He eyes me curiously, his bulging biceps elevating his upper body.

"Since you've got a boner for intel, what better way than a drinking game to get to know each other?"

"First of all, I didn't get a boner," he scoffs, but when my mocking eyes lock on his stirring cock, he sits up straight, trying his best to conceal the evidence of my statement. Guess I'm not the only one here with their libido on high alert tonight. "And second, aren't we a little old for drinking games?"

I place both hands over his mouth and shake my head from side to side.

"No more blasphemous comments out of you. We're going to play, and you're going to have fun. Trust me," I say with a flirtatious wink.

I feel his cocky-ass smirk touch my palms, and I immediately pull away, as if the sun just scorched my skin, leaving a visible imprint on me.

"Fine," he replies, caving in to my demands. "So what are we playing? Some truth or dare thing?"

"Can you be any more bourgeois?" I yawn, feigning boredom.

"Then, what?" He chuckles amused and continues, "Remember, I can't get plastered since I'm your ride home."

"Hmm, you're right," I muse.

I start tapping the pad of my finger on the tip of my nose, trying to come up with an alternative that will keep me both entertained, as well as distracted from wanting to climb Finn like a tree. Still, I don't have to necessarily touch him to have my Finn fix in other ways.

"Now, don't you go and worry that pretty head of yours. I got the perfect game for us," I announce, sitting cross-legged and facing the football god in front of me with good old Jose in between my thighs.

I break the seal and take a pull of tequila to warm me up while I wait for Finn to get comfortable. As much as he tries to shift his bulky legs to sit the same way as me, he just can't master it. Still, I give him props for trying. I mean, his body is all pure steel, so maneuvering such massive machinery must have its kinks. But damn. If Finn's statuesque form is insane with clothes on his tight frame, I can only imagine how hot he looks without them.

"I don't know if I like that look in your eye," he announces when I take too long to respond, thinking of all the delicious ways I can have my fill of his strapping muscles.

"Since you can't drink too much, we need to come up with an alternative—one that will be advantageous and fair to both of us. I say, we ask each other questions, and when we refuse to shell out the dirt, then, as punishment, either we can take a swig out of my man here." I tap the bottle in question before laying my devious scheme on him, "or we can take off a piece of clothing. However, if whoever is in the hot seat does answer, then it falls on the person who did the questioning to drink up or strip down. The wrinkle is that you can't repeat the same punishment twice in a row. Got it? Or was that too hard for you to keep up with?"

"You want to see me without my clothes on?" he asks, half-thrilled at the idea, half-petrified, completely disregarding the little dig I made at his expense.

"Is that your first question? Because, I gotta tell you, that shirt you've got on is out of here sooner than I thought. Yes, pretty boy. I want you to take your clothes off. If I have to endure a night with you, then the least you can do is give me some eye-candy to indulge in. And in return, you have the pleasure of my company. Now isn't that a fair trade?"

He chuckles again and takes the bottle from my grip, taking a healthy gulp rather than rocking my world with his bare chest. I pretend to pout at his poor choice of punishment.

"Don't take the fun out of my game, quarterback, or else it's going to be a long night for both of us."

"I sure hope so," he teases, handing me back the bottle. "My turn to ask the questions."

"Go on."

"You told me you lived in a trailer. Do you still live there?"

I throw my eyes at the sky, unamused and a little disappointed with his line of questioning.

"No. I live back at the dorms in Richfield. Don't worry, Finn. You won't have to go to a trailer park to take me home tonight."

"That's not why I asked," he states, seemingly offended.

"Sure it wasn't. Either way, I don't care. It's my turn on the mic. Do your friends know you geek out looking up at the stars?"

His scowl turns deep, as he grabs at the base of his shirt, pulling it over his head and throwing it to the ground beside me in defiance. My vivid imagination couldn't compare to the real-life sculpted figure in front of me.

"Yeah, I didn't think so," I utter mockingly, trying to conceal how all those deep ridges and steel planes have me panting a little. "Why not?"

"First, I didn't answer your question. And second, wait your turn," he points at me. "It's mine now."

I shrug my shoulders, pretending not to be bothered either way. But, of course, I should have suspected he wouldn't pull any punches with his next question since I was the one who decided to take the kid gloves off in the first place.

"Why do you get all defensive when I ask you something personal?"

Instead of answering his fine ass, I take a long gulp of tequila and stick my tongue out at him once I'm done.

"Fine, if that's how you're going to play this. But fair warning, miss the next one, and it's *your* shirt that falls on the ground."

"Pity you're going to have to wait a little longer, considering it's my turn now."

"I'm not afraid. Give it your best shot, little girl," he taunts, tapping on his cheek and waiting expectantly for the metaphorical punch.

"Have you ever kept any other secrets from your friends?"

"Yes," he deadpans, not leaving much room for misinterpretation.

"So, I guess the grass isn't greener on the Northside either, huh?"

"Everyone has their demons to face, Stone. The place where you're born doesn't factor much into it."

"Got a lot of monsters keeping you awake at night, do you?" I ask skeptically.

"More than most. I just answered three of your questions back to back. Get up, little girl. It's your turn to take it all off," he commands, his voice just as sharp and hard as the bulging muscles he's proudly showcasing.

I flip him off for good measure but stand up just the same. Three questions equal three pieces of clothing. No sweat. I take off my chucks, each one landing in a different location after they've successfully managed to zoom past his head.

"Cute," he goads, his tone still iron-thick.

I then unbutton my shorts and begin to shimmy out of them, making sure I bend just so, keeping my ass up in the air and away from his prying eye. However, my low-cut shirt gives him a nice little view of the ladies just the same. I pick up my shorts and throw them toward his face, but with his cat-like reflexes, he catches them before they've hit their mark. I then sit back down and take a swig of tequila instead of taking off another piece of clothing.

"Three answered questions equal two pieces of clothing and one drink. But nice try, pretty boy."

"You could just as easily have drunk twice and only taken off your chucks," he chimes in, clutching my shorts in his lap.

"I know. Guess I'm feeling charitable tonight."

"Charitable? Right. How come I think your so-called punishment left me in pain instead of you?" he confesses huskily, shifting in his seat while trying to hide the bulge in his jeans.

"Poor baby. You hurting?" I pout exaggeratedly, batting my eyes at him.

"Jesus, you are something else," he says, flustered, running his fingers through his blond mane and tugging at its strands in frustration. "You sure don't have any inhibitions, do you, Stone? You do whatever you want and fuck the consequences, isn't that right?"

"Why live life any other way? Life's too short for pretenses," I answer truthfully, not one bit bothered with his assessment of me.

"Not everyone has the same luxury of being so direct," he scolds.

"You really want to talk about luxuries with me, quarterback? Tell me, just how hard did you have to work for those wheels you've got? Or the clothes on your back? Or even the money in your pocket? Don't lecture me on luxuries when you've lived a life filled with them. Being who I am, with no regard for anyone else's opinion but mine, is one of the few God-given rights I have."

"You're right. But you're also dead wrong, little girl. I might not have worked a day in my life for the things I have, but don't think for a second they didn't come at a price," he replies in torment, catching me completely off-guard.

I bite my lip, seeing how true his words are to him. For a long moment we just sit there staring at each other, creating an odd electricity in the air—thick and heavy—around us. I swallow hard, as the drumming of my beating heart becomes too loud to bear. Finn acting like an asshole is easy to deal with. When he lets down his dickish guard, bringing forth an unexpected vulnerability in its stead, I can't handle it.

I'm about to apologize for losing my cool with him, so we can get back to safer terrain, when Finn places his thumb on my lower lip, unleashing it from the grip of my teeth.

"I'm sorry. I shouldn't have snapped at you," he murmurs, his body suddenly too close for me to pretend his bare chest isn't mere inches away, with his rich, warm, woodsy scent invading all my senses.

"I'm a big girl, pretty boy. It takes more than a short fuse to scare me." I try to play off, struggling to prevent getting lost in his touch.

"I bet nothing scares you," he hushes, staring into my eyes as his thumb continues its torturous trace over my lip.

"What can I say? I don't scare easy."

"You're a better person than me because I'm scared shitless right now," he chuckles huskily, with no real humor behind it.

"What are you scared of?"

"You want the truth?"

"Yes."

"Not kissing you."

Well, I'll be damned. Goodbye, restraint and logic. It was nice knowing you.

His little confession has barely passed through his lips when I do what any hot-blooded woman would do if she were in my shoes—I jump him.

CHAPTER 10

FINN

It takes me a minute to understand what's going on, but I thankfully recover just fine after Stone's unexpected assault. I ease into her kiss, letting her take the lead this time since she did the same with me when I took charge this morning. But just like our impromptu fooling around in her classroom earlier, her kiss leaves me wanting more. Stone's lips are softer than they look. She's so edgy and hard, but her mouth is warm and playful. My hands go to her waist, pulling her on top of me as I lie down flat on the ground. For a little thing, she sure does fit to perfection.

"You taste good," she mumbles into my mouth, nipping at my lower lip in a way that's making my dick want to break free from its confinement.

He's both pissed at me for not been released from his cage yet, as well as giddy for having the Southie in her pretty black panties dry-humping him slightly.

"It's your man Cuervo. Although tequila tastes way better coming from your pretty mouth," I moan out, my hands desperately seeking her. One runs up and down her bare outer thigh, while the other is wrapped around the nape of her neck, keeping her lips exactly where they should be at all times—attached to mine.

"Thanks." She laughs, and the melody goes straight to my head, as well as my oversized cock.

Damn, that sound does something to me.

She kisses me with such passion that I become completely consumed by it. I get lost in our kiss, utterly and profusely. All sense of time and logic slip away when her soft lips are on me, and I wouldn't have it any other way. She leaves a breach open for me, so I thrust my tongue inside her mouth to continue our tortuous battle. The sweet rapture is only heightened when our tongues connect, and I feel the hard steel of her tongue ring, teasing me further. My mind is usually a landmine of thoughts, a jumbled mess pulling my attention in all directions. However, all that white noise takes a back seat at this very moment while one coherent thought holds me captive—I want more.

"Fuck! You taste better than good," I admit, bringing her closer over my crotch, so I can feel her wet pussy put some pressure over my hard, agonized length. In my depraved desires, I secretly hope she marks my jeans with her arousal, even though my dick will hate me for the suffering I'm putting him through.

"More kissing, less talking, pretty boy," she rasps between heated breaths, biting my lip in such a way that has me seeing stars. And not the ones I brought Stone to marvel at tonight.

When she begins dancing on top of my lap, though, all my restraint seems to evaporate. The way she's stroking me, grinding up and down my engorged cock with her barely-clad pussy, is driving me mental.

"Jesus, that feels good," I growl, my fingers leaving imprints on her hips, easing her stroking rhythm. But it's only when I hear the hunger in my voice that I realize I might be off my game a bit more than I suspected.

I'm not a talker when it comes to hook-ups.

I've learned the hard way that if a guy talks during a fuck session, then he can expect the girl he's about to screw seven ways to Sunday to talk her way through it, too. I know it makes me sound like an asshole, but with most girls I've been with in the past, the only good use I ever found for their mouths was to suck me off. Listening to their over-the-top, wanna-be-porn-star wails or their dirty talk never got the end result they had intended. Instead of a stiffy, I'd be limp like a soft noodle. Not exactly something I want to repeat or have talked about. So my rule of thumb for hook-ups has always been—if they want to be fucked so thoroughly that they'll have trouble walking straight for a week, then they have to keep their damn play-by-play to themselves. Moaning and calling out for God at the end was my limit for conversing while fucking.

However, with Stone, it's occurred to me that I haven't enacted that rule. In fact, I'm all for her talking my ear off if she wants. Mostly because half the words that come out of her bratty mouth have me hard anyway, so as far as I can see, it's a win-win for both of us.

"God, I want to taste you all over," I spew out, coaxing her to reply to test my theory further.

"I can help you with that," she teases back, jumping off my crotch and landing on my chest, inching her way up until she's straddling my face. She takes off her shirt, letting it fall to the ground beside me, throwing a little mischievous wink my way, when all I can see are her heavy breasts, so close to where I want them, and yet so far away. "Now, do a girl a solid, pretty boy, and use your mouth for what it was intended for, will you?" she orders provocatively.

Fuck this girl!

"Your wish is my command," I reply dutifully, pulling her skimpy thong to the side, her bare shaven pussy and glistening lips right there for the taking.

Without a second to waste, my tongue takes one large lap, and the nectar it comes in contact with is nothing but pure sugar. I don't need to keep the gentle one-stroke routine for long before getting her pussy acquainted with my tongue. As far as I'm concerned, Stone just handed me her juicy cunt as my prize, and I fully intend on cashing it in.

Unable to contain my raging lust any longer, I grab her ass to keep her in place and eat her out as if she were my favorite dessert. And as much as I try to deny it, all my taste buds tell me she is. Her erratic wails drive me to do my worst, desperate to wring every last drop out of her.

"Fuck! You're really good at that!" she moans out, her hands gripping my hair, holding my face prisoner to where her ache is strongest.

I can't hold back, so my tongue begins to torment the little nub that's hidden away, and then return to plunge into her, giving relief to her torturous need, which only increases my own. My tongue repeats this merciless dance until we're both suffering in equal measure.

"Yeah! Just like that. Don't stop, Finn! Don't stop!" she begs as she fucks my tongue with such fervor, I think I'm going to cum just with her riding my face so unashamedly.

I slap her ass with both hands before sinking them back on her redden cheeks to keep to her ravenous pace, eating her out as if her pussy were my only source of oxygen.

"Shit!" I moan when she lets out a glorious cry, broadcasting to everyone in a ten-mile radius that she's meeting her maker.

From down here, I can't see her face as she falls apart, which is the only downside of the position we're in. So I pull her off my face and turn us over, leaving her flat on the ground with my looming body covering hers. She's still riding her orgasmic high, her eyes hooded and her cheeks pink, when I begin to kiss every part of her flesh. The mounds of her breasts heave up and down as she tries to settle her erratic breathing, but before the night is through, she'll be gasping for air once more. I'll make sure of it.

I kiss and suck her neck, trailing my kisses down until my lips find a puckered nub under her lace bra. I pull the lace down with my teeth, popping out one perfect breast with a pert nipple that looks eager for me. I latch my mouth over it immediately, her rosebud tasting even sweeter than before. I play with the other pebble with my hand, grasping onto her perfect, huge tits with my mouth and fingers. Images of me placing my cock in between them, jerking me off until I mark them with my cum, has me hallucinating.

"Shit, the things I could do to these babies," I groan out.

I give one a light bite before removing myself from such temptation, and slide my tongue further down to kiss her flat stomach. When I smell her desire increase so close to her needy pussy, it tells me her craving to ravish me is just as fierce as my own.

"You really do talk a lot when you're horny," she jokes, pulling at the strands of my hair so she's the one calling the shots.

"Want me to stop?" I ask, wondering if my dirty talk is putting her off, the same way I was by so many girls before I implemented my no-talking rule during sex.

I don't know why, but that one silent second that passes by without her answer has my insides all twisted up.

"And why would I want that? When that mouth of yours knows exactly what to say… and do."

She smiles at me, and won't you know it, the knots inside my throat just evaporate into thin air. Unable to stop myself, I crawl my way back up and kiss her as if my life depended on it. Her taste is still on my lips, and our maddening kiss just makes me want to lose control and fuck her senseless once and for all. However, I was raised never to assume that, just because I got a girl off, she would be down to fuck right after, so I have to ask.

"I kind of need to fuck you, Stone. So if you're not okay with that, now would be a good time to tell me to fuck off."

Okay, so maybe I'm not for pretty words and romantic gestures and all that, but at least I'm being honest. I'm about to explode in my goddamn jeans, just with the taste of her pussy still lingering on my tongue and her soft, pliant body beneath me. So why make a big production that I'm anything but turned the fuck on?

Luckily for me, the desire in Stone's eyes doesn't look satiated enough either, so when she turns me onto my back, I'm all too happy to comply.

"You have a condom on you, quarterback?"

I repeatedly nod like a fool, my hand already taking the wallet out to retrieve a string of condoms. She takes the bunch out of my hands, placing another earth-shattering kiss on my lips as her hands trail down my chest. When her deft fingers find my engorged cock she purrs in delight.

"You gotta stop making those fucking noises, Stone," I warn.

"Why?" she asks, unbuttoning my jeans and shimmying them down just enough for her to see my aroused state.

Her sneaky hand finds itself inside the flap of my boxers, grabbing my junk with all the confidence in the world. Without wanting to, I do the girly thing of letting my eyes fall to the back of my head as she begins to pump my weeping cock in her delicate hands.

"Cat got your tongue, Finn?" she hums again, only intensifying my suffering.

"Stop being such a brat, Stone. You're going to make me cum, and I really want to do that inside you, if you don't mind," I beg, and she lets out another little laugh, triggering my dick to bob and leak in happiness.

"I didn't think you would be a one-pump chump. Don't disappoint me now," she teases, taking her hand away from my cock and licking the pre-cum off her palm.

"I won't. Don't you fucking worry," I grunt out loud.

With my manhood threatened and the sexy-ass display of her licking my taste off her skin, my dick hollers at me, promising he's got his act together and wouldn't dare let me down.

"We'll see about that," she mewls, ripping one condom with her teeth.

'Shit, that's sexy,' my cock swoons.

'Nope. No fucking swooning. This is war,' I yell at my dick.

'Right. Sorry. It's just… damn, this one is so fucking hot.'

'Don't you think I know that?! Now, man the fuck up. I swear to God, if you cum on the first pump, I will castrate your ass,' I yell inwardly at him.

'Damn, Finn. Don't have to be all Henry VIII with the beheading and shit. I got you. You'll see.'

'You better. Otherwise, the only action you're getting is my right palm.'

'Jesus, you're a prick when you're horny.'

'Takes one to know one.'

Another giggle slices through my wayward thoughts, bringing me back to the girl straddling me.

"You know, it's cute when you're all up in your head like that. I'm starting to get used to the hard scowl your face makes when the conversation you're having with yourself doesn't quite compute," Stone teases, but her features are now something the hard-ass girl rarely is—sweet. "You want to tell me what's going on in there?" she asks, her fingers raking gently through my hair.

"You'll laugh."

"Try me."

My hands go to fondle her breasts instead of satisfying her curiosity, but the infuriating girl just slaps them away.

"Tell me, Finn. Don't be shy now," she taunts, her hands finding the hook of her bra behind her and unstrapping it, leaving those exquisite breasts of hers out in the open.

I bite my knuckle because I'd do just about anything to touch those babies. But allowing Stone a peek into my crazy mind seems too big a price to pay.

"If you tell me, I'll let you play with the girls," she goads, toying with them in her hands, taunting the fuck out of me.

"I was telling my cock if he doesn't rock your world, the only action he'll get is my calloused hand," I blurt out, failing miserably against her cunning ways.

"Is that so?" she replies, intrigued.

I nod because, at this stage, there is no point lying any more than I already have.

"Which hand?" She cocks her brow.

I hint at my right hand, which she unlatches off her hip, placing a kiss on my open palm.

"Just in case he doesn't live up to the challenge, at least he can have some fun knowing my lips were here too."

"That's it, little girl," I growl, slapping her ass. "I'm done talking. Jump on my dick already."

I take the foil wrapper away from her hands and wrap up my eager and ready-to-roll cock.

"So impatient," she taunts, licking her lips.

I go in for another kiss, either because I can't handle another teasing remark out of her, or I just crave it too much. When we part, we are both panting wildly, our eyes locked together, anxious for what's about to happen next.

I watch in awe as Stone slithers her delicate hands down my chest until one is wrapped around my eager cock. I try to think of every obscure fact I can to distract myself with, because her hands alone feel amazing on me. But, fuck, nothing—I mean nothing—is better than when she positions my dick at her opening and slowly sinks herself down to the hilt.

"FUCK!" we both shout at the same time.

I'm trying really hard not to be a one-pump chump like she said, but come on! Did her pussy really have to have magical powers or some shit?

Stone's head falls back, her hands pressed on my chest as she slowly lifts her ass up and down on me. It's cruel torture, as well as one of the most beautiful things I've laid eyes on. Her naked body, shimmering with glistening sweat against the night-sky backdrop, will be engraved in my memory forever. All of her is a vibrant color. The dark sky, contrasting with bright stars that kiss her skin, makes Stone look like a decadent work of art. It's as if she's one of those voluptuous women in a museum, carved in cold, white marble, and someone graffitied a rainbow of colors on her to showcase her true beauty.

When Stone's pace increases, riding me like a woman on a mission, my nails pierce through her skin, and a soft moan falls from her lips. I lift a little bit higher just so I can have her full, plump breasts bouncing close to my face. It's too damn mouthwatering not to get a taste. My mouth sucks on each pebble, lavishing them both with the same care and devotion while she continues to drive me insane with the way she's fucking my brains out.

God, she feels good.

Too good.

"Pretty boy, you look like you're not enjoying this," she purrs, swallowing my cock for all its worth, as she rakes her fingers through my hair.

She tilts her head down to look at me, but if I see the lust in her eyes, I know it will be my undoing.

"Don't talk, Stone, or this is going to end real fast," I warn her, biting her puckered nipple before sucking it into my mouth.

I think I could spend days on end playing with her breasts and never be satiated. Nope. I don't think. I know I can.

"I knew you were weak." She tries to laugh, but when I thrust inside her with all my might, I watch her head fall back, her hair cascading beautifully as she cries out into the night air.

"Let's see who the weak one is," I threaten, taking over her steady pace.

Her moans increase as I begin to play with her body, making it jump on me until all she feels is my hard length expanding her tight walls. With one hand still gripping her waist to keep her steady, the other wraps itself around her raven hair, tugging at the boundaries of pain and pleasure. My mouth never leaves her tits, nibbling and teasing them in turn, while I make sure my cock ruins her pussy for any other motherfucker that follows.

"Okay, I get it. You've got some moves in you." She pants, trying to regain some control, which isn't going to happen.

"You haven't seen anything yet."

I continue to pump into Stone, her pussy clenching ever so often. I'm so close to cumming that I don't even know what to do with myself, much less follow through with my threat. Her soft moans, along with our sweaty bodies gliding against each other, are all the stimulation I can handle. Seeing as I'm on the brink of losing it completely, my thumb finds her hidden nub, strumming it with all the fierceness and resolve I can muster. Her cries become louder as her core clenches around my cock like strangling ivy, blanking my mind completely, leaving sensation as the only ruling dominant.

"Just like that, Finn. Keep fucking me just like that. I'm so close," she whines, her own nails sinking deep into my shoulders.

This girl is going to be the death of me.

Who would have known that Stone, seconds away from unraveling, could be the sexiest thing ever and the driving force pushing me over the edge? Unable to keep my shit together, I kiss her to prevent her from saying anything else.

Madly. Possessively. Savagely.

She returns my kiss with the same fiery passion, and with our bodies fully aligned in every way that counts, she cums. I'm right there with her, eating up her screams with my hungry lips, as I let go and have the mother-of-all orgasms enticed by her tight little pussy.

Once we're spent, I fall down to the ground, taking her body with me. The satisfied purr she makes has my fucking cock hard in seconds and ready for round two. I'm still trying to catch my breath while my dick is looking at his watch for me to get a move on.

"You're better than you look," Stone rasps, also trying to steady her erratic breathing.

"You thought I didn't know how to fuck?"

"Oh, I was positive you knew how. I just wasn't sure if you were any good at it."

I slap her ass, and she lets out another one of those cute little laughs.

"You really are a brat. So, does that mean I got your stamp of approval?" I taunt back, running my fingers up and down her bare back.

"Sorry, quarterback. I'm not here to stroke your ego. But I've had worse."

"Geez, thanks."

I roll my eyes since she can't even give me this, but when I hear another light chuckle followed by butterfly kisses on my chest, my insides go all soft and gooey.

The fuck is that all about?

As I begin to think that I may be turning into a pussy, Stone crawls up my body like the little eager monkey she is and delivers one hell of a kiss. I'm still reeling when she gets off me and begins to put her clothes back on.

"Hey? Are you cold or something?" I ask in concern, squeezing her shoulder.

"No, pretty boy. Just need to get home," she answers without even looking at me as she laces up her chucks.

"Already?" I ask, internally torn at this being over already, since my cock had his heart set on her riding him again tonight.

"Some of us have to work in the morning. But this was fun," she replies with nonchalance, as if I just spent the night playing Monopoly with her, rather than being balls deep inside her.

When she slaps my knee for me to get a move on, it's the bucket of ice water I need to get us the hell out of here.

Now I know why the girl's name is Stone. She's hard as a rock and just as unfeeling.

Isn't that a kick in the junk?

CHAPTER 11

FINN

"What's your problem? You look like someone keyed your beloved Porsche or something," Easton jokes as he takes the seat next to mine.

"It's nothing." I slump back, pressing my lips in a slight grimace.

"Doesn't look like nothing to me." He eyes me suspiciously. "Did you get another letter?" he whispers in my ear.

"No," I grunt, pulling back away from him and snapping my pencil in half, with just the mere mention of another letter from The Society showing up on my doorstep.

It's because of this stupid society and their threatening letters that my head is all screwed up in the first place. Sure, I was already in a pretty fucked-up situation before they were added to the equation, but they sure as shit raised the stakes with my fragile sanity.

"Hey, chill, Finn. Remember, whoever sent it is probably watching you. Watching all of us," Easton warns, discreetly scanning the classroom to see if anyone caught my little meltdown. "Don't give them the satisfaction of knowing they're getting to you. Remember what Lincoln said—act cool until he and Colt can figure out who the hell is behind this."

"I am acting cool, asshole," I bark back, infuriated with him for talking to me like I'm the weakest link in our foursome.

But who am I kidding? I probably am, and that's why The Society chose my stupid ass to do their bidding first.

"You're cool, huh? Oh, I totally see that. You're a regular fucking iceberg, dude," he mocks, nudging my shoulder with his, trying to lighten my dark mood.

I huff out and grab another pencil from my bag, pretending to be taking notes. Yes, pretend, because my head isn't in the right frame of mind to actually care what my philosophy professor is talking about, much less take notes. But if it will get Easton off my back, then I'm willing to at least try and act like the dutiful scholar. However, before I even have a chance to put pencil to paper, he grabs it from me and starts tapping his knee with it repeatedly.

"Spill, Finn. I can see from here that mind of yours ready to burst. Whatever it is, we can hash it out."

"I don't want to talk about it."

"Really? You're going to make me guess? Okay, I'm game," he replies, now tapping the eraser end of my pencil on his pouty lips in deep thought.

Yeah, he can keep it now. No way do I want it back. Who knows where his mouth has been? And no, I'm not being a dickhead. Easton isn't known for being picky with his conquests, and since I didn't lay eyes on him all weekend, who knows where he's been holed up. Or, more importantly, with who.

I rummage through my book bag again to see if I've got anything else I can write with, when Easton starts throwing out possible scenarios of why I'm all riled up, only resulting in aggravating me further.

"Your dad give you shit this morning?"

"No."

"Your mom?"

I slightly turn my head his way, slanting my eyes at him at the absurd statement.

"Yeah, that woman is a peach. I don't see her busting your chops so early on a Monday morning. So, it has to be your coach. He's the one on your case, right?"

"No, asshole. He's fine. Dad's fine. Mom's fine. Everything is just fucking fine!" I whisper-yell, giving up completely on my endeavor in finding a pen or a pencil.

Fuck it. I'll just try to memorize whatever Professor Donavan is excitedly talking about on the podium below. That is if my insistent best friend ever shuts his pie hole, which I doubt very much.

"Fine, huh? I can totally see how *fine* things are from the vein threatening to pop on your forehead. You know, if you scowl any harder, those wrinkles are going to be a permanent thing. You'll look fifty before your twenty-third birthday."

I let out an exaggerated exhale and turn to face my inquisitive friend.

"Can you please just let it go, East? Seriously, I'm not in the mood for your twenty questions or your sarcasm."

"No can do, brother. That's the price you pay for being my best friend. I'm a curious fucker." He chuckles, squeezing my shoulder.

"Emphasis on fucker," I quip back with a small smile, slapping his hand off me.

"A joke. I'll take that as progress," he teases.

Even though he's a cocky motherfucker, I love the asshole for trying to uplift my spirits. But as grateful as I am for his stubbornness in trying to change my disposition, I'm equally pissed off when he mentions the one person that has been constantly on my mind for the past two days.

"I got it! It's the Southie, isn't it? She's the one who has your panties in a twist." My face must rat me out because the victorious smile cresting his face is so damn wide that I want to slap it right off him. "I must be losing my touch. She should have been the first person to come to mind. I knew she'd give you trouble. So, what happened? I thought you were finally gaining some leeway with her."

"Nothing happened. And I was… I mean, *I am* gaining some leeway," I mumble, frustrated and confused.

"I can see that. So, Friday night didn't go as planned, huh?"

"It went as expected," I reply through gritted teeth, not really interested in giving Easton the specifics of what went down with Stone.

"Is that all you're going to give me? Come on now. Something must have happened for you to be all bent out of shape. What did she do? Mace you? Kick you in the junk? Break a bottle over your head when you tried to kiss her? What? Because with a girl that feisty, my imagination can paint quite a picture." He chuckles, stretching his long legs and resting his big black army boots over the headrest of the vacant seat in front of him.

The girl sitting hunched over right next to it shakes her head profusely, unimpressed with his comfortable, yet disrespectful pose. I knock his feet off and mumble a pathetic 'sorry' to the top of the girl's head, apologizing for my friend's poor manners.

"Stop being a dick, East," I reprimand in a low voice, but he just shrugs it off 'Easton-style'.

He relaxes his shoulders, placing his entwined hands behind his head, and looks up at the high ceiling while manspreading, as if he had all the space in the world, which he doesn't. These auditorium rows hardly allow enough room for me to sit comfortably, and Easton eating up my precious space is not going to fly. I slam my knee against his, commanding the fucker to close his legs and give me back my legroom, only to have him chuckle in my face some more.

"You don't want to talk, then don't. I'll get it out of you eventually. One thing's for sure. We lucked out on whoever is trying to fuck us over. I can think of a whole list of ways that they could be making our lives a living hell. Sending letters ordering your ass to spend time with a Southie hottie doesn't feel like one of them. I mean, we should be groveling for mercy, or running errands for them so fucked up that it would sicken us to our very core. At least that's what I would be doing if I were in their shoes. Not ordering us to chat up pretty girls like Stone Bennett. But, hey, that's just my two cents for you."

"I guess we should all feel lucky you're not the one who's calling the shots then," I mumble.

"Ah, but what fun I'd have if I were." He laughs out loud, not caring about his deep, throaty laugh interrupting the class.

"Jesus, can't you take anything seriously?" I bark at him, not impressed that he is talking about this whole society thing so cavalierly.

"When the shit hits the fan, then I'll take things seriously. Now, are you going to spill, or what? I'm getting more bored by the minute, which may actually force me to start paying attention to this lecture if you don't talk." He yawns loudly.

"Oh, dear lord!" exclaims the brunette in front of us, throwing her hands in the air in aggravation before turning over her shoulder. "Will you two ever shut up?!"

Her ponytail, which is tightly bound on her head, and her dark-rimmed glasses poised to the brim of her nose make her look twice her age and just as stern. She's wearing a light-beige grandma sweater, which is a little bit ridiculous since it's still late August and eighty degrees outside. If the girl was going for an unflattering and dull look, she hit the nail on the head with her choice of wardrobe and hairdo, which is a shame, since she isn't that hard on the eyes.

"Oh, I'm sorry. Were we too loud for you?" Easton feigns concern with his open palm to his chest. Always with the dramatics this one.

"As a matter of fact, yes, you were. Some people here actually came to learn, not listen to you two bickering like an old married couple," she scolds, pushing her glasses up the bridge of her nose.

"Too bad for you, I'm not one of those people." Easton shrugs unapologetically, back to his dark, who-the-fuck-cares persona.

The black look she throws at him only deepens as she white-knuckles the pen in her hand, pointing toward him in a way that looks like she wants to poke his eye with it.

"Just keep your conversation to yourselves, will you?"

"Why? You were the one eavesdropping on us, not the other way around."

The girl's brown eyes become two large saucers, bugging out to the point that not even her glasses could keep them contained on her face.

"I was not eavesdropping! For me to do that, the two of you would need to have a coherent conversation. Not grunt and cackle every few seconds," she snaps enraged.

"For a girl who says she's here to study, you sure do pay a lot of attention to strangers' intimate conversations," Easton argues, stretching his legs once more onto the empty seat next to her, his boots inches away from the angry girl's face.

"Just keep it down." She tries again, ignoring the boots swaying left to right beside her head.

"No promises, your highness. Now be a good girl and turn around. You're boring me."

She rolls her eyes before straightening forward, but both Easton and I hear her loud and clear when she mumbles 'asshole' beneath her breath.

Damn it. She really shouldn't have said that.

Easton, never being one to let anyone have the last word, takes his feet off the headrest to lean right into her. Her back is visibly stiffened by his move, which makes his menacing grin split his face in two. He then pulls at her ponytail to bring her head back, making her gasp out sharply, and putting his mouth right next to her ear, he says, "You know, if you ever want to remove the stick up your ass, I could deal with that problem for you. A few orgasms will definitely relax that stiff upper lip."

"I wouldn't sleep with you if you were the last man on Earth," she snarls with a hostile stare, leaving no misinterpretation about her thoughts when it comes to my best friend.

"Ah, isn't that precious. Baby, all I have to do is snap my fingers, and you'd come running. They all do, so what makes you any different?"

She lets out a loud scoff as she looks him dead in the eye.

"You wish. Not everyone wants a piece of Easton Price."

"And yet, you know my name, whereas I have no clue about yours. Nor do I care. I don't need a name to make you see God, sweetheart. Too bad for you, I don't fuck uptight bitches."

"And too bad for you, I don't screw entitled assholes. Guess we both lucked out," she rebukes, turning her head away, forcing him to let go of her hair.

"Feisty. Maybe I was wrong." Easton sinisterly laughs out in amusement. "Maybe you wouldn't be a lousy fuck after all. As long as you brought those claws with you, we could have a go at it. What do you say? Want to find a janitor's closet and put it to the test? I'm bored, and you seem like you need a good fuck. Don't worry. I won't turn the lights on."

"Don't flatter yourself," she retorts without missing a beat. "As I said, you'd be the last guy in all of Asheville I'd ever be alone in the dark with."

Easton's gunmetal eyes burn an eerie shade of gray, the tug of his upper lip looking pleased with the challenge.

"Will you stop?" I chime in, pulling his shoulder to force him to sit back down, all the while wondering what the hell has gotten into him. Unfortunately, Easton just shrugs me off, ignoring me completely, too wrapped up in his little game of harassing the poor girl.

"Are you afraid of the dark?" he hushes in her ear. "Why? Do the things that lurk in the shadows scare you?"

I see a small shiver running through her body while the nape of her neck bursts with goosebumps, proving how much Easton is freaking her out. And purposefully, too. After all the shit we have to deal with, he should be more sensitive and self-aware of his intimidating ways.

"Enough, East," I warn, not one bit happy with his attitude.

He tilts his head my way, his shark-like grin intact, utterly unaffected by my warning.

"For now. Just one more thing."

He then turns to the brunette one more time to rasp his last, ruthless, pestering comment in her ear. As hard as she tries to pretend he's not getting under her skin, her body betrays her the minute his breath touches her skin.

"You just made it on my radar, sweetheart. I hate to tell you, but that's not a good place to be. I'd be careful if I were you."

She snaps her neck toward him with burning fury covering her eyes, even though every cell of her body is clearly showing how terrified of him she is.

"You don't scare me," she lies.

"Ah," he coos, gripping her chin so their faces are just inches apart. "But I think I do, don't I?"

"Mr. Price! Is there anything you want to share with the class?" Professor Donavan asks, confirming we got his attention.

Easton takes a full minute to stare the girl down instead of letting her go. When she finally submits and lowers her eyes from his, Easton releases his grip from her chin and leans back in his seat, looking right as rain.

"Nah, teach. I'm good. What I have to share is only for a selected few, if you catch my drift?"

The few smirks and giggles from the other students invade the classroom, taking Professor Donavan a minute to restore order.

"Please try to refrain from repeating things of that nature, Mr. Price. This is a Philosophy class not Sex Ed."

Another slew of chuckles ensues, but Professor Donavan is able to keep control and continue with his lecture quickly enough.

"What the hell was that all about?" I interrogate him once we're no longer the center of attention.

"Don't worry about it. You've got other things to focus on." He pretends to pick off lint from his shoulder, not caring to look me in the eye.

My brows pinch together as I scrutinize my best friend from head to toe. Easton is a cocky asshole, but he isn't a mean one. That's Colt's area of expertise. So, what gives?

I slant my chin toward the brunette, who is now crouching down in her seat, making a serious effort to not gain Easton's attention again.

"You know her, don't you?" I whisper, making sure no one else is listening. East offers me a curt nod, confirming my suspicion. "And she just happened to get on your shitlist how, may I ask?"

He leans his head back on the headrest, pensively looking up at the ceiling again.

"She's good. I'm bad. Do I need a better reason?"

"Sometimes you can be a real dick, you know that?"

"You've got bigger fish to fry than worrying about me, Finn. I've got my shit handled."

"Whatever," I huff out with little to no steam behind it.

At the end of the day, he's right—my plate is already full enough. Wasting my time on Easton's mercurial moods, or who got on his bad side, is not going to help either way.

I try to focus on what Professor Donavan is saying for a while, but truth be told, I'm not remotely interested in anything he has to teach today. When the bell rings, announcing the end of the class, I'm all too relieved to hightail it out of here. Not as fast as the brunette in front of me, though. The way she scurries out of the classroom has me feeling a little bit guilty that I didn't put a leash on Easton.

I'm about to reprimand him again for intimidating the poor girl when he wraps his arm over my shoulder with a wide grin spread on his face. He's all bubbly and shit, as if he didn't just put the fear of God into one of our classmates.

"You know what we need? A large dose of caffeine from The Grind. Maybe some of their sugary treats, too. You with me?"

"Yeah, why not?" I nod.

It's not like I'm going to pay attention to any of my classes today anyway, so ditching one won't make much difference. It will also serve as the excuse I need to keep me from going to the other side of campus in search of the current bane of my existence—the stunning, green-eyed girl with thick, tattooed thighs, and a razor-sharp tongue.

I've thought of nothing else for the past forty-eight hours, and three things have become painstakingly clear for me. The first is that Stone is going to be harder to crack than I thought. The second is that I must be a fucking masochist to even try. The third is a nasty pill of truth, way more difficult to swallow—The Society isn't the only reason why I'm invested in gaining Stone's favor, and I'm not sure I like what that means.

I don't do feelings. And I sure as shit don't get them for smart-mouthed girls with too much attitude for their own good.

So why the fuck am I feeling dejected? Why is she all I can think about lately?

Girl's going to be trouble. I just know it.

Fuck my life.

CHAPTER 12

FINN

Easton drives us to The Grind in his truck, luckily not asking too many questions about my sullen mood on the way, preferring just to sing along to the new Post Malone song playing on the radio. However, when we enter the coffee house, my luck takes one hell of a nosedive. Lincoln and Kennedy are talking animatedly with each other in one of the booths, but stop the minute they see us walk into the place, and instantly call us to join them.

Any other day, I'd be more than happy to have Kennedy Ryland for company. Today, though, not so much.

The thing about Kennedy is that she has an uncontrollable need to try and fix everything. She can't see something broken without attempting to put it back together. She's like the Mother Teresa of fuck-ups, which means my moody behavior will definitely pique her interest.

I sit next to Linc, hoping the small distance will be enough to keep me off her radar. But my ass hasn't even hit the seat when, from under my lashes, I see Kennedy shaking her head left to right as she makes a small tsking sound of concern.

"Oh, no. What's got you down, honey? You look like a wreck."

"Nothing, I'm good," I mumble with a fake smile plastered on my lips.

"No, you're not. Come on, big guy. You can tell me. What's the matter?" she coos, patting my hand over the table soothingly like a mother hen.

"I'm good, Ken. Swear on a stack of bibles. So, what's up with you two?" I ask, hoping to steer the conversation away from me.

I look at Lincoln, silently imploring him to help me out with his girl, who is comfortably sitting across from us. But the fucker just shrugs at me with a stupid-ass grin on his face.

"Sorry, Finn. You're on your own. You know Kennedy isn't going to drop it. You do look like shit."

"I told you I'd get it out of you one way or another." Easton chuckles while ordering two coffees and a couple of blueberry muffins from the barista.

"You knew she'd be here, didn't you, you fucker?" I grunt over at East, unimpressed with the ambush.

"You're only getting that now?" He winks unapologetically.

"Dick."

"Come on, Finn. Don't be bitter. Tell me all about it," she insists with a genuine smile.

I let out a long exhale, cracking my knuckles and wondering who I'd like to punch first for their traitorous ways—Linc for not distracting Kennedy when I need him to, or Easton for bringing me here in the first place.

I swear that I have assholes for friends. Whatever happened to bro code? Or does that mean something else? Yeah, I think I might be mixing up analogies, but who gives a shit. There must be some form of unwritten rule not to let your friends become one of Kennedy's pet projects. And if there isn't, I vote in favor of one.

"Hey, big guy!" She snaps her fingers in my face, startling me. "No retreating to Neverland like you always do. Tell me what's got you down, Finn. Maybe we can help," she says cheerfully, looking at Linc and East for support in her cause.

I'd roll my eyes at her if I didn't think she'd kick my ass for it. See, Kennedy Ryland can be the sweetest southern girl there is. Sweeter than warm apple pie. But since she was raised with the likes of us, she has a mean streak to her, too—one you really don't want to mess with.

You wouldn't think so, just by looking at her, though. With her long, golden hair, perfectly clear, blue eyes, and a face of a goddamn angel, most would consider her the epitome of southern belle propriety. She's every mother's wet dream and a shotgun-carrying father's worst nightmare. The thing that makes her one of a kind is that she can play dress-up with all those frivolous debutants just as easily as she can play touch football in the mud with us guys.

Not that she has many girlfriends that I can recall. It must be tough on her. All her best friends are guys, making her a certified tomboy to us while, at the same time, bringing out every green-eyed monster lurking within most of

Asheville's female population. However, I never heard her complain about it. Not once. She loves the fuck out of us too much to be bothered with petty jealousy from the other girls, and in turn, we adore the hell out of her, too, except for Linc, who has a total boner for her.

Kennedy is like our kid sister. She's family. The only problem in that scenario is that she pries like family, too. And right now, her prying is the last thing I want to deal with. Fucking East led me right into her trap with promises of richly brewed Colombian coffee and moist muffins as bait.

"Sucker." His eyes beam at me while I flip him off for the betrayal.

"Finn, I'm waiting, buddy," she cajoles again, her fingers tapping away on the table between us.

"Fine," I grunt, but I don't say anything further as the barista arrives and places our order on the table. The minute her back is turned and we have our privacy back, I point a menacing finger at both my best friends and say, "I want it on the record that you two are fucking dicks for not backing me up. When Kennedy comes for one of you, I'll hand-deliver your asses on a silver platter myself."

"I'm good with that. Are you good with that too, Linc?" Easton asks while shoving a piece of muffin in his mouth, not one bit bothered about my little threat.

"Hmm, let me think about it. Are you okay with Finn hand-delivering my ass to you, darling?" Lincoln questions with a deep drawl and a flirtatious smile.

Her cheeks flush crimson, but her sharp tongue sure as hell isn't embarrassed.

"Continue flirting with me like that, and all your ass is going to get is a spanking."

"Is that a promise, Ryland?"

"Test me and find out, Hamilton."

Okay, now I do roll my eyes because come on! These two should just fuck already and get it over with. He likes her, and she likes him. It isn't rocket science that they should bang. The only drawback I can see to it is that her fiancée might not be too happy about her two-timing him. But where is it written that life is fair? Not in any book I've ever read. Kennedy shouldn't even be engaged to Thomas Maxwell anyway. She and Lincoln are destined for each other. Anyone can see that.

Well, except maybe them.

And Tommyboy.

And her brother, Jefferson.

Okay, so her dad would also lose his shit if he ever found out.

On second thought, maybe a lot of people are none the wiser that the two are crazy for each other. Huh. Guess I'm more clued in than most. Who would have guessed?

"Focus, Ken," Easton coughs into his fist, and I kick the fucker under the table for bringing Kennedy's attention back onto me, when she was perfectly fine making googly eyes at Lincoln.

"Asshole," I mutter under my breath, earning his cocky smirk and an added wink for my troubles.

"Right." Kennedy claps cheerfully, making me her main point of focus once again. "Come on, big guy, spill the beans. Why do you look like someone just ran over your dog?"

All three sets of eyes look in my direction, and if there were a hole I could crawl into to hide myself from them, I would. But since my life has been one shitshow after another, coming clean with what happened between Stone and me doesn't seem all that bad. I mean, let's be real. In the grand scheme of things, Stone doing a hit and run on me last Friday night is pretty goddamn mild compared to the shit I've done this past year.

"I know your heart is in the right place, but I think this is more of a guy thing," I explain, my last attempt to avoid this awkward-as-fuck conversation.

"Well, you're in luck. You've got two guys right here," she beams at my two best friends, nudging Easton's shoulder with her own. "But something tells me you'll do better with a woman's point of view than one of these guys. A certain tattooed girl with vibrant, black and blue hair giving you a hard time, is she?" she singsongs with stars in her eyes.

My jaw falls flat on the table. Not only is Kennedy intuitive as fuck, but she also might be a goddamn witch.

"How did you know?"

She leans back into the leather cushion with an all-knowing smile splaying her lips, looking pleased for nailing my current predicament right on the head.

"Oh, come on, Finn. Did you honestly expect to keep it a secret for long? I mean, Richfield's star quarterback cannot be seen trailing after a girl from the Southside for over two weeks without setting tongues wagging all over town. You two have started quite a stir, I tell you."

"Shit," I mumble.

I don't like the idea of being the center of gossip, and I know for a fact that Stone is going to fucking hate it, too. It's just something else to add to her cons' list where I'm concerned.

"So, what's going on with you two?" Kennedy continues, cupping her chin with her hands and gazing at me like one of the rom-coms she loves to binge-watch on Netflix.

"Honestly, I don't know," I confess exasperatedly, making her brows furrow together at witnessing my frustration.

"Okay. How about you use your words and explain why you're in such a sullen mood? Baby steps, Finn. You can do this," she insists patiently.

"Fine. Whatever. You'll bust my balls one way or another."

"I think our boy is finally getting it," East jokes, leaning into the table right alongside Kennedy so he doesn't miss a second of my humiliation.

I look at Linc, and he's just as attentive.

Curious fuckers, the lot of them.

Guess I've got to bite the bullet, or they'll never leave me alone. But fuck, this is going to be a hard one to live with once I come clean.

"So, have you ever been with someone, and uh… had an incredible night together, uh… had mind-blowing sex, and then two minutes afterward, they're, uh… they're ready to bounce like it never happened?"

"You mean hit it and quit it like you usually do, motherfucker?" Easton teases with a laugh.

I flip him off again while Kennedy jams her elbow in his gut.

"Ouch."

"Stop being a dick and answer him, East. Can't you see Finn's really torn up about it?" she pleads, which makes me feel like shit because I must look really fucking bad for Kennedy to be coming to my defense.

"Why can't Linc answer him? He gets around just as much as I do," East defends, tilting his chin in Lincoln's direction while holding his stomach to prevent her from hitting him again.

Even though Kennedy doesn't waver her sights from my dark-haired friend, I don't miss how she flinched with Easton's statement. And I doubt Lincoln did either.

"Kennedy asked *you* to do it, asshole. So talk," Lincoln orders, not exactly ecstatic about East throwing him under the bus to save his own hide.

"Whatever," he mumbles, and then pretends to take a minute to really think about it. "So, I've had some clingers. I've definitely had some seconds. I also had my share of one-nighters, but never one who was ready to hit the road after only one fuck. You sure you rocked her world, man? You do

184

know your hands aren't just for throwing around a football, right?" he goads, wiggling his fingers in my face.

"First of all, fuck you. Of course I know how to use my goddamn hands. And second of all, I know when a girl is faking and when she's not. And Stone was definitely not faking."

"Had a lot of experience with girls faking it, have you?" he jokes, gaining a muffled chuckle from Linc at my side.

"Again, fuck off!" I seethe through my teeth at him, but the fucker just laughs away at my misery. "I knew this was a bad idea," I groan, slumping in my seat, pushing the plate of muffins away.

These assholes have managed to take away my appetite, and that's saying something. I'm a big guy, so I'm always down for a snack. These idiots just ruined any craving for sugar I could have had.

Assholes.

"Will you two stop?" Kennedy reprimands, grabbing my clenched hands in hers. "Don't pay attention to these two fools. You said you and Stone had a good time together, right? So perhaps she was in a hurry because she had something to do the next day. Or maybe she was tired because you wore her out, big guy." She tries desperately to soften the blow on my ego.

"She did say she had to work," I mumble, still unconvinced.

"See? She was just being responsible. Don't take it so personally. You both had fun. That's what you should be focusing on."

"I guess."

Shit, I think I might even be pouting. The fuck is wrong with me? Am I becoming a pussy all of a sudden? I'm looking down at my crotch and see that all my male parts are still intact, but it sure feels like my balls have taken a leave of absence along with my dick, leaving me high and dry on this one.

Kennedy tilts her head to the side, taking a long, hard look at me and asks, "You like her, huh?"

I feel my forehead wrinkle and my nose twitch at the question, but before I'm able to organize my thoughts and give Kennedy an honest answer, Easton interjects in my stead, "It's not like that, Ken, so don't you go off and start planning a double wedding just yet. Finn here just got his ego hurt instead of stroked. That's all this is."

"I don't think so," she sings.

"You're wrong," he deadpans.

"I'm right."

"Not on this one, Ken."

"God, you're infuriating."

"Is East right? Is that all?" Lincoln hushes beside me while Kennedy and East continue to bicker with each other.

I turn to face Linc, and although his features seem carefree and bright, beneath his ocean-blue eyes I see a storm brewing—one provoked by fear and regret. He knows, as well as I do, the threat looming above us. Stone is only a target for The Society. Nothing more, nothing less. For all our sakes, it will pay me well to remember that.

I give him a curt nod, which seems to lighten the weight of the boulder on his shoulders, even if just by a little bit. His instant relief throws rocks into the pit of my stomach, making my insides twist and coil at the unexpected assault.

Why do I feel like I just lied to my best friend?

"Yeah, I don't buy it," Kennedy continues to debate with East. "I think Finn's way more interested in her than you realize. Otherwise, why would he be upset with her leaving their first date so fast?"

"It wasn't a date!" all three of us answer her in unison.

"God, you guys are being such weirdos. What's the problem if Finn likes this girl or not?"

"Finn likes who now?" a deep velvety voice questions, announcing an uninvited presence.

Shit.

We all look up in unison and are confronted with the other two men in Kennedy's life; Thomas, her fiancé, and Jefferson, her twin brother—two pricks who I wish hadn't overheard our private conversation.

I don't mind Jeff so much, even though he can be a tool when he wants to. But he's a pussycat compared to the senator's son at his side. That's the asshole I can't stand. Maybe it's my loyalty to Linc that makes me biased, but there's just something about the guy that rubs me the wrong way. And it has nothing to do with the fact that he likes to play for both teams. I couldn't give a fuck where he likes to stick his dick. I'm just not entirely convinced that he'll stop getting his cock sucked by all genders, once he gets Kennedy's ring on his finger. His own daddy is famous for his side pieces, so something tells me that the apple doesn't fall far from the tree when it comes to Tommyboy over here.

"So? Don't leave us in suspense. Who does Walker here have the hots for?" Jeff jokes, messing with my hair, leaving me all disheveled. I slap his hand away, but the fucker takes it as his invitation to sit next to me.

"Did the Tin Man get a heart? I thought you were forged in steel, not mush," Tommy jokes, blowing a kiss at Kennedy.

Tommy prefers to stand instead of sitting next to East. If I dislike him, then Easton hates him with the power of a thousand suns, something that Tommyboy knows all too well.

"Don't be an asshole, Tom. It doesn't suit you," Kennedy snidely interjects in my defense, something she is accustomed to do when her fiancé comes after one of us.

"Chill, babe. I'm only busting his balls. Who's the lucky lady that's grabbed young Walker's attention?"

None of my friends open their mouths, but since I don't want him to think I'm ashamed or something, I give him the name he wants to hear.

"Stone Bennett."

"Are you serious?" Jeff whispers beside me.

I see concern tainting each of his words, but I don't have time to answer him since Tommy acts like I just told the world's funniest joke.

"Oh my God, so it's true?" He continues to laugh, slamming his open palms on the table so hard that it startles a few of the coffee goers in this place. "You *have* been slumming it down on the Southside. I'd heard the rumors, but I thought it was fake news like most of Richfield's gossip. So, how's that going for you, Walker?"

"It didn't pan out," I reply with gritted teeth.

I wish I could punch the asshole in his fucking smug face, but then I'd have to deal with a pissed-off Kennedy. Believe it or not, Tom being a dick to me is the lesser of two evils.

"Maybe it's for the best," he retorts after he's done laughing like a fucking hyena. "Some people just need to stay in their lane. You know what I'm saying?" He cocks his brow.

"No, asshole, he doesn't. Explain it to him," Easton belts out.

Tommyboy sways his head toward Easton, giving an elitist sneer that is all sorts of fucked up.

"Oh, I think you don't give Walker here the credit he deserves. Some people shouldn't mix, and your boy knows it. White trash is just that—trash. No matter how pretty the packaging is, some things should stay in the gutter where they belong," he explains with a scornful glower, the dig evidently intended for Easton's mom as well as Stone. He then tilts his head my way, and I have to curl my hands into fists under the table to keep my level head. "You got my meaning well enough, didn't you, Walker?"

"Yeah, I got it."

I know the bastard is dying to say something else, but he's interrupted by Lincoln's mocking whistle, which breaks his focus and gains the attention of all of us.

"You are so fucking full of shit, Tommy. Phew. I can smell your stench every time you open that trap of yours. Why don't you do us all a favor and choke on it instead of spewing it in our direction? Go on now, Tommyboy. Get," Linc orders, waving Tommy off as if he were an errant puppy needing to be hit on the nose with a newspaper.

Tom turns every shade of red in a crayon box, but he shuts his mouth, knowing that, against Lincoln, he is shit out of luck. Tommyboy might be the only son of the great Senator Maxwell, but Lincoln owns most of the Carolinas. You can't throw a rock in all of Asheville without it hitting some monument with his family name on it. Senator Maxwell knows that if he wants to be reelected, he'll need the support of the last heirs to the Richfield dynasty—Lincoln Hamilton and Colt Turner, the two men Tommyboy can't say shit to, or about, if he doesn't want to get on his daddy's bad side.

Sensing the mood, Kennedy discreetly asks Easton to let her pass, so she can do some damage control.

"Good thing my time is up since this is too much testosterone for me. I best be heading back to Richfield, or I'll be late for class. Drive me, Tom?"

"Sure, babe," he answers, dropping a kiss on her lips.

I feel Linc's body stiffen next to me, but he doesn't say anything further to antagonize the asshole.

"Are you coming?" Kennedy asks her twin, trying hard not to look at anyone else sitting at the table after that unsolicited kiss.

"Yeah, I'll meet you both outside. Just need to talk to the guys for a quick second." He smiles warmly at her.

Kennedy gives him a nod and an awkward wave to the rest of us as she pulls Tommyboy by the elbow to follow her.

Jefferson waits until his sister and that asshole he has for a future brother-in-law are out of view and earshot. He then stands up to address us all on what's so goddamn important that it couldn't be said in front of them.

"I know Tom is a dick, but he's Kennedy's fiancé. If you love her as I do, then you have got to get over your wounded pride. He's important to her, which means you have to cut him some slack. You three feel me?"

The question is aimed at all of us, but Jefferson's eyes are fixed only on Linc, demonstrating who he's really concerned about.

"Whatever you say, Jeff. We'll be good little boys from now on. Pinky promise," Easton replies sarcastically, crossing his heart with his middle finger.

Jefferson just shakes his head and leaves without adding anything further to his diatribe. He said what he needed to say, and it was enough.

"What does Kennedy see in that douche anyway?" East belts out once the door closes behind Jeff. "Are you really going to let her marry that dickwad?" he queries the friend at my side.

Linc leans his head back on the headrest, looking exhausted all of a sudden.

This new split personality that Linc's got going still takes a little getting used to. When he's with anyone but us three, he acts as the same carefree guy with no worries—the one he used to be before *it* happened. Now, the scars and damage of what we've done are only visible on his face when we are alone and away from prying eyes.

But then again, aren't we all leading a double life? Aren't we acting like we've got our shit together and everything is above board when, in reality, we are slowly drowning in a sea of despair? We are all wearing masks. Lincoln, Easton, Colt. Even me. We are pretending to be something we will never be again—innocent.

"Well, don't just gawk at the sky, dude. Answer me! Are you going to sit back and do nothing? Just hand over your girl to that fucking prick?"

"She's not my girl, East. She never was and never will be, so just drop it," Lincoln replies in defeat.

"The fuck are you—"

"I said, DROP IT!" Linc yells this time, slamming his fists onto the table for good measure.

The eerie silence that transpires has me sweating bullets. East should know by now that Kennedy is a sore subject for Linc. Not that I understand his reasoning behind not pursuing the only girl he ever cared for. But hey, that's Linc's prerogative, not mine. And certainly not East's.

As a distraction, I order some sweet tea, entirely disregarding the coffee in front of me. Easton just slumps in his seat and crosses his arms over his chest like a spoiled child, scowling around the coffee shop rather than looking at either of us.

I sip on my tea, trying hard not to get too lost in my head, waiting for one of them to set aside their differences and call a truce so we can get back to normal. That's the thing about our little band of brothers—we can be swinging punches at each other one minute, and by the next, we're joking around, not even remembering why we were pissed off in the first place.

"So, things with Stone aren't going as The Society would have liked it, huh?" Lincoln asks, being the first one to break the silence.

He has always been the pacifist in our foursome, so I'm not surprised he's the one to drop the olive branch to get us back to our norm.

"Honestly, I'm not sure what they want. They told me to befriend her, and in a way, I have. I just hope it's enough for them."

"Is it enough for you?" he asks cryptically.

"Just say what you mean, Linc."

"If you're starting to care for this girl, I don't want you to do anything you don't want to," he replies, sincere apprehension to his tone.

My brows furrow tightly, trying to decipher the right words that he wants to hear from me, but to be honest, I don't know what they are.

"He's fine, Linc. I mean, have you ever seen Finn like any girl in all of the time you've known him?" East interjects with a scoff, as if the idea I might fall for a girl was utterly preposterous. However, Linc's expression tells me he's not as easily convinced.

"Just because it's never happened before doesn't mean it can't."

"If it does, it won't be with Stone Bennett. Tell him, Finn," East commands, but for the life of me, the words seem trapped in my throat, unable to come out.

"Tell him," East insists, growing more impatient with my silence.

But the only reply I can come up with is the one I know still rings true to my ears.

"I'll do what I have to, Linc."

Linc lets out a long exhale, his back dipping further into his seat.

"I think that doing what we *had to* is what got us all in trouble, to begin with."

"Have you or Colt found out anything about The Society yet? Anything that could help us get out of this mess?" I ask, wondering if they are faring any better at their task than I am at mine.

"Not really. But the minute we do, I'll let you both know."

"Where is that motherfucker anyway?" Easton asks, only now noticing Colt's absence.

And I'm the slow one of the group.

Linc picks up his phone, the first genuine smile tracing his lips, as he shows us a picture of a flustered Colt talking to an unimpressed librarian.

"Well, I'll be damned. I don't know what surprises me more—Colt actually doing some groundwork that doesn't involve pussy, or that he knows where the library is to begin with." East chuckles.

"His name *is* on the building," I counter. "He should at least know where the damn thing is located."

We all laugh at that because Colt isn't the type of guy you'd ever expect to encounter in a place that doesn't offer the potential of getting laid. The girls' locker room, yes. The library, hell no.

After our laughter dies down, I can't help but look to Lincoln one more time for guidance.

"So, how are we going to handle this in the meantime?"

"Just as we have been. Act normal and wait for further instructions."

"Instruction from The Society, you mean?" I ask just to be clear, getting from him a stiff nod in reply.

"What if they know that Finn blew his chance with the Southie, though?"

"You think I blew it?"

"I love you, dude. Like a brother, I do. But I gotta tell ya, when a girl is ready to bounce after a fuckfest, it usually means she's running home to finish herself off and get the orgasm you were meant to give her. Sorry to burst your bubble, man." East shrugs, not as apologetic as his words sound.

"Why didn't you say that shit earlier?" I grunt, annoyed.

"Because! Kennedy was here, and I didn't want to be all crass and shit in front of her," he counters defensively.

"It never stopped you before, asshole," I yell.

"Guess I'm evolving."

"Evolve this motherfucker." I slap him over the head, which is kind of hard since he's all the way across the table.

The jackass, instead of getting pissed at me, just laughs harder.

"Don't worry about it. You just have to convince her that the second time around will be better. That you are going to wow her as a second act, rather than a first. I mean, sequels can be better than the originals, right? It's not totally unheard of," he goads.

"Funny. But what if she doesn't give me a second chance?"

"Have you at least called her to find out?"

"I've texted, but she hasn't replied. Pretty sure she's already blocked my number from her phone," I admit.

I mean, why else would she not reply? It's the only plausible reason I can come up with to explain the radio silence I got from her all weekend.

"Yikes. Jesus, how bad a lay are you?"

"I'm not!" I shout at him, but the fucker just keeps laughing.

Linc, unable to hold it in, follows suit, and pretty soon, I join in, too. Because what am I going to do? Cry? Fuck that.

Linc wraps his arm over my shoulder and tilts his head next to mine.

"Finn Walker, you might not know this about yourself, but you are a fucking catch. If this Stone girl doesn't see it, then fuck it. No skin off your back. But we still need her, brother. Whatever harebrained scheme The Society has in mind, Stone is at the very center of it. You think you're cool with giving it another go?"

Do I even have a choice?

"Of course he is," East replies on my behalf. "His cock is ecstatic at the idea of getting near that Southie hotness again. I mean, you have got to see this girl, Linc. So damn hot, your cock would be weeping for weeks," East jokes, but I feel my features grow somber, not one bit happy with his remark about Stone.

"Don't talk about her that way. She isn't like the girls you're used to."

"Oh, no? Yeah, I'm sure she's a goddamn peach. The Southie looks like she can handle her own shit, Finn. No need for you to be playing the knight in shining armor to defend her honor. I wouldn't dare to say half the shit I am in front of her. Something tells me she'd cut my balls off and make them earrings. Parade them all around the quad, too, like trophies."

"That's true. She is a tiny badass, isn't she?" I ask, somewhat proudly.

"Please don't make me barf up my muffin," he quips, looking nauseated. "And take that stupid-ass grin off your face. Seriously, it's giving me the creeps," he adds, shivering his body like a cold gust of wind just went through it.

Linc's phone starts to vibrate, and I can see him receiving another picture from Colt. Only this one differs significantly from the last. His arms are around two freshmen's shoulders, giving us the thumbs-up as they head into the dead languages' section of the library. In other words, he's about to fuck them both, instead of continuing with the research on The Society as he was supposed to.

"I have to get back to school. Colt gets easily distracted with shiny new things," Linc jokes, finishing up his coffee.

"Yeah, we should get back, too," I add as I'm about to move my ass out of the booth, but stop when Linc grabs my forearm, giving it a light squeeze.

"Thank you, Finn. For everything," he hushes out genuinely.

I know his words are sincere, and I wish there wasn't this small part of me—hidden away in the confines of my hectic being—holding a little bit of resentment for the reason behind his genuine gratitude.

I shrug the hateful sentiment off, not wanting to give it any credence, and throw him a half-assed smile instead of uttering a word.

I mean, what's the point?

We are all in this boat together. It's not only Lincoln's fault we have fallen prey to The Society's demands. We all played our part that night, and as much as I try to push it to the back of my mind, my hands are just as bloody as his.

On the ride back to campus, I try to think of how I'm going to deal with the whole Stone situation, instead of focusing on past fuck-ups. Maybe I should give her some space to breathe. Give her enough time to miss my stalking ways. Isn't that how the old proverb goes? Distance makes the heart grow fonder, or some nonsense like that? Couldn't hurt to try and see if it will work. It sure as hell beats the alternative—me groveling for her attention. Unless, of course, backing off is exactly what she wants from me.

Fuck.

This shit is hard. Do all guys go through this when they want to win a girl over? Because if they do, then I wasn't missing much.

By the time we get to Richfield, I've decided to give Stone a few days for her to get in touch with me. A week should suffice. Okay, maybe less than a week. Three days tops. But do I count Saturday and Sunday, or do I give her three days starting from today? Hmm. Isn't there some sort of manual on how to deal in these types of situations?

I'm about to google it when Easton parks the car. Since I don't want his ass to tease me any further for my lack of experience, I stash my phone away, making a mental note to check later for the correct protocol on how to deal with chicks.

However, when we both get out of the car, our attention is quickly grabbed by a herd of college kids in the parking lot, all excitedly on their phones, taking pictures of something I can't quite make out.

"Wonder what that's all about?" Easton queries next to me, as we walk closer to the gawking crowd.

With each step I take, there is a twisted feeling in my gut, telling me I'm not going to like it one bit.

"Finn, don't you usually park your Porsche on this side of the lot?"

I just nod because words fail me as soon as I set my eyes on what everyone is gaping at. My silver Porsche, drenched from hood to tires in pig's blood, with one single word fingered on the windshield for the whole world to witness— KILLER.

I swallow dryly as the kids around me slap my back in approval. From the strands of endless gibberish coming from the crowd, I realize they are all thinking that this is just some fucked-up hazing from a rival team, wanting to mess with my head before a big game. Thing is, there is no big game this weekend, and if these kids used the same brain cells they are wasting to upload pictures of my wrecked car on every social media platform there is, they would also put two and two together.

"Remember when I said that I would take The Society's hoopla seriously when shit hit the fan?" Easton asks beside me, nodding at the student body around us as if joining in on the joke. "Well, this is our motherfucking wakeup call that these cunts mean business."

I crack my knuckles, trying to keep my fake, standoffish grin on my lips, rather than letting the dread set in.

"What do we do now?" I mutter under my breath, not wanting anyone to pick up on my panicked question.

"*We* don't do shit. *You* are the one who has to step up their game."

"And how exactly do I do that?"

"You know what you have to do, Finn. Go see Stone, man. It's her they want."

CHAPTER 13

STONE

"You look like shit," Janet laughs, eyeing me up and down after giving me her table's order.

"Geez, thanks, bitch. Don't hold back or anything," I grumble sarcastically as I pour three shots of Jack for her.

She slants her eyes and leans closer to the bar counter, making sure tonight's clientele get a good eyeful of her ass in that wide belt she insists on calling a skirt. It's pathetic the lengths my colleague will go to get these rejects grabbing their balls and drooling at the corner of their mouths for an ass that can be bought with a few dollar bills or a line of coke.

I've seen Janet too many times on her knees in the storage room, working on her 'extra income'. If she was trying to earn money to keep her lights on or her fridge stocked up, I'd think it as a sad situation. Still, since it's just for her to snort up her nose or shoot down her vein, I couldn't be more repulsed about how she comes by the extra cash.

The problem with Janet giving her hoochie away like it's Christmas morning is that some of these losers think I'm just as skanky and easily bought. Though they quickly learn how that isn't the case when they try to put their hands on me. I don't fall to my knees unless I'm in the mood, and only in front of who I damn well please—the losers that come every night to Big Jim's don't make the cut.

"Don't get pissy, honey. I'm just calling it as I see it," Janet placates with her deep southern twang, as if that will take the sting away from her insult.

"Oh yeah? And what do you see?" I cross my arms over my chest, not really giving a rat's ass about what she thinks one way or the other.

"A girl who isn't going to get any tips looking like that," she rebukes, her red acrylic nail drawing an invisible line up and down my short frame to make her point. "I thought you were a smart college girl. I guess you're just as stupid as the rest of us," she taunts, wiggling her brows and prancing off to the customers that ordered the whiskey.

Even though my resting bitch face is permanently stitched on, I know the skank is right—Big Jim's isn't classy. There's no dress code for staff, but the scruffy-looking clientele will pay a little extra if they see some cleavage or leg. And tonight, I'm definitely not giving them their money's worth with an old pair of skinny, black jeans and a raggedy 'The Smiths' T-shirt that should have been thrown out ages ago due to its overuse. The clothes covering all my prized treasures from these horndogs' eyes won't win me any brownie points or pay Mom's grocery bill this week.

Damn it, I must be slipping.

I should have reconsidered my clothing choices before I left for class this morning, but I was planning to drop by the dorm before clocking in. Unfortunately, I ran late from my study session at school this afternoon, and before I knew it, it was time for my shift at this dump, so I didn't have time to go back to my room and slut it up.

The worst part is that I know I'm bound to drop the ball again. I get so razor-sharp focused on schoolwork that everything else just ends up being white noise. I forget there is a real world that I still need to deal with outside Richfield's walls, and dressing it up for these creeps is part of my everyday life. Since today I failed miserably to remember my norm, my tips are going to suck ass.

I just have to think of another way to make up for it. I could flirt with these assholes to get some extra money in, but giving them their daily dose of eye-candy is as far as I'm willing to go for a bit of cash. Flirting leads men to have expectations, and men with expectations usually get handsy, which then leads me to either punching their lights out or kneeing them in the junk. And then all my tips go out the window, along with my job. As much as I wish I could kick this sleazy shithole to the curb, I need the money. No way around that.

I look over at Janet working the crowd, sitting on laps and giggling like a schoolgirl, throwing me a wink to rub it in my face how she's going to make bank tonight. I might not like the bitch much, but I do envy her hustle. She's thirty if she's a day, and still wearing fuck-me short skirts and tops loose enough for the men here to get a peek at her goods.

It's a smart move on her part because, let's face it, men are stupid. The minute they open their wallet to pay her, they're more than happy to shell out another five bucks just so they can have a few more seconds staring at her rack. And Janet is all too happy to relieve them of their money and let them have their fill. Of course, for Janet to feed her habit, working these suckers who only came in for a beer or two is just pocket change. The real big spenders get to take a trip with her out back, where she shows how accommodating she can be for an Andrew Jackson or a Grant.

No Benjamins here, I'm afraid. This is Southside, where even a ten-dollar bill is a hard commodity to come by.

"Fuck," I mumble under my breath, aggravated with myself for being so careless.

I have to be more mindful of having my head in the game. My scholarship may pay for my tuition and board, but if I want to eat and keep the lights on at my mother's, this job needs to pay me accordingly. And the measly eight dollars an hour that Big Jim pays me doesn't cut it.

I only have one more year to muddle through this anyway, and then I'm out of here. Next summer I'll be at my internship, and hopefully, they'll keep me on as a paid aid while I get my law degree. This is the last year I'll have to wash puke off the floor, cum off tabletops, or be some asshole's pin-up girl for him to spank off to the minute he gets home. I've worked too hard to let it all fall apart in my last year. They want tits and ass, then that's what they'll get.

While making an inventory of all the slutty clothes I have, someone clears their throat behind me, interrupting my reverie. I plaster on a fake, sultry smile and get ready to put on my charm. Even looking like a day-old mess, I need to see if I can still work my magic and shift a few bills out of this shmuck's pocket into my own.

Of course, when I turn around, the man sitting at the stool is the last one I ever thought would show his pretty face in here again.

"You lost, quarterback?" I ask with my hands on my hips, looking at the guy who gave the start of my senior year an unexpected twist.

"It's rude not to text someone back after hanging out, you know," he reprimands, without so much of a hello. Not that I care since the small pout he's trying damn hard to hide is all the reaction I need, not to mention it's sexy as fuck.

"Is it?" I ask, leaning against the counter, pushing the twins in his face just to get a rise out of him. Sure, Mary Kate and Ashley are all covered up, but I know my perky girls get him riled up anyway. "So, you're telling me that you call back all the girls you hook up with?"

He looks down at his feet with guilt, and I know I got him pegged.

"Yeah, quarterback. I didn't think so. Now, how about we do this little bit again, shall we? I'm sure your momma gave you more manners than that."

"Hi, Stone," he replies sheepishly, giving me the greeting I deserve while looking way too out of his comfort zone.

I bite down the chuckle that wants to leave me because, honestly, it's too damn funny watching Finn try to fit in when he is miles away from his natural habitat. Why he's even here is mind-boggling, but it will surely be entertaining to watch him squirm and cringe at being in my neck of the woods.

"Hi, yourself, pretty boy. I have to admit, I didn't think I'd see you in here again. Has the Northside become too boring for you? Is it not giving you enough action, and now you have to drive here to get it?" I tease, leaning my hip on the counter.

"I just came to see you. That's all," he mumbles, still looking like he'd rather be anywhere else but here.

"Me? You came to see me?"

"You say it like it's unfathomable or something. Yeah, I'm here to see *you*. Haven't I stalked your ass enough around school for you to know I like looking at you?" he grumbles, and although the words coming from his mouth seem as if he resents the fact that he's here, the reason behind it is kind of sweet. I guess as sweet as a guy like Finn can be.

"Yeah, I like looking at you, too. Still, I wouldn't drive miles out of the fancy part of town to visit this hellhole to do it."

"You didn't answer your phone, and things got a little bit hectic back at school today, so this was the only way I could catch up with you."

"It's been just two days since we saw each other, Finn. You're not catching feelings, now are you?" I joke, but my tone sounds as if the idea of such a thing were worse than catching an infectious disease.

"It's not like that," he counters defensively, this time being man enough to look me in the eye.

Now that's more like it.

I take a minute to answer him because, damn, he's pretty. I mean, men shouldn't be this fucking pretty. It makes smart girls do stupid things, and I'm way too smart to be this stupid. But still, I take my time to give him a once-over and let my eyes enjoy the view for a minute.

If I lick him, could I claim him?

Cause I definitely wouldn't mind licking those abs from top to bottom.

Sweet baby Jesus. He's too damn gorgeous for his own good.

"Stop looking at me like that. I told you, I just wanted to see you. That's all," he explains, completely misreading why I'm gawking at him.

"I sure hope so because you might be cute, but I don't do feelings," I warn him, making it clear where I'm at and hoping to God Almighty he didn't see me drool there a second ago.

"Neither do I."

"Good to know." I throw him the first smile as his reward for giving me the right—and only—answer worth my time. "So, what can I get you?"

"As long as it comes from a bottle, anything will do."

I grab him a beer and slide the bottle back to him, ignoring the other customers at the counter who also want their liquor. They can wait. Pretty boy here can't.

"That will be fifteen dollars."

"Last time, it was six." He furrows his brow.

"Last time you didn't have the pleasure of my company, now did you? Consider it tax." I smile sweetly, batting my eyelashes at him.

He passes me a twenty, and I start heading to grab his change, only for him to tell me to keep the rest.

Don't mind if I do.

I watch him clean the bottle ring with his shirt, looking like he's afraid of getting an STD just by wrapping his lips around it. The urge to tease him is strong, but another customer calls out to me, so I lose my shot at busting Finn's balls for his cautious ways, which is a shame since I kind of like seeing him all riled up. I've seen firsthand what a little fire burning in his veins does to him, so it's just too delicious and tempting to pass up.

Before I know it, I'm deep in rush hour on autopilot. You wouldn't think a place like this has a rush hour, but it most certainly does. Everyone from this side of town knows Big Jim's is the place you want to be at to blow off some steam after a long-ass day of underpaid work.

I have to say, I'm kind of happy that Big Jim let me switch to bar duty this week since the demand makes the time pass quicker. I'm so occupied that I totally forget that pretty boy is squirming away at the far end of the bar counter. I only remember his presence every time he asks for another beer, enabling me to make a few extra bucks off him. A better woman than me would feel remorse in taking advantage of him, but if I have to pick between dignity and an empty stomach, then it's an easy decision to make.

It does make me wonder why he's here at all, though. My bet is that his usual groupies aren't cutting it for him anymore, and he thought he'd get his kicks with an easy, white-trash blowjob. I'm fine with a booty call, and pretty boy isn't just nice to look at since he definitely has some moves on him in the bedroom department.

The only thing is, he's a distraction I don't have the luxury to indulge in. I've got too much on my plate as it is.

Sure, I still have my sex drive on high alert, but nothing I can't fix with my trusty vibrator and a bit of good old-fashioned Tumblr porn. Getting off solo means I don't have to deal with clingy-ass guys who always end up blowing up my phone, demanding my time, and getting pissed off when I don't have any fucks to give.

Although, Finn doesn't strike me as the needy kind. If he were, his ass would have been sitting in that precise spot he is now the very next day we bumped uglies. But he wasn't. All he sent was one lousy text all weekend.

Can't stop thinking about fucking that bratty mouth. We should do this again.

Any other girl would probably be offended by it. Me, though? After he planted that mental picture into my skull, I had to take out the above-mentioned vibrator and put it to good use. I came good and hard, picturing pretty boy here making my mouth his fuck toy. See? A distraction.

Finn showing up tonight might spark up my curiosity, but not enough that I want to spend my precious time thinking about it. As I said, I've got too much going on—finishing up school, my mom, my internship, and my goddamn life to worry about. And as much as I'd like nothing better than to lose myself for a couple of hours straddled over his tree trunk of a body, it's just time taken away from more important matters. A girl has to have her priorities in check if she wants to make it in this world.

When the night starts to dwindle down, and most of the clientele have had their fill, my eyes lock on Finn, who is playing around with the napkin, the one I gave him to swipe his beer bottle with, rather than using his shirt all the time.

"Okay, pretty boy. You've been here long enough. I think it's time you called it a night. You look like you're bored out of your mind."

"Can I get another beer?" he asks, instead of doing as he's told.

"Are you driving?"

Finn had six beers already, and although he's a big guy, I don't know how much tolerance he has for his liquor.

"No. Going to call an Uber."

I can't help but laugh. As if an Uber was going to come to this side of town to pick his ass up.

"Good luck with that."

I fetch him another beer, and since things have slowed down, I take a minute to talk to him. I lean against the counter, stripping the empty beer bottle of its logo, and ask, "Why did you come tonight? Not only do you not belong here, but you also look like you don't want to be here either. So why waste your night slumming it up in a place like this?"

"I just needed to see you," he mumbles, taking a swig of the bottle, his light-blue eyes intent on mine.

"You already said that. But why?"

"I don't have a reason to tell you," he explains incoherently, taking a larger pull of his beer this time.

"Oh boy, I think you drank more than I should have let you."

It's my fault, really. Any other guy I would have cut off earlier, but I made at least eighty bucks off Finn, which is more than enough to fill up my fridge and still have some left over for my mom. I either got distracted or greedy. Take your pick.

"It's okay. I told you I didn't bring my car," he tries to pacify me.

"Why not? Were you worried someone would steal it?"

"Something like that," he admits, and I can't help but laugh. "I like how you laugh," he adds in a sultry tone, his fixed gaze dropping to my lips, making my insides start to liquefy.

"That's it. No more beer for you, mister," I reply sternly, hoping it serves as an excuse for him not to say shit like that to me. I mean, a girl can only take so much.

"I like how your plump mouth opens just a tiny bit when you do it. And the sound is sexy as fuck."

"Now I know you're drunk, quarterback," I play off.

"I'm not drunk," he utters steadfastly.

"Well, you're not making any sense either. Just pack it up for the night, pretty boy. Whatever you came here for isn't happening tonight."

"Yeah, I can see that," he replies before drinking the remainder of his beer in one fell swoop and slamming the bottle on the bar. "Guess I'll just have to take my chances tomorrow," he adds, this time leaving a crisp hundred on the counter for me.

I pick it up and put it inside my bra, next to the other bills he's given me tonight. Against my better judgment, I halt his step before he leaves and say, "Finn, don't come tomorrow. You're wasting your time."

"We'll see."

Chapter 14

Finn

Just as I promised Stone, I'm right back at the bar the next night, sitting on the stool by the counter. I'm here every night she's working, knowing the only day I can stay clear out of this rat hole is on Thursdays when she has her night off. Unfortunately for me, Big Jim's Bar has become my second home for the next couple of weeks.

Even though I'm here to make my presence known, I'm unsure if I'm making any real progress. I don't know if I'm playing by The Society's rules and being the good little soldier they want me to be, or if I'm missing the mark entirely. At least they haven't made any more demands, nor have they gone after me or any of the guys. I think they made their point loud and clear on the day they wrecked my car with pig's blood.

Killer.

That's what they called me.

That's what everyone will call me if the truth ever gets out.

I can't let that happen. If coming to this dump every night for all eternity is my penance, then so be it. I'll do whatever I need to do to keep the truth under lock and key. I thought the only downside to this arrangement would be spending a few hours in this shithole, filled with cockroaches and filth. But as each night passes, it gets harder and harder to be here for a whole other reason entirely; the very one The Society has forced upon me—Stone Bennett.

I spend my nights scowling at every guy in the joint. And when I say every guy, I mean every last one of these fucking assholes who can't keep their eyes in their skulls whenever Stone is bartending. She sure as shit doesn't make it easy on me either. She comes in every night looking even hotter than the night before. Most nights she's wearing booty shorts or miniskirts that show off her tanned legs, along with her phoenix tattoo, making every dipshit in the place imagine those legs wrapped around their waist, or worse, around their head. Don't even get me started on those ripped up T-shirts she's always flaunting around.

Case in point, the one she's wearing tonight is just a tear away from leaving her stark fucking naked. I wouldn't even have to put much effort into shredding the flimsy garment apart since there's barely any material to speak of. Not only does it leave her belly button fully exposed, showcasing her flat stomach and slender waist, but it also ends up drawing even more attention to those thick thighs of hers, not to mention the amazing ass that you just can't help but want to sink your teeth into. Still, more relentless is the deep, V-shaped neckline that does fuck all to cover the swell of her breasts. The damn woman even has her hair up to show off her long neck, highlighted by the sterling hardware she adorns on her eyebrow and both of her ears. The loose strands of blue hair that fall to her face, added with all that ink, make it that she's a wet fucking dream for every guy who walks into the biker's bar. Present company not excluded since, for nearly a month, she's been the only one I imagine while beating my cock into submission. Always looking savage and dangerous, and—God help me—sexy as sin, too.

Shit!

This is more than my atonement for the wrongs I've done. It's downright cruelty. Having to sit here and do nothing while all these fuckers are jonesing to get in her pants is beyond anyone's tolerance threshold. Funny thing is, I can't even blame them. My name is right at the top of her list of admirers since I know exactly how sweet every part of her tastes, something that I highly doubt any of these assholes even has a clue about.

I really don't know how much longer I can take this.

Shit, I'm not sure if me being here even registers on her radar.

Some nights, Stone throws me a bone and spends a few minutes with me, while on others, she completely ignores my very existence. Not to mention that every time I do come into the place, she flushes me out, leaving me penniless. I know she doesn't charge the other dipshits here as much as she does to me, but knowing Stone, it's her not-so-subtle way of telling me to go away unless I want to get played. Little does she know that I'd pay triple the amount I leave here every night if only she threw me one of her genuine smiles. Or just one of those deep, sultry laughs of hers.

Yep, the brat has turned me into a pathetic mess of a man. That's why tonight I changed my game plan and brought something to keep my mind occupied.

"What do you have there?" I hear her ask, pulling the book from my hand to see the cover. "*NightWatch* by Terence

Dickinson," she whispers, flipping a few pages of my astronomy book.

It's an old worn-down copy that I got almost a decade ago, but every once in a while, I like to go back and reread it. It always seems to teach me something new every time I do.

Stone carefully hands it back to me, and I wait patiently for her to start hassling me about it. Surprisingly enough, though, she doesn't. What she does is place both her elbows on the counter in front of me with her open palms under her chin, just staring directly at me, curiosity tainting her every feature.

"Can I ask you a question?"

I nod because I'm a little lost for words with her deep-green eyes transfixed so intently on mine.

"Why do you like stars so much?"

It's a simple question, but it's one that I haven't been asked often. Anyone would assume I'd need a minute to think about it before answering. Still, when it comes to my passion for astronomy, there really isn't much to think about.

"You know when it gets a little too much up here?" I say, pointing to the center of my forehead. "Well, with me, sometimes the noise is so loud that I get a bit overwhelmed. My mind is a turbulent place to be in, and every now and again, I need to switch it off just so I can breathe, you know? Astronomy does that for me. Looking up at the night sky and seeing all those stars shining on the deep, rich, vast backdrop of the universe allows me to experience the silence that exists far from this planet. I like the idea of that. It mellows me out."

Her eyes turn half-mast as she softly bites her tongue just below her piercing. She starts to open her mouth, ready to say something, but some asshole calls out her name, demanding his order. And just like that, she sashays away, keeping those words locked away in that beautiful mind of hers.

Defeated, I return to my book, hoping its images can quiet my current torment, but just as my mind starts to ease, Stone's voice slashes through the calm.

"Hey, pretty boy. You think you can help me out back and grab some beer crates with me?" she yells from the other side of the counter.

"Sure," I mumble, thinking that some heavy lifting is preferable to her giving me the silent treatment.

I watch Stone tell one of her colleagues to manage the bar while she goes on her errand. It's one of the more blatant cougars this dump employs to keep the customers happy. I've seen her around before. Kind of hard to miss since she's been eye-fucking me every chance she gets. Too bad for her that my ass only seems to be interested in one particular Southie, and it sure as shit isn't her. The night is almost through anyway, and the crowd is dwindling down so it won't be too hard for the barmaid to manage.

After I help out Stone, I should be heading back home myself. I've got a few drinks in me but not enough to do any damage. I learned the hard way that relying on Uber to pick me up from this side of town isn't an option. Assholes don't like coming here. The last time, I had to walk a few miles before I got picked up by one. So now I drink less and bring one of my brother's cars. If it gets stolen, I won't be too sad to see it go since it's not my baby.

Stone ushers me through into a poorly lit hallway behind the bar, leading to a door down a corridor. When she pushes it in, I observe a dark, cramped room just as humid as the bar itself. The door swings, closing behind me, and before I'm able to ask Stone to turn on the lights, I feel her hands push my back against it.

"Stone?"

"Shut up, pretty boy. This is going to have to be quick and dirty."

"What is?" I ask stupidly, but when I feel her hand on my hard cock—no surprise there since it's always hard whenever I'm around this woman—I get a clue to what the brat has in mind.

She unzips my jeans, pulling them down along with my boxers, just enough to let my stiff shaft feel the cool air. Stone then falls to her knees, making me slam my head on the door and biting my knuckles to keep me silent, all the while impatiently waiting for her next move. The minute I feel her smooth tongue play with the slit of my cock, I curse out loud, unable to keep it in.

"Fuck, that feels good."

"Promise it's going to feel even better in a minute," she taunts and then wraps those plump lips of hers around my dick, making the bastard cry tears of joy.

God, this girl sucks cock like she does this for a living.

Stone hollows her cheeks, sucking me to oblivion while leaving her hands free to grab my ass and push me mercilessly further down her throat. Unable to keep still, my hands start to feel along the wall in search of a light switch, and when I reach one, I swear I hear angels sing. I flick it, letting the sudden light into the darkened room, which only deters her for half a second. She recovers in record time, resuming her vicious assault on my dick.

My eyes can't help but appraise the raven beauty on her bare knees. I grab her by the bun, so she has no choice but to look up while she deep throats me. Her light eyes smolder with every inch she gets inside that pretty little mouth of hers, and I'm sure mine are just as hooded. The will to face-fuck the hell out of her is brutally strong, but I curb the roaring beast within me, not wanting to scare her in such a vulnerable position.

But Stone, being Stone, never makes life easy for me. She plays with my cock like it's her favorite toy, teasing each vein with the tip of her tongue, letting the smooth steel of her piercing press against my sensitive skin to madden me further.

"Fuck, Stone. You're too good at this," I mumble, my head slamming against the door repeatedly to keep it together as my fingers weave themselves into her hair forcefully.

The sound of her mouth sucking me in, while she purrs out in triumph, undoes me just as much as her sass always seems to. But, fuck me, if this isn't the best feeling ever. Her warm, wet mouth seeks every part of me as if she's been starving for my cock, which weakens my restraint, completely withering it when she starts humming around me.

"Damn you, woman," I groan, unable to take this excruciating torture any longer.

I grab her by the hair with enough strength to bring her slight pain, and the small whimper of satisfaction that leaves her lips emboldens the wild animal in me to come out.

Without delay, I thrust all of me inside her until I feel the back of her throat clench with my size. With my eyes fixed on hers, I look for reassurance that she can take the beating that I'm offering. Her gorgeous, dark lashes beating twice is the only sign I get, baiting me to do my worst.

A better man would warn her. A better man would ask and gain her verbal consent first. A better man would handle this situation very differently.

Unfortunately for her, I'm not the better man.

I lost the right to call myself that months ago.

All that remains is this—a caged animal that pretends to be a docile creature to do a worse man's bidding. I'm nothing but a starved beast, ready to pounce on its unassuming prey upon drawing the first scent of blood. Thirsty for flesh, craving to tear it from bone until there is nothing left but raw passion. There is nothing more I want to do than to sink my sharp teeth into this precious stone until I shatter it—piece by glorious piece. She opened the door, inviting the monster in, unaware of the devil that's about to possess her.

I repeatedly thrust deep into her mouth, in search of the release that has escaped me before. The night she let me taste her sweet cunt for the first time, only to deprive me ever since. My fingers bite into her scalp as I push her to take in all of me, the sound of her gagging, making the sick, twisted part of me rejoice.

"Is this what you wanted?" I curse out when I watch the tears smudge her black eyeliner.

As Stone cranes back her head, I prepare myself for the disgust I'll likely see imprinted on those emerald jewels of hers. But instead, I find in them a river of desire break out in a fire, torched by my lack of restraint. I feel her nails bite into my ass cheeks, ordering me to keep up with my harrowing tempo, making me groan out.

This woman will be the death of me.

"Oh, fuck, Stone. What are you doing to me? You want it, I'll give it to you," I threaten wholeheartedly.

The fiend she's confronted with next is something I've never shown any woman I've ever been with. The debutants, cheerleaders, and groupies will fake that they like it rough behind closed doors, just so they're treated tenderly out in the open. But I know it's all for show, so they never get a taste of my true, coarse, obscene nature. They are all too damn vanilla and would probably whine my ear off if I left a single bruise on their flawless skin. And that is just the sort of headache I've always tried to stay clear from.

Stone, however, isn't as delicate.

Her busted-up knees on the grimy floor, swallowing my cock like there's no tomorrow, tells me as much. With those other girls, I never really let go. They didn't care that they were getting just a smidge of me, as long as they were seen on my arm at some party we met. For them, it would be enough of a reward for my little brutality.

With Stone, though, it's a whole other ball game. She'll never be content with less than my true self. Aside from that, she couldn't give two fucks either way if people see us together or not. She doesn't expect me to call in the morning after I've fucked her brains out. She's doesn't want to talk about feelings or take me on long walks on the beach. She doesn't want jack shit from me. I'm not sure she even *likes* me. At this very moment, all she wants is my cock in her mouth, dominating her completely. And for the first time in my entire life, I'm all too willing to comply with a woman's demands.

I give everything I have—all of it and more.

I fuck her inviting mouth like it's the last hole I'll ever be in. As her tears start trickling down her face, the sparkle in her eyes keeps fixated on mine, demonstrating she's loving every minute of my abuse. I can't help but marvel at how her cheeks are flushed pink from unashamedly taking my cock.

Stone has plenty of tricks up her sleeve, too. She continues to hum, making me realize that it's not only to drive me insane but also to relax her gag reflex just so she can take me in deeper.

The praise for her that ensues, surprises even me, "How can a bad girl like you look so good on your knees sucking cock, Stone? I swear I've never seen anything more beautiful."

She moans as she shuts her eyes, loving the dirty words she's coaxing out of me while sinking her nails into my skin hard enough that I'm sure she's cut into me. Her nails are definitely going to leave half-crescent moons on my ass, but I'll wear those fuckers like a badge of honor once I'm done with her. I'm so fucking lost in the world this girl has created for me. This little piece of heaven is stored away in the backroom of a filthy bar where all the devils come to play.

"I bet that pussy of yours is drenched just by sucking my cock. Isn't that right, little girl?"

She squirms, pushing her thighs together and trying to get some friction to relieve her own ache, confirming my suspicion without her having to say a word.

"You make me want to be rough with you in so many sweet ways," I confess, one hand still pulling at the blue tips of her hair, while the other caresses her wet cheek, offering nothing but adoration.

"I'm going to cum in that mouth of yours, Stone, and I want you to drink every last drop. Then afterward, I'm going to eat your pussy until my name is the only word you even remember. Is that understood?"

The little complying nod she's able to give while being fucked in the mouth so ruthlessly is an extraordinary feat. I vow to make this girl cum so hard that she'll see her fucking maker tonight. I'm so enraptured by the awe of this moment—not only am I fucking Stone's bratty mouth as if my life depended on it, but she's also just as eager to swallow me whole, not once waving the white flag. It dawns on me that Stone must have her own starved animal trapped inside her—one with sharp claws and hungry teeth ready to cut me open and eat me raw.

The epiphany has me instantly unraveling, leaving me no time to warn her. My eyes slam shut, blinded by white light, as I empty myself inside her in a way I've never done before. Like the goddess that Stone is, she laps it all down, hungrily cleaning my cock with her hot mouth and velour tongue. Unable to take another second without tasting this temptress, I unbind her hair from her bun, wrapping it around my wrist so I can pull her up to her feet and kiss her madly— possessively and feverishly.

"Finn," she moans out desperately, and I relish my name on the tip of her tongue, wishing I could tattoo it to always be there.

I pick her up from her waist, my lips still locked with hers, as I carry her to sit on a freezer at the other end of the storage room. When my hands travel down to her thighs, she unabashedly opens her legs for me.

That's Stone for you. She has no inhibitions. No worries or cares. She knows what she wants and demands to have it, one way or another. And I'm the lucky asshole who won the golden ticket to satisfy her every order and command.

When my hand feels her wet thighs dripping with want, I lose it, going instantly to my haunches, yanking her panties to the side. I pull her toward my face so that I can get my own sweet mouthful. The taste of honeyed peach wrecks my senses, her soaked pussy becoming the only source of sustenance I need. My tongue laps at her entrance, cleaning her until it finds the hidden nub that pleads for more attention. I tease her sweet spot, nice and slow, taunting her to latch her hands into my hair and demand me to fuck her senseless with my tongue.

The instant she caves and unleashes her own inner demon, I go to fucking town on her tight little pussy, eating it with such ardor that her wails can't keep contained in the small room around us. When Stone is at her brink, right at the edge of madness, I go for the kill, flattening my tongue on her clit while fucking her cunt with my fingers, curving them ever so slightly until they find that one tiny spot inside her walls that has her seeing the heavens and beyond.

"Finn!" she screams out while riding my face, pushing all previous orgasms to the end of the list and telling them they all sucked compared to this one.

I take my time with her, letting her ride it out as I continue to show her sweet little pussy the same attention she showed my eager cock, who is already bobbing in the air, hard as a rock, ready for round two.

With her chest still heaving, she tries to straighten up. Before she even thinks about saying what I think she's about to, I wrap my hand around her throat and deliver the mother of all kisses. When we break apart, her breathing is even more erratic, and her eyes heavy as she tries to keep her focus on me. With my thumb still caressing her throat, I lean in closer so she can hear me loud and clear.

"We're not done," I grunt, shutting down any ideas she may have had about making excuses to walk out this door.

She might have played that card on the night I took her to my secret hangout, but she has another thing coming if I'm going to let her walk away just as easily the second time around.

This time, *I* say when this ends. I don't want her bratty lip, unless it's to kiss me stupid.

What I want is to sink into her wet core, which is dripping with need, so I'm not leaving this room until I have all of her.

I pick her up and turn her around, bending her over the freezer. With her butt in the air and her mini skirt scrunched up around her hips, I can't help but slap that exposed gorgeous ass, promising to give it its own little debauchery one day. I slap it again, loving how her ass cheek jiggles while turning such a lovely shade of red. Maybe someday, I'll slap it so hard that I'll leave my five-digit imprint permanently marked so that the next fucker that comes around knows he will never live up to me.

Fuck the next fucker! She's mine now.

"Finn?" she mewls over her shoulder, docile and panting, her legs still shaking, but holding on tight to the freezer so I can have my way with her.

God, I'm in trouble.

A snarky Stone gets my motor running like crazy, but this sweet, lust-filled one is killing me.

"Shhh. I got you," I tell her, slipping my fingers under the edge of her panties and ripping them to shreds at the sides.

I don't throw the garment away, though. Instead, I shove the piece of fabric in her mouth, placing my hand over her lips. I lean down next to her earlobe, nibbling and sucking on it, feeling her heavy breathing up close.

"This is because you're going to be too loud, and I don't want to be interrupted by some curious asshole outside."

With her green eyes still at half-mast, she nods understandingly. She then proceeds to wiggle her ass at me, making me want to fall on my knees again just to have that juicy ass in my face so I can bite it and properly introduce it to my tongue.

But first things first.

"Are you clean, Stone? Do you take the pill?" I ask her, and she gives me another soft nod.

"Good, because I'm going to take you raw. You okay with that?"

The little satisfied, muffled sigh that leaves her has my shaft applauding the vixen. For praise, I slap her other cheek with a little bit more power behind it.

"Humph," she mumbles through the lace.

I love the fact that she's tasting herself through the fabric, mimicking the same lingering sweetness I still have dancing on my tongue.

I push her skirt higher up to her waist, kicking her legs to open wider. I run my hand up and down her entrance, making sure she's ready, while her whimpers of anticipation only harden me further. Unable to prolong our suffering, I shift my stance so my mushroom head can feel her dripping lips on it. I get it nice and slick, and without warning, I plunge deep inside her, making her head arch back while mine finds its resting place on her spine.

Shit! Skin to skin, she feels even better.

Jesus, Stone!

I start off slow just to get my size reacquainted with her tight fit, but sooner than I expect, she's slamming her ass onto my crotch, enticing my inner beast to take her the same way I took her sweet mouth. I do as she orders and thrust into her without pity. Without mercy.

The otherwise loud wails, which are muffled by the panties in her mouth, become beautiful cries to my ears. I pound into her, telling her how gorgeous she looks while taking me inside her. I'm not one for pretty words, but they all spill from me like a waterfall of lust and desire.

The sensation of having her tight pussy strangling my bare cock is just too much for me to take. Knowing I'm on the precipice of cumming and not wanting to leave her hanging, I strum her clit as I savagely thrust into her. When she bursts on my cock and on my hand, the cry, even if suppressed, is loud enough for everyone to know what we're doing, leaving me just enough time to pull out and cum on her ass.

"Fuck," I grunt in awe of the small puddle on the floor beneath us.

Shit, that's sexy! This fucking woman is going to ruin me.

Her body is still trembling with aftershocks of her explosion when I grab the lace material from her clenched teeth and wipe my cum all over her backside. She turns around after I clean most of it, but it's not like I did such a thorough job. The sick bastard in me likes knowing she'll have to spend the rest of the night with me on her.

I place her thong into my pocket, which makes her pierced brow cock up and a flirtatious grin appear on her face, as she taunts, "Are we keeping souvenirs now?"

I straighten up her clothes, taking extra care to fix her hair since I left it in utter shambles, and reply, "Don't know when you'll let me do this to you again, so why not save a little keepsake?"

She bites her lower lip, grabbing a handful of my shirt and pulling it toward her, leaving me no choice but to lean down until her mouth is mere inches away from my ear.

"Pick those crates up, pretty boy," she orders, tilting her head to the corner of the room, back to her usual tongue-in-cheek swagger.

She gives my lobe a quick bite and then proceeds to walk over to the door. A small chuckle leaves me, seeing how she's reduced me to being her little bitch after I fucked her in every which way. To be fair, I'm completely fine with it.

Once I have the crates in my grasp, I walk over to Stone, who's holding the door open for me. But rather than letting me pass, she puts herself in front of me and goes to the tip of her toes, pressing her lips on mine.

"You can keep the panties, quarterback. But just so you know, those are the only ones you get. Next time we do this, I won't be wearing any."

CHAPTER 15

STONE

Another loud moan leaves me, and the slap that comes with it is something I've begun to enjoy. My legs are spread wide, and my arms up high against the pool table as Finn eats my pussy in a way that no man has ever done before. He doesn't just do the lame three licks and done shit as most college guys tend to do. Nope, not pretty boy here. When Finn goes down on me, he takes no prisoners. It's just too fucking good, and even though I know I should be back at the dorm studying, I can't seem to stop myself from creating small windows in my life just so Finn Walker can fuck me senseless.

Tonight's excuse was telling him I needed help cleaning up after closing. Twice a week, the endeavor falls on me to be the last one to leave and clean this pigsty as much as possible. In all fairness, Big Jim doesn't expect more than a quick sweep of the place, clean tabletops, and put the glasses in the washing machine, ready for tomorrow. And frankly, that's as much as I'm willing to do here anyway. It would take a whole lot of strong-ass chemicals and at least a month to get this place up to code, and I don't get paid enough for that. And since the clientele doesn't care either, why bother?

Of course, not five minutes into the so-called cleanup, and my back was laid out on the pool table, my panties torn to shreds, and pretty boy's tongue lapping me up. I should have known better than to wear panties in the first place. Every time I do, they end up in his pocket, ripped to pieces.

"OH, GOD!" I scream out when Finn grazes my sensitive nub with his teeth, plunging a digit inside my hot core.

For someone who doesn't know the first thing about me, he sure has discovered how to play my body like a fiddle. My ass leaves the green tabletop as he pulls my legs to wrap around his head so he can get all in there.

Damn the man!

I don't even have time to curse him out when the earth begins to shatter around me, my orgasm splitting me in two. My whole frame rises from the table, trying to escape, but he plants his open palm on my belly, commanding my body to endure the ecstasy until I'm left a blubbering mess.

He lifts his head, licking his wet lips as if my pussy were the best thing that ever came across them, and the lethal way his eyes take stock of my body lets me know we aren't done yet.

Good.

Because seconds with Finn is even better than his first go around. My chest heaves under his lust-filled stare, my heart already doing summersaults, anticipating his next move.

"You see anything you like, pretty boy?" I joke, my tongue playing with my lower lip.

"Take that damn top off," he commands, his dominating demeanor making me drip onto the green fabric.

The stain I'm leaving on the pool table is going to be a bitch to explain to anyone bothered enough to complain about it, but fuck it. This is so worth whatever embarrassing conversation might come tomorrow.

My trembling fingers go behind my back and pull the flimsy string of my halter top. I pull the rest of it up over my head, revealing my ample, bare breasts to his scrutinizing eye. He roughly grabs one in each hand, and the hiss that leaves his lips makes me crave every touch.

"These fucking tits have been taunting me all night. Seeing your nipples point out at me, begging for a bite, while I couldn't do anything about it."

"They must have a mind of their own," I tease, but when he leans down and takes one pert nipple into his mouth, my next taunt is replaced with a moan.

"I think you like turning me on like this. Making me angry and hungry for you."

A little laugh rises from my throat, but it quickly turns into another lustful wail.

"Why do I make you angry?"

"Because while you prance around here with that sexy body of yours, wearing no bra and a shirt I could tear apart with my teeth, every last fucker in here is thinking the exact goddamn thing. Fantasizing how they want to have these beautiful breasts in their hands while fucking you raw and hard until you see stars. I hate you for it," he says, lavishing my other breast with the same care and dedication.

"It doesn't look like you hate me at all," I moan out when I feel his jean-clad cock grinding over my sensitive core.

"Oh, but I do. I fucking hate you so much, Stone. So fucking much," he continues to coo lovingly while I'm starting to lose my own goddamn mind with his dry-humping.

I lift off the table, my hands frantically going to his waist, and it's only when I find his belt buckle that I relax back down. His lips are now sucking and biting my neck, giving me room to get what I want. When I feel his hard cock in my hands, I almost cum with relief.

"Put me inside you, Stone. Let me show you how angry I am," he groans, biting my shoulder in such a way, my eyes fall to the back of my head.

My slick pussy doesn't wait for my permission and swallows his impaling cock as if it were her new favorite toy. She's always been a hussy bitch, but for the past two weeks, all she does is dream of the next time she'll ride Finn Walker's ten-inch cock to oblivion. I can't say that I blame her.

Everything about Finn is big. Broad shoulders, muscular thighs, steel abs, and a dick that looks like it's about to eat you alive. All of him is larger than life, and for a few brief moments, he makes mine light up. Although he grunted out that he hated me a few minutes ago, the way he fucks me has nothing to do with hate and more to do with possession. I feel like he wants to embed himself inside me, capture me and keep me, making his hate the sweetest thing I've ever tasted.

"Finn!" I cry when he hits that one spot inside that has me clamping down on him.

"Fuck, this pussy! I want to rip it apart with how good it is. Make you just as crazy as you leave me."

I want to tell him that the feeling is mutual, but my mind isn't capable of coherent thought, much less stitch a whole sentence together. My hands fall to his ass, loving that I can still push him deeper, even though each thrust seems like he really is going to tear me apart.

The quarterback might look all nice and proper, but he's got a dormant animal inside him. One that comes out when he's this exposed, this vulnerable, and it gives zero fucks what anyone thinks. All he cares about is fucking me so hard and good that I become addicted to it. Crave it. Need it. And God, I think he's succeeding.

I feel the bitter taste of iron reaching my tongue, as my teeth cut my lip just to keep control of my loud cries. But fuck if I care. Hurting in Finn's arms is one of the best sensations I've ever experienced. I'll take the little blood, the bruises, and the pain, just so I can feel this rush, this ecstasy that burns through me.

Finn's eye catches the small cut on my mouth, and with brute strength, he lifts me completely off the table. One hand under my ass, the other cradles the back of my neck, caressing it as his tongue gently cleans the blood away, sucking on my lip like a man possessed.

"Everything about you tastes sweet. Even when you're not."

In this position, I feel so full, as if there were a hollow void inside me that only he could fill.

"Don't stop. Don't stop, Finn."

"The only way I'll stop is when I hear you scream out my name while balls deep inside you."

Fuck, his dirty mouth only leaves me more depraved and wanting.

"And then I'm going to fuck these tits and come on you like the bad little girl that you are."

I just nod, panting madly as he keeps driving himself inside me, making me clench around him with each filthy word that escapes his mouth.

"You'll lap it all up, won't you?"

Yes! God, yes!

"And if you are really good, then one day I'll fuck that tight ass of yours. Fuck! Just thinking about it is going to make me cum!" he grunts, his tempo reaching all new heights.

He's hitting all the right spots, and when the sky begins to rip itself apart, I'm not one bit surprised.

"That's it, Stone. Cum for me," he orders, coaxing my brutal orgasm out, leaving every bone and muscle in me limp and sated.

Finn then sets me on my feet and presses on my shoulder—forcing me to squat down just low enough that his cock is perfectly aligned with my breasts—and starts strumming it in between them at a frantic pace. I push the twins together with my hands as he repeatedly assaults the space between them until jets of cum cover my chest beautifully. Knowing that it will drive him insane, I swipe a little bit of it onto my finger and suck on his salty taste, awakening something feral in him.

I'm about to go for seconds, but Finn blocks my attempt, pulling me up once more just so he can kiss me, furiously and maddeningly. I let him take my mouth hostage all too willingly, as his tongue reaches out for my own, worshiping it just as he did my body. When we finally break apart, he holds me tightly to his chest, kissing the top of my head over and over again while combing my hair back with his fingers.

The tenderness that always arises after he's had his way with me leaves me uncomfortable. His gentle touch as he dresses me and arranges my hair, creates a strange sensation to bloom inside me, one that I have no intention in deciphering. After Finn's made sure I've been properly taken care of, he tilts my head, craning it all the way back to lavish me with yet another soft kiss.

Always sweet.

Always frightening.

His clear blue eyes turn soft as he looks down at me, only adding to my dread, making me swallow dryly.

"I'm going to miss this next week," he hushes, running his thumbs over my cheeks, keeping my head in place so that my eyes never leave his.

"Oh? Are you going someplace?"

He shakes his head, his shoulders slumping a bit.

"The Sharks have their first game on Saturday. Training is going to be brutal for the next couple of days, so I'm not sure if I'm going to be able to come over and see you as much as I'd like."

"See me? Or *fuck me*, quarterback?" I cock a brow teasingly, trying to lighten the solemn mood he's just created.

"Seeing you. Being with you. Fucking you. I'm going to miss it all," he admits, running his thumb over my lip, watching my mouth intently.

My chest begins to feel heavy and constricted, so I playfully push him aside to get some well-needed space. I walk over to the table beside us and start placing the chairs upside down on it, resuming what I should have been doing in the first place—which was preparing to get the bar locked up—all the while making sure my back is turned from his melancholic expression, so he can't see how it affects me.

"You do you, Finn. You know where to find me."

My beating heart is pounding so hard, it makes the silence between us that more unbearable. Just when I'm about to go over to the next table, I feel his warm arms envelop me in an embrace from behind, his chin nestling on the crook of my neck.

"I was thinking that maybe after the game, I could pick you up and we could go out."

I feel my whole body stiffen, and so does he.

"We could do it next Thursday, on your night off, if that's the problem," he adds, misreading my reaction.

"I'm good," I coolly reply back.

He spins me around, his hands on my waist keeping me from toppling over.

"You're good?! What the fuck is that supposed to mean?"

"It means I don't do dates."

"Ever?"

"Not while class is in session, pretty boy."

"You can fit me in. You have for the past couple of weeks," he replies with a cocky smirk tugging at his lips.

"A quick fuck isn't the same thing as dinner and a movie. I have no time for it," I reply sternly, crossing my arms over my chest so that he sees I mean business.

He takes two steps away from me, his features taking a scowl of their own as he mimics my stance.

"No date, no sex." He utters the ultimatum as if it were his winning trump card against this argument.

"Please, as if you could ever follow through on that threat."

"Try me," he deadpans, resolve ingrained in each of his beautiful features.

I roll my eyes at his cockiness and shake my head.

"Not happening. Dating isn't on the table," I retort with the same stubbornness.

"Then neither is this," he replies stoically, pointing to his sculptured physique.

"Fine. Have it your way. So, this has been fun, but I've got shit to do," I say, going back to the task of cleaning this dump and turning my back to him once more.

I feel his eyes on me as I wipe down another table, but he doesn't say a word. I try to act cool as the silence prolongs, but I really wish he would just leave so I could do my job in peace without his presence looming over me.

"See you around, quarterback," I mumble, hoping he takes the hint.

The beat of my heart pounds in sync with each passing second that I have to endure his silence. Luckily for me, Finn isn't just a pretty body and face. He's got plenty of brains to go with all that heavy artillery.

"Call me when you change your mind," he hollers at the door.

"Don't hold your breath," I rebuke, not once looking up at him.

"I won't need to. You'll miss me soon enough."

"Not likely," I answer, feigning boredom and cleaning the damn table just a little bit faster, all the while wishing he would just go already.

"You will, Stone. You just don't know it yet."

I scoff at that, but when the asshole finally leaves, I throw the damn cloth to the floor.

I hate the feeling that pretty boy might know something I don't. That somehow, he is more in tune with my inner workings than I am. And that frightens me more than his absence ever will.

"Good riddance," I mumble to the empty doorway.

But as my heart sinks to the pit of my stomach, I wonder if the one to break first will, in fact, be me as he predicted.

The bastard was right.

And how I hate him for it.

It's been five days. Just five measly days without laying eyes on Finn, and wouldn't you know it, I *do* miss the cocky asshole. So much so that, when I realized this afternoon was his big game, the most idiotic thought flew by my head—to call in sick and see him play. Thankfully, sense slapped me upside the head before I did something as stupid as going to a college football game just to see the quarterback strut his stuff. There will be plenty of jersey chasers there for him. He doesn't need me to make a cameo and add to the slew of girls calling out his name, eager to lick the sweat off of him after he's led the Sharks to another win.

No way am I putting myself in that position. Maybe I'd forget the bastard entirely if he didn't send me a text every day to remind me of his existence. It's not like he hears a peep out of me.

Monday – **Pretty Boy:** *Miss me yet? I bet you do.*

Tuesday – **Pretty Boy:** *You're such a stubborn little thing, aren't you? But you'll break.*

Wednesday – **Pretty Boy:** *Still not backing down, huh? Always the brat.*

Thursday – **Pretty Boy:** *I dreamed about you today. I can still taste you on my lips.*

Friday – **Pretty Boy:** *Are you even getting my texts? Maybe it's for the best if you aren't.*

Today – **Pretty Boy:** *I miss you in my arms, Stone. I really fucking do.*

Damn it all to hell!

How is a girl supposed to hold out when she gets texts like these? I swear he must love seeing me squirm. But it will be a cold day in hell before I admit to his face that I miss him too. That I think about him non-stop when I have other things I should be focusing on. I knew he'd be a distraction, I just never assumed he'd be this all-consuming.

I hate the Northside prick. He's ruining everything.

I hear someone clear their throat behind me, reminding me that I'm at work and should have my act together.

"What's your poison?" I ask, turning toward another drunkard who has nothing else to do but come to Big Jim's on a Saturday night.

"Poison, huh? If it's all right with you, I'll stick to beer."

I place both hands on my hips, staring down Finn's black-haired—and probably black-hearted—friend.

242

"Easton Price. As I live and breathe. This is your second visit in just a few months. Let me guess. Is the Southside growing on you?"

Easton looks left and right, his bored expression rivaling my own. I've got to admit that, while Finn is beautifully transparent with his emotions and thoughts, Easton is the exact opposite. His slanted smile holds secrets while his silver eyes give none of them away. The man that sits before me is an illusion. I pity whoever falls prey in wanting to unravel his puzzle. Some things are just better off not being solved.

I get him his beer, but he makes no move to even touch the bottle. Instead, his eyes lock on mine, making sure I stay rooted to my spot.

"If you have something to say, Easton, why not do us both a favor and just say what's on your mind."

"Can't I just enjoy the view?" he asks with a knowing look, eyeing me up and down.

"Nothing here for you to look at," I reply sternly, not one bit pleased with his flirtatious act. "If that's what you came for, you're shit out of luck."

"Good to know," he says with a thin smile. "But you're right. I didn't come all this way to drink or take in the scenery. I came because Finn's my friend."

"Is he now?"

"He is. The best one I have," he adds with such conviction that I almost believe him.

"And what does that have to do with me?" I reply, looking at my nails to avoid his harsh face.

"Don't act cute, Stone. That shit might work with Finn, but not with me."

"Is that so?" I mumble, not at all bothered by his dark tone.

He lets out an aggravated sigh, this time picking up the bottle of beer and taking a swig. He keeps the bottle in his hands as he stares at the ring instead of looking back at me.

"I think you know by now that Finn isn't like you and me. He's not jaded, and he's not used to people playing him, either."

"And you think I'm playing him?"

He lets out a sinister laugh, and this time he does look me dead in the eye.

"I know you are. Now, if it were up to me, I'd keep this so-called friendship of yours low-key, but against my better counsel, Finn has taken a liking to you. He doesn't have to tell me point-blank for me to know you're fucking with his head. So I'm here to tell you to stop."

I bite my inner cheek just so I don't slam the bottle over his head.

Who the fuck does this jerk think he's talking to?

"Finn's a big boy, Easton. He can handle his own shit. He doesn't need you to come to his aid and scare me off."

He places the bottle back on the counter, standing back on his feet while taking out a twenty from his wallet to pay his tab.

"You're not stupid, Stone, so don't deem to insult my intelligence, either. Unlike us, Finn's a good guy. Don't fuck with his sanity. Just have your fun and leave him be. Both of you will be better for it in the end. Trust me."

He doesn't even give me time to flip him off, turning his back to exit Big Jim's in record time, leaving me fuming where I stand. I'm so mad at his insolence, that before I can talk myself out of it, my phone is already in my hands to type away my first text message.

Me: *Okay, pretty boy. Let's see what this dating thing is all about.*

Pretty Boy: *Say, please.*

Me: *Fuck off. I don't beg.*

Pretty Boy: *We both know that's a lie.*

Me: *Take it or leave it.*

Pretty Boy: *You already know the answer to that. When?*

Me: *Tomorrow.*

Pretty Boy: *What about the bar?*

Me: *What about the bar? Just pick me up at my dorm around seven.*

Pretty Boy: *I'll be there.*

Pretty Boy: *Stone…*

Me: *What?*

Pretty Boy: *It's a good thing you didn't beg. You know how much I like it when you plead for mercy in person.*

Me: **middle finger emoji**

Pretty Boy: *I missed you too, brat.*

CHAPTER 16

FINN

When I arrive at Stone's dorm and have to wait in the lobby for over twenty minutes, I immediately know that something is wrong. The girl at the front desk sits twirling her hair and popping her irritating pink bubble gum, while unashamedly ogling me from head to toe, apparently unable to check on Stone like I asked her to.

"Sorry, but I don't know any Stone."

"She's this high, with big, green eyes and long, jet-black hair with dark blue highlights. She also has too many tattoos and piercings to keep track of, and a rocking body to go with the mean mouth she has on her. How can you not know her?"

"Sorry!" She shrugs. "But if your girl doesn't show up, maybe we can do something?"

"Not likely," I grunt.

It's not like this type of thing doesn't happen frequently. Being Richfield's star quarterback—one who is set to break every record this school has ever had—I am bound to get some unwanted female attention. Even from those who don't enjoy the sport. However Miss Pigtails isn't who I want checking me out. Not in the slightest.

Every time I look at my phone and see the minutes pass without a word from Stone, a sunken feeling in my gut tells me she's changed her mind about our date.

I think I've fucked this up.

Maybe I should have kept our situation as it was—easy-breezy without the hassle of actually going out. It's not like The Society is adding any pressure on me, either. They seem just fine with me only hanging around Stone at her workplace. At least I think they do since they haven't sent me any of those pesky black letters of theirs in weeks.

I still have no idea why they even want Stone in the first place. I wish I knew why she's so goddamn important to them. Maybe taking this next step in our complicated relationship will help me gain some perspective into why they've set their sights on her, to begin with. At least that's what I keep telling myself. But I know its bullshit because I was the one who was no longer happy with how things were going between us, not The Society.

Watching Stone from a barstool all night was no longer cutting it for me. I wanted more, so I manned up and asked as much from her. Sure, she let me fester in uncertainty for a whole brutal week before she gave in, but that's just the type of girl Stone is. She'll make it hurt first before she makes it better. And like a sucker, I've begun to crave both—her pain and her sweetness. But I've gone without either for a week now, so I've hit the limit on how patient I can be.

Tonight was supposed to be a beginning for us. Of what, I'm not sure, but it was still going to happen. I need it to happen. So where the fuck is she?

I begin to pace the ugly, brown carpet in anxiety. I'm two seconds away from running up these stairs, bypassing miss pigtails altogether just so I can knock on Stone's dorm room and find out what her deal is. She agreed to go out, and she isn't exactly the type of girl who says yes to anything unless she really means it. I know that for a fact since all her sweet yeses usually include me being a brutish beast with her.

My doubts start to ease when I finally hear feet rushing down the stairs. When my eyes land on the girl I've been waiting for an eternity, my heart cracks a little bit.

Fuck, I've missed her.

She looks beautiful tonight. So fucking beautiful that I get a little tongue-tied.

Her long, raven hair is curled in loose waves running down her back, so her face is perfectly in view. A dark blue dress that hits her just mid-thigh is painted on her body, revealing only a bit of her stunning ink, yet showcasing all of her curves. The black army boots with skulls on is the final badass touch to the ensemble. Being a girly-girl is just not her style. But damn, if she doesn't look like a dark angel, regardless if fallen from heaven or risen from the pits of hell. Either way, I'm still the luckiest asshole there is for being her date tonight.

Shit, I think I'm a little pussy-whipped.

Fuck it.

I don't even care. Not when I haven't seen Stone in so long that the very sight of her has me feeling all warm and shit.

"Sorry I'm late, pretty boy. I had some stuff to sort out," she exclaims, and the worried scowl on her face is enough to take me out of my lust-filled reverie, allowing me to realize that my girl is a mess.

Hold up! Did I really just refer to Stone as my girl?

Snap out of it, you pussy! You're going to scare her off before you've even set foot out of her dorm!

"What's wrong?" I ask, instead of revealing the chaotic thoughts rummaging around in my head.

"Nothing. It's sorted. Or at least it will be, once we're done with this date."

"Oh no, you don't! Like hell, do I want you spending our night with whatever shit you've got going on hanging over us. I know exactly how this is going to play out. You'll act like you're present when, in reality, you're miles away. Then you'll do everything in your power to end the night faster and send me packing, just so you can deal with whatever clusterfuck has got you pissed off. Not going to happen, Stone. Whatever it is, out with it. We can deal with it now and go on about our date after."

"Kind of bossy tonight, huh, quarterback? Just because I'm going to let you pay for dinner, do you think I'm going to let you in on my personal affairs and order me around?" she says teasingly, with no heat whatsoever behind her reprimand.

I eat up the small space between us and lift her chin so she can tell that I'm not playing her little games. Not tonight.

"I haven't seen you in almost a week, Stone. Now, that shit might not affect you as much as it affects me, but no way in hell am I starting our first date together on a sour note."

"Okay," she susurrates, her long lashes batting a mile a minute.

My hand goes to cradle the back of her neck, and for a minute, I get lost in her green meadows.

"Tell me what's wrong. Let's see if two heads work better than one, and sort out whatever problem you've got going. We're friends, right? And friends look out for each other," I explain hoarsely, feeling my eyes smolder as her cheeks begin to flush.

"Friends, huh? Is that what we are?" She mauls at her lower lip, her eyes becoming just as hooded as my own.

"Yes, friends." I nod, licking my own lips, my gaze lingering on her plump mouth.

"You mean friends who fuck?"

"Whatever label you want to put on it. I don't give a shit," I answer, tugging at her waist so that she's rubbing right up against me.

The little sigh that leaves her lips is all I'm able to handle. My hand puts some small pressure on the back of her neck just so she can crane a little bit further as I lean down to kiss her. My cock jumps to attention the minute my tongue breaches through and wrestles with its counterpart. Her soft body melts seamlessly into mine, and it takes every ounce of restraint to pull away from her. We aren't alone, so I can't just take her here in the middle of her dorm's foyer.

"Is this how tonight is going to go? You're just going to take what you want, when you want it?" she asks, her tone thick and heavy with the same desire I feel burning through me.

"Don't tempt me, little girl. I've made plans for us tonight. But if you keep looking at me like that, I'll just put you over my shoulder and go back to your room to fuck some submission into you."

"You can try." She laughs softly.

Always my little brat.

"Tell me what's wrong, Stone?" I ask, instead of falling for her well-laced trap. She can seduce me later when we're alone.

Stone looks over my shoulder to where little Miss Pigtails and Bubble Gum is and throws her a dirty look, obviously not being a fan of hers.

Didn't know Stone my ass.

"Not here," she hushes low, and my spine instantaneously reacts to those words, going ramrod straight, directly into protector mode.

Without a minute to lose, I take her hand in mine and walk us out of the building, ushering her into the passenger seat of my Porsche. I open the door for her, even though I know she hates that type of chivalry. Yet I can't help but want to do it. She either humors me and doesn't call me out on it, or is too into her own head to even notice. I run to the other side of the car, slamming the door, impatiently wanting to get down to the reason that has her all bent out of shape. But just as I'm waiting for her to come clean, my stomach begins to twist in knots.

Fuck! Is this about The Society? Is that it? It must be. What else could have Stone all red in the face and upset like this?

"I'm not hearing any words coming out of that gorgeous mouth of yours, Stone. Start talking before I put you over my knee and make you."

"Such a charmer," she rebukes, feigning annoyance.

I know the idea of her sitting on my lap to get spanked already has her squirming in her seat. But that will have to wait for later. I'm all too interested in whatever shitstorm is going on now.

"Stone!"

"Alright already. Geez! You are one impatient asshole when you want to be."

"Don't act offended or surprised. You know that about me already."

"Yeah, I do," the enticing Southie replies huskily.

"Don't sweet-talk your way out of this one, either. Just tell me what's going on," I plead in earnest, clasping her hands in mine.

After a long, pregnant pause, her shoulders deflate, and she bows her head, not wanting to look at me while she confesses her worries.

"It's my mom," she mumbles under her breath.

"Your mom?" I ask, surprised.

I was expecting the words stumbling out of her mouth to be about The Society, not her mother.

"Stone? What about your mom?"

She releases a long-winded sigh, her head falling to the headrest.

"She let that ass of an ex-boyfriend in her trailer again last night. Probably for one last hurrah, a hate fuck, or whatever. I don't know, and I don't care. Thing is, when she woke up this morning, she saw he had gone through her stuff and took the little money she had stashed away," she explains, aggravated. "And since I'm not working tonight, I can't get any tips to run over to her place and give them to her. I'm on my last twenty as it is, after leaving her most of what I earned last week," she adds subdued.

"You give your mom your paycheck? Why? Can't she work?"

"It's not that simple." She shakes her head. "It's hard getting work in this town when you have a disability. And welfare only goes so far. The measly food stamps she gets don't exactly cover everything."

"Where does she live?" I ask, pulling the seatbelt over her, locking it securely in place.

"Why?" she questions suspiciously, scrunching her eyebrows together.

"Because we're going to her house now. We'll get this sorted, and then we can start our night."

She slaps her palms on her bare knees and throws me a dirty look.

"I just told you, Finn. I don't have any extra cash to give her."

"You don't, but lucky for you, I do," I quip back, turning the ignition on.

"I don't need your charity," she snaps.

I switch off the engine and unlatch my seat belt to get in her face.

"Look at me, Stone. Really look at me," I order, grasping her chin in my grip. "Do I look like the type of guy who is charitable in any way? Fuck no. I'm a selfish asshole, and I own it. This has nothing to do with trying to help your mom out. This has to do with making sure her daughter is in the right headspace and, in a couple of hours, is jumping on my cock as if it were a trampoline. That's it. That's all this is," I lie, schooling my features to hide my bullshitting.

She sucks in her teeth, staring me down, and when I don't budge, the playful tint in her eyes return.

"Are you so hard that you're willing not only to meet my mom on our first date but also to help her with her electric bill?"

I grab her hand and place it on my bulging cock, to which the fucker instantly bobs at her mere touch.

"Hard enough for you, little girl?"

She slants her eyes at me, but the playful grin stitched to her lips is all the confirmation I need that she fell for it hook, line, and sinker. It doesn't matter if she believes me to be that egotistical and self-centered. As long as Stone is good, that's all I care about. Sooner or later, I'll probably be the one to hurt her anyway. The Society will make sure of it. So if I can care for her now, and for as long as she'll let me, then how I go about it doesn't matter. What she believes my motives to be behind my altruistic actions shouldn't matter either.

Nothing matters.

All that does is keeping that glorious smile of hers on her face for as long as I can.

Or for as long as The Society will allow it, anyway.

CHAPTER 17

STONE

Damn it all to hell. She's wasted.

I should have known. Shit!

I really wish Finn would've just left things alone. Why did he insist on coming here? And why the hell did I give in so easily? I wasn't lying about not needing his charity. I would have come up with another way to get her some money. It's just, I really needed to see her. The way she was so erratic over the phone, taking forever to calm down, really hit a nerve. That's my mother for you, though. Up one minute and down the next.

I've read plenty of articles describing how people who have her condition can lead perfectly normal lives once they have the right medication. The only thing they leave out is the hefty price tag that goes along with playing the game of 'let's see what meds work for you, Ms. Bennett.' When you've grown up dirt poor, even cold medicine is a luxury. So adding my mom's bipolar meds into the equation, we couldn't exactly jump from one test drug to the next if we wanted to make sure we had a roof over our heads and food in our bellies.

"Baby girl! You came!" she slurs with a happy tone.

I look around at the empty whiskey bottles and cans of beer and see she at least bought enough booze before that dipshit ex of hers stole all her money.

"I just wanted to check up on you."

"Always the dutiful daughter. How did I ever get lucky enough to raise such a good girl?" she continues with a wide smile, hiccupping at the end of her rant.

Her steps are clumsy and her pupils dilated, so when she begins to sway from left to right like walking on a boat, I know she's more than shitfaced. She's high as a kite, too. I should have figured—booze and meds don't mix. Before she stumbles to the floor, I run to her side and help her keep her balance.

"Had too much to drink, Momma?"

"Just a little, baby. Just enough to calm my nerves." She grins.

My mother is one of the most beautiful women I have ever seen when she's smiling. And when she's having a good day, she's always smiling. When Dad was around, he took care of her and made sure she always had a reason to show her pearly whites. He knew exactly what to do to keep her happy, to keep her stable. And when her moods would shift, he kept her sane enough just for me.

That all changed when he got locked up, though. That's when Mom fell off the deep end and never recovered entirely. She never smiles quite like she did when Dad was around. But for the past twelve years, I've been the one looking after her, doing my very best to make sure she still has a reason to smile every day.

"Who is this tall glass of water?" Mom asks inquisitively, looking over my shoulder.

"Um…" I begin to stutter when I realize that Finn is at the door and not in the car where I ordered him to stay.

"My name is Finn, Ma'am. Finn Walker. I'm Stone's friend," he replies, taking a further step inside the trailer.

"Friend, huh? You look more like a heartbreaker to me. You're not going to break my baby girl's heart, are you, Finn?" she coos, looking deep into his eyes, half-joking, half-serious.

Finn rakes the back of his neck with his hand, obviously embarrassed with her comment.

"Momma—"

"Hush, baby. He's got a mouth on him. He can talk for himself." She lets out a little giggle.

"No, Ma'am. I'm not going to hurt Stone," Finn replies shyly, looking to the floor rather than meeting her gaze.

My own frown surfaces, not liking how he's unable to meet my mother's drunkard glare, but I don't say anything to call him out on it.

"You say that now," she warns warmly, playfully shaking her finger at him, making Finn's brows furrow even tighter together. "But eventually, you will. They all do."

"Momma, stop," I plead softly.

My mother turns my way and grabs my face gently in between her palms. Even in her worst fits, she was never capable of striking me down or hurting me. When it got really bad for her, she fought hard to keep lucid enough to recognize me. And in her internal battle, even on the days she had no idea who I was, she was always sweet, always kind. Maybe that's why Dad and I had to be so hard all the time. Because she couldn't be, and we knew there are plenty of people out there who would love nothing more than to exploit such a tender soul.

"Momma, please." I try again, hoping she will take the hint and not say anything in front of Finn that I can't take back later.

She just shakes her head, almost losing her balance, but not enough to dissuade her from saying what is obviously lodged in her throat and needs to come out.

"My baby girl looks tough, but she isn't, you know? Under all this bravado, she's fragile and soft, so soft. Just like her daddy. She's the most precious thing I have, and I don't know what I'd do without her," she susurrates, teary-eyed.

"Momma, you're talking gibberish now. Come on, let me get you cleaned up and take you to bed. You need to sleep it off."

"But what about Rhett? Are you going to talk to him? Please don't. I don't want you near him," my mother pleas in concern, the last bit of sobriety announcing itself, worried about me trying to go after her ex.

Yeah, like I'm going to go on the lookout to talk to that piece of trash. He's probably spent my hard-earned money already, shoving whatever he could buy up his vein. That cash is long gone by now, and I'm not going to waste my time trying to get it back. There's no point.

"He might get angry if you do. Just let it go, baby. I'll make do somehow," she continues, her long lashes stuck to the tears she's shedding out of pure worry for my welfare. God, how I wish she could take care of herself.

"Come on, Momma. I don't want you to worry about that, okay? I'm going to leave some money in our secret stashing place. But if that asshole comes back, don't let him in. You hear me?"

"I'm sorry, baby. I know I shouldn't have opened the door for him. It's just, I get so lonely sometimes."

"I know, Momma. I know." I hug her to my side and make my way to the back of the trailer where her bedroom is. I tilt my head over to Finn before I close the partition.

"You can either take a seat or wait outside. I'll only be a minute."

"Sure," he mumbles.

I watch his eyes take in our tiny couch, knowing there's no way he'll be comfortable there. I expect him to rush outside, but instead, he looks at the kitchen and stays put.

I don't have time to placate his need for comfort since I want to make sure Mom is in the safety of her bed. I don't want to worry that she may end up outside while being this messed up. Not that she would go out willingly on her own, but I'll rest easier knowing she's safe, sleeping it off.

She doesn't complain when I remove her shirt and use a wet towel to wipe the day's sweat off her skin. Once she's clean enough, I pull a camisole over her head and help her into the bed.

"He's very handsome," she says all of a sudden, her eyes twinkling with mischief.

"Hmm," I mumble, straightening up her bedsheet.

"Do you like him?"

"I like him enough."

"I think you like him more than enough," she singsongs.

"Hmm."

"Just be careful, baby. First loves have a way of hurting more than the others," she adds with a cautious tone to her slurred words. Her eyes look up at the heavens, and whatever is on her mind steals the little smile on her face, turning it into a saddened frown. "I miss your father," she laments softly, finally revealing what ails her.

"I know, Momma."

"I was thinking that maybe next weekend we can go visit him," she adds expectantly, and I hate to be the one to damper the small flicker of hope in her eyes.

"I don't think that's a good idea," I mumble under my breath, knowing Dad still hasn't added her name back on his visitor's list.

Last time I went to the big house to see him, Dad was still adamant that Mom shouldn't be in an environment that could only trigger her. Although they haven't been together in over a decade, he loves her just as fiercely, and wouldn't want to do anything that could harm her stability.

Like we had any after he was locked away.

"Yes, of course. You're right," she replies disappointedly, turning to her side, away from me.

"Sleep now, okay? Tomorrow, I'll come over and have an early dinner with you before going to work. I'll even bring you some fried chicken from Mable's Diner, the one you like so much. Does that sound good?"

She gives me a sheepish nod, but I know fried food isn't going to make things better for her. I don't think anything will, really. Her mental state, combined with a broken heart, just leaves too many scars for her frail mind to overcome.

Life hasn't been fair to her, but hopefully, the tides will change in our favor. I've been working my butt off at school to make it so. I'm going to do everything in my power to change our lives. To get us out of this shithole of a town and give her the proper care she needs. Dad had tried his best, but I'll make sure to succeed where he failed.

I wait for a few minutes until I hear her breathing simmer down into a soft pace. Once I'm sure she's out cold, I step outside her room, ready to get pretty boy out of here. God knows he must be counting the minutes for us to leave. However, I can't help the smile that crests my lips when I see him washing my mother's dirty dishes, looking right at home amongst all the mess.

"I never imagined you were so well house-trained," I tease, behind him.

"I umm... I mean... is this okay? I just couldn't keep still," he stutters in embarrassment, placing another plate on the rack.

"I see that. Knock yourself out, quarterback."

He throws me a meek grin and continues on with his task.

"How is she?"

"Okay. Okay for her, at least. Luckily it's not one of her worst days."

"What's wrong with her?"

"What isn't wrong with her?" I sigh out. "She's sick. Body, mind, and soul. But if you want to get technical, she suffers from bipolar disorder according to the doctor's diagnosis."

The confused look that shadows his features, trying to make sense of my explanation, is priceless. His forehead is wrinkled, and his clear blue eyes are focused on the soap suds while furiously scrubbing the plate in his hand. He seems lost in his head, trying to solve what looks to be the world's hardest algebra problem.

"And this was a good day, you say?" Finn questions, confused, trying to get more data to help him process what he just encountered—the mess that is my life.

"Surprisingly so. After her frantic call earlier today, I was sure to find her worse off. But I guess the bourbon helped." I sigh, picking up an empty bottle and throwing it in the trash.

"Should she be drinking at all? I mean, won't that mess with her meds?"

"Now you're talking like a true Northsider. What meds, pretty boy? You think she can afford the good stuff?" I retort back harshly.

"It was just a question, Stone," he answers softly, making me feel like shit for snapping at him.

"I know it was," I huff out, feeling exhausted all of a sudden. "Are you almost finished? I need to get out of here and breathe some fresh air."

"Are you still in the mood for dinner?"

"Yeah, I am. But I don't think I can handle whatever fancy place you picked out. Mind if we go somewhere else?"

"I'm all good with whatever you want, Stone," he replies with a little sparkle in his sapphire eyes as he dries his hands with a dishcloth.

I try not to read too much into it, and instead walk over to the cereal cabinet and take out the box of Raisin Bran. No one eats this vile stuff, so if my mom's ex, Rhett, decides to pay her a little visit again, this will be the last place he'll look for cash. I take out the last twenty-dollar bill from my purse and stuff it inside, so she at least has money for bread and milk tomorrow morning. From the corner of my eye, I see Finn going to his back pocket, taking out his wallet and grabbing a few bills, too.

"Stop," I order, putting my hand on his chest to halt what he's about to do. "I told you, I don't want your money."

He grabs my hand, keeping it locked and pressed against his beating heart, making me shift from one foot to the next, uncomfortable with his penetrating gaze on me.

"I know you don't, but I'm not giving it to you. I'm leaving it for your momma," he explains softly.

"Whatever," I mumble, squinting my eyes at him, and take back my hand trapped on his grasp.

When I see him drop a few Benjamins into the box, my lips thin. I know my mother will go nuts when she sees all that cash but still doesn't feel right. There are always strings involved whenever accepting such a generous gift. No one does anything out of the kindness of their own heart. That's just not the world I live in. Everything comes at a price—even kindness.

"You ready to blow this joint or what, quarterback?" I ask anxiously, needing to get Finn out of my childhood home as fast as I can.

"Lead the way. I'll follow wherever you go."

"Sure you will," I retort, unamused at his knight-in-shining-armor routine.

Finn doesn't look even one bit perturbed that I'm not falling for his one-liners. In fact, he looks almost happy. He really is a weirdo.

"Keys," I demand the instant we get outside.

"And who says I'm going to let you drive my car?"

"I do. Keys. Now."

"And I'm the one who's bossy? Woman, you invented the word." He laughs.

"And don't you forget it." I smirk at him as he tosses me the keys to his beloved Porsche.

Sinking into the seat, I instantly love being behind the wheel of such an extraordinary piece of equipment. I can't help the smile that splits my face when the powerful engine purrs to life. This is going to be fun.

Finn takes ages to set the passenger seat, trying to get enough room for his bulky legs. I'm sure he's just stalling, worried that I'll wreck his baby the minute we get on the road. I've never seen a man have such a hard-on for a car. I'm not sure if it's a guy thing or a Finn thing, but honestly, I don't care. Who knows when I'll have the opportunity again to drive such a fast machine? I'm going to milk it for all it's worth, that's for damn sure.

"You ready?" I raise my brow.

"As I'll ever be," he replies, not convinced in the slightest.

"Then strap in and hold on tight!"

Without warning, I pull in reverse and turn the car so fast it gives Finn whiplash.

"Jesus, Mary, and Joseph! Woman, don't kill us!"

"Don't you worry that pretty head of yours. I got this," I laugh out loud, pushing the car as fast as it can go.

After a few minutes, I half-expected Finn to go crazy on me and tell me to slow down, but to my surprise, he doesn't.

Instead, he looks chilled and relaxed in his seat, as if this weren't the first time I was driving his car. And when he puts on some music, and my jam begins to play, his smile turns ten feet wide the minute I start singing along. I roll the windows down to let the wind blow on my face and just enjoy the moment. After seeing my momma in that state, this is exactly what I needed—freedom to fly and spread my wings without the constant worry of my obligations chaining me down.

I've lived all of my young life responsibly, so doing stupid shit sometimes reminds me that I'm still young with the best years still ahead of me. It's oddly liberating, being reckless every now and again. We only live once, so we should grab life by the balls whenever the opportunity presents itself. Life should be a string of moments lived to the fullest, not full of regrets.

And for the next twenty minutes, I do just that—enjoy my youthful recklessness with the wind in my hair, good music on the radio, and Finn's light chuckle ringing in my ears. If I didn't know any better, I'd think this might be as close to content as I've ever been.

I take a peek at the man at my side and see a damn smile still widely planted on his face, mimicking my own and making me melt further into my seat.

Once we get to our destination, I make a ruckus with my sharp-break parking, announcing our arrival to everyone at the food truck. Now I know why Finn loves this car so much. This silver number is all sexy curves with a powerful engine begging to be driven to its limit. She sure does drive like a dream. I almost feel like I'm cheating on my poor beat-up truck. Sure, it's not much to look at and takes forever to get from A to B, but at least it's reliable. And if I had to choose between Fast and Furious or Driving Ms. Daisy, I'd take the latter.

Going fast in life leads to trouble, and I've got too much of it, to begin with. My father taught me that, at least. To be cautious. He was the perfect example of how, with one false step, everything you love can be ripped away from you. So, as much as I adored the adrenaline rush when driving Finn's ride, I don't want to get used to the feeling. I don't want to get addicted.

Am I still talking about the car or its owner?

"Is this where you want to eat?" Finn asks, calling me away from my pensive thoughts with his question.

"This is the place," I reply, trying hard to school my features. "Do you have a problem with that, pretty boy?" I ask with my usual sass, my hands on my hips and brow raised high.

Instead of Finn using his words, he just bridges the gap between us, leans in, and grabs me by the neck to deliver such an intense, passionate kiss that I'm sure I leave a puddle on the floor.

"No problem at all." He grins once he's had his way with me, his heavy eyes staring into my own. "Just needed to do that first."

"Satisfied now?" I smirk back at him, a little too breathless to play off that he didn't just kiss me stupid.

"Not by a long shot, but it'll do for now."

"Come on, quarterback. I bet you're starving."

"You have no idea," he replies flirtatiously, biting his knuckles as he scrolls his eyes over my body.

"Will you stop?!" I slap his chest, laughing at his lame-ass innuendos.

"Then don't make it easy for me!"

"Just move those feet," I order, and with another chuckle he begins to walk beside me toward the food truck, but not before grabbing my hand in his.

"You know, you might be a little too dressed up for truck food."

"And who says that?" I taunt.

"Sorry, you're right. My bad." He laughs.

I order three chili burgers, some fries, and two sodas while Finn passes another crisp bill to the vendor to pay for the food.

I eye him up and down and see he really did clean up nice to take me to whatever place he had in mind. A small sense of guilt rises within me, making me think that perhaps I ruined his plans with my drama. It's an emotion I'm unfamiliar with, and if I'm honest with myself, spending time with Finn brings out other feelings that I'm trying hard to push down and ignore.

"Hey, you okay?" he asks once I've gone silent.

I give him a tight nod and a fake smile while walking us over to one of the free tables. He sits in front of me, always observant with that watchful eye of his, making me inadvertently bow my head.

"Stone, you sure you're okay?" he asks suspiciously when five minutes pass without barely touching my food.

I bite the side of my lip while playing with my fries, not one bit thrilled to feel this way.

"I was just thinking, maybe this isn't exactly your style? I mean, have you ever eaten at a food truck before?"

"Are you kidding? Of course, I have. You think you're the only one who likes greasy food?" he laughs out, taking a huge bite of his burger.

"Are you sure you wouldn't prefer to eat lobster or caviar, or whatever you Northside, rich folk eat?"

He takes another big bite of his chili burger, closing his eyes while letting out an exaggerated moan, looking like he just took a bite of heaven itself. He then shakes his head and replies, "I'm good, Stone. Food is food. It's the company that matters."

I can't help but chuckle at that little comment.

"You're such a dork," I exclaim with a little laugh, feeling more relaxed.

"Whatever. Just eat your burger."

I laugh again but do as he says. The peaceful silence that arises while we eat our dinner is oddly comforting. I can't help sneaking in a peek at him every once in a while, chuckling as he shoves his food in his face, perfectly content with the setting.

After we're finished, Finn goes back to the truck and orders a couple of sundaes. He wolfs his down before I've even taken two bites of mine. But I guess Finn must need some serious calorie intake every day to keep his body as fit as it is. When I'm done with my dessert, he takes my hand and walks me back to the car.

"You tired?"

"No, not really. Why?"

"I want to take you back to my spot. You game for that?" he asks nervously, his blue eyes as clear and bright as a summer's day.

I just give him a little nod and follow him to the car, this time letting him take the wheel. He puts on some music, and again I feel that peaceful silence between us.

"I'm not used to you being so quiet," he states, the back of his knuckles slightly grazing my cheek.

I hold his hand and open his palm to land a small chaste kiss to it. It's the only answer I have for him. Anything else will be messy. Explaining how he turned a bad night into something serene and normal is not something I want to discuss.

He leans in closer, gently pressing his temple against mine, making his woodsy scent kick-start the beat of my heart. His eyes are shut as he takes a minute just to breathe me in. I lick my lips, letting my eyes close of their own accord, to try steady my foolish heart.

"Just take me to see the stars, Finn. I've missed them."

"Not as much as they've missed you. Not nearly enough."

CHAPTER 18

FINN

When we get to the secluded gazebo, I scratch at my throat, hoping the lump in it will miraculously disappear. Deep down, I know the fucker will only go away once Stone opens that beautiful mouth of hers and tells me she likes what I've done with the place. It took me all afternoon to make my small corner of the world look presentable for our date. With colorful cushions spread out on the lawn, and comfy blankets, I tried as best I could to make it comfortable and cozy. The first time we were here, I only had two sweaty gym towels for us to lie down on. This time around, I made sure to go all out and make this place look and feel somewhat romantic. Even got scented candles and shit.

"You've been busy," she marvels, taking in the scenery.

"I wanted tonight to be perfect," I confess, hugging her from behind, placing my chin on the top of her head. "So, did I do good, brat?"

She turns around in my embrace, her emerald eyes shining with an unnamed emotion behind them.

"You did good, pretty boy," she whispers huskily, batting her dark eyelashes at me, making my chest tighten and my cock harden.

I'm about to go all in and kiss her senseless when she lightly pushes me away to stroll around the small lawn and investigate further what else I've done with the place. Without her watching, I discreetly maneuver my stiff cock to make him behave. We have all night for him to call the shots, so he can be patient. At this moment, all I want is to enjoy Stone in any way she'll let me.

My eyes never leave her as she walks slowly over the decorated lawn. When I hear a little laugh fall from her lips, I know she's found the cooler. She picks up the bottles of Jose and Jack, looking amusedly at them, lifting them up to her head and swinging them in my direction.

"Couldn't do all this and not have your plan A in mind, now could I?" I joke, taking a seat and leaning open-armed against one of the larger cushions. "Had to make sure you'd have a good time one way or another."

She places the bottle of whiskey back in its original place and begins to stroll over to me with her beloved tequila in hand.

"There's some limes and salt there, too," I add before she takes a further step.

"You *have* thought about everything, haven't you? I have to say, I'm impressed, quarterback," she teases, going back to get the small Tupperware of sliced lime wedges and salt shaker. "If memory serves me right, you said you were bad at this dating thing," she adds, walking back over to me, her hips swaying left and right.

Instead of the banter she's looking for, I just shrug in reply. I mean, what can I possibly tell her? That she's the only woman who has ever made me want to do this type of thing? That I wracked my brain for hours on end last night, thinking of ways to bring a smile to her face? Nah! No way can I tell her that. Stone spooks easily, and after almost a week of not being around her, I'm not going to shoot myself in the foot by telling her the truth—that I'd do just about anything for the tattooed, fearless Southie.

Unsuspecting of the insanity rummaging through my brain, Stone toes off her boots, hikes her dress up to her hips, and sits cross-legged beside me, cracking the seal on the bottle, creating a nostalgic sense of déjà vu around us.

"Are we going to play another one of your games? If it ends the same way it did last time, I'm all for it," I taunt with a wicked smirk.

"Funny." She wiggles her brows. "Actually, I was thinking tonight we tell each other our secrets without having to take our clothes off."

"If I'm going to spill any of those, I'll need a good incentive."

"Oh, yeah? And what type of incentive are we talking about?"

"Get your sweet ass on my lap, and I'll show you."

She rolls her eyes at me but follows my command, straddling me like I've envisioned in my dreams every night now for almost a month.

"Much better," I groan, placing my hands on her hips, pressing her down on my hard length.

"You're such a horny asshole," she teases with a whimsical giggle.

"No, I'm not. I just needed to be close to you. If I'm about to tell you all my deepest, darkest secrets, then I want to get lost in your eyes while doing it," I confess, blurting out my first hidden truth.

"I like your eyes, too," she cajoles, her fingers playing with my hair as she looks deep into my crystal blue eyes.

"I more than like yours, Stone."

I fucking live for seeing my reflection in them as if it were meant to always be there.

A faint, red flush colors Stone's cheeks, and when things start getting intense, she picks up the bottle of tequila and swings it in between us.

"You ready for it, pretty boy?"

"Hit me."

Stone picks up a lime wedge, sticking it between her teeth while sprinkling her knuckle with a line of salt. She lets me lick the line off before pressing the ring of the bottle to my lips, spilling a bit of the sour liquid over my tongue. When she pulls the bottle away, she leans forward to push the lime wedge inside my mouth for me to suck on. I grasp the back of her head and kiss her, thinking that, as long as I keep her lips gently pressed against my own, the bitter taste of the citrus feels like heaven.

"Do you like this game so far?" she taunts, feeling my shaft bulging up against her.

"What do you think?"

She looks down at my crotch, the pull of her upper lip teasing me, and replies, "I think you like playing with me just fine."

"I think you're right," I taunt back, lifting my hips so her swollen clit can feel just how much I enjoy her little games.

I go to grab the tequila bottle from her, ready to make her suffer in the same way, when she hides the bottle behind her back.

"Not yet. I haven't heard a secret yet," she explains mischievously.

"So it's like that, huh? Fine. What do you want to know?"

"Tell me something no one knows about you. Not even your closest friends. And geeking out over astronomy doesn't count. I already know that one."

I grunt as I slap her behind, eliciting a little, excited 'humph' to fall from her lips.

"Always the brat."

"Come on now, quarterback. Don't get shy on me."

Secrets.

She wants my secrets.

Shit. Which one do I pick? There are so many of those fuckers, sometimes even I lose track.

"Tick-tock," she goads, shifting up and down my crotch, increasing my misery.

"Okay. Here it goes. Last summer, I lied to everyone. My family. My friends. Everyone," I admit, to which she pauses her dry humping, sensing the seriousness of my tone.

I let out a long exaggerated breath, and lean my head forward against the small swell of her breasts.

"What did you lie about, Finn?" she asks, combing my hair lovingly, her voice calm and tranquil, not one bit judgmental.

"They all think I spent the summer with scouts from the Miami Dolphins, training with the team and whatnot, preparing me to go Pro next year. But it's bullshit. Instead, I went to Florida Tech and did their summer Astronomy program. It's one of the best schools for it on the East Coast, and since it's just a few miles away from NASA and the Kennedy Space Center in Cape Canaveral, I jumped at the chance to go. No one knows. They don't even suspect it. I've never told a single soul about it. Not even East."

"Oh, baby," she whispers under her breath, saddened for me, kissing the top of my head repeatedly, the endearment wrapping itself around my heart, making the fucker bleed out for her.

I lean my head back, keeping it still so that we are just a breath apart from each other.

"Your turn. Be real with me, Stone. Tell me your secret."

Her eyes become hooded, staring down at my lips.

"I'm leaving Asheville at the end of the year."

"What?!" I blurt out in a panic, pulling back a little bit to face her as she breaks my heart.

But Stone just continues to play with the ends of my hair, locking her legs tightly around me, as if she didn't just punch me in the gut.

"It's not a done deal yet, but it looks promising. I applied to Columbia to get my law degree, and they are willing to give me a scholarship as long as I keep my grades exactly as they are. Now, their scholarship won't cover all my expenses, but I already have a plan. I'm currently in the running to become a legal aid at Watkins & Ellis, one of the most prestigious law firms in Manhattan. At the moment I'm tied with three other candidates, but the feedback that I've gotten from them is encouraging. So, if I get the job, I'll be able to accept the scholarship at Columbia, too."

"I thought you were going to stay in Richfield for your law degree," I stutter, feeling like someone is carving my insides out.

"I mean, I can. Richfield offered me a full ride, so it would make sense for me to stay, especially because of Momma. I know that leaving for New York will be tricky, and I'll have to work extra hard so that she is properly taken care of. But, Finn… it's New York City! I'm not like you. I've never left Asheville in all my twenty-one years of life. This is my chance. Not only to leave Southside but also to be in a better position to help my momma in the future. You understand that, don't you?"

Her eyes search mine, and I try my best to hide how her good news has just shattered me—utterly and completely.

"Of course, I understand. I only wish I could be there when you make New York City your bitch," I joke half-heartedly, gaining a shy smile out of her.

"You want to tell me another secret?" she asks inquisitively, completely oblivious of my inner turmoil.

"I sometimes wish I could just disappear," I tell her, the honesty spilling from my lips without hesitation.

"Why do you feel like that?" She furrows her brows in concern.

"Because if I could, then maybe I could finally be happy," I confess.

"And you're not now?"

"No."

"Why not?" she asks, her lips thinning into a frown.

"Everyone expects me to be something I'm not."

"And what's that?" she whispers in my ear, bringing me closer to her, wrapping her arms around me as my eardrum pulses with her beating heart.

"The obedient son. The loyal friend. The all-star football player."

"And you don't want to be those things?"

"I just want to be me," I hush out, my body beginning to tremble in her arms.

"And who are you, Finn?" she continues to coax.

280

I lean back, grabbing her chin with my hands and telling her the one secret that is as true as the day is long.

"A guy who likes losing himself watching the stars above him, nearly as much as he likes getting lost just looking into your eyes."

"So, I'm not one of the people you want to escape from?"

"No, Stone. You're not. Does that scare you?" I ask cautiously, but thankfully my fears are assuaged when she shakes her head, tenderly moving her nose left to right on mine. "Do you ever want to start over?" I ask her, diving deep into this vulnerable moment we're sharing.

"Honestly? No. I know my life isn't all flowers and rainbows, but it got me this far. Maybe if I were someone else, I'd forget that."

"And you don't want to forget? Not like I do?"

"No, I don't," she replies saddened for me.

"I envy you."

"Me?"

"Yes. You know exactly who you want to be, and you're willing to fight to be that person."

"I think you know exactly who you are too, Finn. You just have to find the courage to be who you want, rather than being someone who everyone expects you to be."

"It's not that simple," I lament.

"It is, Finn, if you want it bad enough. Don't let others dictate your life for you. You are the master of your own destiny."

"I don't feel that way. I feel like everyone is always pulling on my strings, making me dance to their tune."

"Then change the station," she lightly jokes, kissing the tip of my nose.

"Ah, Stone, you make it sound so easy."

"Life is never easy, Finn. But you shouldn't let others complicate it for you, either."

"Hmm."

"Do I complicate your life?" she asks meekly after a long pause.

"Yes."

My life might have been chaotic before Stone was forced into it, but now that I know she's going to vanish from it completely, I feel more lost than I ever did.

"Do you want to disappear because of me?"

"No. You're the only thing that I want to hold onto," I answer her sincerely, her face scrunching. "Does *that* scare you?"

"Yes."

"Me too."

She leans in and presses a light kiss on my lips, and just as I succumb to her emerald gaze, I get lost in her tender kiss, too. When she breaks away—far too soon for my liking—I hold her face in my palms.

"If I could disappear, I'd take you with me," I utter with conviction.

"But I'm not going anywhere yet, Finn."

"Then, I won't either."

"Even though you want to?"

"Even though I want to," I admit.

She kisses me again, and this time she deepens it. I let the kiss consume me as it always does. The little sighs she makes begin to boil my blood, and the need to have her becomes the only thing I can focus on.

"Stone," I mumble between erratic kisses.

"Yes?"

"I need you," I beg.

She doesn't say a word and begins to grind over my stiff cock, knowing exactly how big my need for her truly is. Her tongue plays with mine, my hands gripping on her exposed thighs, pushing her dress up until I feel her bare waist in my hands.

"What do you want, Finn?" she asks as she straddles me, rocking on my lap, dry humping me into a frenzy.

"You. I only want you."

"Then take me," she orders, making my mind go blank while my body goes into overdrive as she bites my chin, licking her way down.

With one hand on the nape of her neck, I bring her lips back to mine while my other hand slips under the strap of her thong and follows the material down between her cheeks to stroke her slick folds. Her own hands become erratic as they pull my zipper down, releasing my angry cock. His anger for being deprived of her for so long simmers when he feels her delicate hand wrap around him. I rip the ends of her panties, knowing that one day I'll have to buy her new ones. I always end up either going all caveman on her lingerie and shredding it or taking the damn things as souvenirs.

Her wild panting in my ear begins to drive me insane, so I slap her ass hard, the echo slicing through the silence around us and giving me another lovely sound to focus on. I know she's jonesing to jump on my cock, but right now, *I* need to be the one in control.

I pull Stone by her waist, lifting her completely off me and setting her at my side. Her confused expression lingers on her face only for a second, lighting up the very next when I unleash my command.

"Take your dress off," I order while stroking my cock.

Without delay, she pulls the blue fabric over her head, proudly showcasing all her curves.

"Forget your bra at home, little girl?"

"Didn't think I needed one for tonight. I would have gone commando too, but I know how much you like tearing my panties. Didn't want to disappoint you," she replies cheekily, but her cocky grin falters as she becomes transfixed on me beating my dick into submission, pre-cum glistening at its head.

I wet my lips as I take stock of every lush curve and valley, letting that image sink into my brain and scorch its way into my memory. After I've had my fill—or as much as I can withstand without touching her—I go to my knees and pull her to me. She gasps out sharply when I bend her over, making sure the brat is naked and on all fours in front of me. I slap her ass cheek again, so I can watch it redden and then soften the sting away with my lips and tongue.

"Hold still," I grunt as I trail my tongue down lower until it meets her wet entrance.

I grab her hips to keep her in place since I know the minute I start eating her out, she won't be able to control her movements no matter how many times I order her to keep still.

And eat her out is precisely what I do. I fuck her wet cunt with my tongue until her moans are so loud that they reach the town far below. But it never seems to satisfy me enough. I want her to howl at the moon while I lick her clean.

"Finn!" she yells as I lap at her, my tongue coated with her arousal.

I slap her ass again, hard and ruthlessly, making her leak even more onto the flat of my tongue.

"You always taste so fucking good," I moan into her, wanting desperately to make her cum just like this—ass up in the air and my face in between her thighs.

My own cock begins to plead for mercy, needing inside her pussy, but I internally yell out at him to wait his fucking turn. I need Stone to cum for me just like this—vulnerable and entirely at my disposal. I need her to walk over the precipice, knowing I'll be right down there to catch her when she falls, loving her afterward.

I just need…

I just need…

Her.

"Finn!" she shouts, reaching that almighty high and drenching my tongue with all of her juices.

How can I ever say goodbye to this?

I pull back onto my haunches, and while she is still riding the rush of her orgasm, I make it my mission to eviscerate it with the next one. And with one fast thrust, I'm exactly where I need to be—inside her sweet pussy, dominating her in the only manner she'll allow me.

"Being inside you is the only thing I want to keep from this life," I tell her as I use my grip on her hips to slide her along the full length of my shaft.

At first, our tempo is deliciously slow and soft but quickly gains speed, becoming the pure fire that we are addicted to.

"I'm starting to see that," she teases, but the lust-filled mewl that comes out of her right after has my Adam's apple bobbing, my ribs constricting the organ that I feel is about to break with the wonder of having Stone in such a way.

"Tell me you feel the same, Stone. Tell me you live for me fucking you like this."

"Oh, God!"

She begins to climb again, but I don't want her to meet her maker before she gives me a bit of herself too. A bit of her soul.

"Tell me, Stone! Tell me you feel this as much as I do!" I command, grinding my teeth as I impale her hot core with my merciless cock.

"Finn," she wails, her hands grasping onto the blanket beneath us to keep herself steady.

Her raven hair is cascading beautifully around her, but since it deprives me of her face, I unlatch one of my hands from her hips to grab her dark, rich locks. I forcefully pull on the blue tips, so she has no choice but to crane her head back so I can have a perfect view of her wanton face. I love the sight as much as I love her pussy clenching around me with my inflicted pain.

"Has anyone made you feel this wanted? This perfect?"

She purrs again, riding me as if lost in motion, hitting her ass on my crotch so I can sink into her deeper.

"Has anyone cared for you this much? Tell me I'm the only one. I want to be the only one."

"You are, baby. Please, you are," she pleads, so close to falling apart.

Goddamn, those words on her lips almost push me over the edge.

"Fuck! I love it when you call me that," I admit, fucking her so hard it will be a miracle if she can walk afterward.

"Baby?" She pants wildly.

"Fuck, yes!" I profess, pulling her hair further so that she has no choice but to go up onto her knees, her glistening back soaking my shirt.

In my deranged lust, I didn't even take one piece of clothing off, but somehow, being fully clothed while she's stark naked, just makes the whole spectacle even hotter. I pull her chin closer to her shoulder and kiss her madly, my teeth sinking into her lip.

"Just like that, baby. Keep fucking me just like that," she breathes against my mouth.

My hand falls from her face to grab onto one heavy breast, and I begin to play with it, kneading it while eating up her cries.

"Oh, God!" she stammers, unable to decide if her air intake is preferable to my unyielding kiss.

I keep my hand groping her tender breast while the other slides down to her bare mound, instantly finding her swollen clit. I start stroking it until she's far gone, leaving only our bodies entwined along with our entangled souls.

"I'm going to cum, baby! I'm going to cum so hard!" she roars in the throes of passion, jumping on my stick until her orgasm rips through her.

"Fuck, Stone, you're so fucking perfect. That's it, ride me. Take all of me. It's fucking yours."

Her pussy deliciously clenches on my cock as she cries out my name, cumming fast and hard in a perfect dance of passion. I can't help but follow her over, loving that I'm filling her up and marking her as mine.

Unable to keep my trembling knees from shaking with such an earthshattering sensation, I fall to my back, bringing her down with me. She melts against me with her head on my shoulder, and I run my fingers into her hair as she purrs in contentment.

"Do you still want to disappear?" she asks after we catch our breaths.

"Not when I'm with you. When I'm with you, I can be myself."

"Then maybe it's about time the world meets the real Finn Walker. I like him just fine," she coos, tracing a finger over my lips.

I pull her hair back softly just enough so she can see my face.

"What if I don't want you to like me? What if I want more than that?"

Her brows furrow, and her beautiful, sated smile turns somber.

"Finn," she begins softly, but my heart crumples into a mangled mess with just the hesitation in her tone, accompanied by a panicked look in her eyes.

I school my features as best I can and shake my head before kissing her nose.

"It's okay, Stone. I'm used to disappointment."

And just like the last time we were here, she slowly begins to get up to find her clothes.

"I… umm… I'm a little tired now. You mind taking me back to the dorm?" she asks, once her dress is fully back on her body.

"Sure." I try to smile, but I'm not fooling anyone.

I opened up, and she slammed the door in my face. But I guess I really should be used to it; expect it even. Stone is just like her namesake—hard and impenetrable. She's not going to give in to me so easily. I've probably gotten closer than most, so I should take that as a victory, right? Then why do I feel so raw? Why does this feel like I'm fucked beyond measure? Like I'm losing her? And how can you even lose something that was never yours, to begin with?

All these miserable thoughts plague me on the silent ride over to her dorm. Upon parking the car, Stone places a chaste kiss on my cheek, giving me all the confirmation I needed—it was too much, too soon for her.

Fuck!

I wish I knew how to do this shit. I wish I had some sort of clue to guide me on the best way to reach her. But I don't. Stone is the first girl to make me feel this way, whatever *this* is. And I'm not sure she feels the same. Actually, I'm not sure she's even capable of it.

I walk her to her door as I still want to be near her in spite of the clear rejection. But maybe I shouldn't. She's protecting her heart while I'm throwing mine on the ground, allowing her to trample on it with her skulled boots. Maybe I'm the sucker who should know when to cut his losses and bail.

"Are you coming over to Big Jim's tomorrow, or do you have some big game to train for?" she asks, sounding indifferent, but the distraught look in her stunning green eyes tells me otherwise.

"I have some assignments to hand in this week. I should probably focus on those. But I'll call you," I tell her, her face not giving me anything to work with.

"Okay, so I guess I'll see you around, quarterback," she responds nonchalantly, throwing me a meek smile, before heading into her dorm without giving me a chance to say goodbye.

"I don't know if you will, Stone," I mumble to myself, kicking the air at my feet, feeling like shit as I walk back to my car.

I feel like a total asshole driving home, too.

Maybe this is for the best. Some space will give me some perspective. It will give me time to simmer down these unknown feelings until I understand them. Until I'm able to curb them into something similar to what Stone is feeling. Perhaps we are *just* about sex. And what's wrong with that? I mean, she's leaving at the end of the year anyway, so a no-strings-attached fuckbuddy scenario is the way to go. Most assholes would sell their own grandmother to be in my shoes.

I guess I should be happy, right?

But I'm not. I'm fucking miserable.

And because life just loves to fuck with me, the minute I get home, I'm confronted with yet another clusterfuck of immense proportions. Sitting pretty in my foyer, just waiting to shove the branding iron up my ass—sans lube, I might add—is another mandate from The Society, reminding me exactly who the fuck is calling the shots.

Fuck this night!

I'm so fucking over it already.

CHAPTER 19

FINN

After last night's events, I twist and turn in my bed, trying to think of a way to get out of the mess I'm in. As hard as I try, nothing comes to me. All I end up doing is staring at the ceiling of my bedroom, reliving that one night from last May, which turned out to be a catalyst for my current state of affairs.

Because of that one moment—that one fatal mistake—my life is in shambles.

Not only am I being blackmailed by the boogeyman, but because of them, I met the only girl on God's green earth that has ever meant something to me. No matter what anyone says, ignorance *is* bliss. If the foul-mouthed Southie never landed in my crosshairs, if she didn't piss off The Society somehow, then I wouldn't be feeling like I'm being backed into a corner, ordered to choose between her life and mine.

When dawn arrives, laying the sun's early beams on my face, I instantly curse out at it. I hate the fact we're going to have yet another sunny day in Asheville when all of me feels nothing but dreary desolation. It's September, for fuck's sake. A time upon when the trees should be shedding their aged leaves, letting them fall to the ground to remind us that nothing lasts forever. Although, it's not like I really need the reminder.

I pull my arm over my eyes, trying to shield them from the sunlight, but it's no use as my mind is already fully awake. Shit! Who am I kidding?! The chaos that is my mind hasn't stopped for even a minute. It's working double time, not showing any signs of slowing down since I got home from my disastrous first date with Stone.

Not that all of it was bad. Most of it was pretty fucking incredible, actually. It was just that last bit at the end that was a mean soul-crusher.

Fuck!

I can't continue to think about this shit, or I'm going to lose my goddamn mind.

I sit up and hold onto the edge of my mattress as I place my bare feet on the oak-finished floor, latching my eyes onto the other SNAFU in my life—the little black box sitting on my nightstand The Society was kind enough to send me.

Being a sucker for punishment, I pick it up and open the lid, revealing a brand-new phone inside, nicely wrapped in its pristine packaging. If anyone came in and saw me now, they would assume I had just bought the piece of shit and hadn't had time yet to fiddle around with it. But they would be wrong. I have no intention of even touching the damn thing just yet. If I thought I could get away with it, I'd bury it in the Oakley woods and let that be the end of it. But I'm not so fortunate.

Inside the black box, right beside the phone, is the third letter I've received from The Society. And if I cave in to their demands, it looks like it will be my last.

The masochist in me clutches the black stationery, its golden lettering revealing their final command.

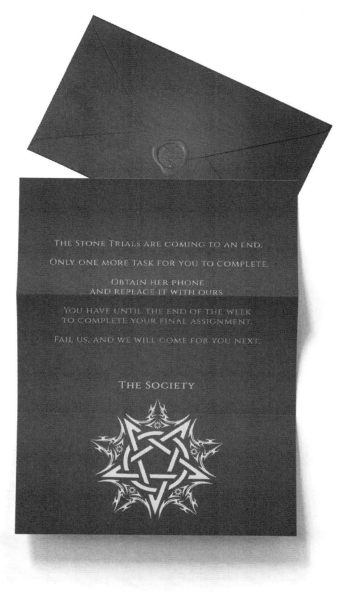

THE STONE TRIALS ARE COMING TO AN END.

ONLY ONE MORE TASK FOR YOU TO COMPLETE.

OBTAIN HER PHONE
AND REPLACE IT WITH OURS.

YOU HAVE UNTIL THE END OF THE WEEK
TO COMPLETE YOUR FINAL ASSIGNMENT.

FAIL US, AND WE WILL COME FOR YOU NEXT.

THE SOCIETY

Fuckers!

I swear, when Linc and Colt finally figure out who is behind this society bullshit, I'm going to beat them into a pulp, skin them alive, and make them swallow each and every letter they've sent me with the intention of ruining Stone. I'll only stop when I've made sure they feel as powerless as they have made me.

Fuckers. The lot of them!

I shove the letter back into the box, unwilling to have it in my hands for another second, and walk over to my closet. I fall to my knees and hide it at the far corner in the back, placing some old football gear in front of it, just in case someone snoops around.

"That's the end of that," I grunt, wiping my hands on my sweat pants, feeling filthy just by having touched the damned thing.

These assholes gave me a week. By my count, that's how long Linc and Colt have to get their act together and find something that we can use to finally get rid of these bastards once and for all. I'll even help with the research if it speeds up the process. However, if nothing comes out of it, if we still can't find shit about the members of The Society, then I guess I'm fucked no matter what decision I make.

I'm too screwed-up right now to think that far ahead, though. My jumbled mess of a brain is still trying to play catch-up to my mangled heart. Let me lick my wounds for a few days before I'm forced to make a decision, one that will impact either my life and the guys', or Stone's.

After a quick shower, I run downstairs for some breakfast, but I hesitate for a second upon seeing my dad at the kitchen table, reading his newspaper. Mom is trying to feed my brother Calvin's one-year-old boy, getting more orange goo on her silk blouse than into little Noah's mouth.

"Morning," I mumble, after gaining the courage to enter the room.

"Hmm," my father mumbles as a reply, his eyes never wavering from the sports section.

I walk over to my mom, bending down to kiss her on her cheek before making myself a plate.

"Everyone missed you yesterday for Sunday dinner," my mom says in between the plane noises she's making at Noah, trying to convince the little guy to open his mouth and eat the pumpkin mush.

"Sorry," I answer, taking a seat at the table, stuffing my mouth with delicious, crispy bacon.

"Why couldn't you come again? It's skipped my memory entirely," she adds inquisitively, acting as if she didn't have the foggiest notion as to why I was out last night.

She's acting all clueless and aloof, which are two characteristics that have nothing to do with my mother. Nothing gets by Charlene Walker, including the reason for my absence last night.

Sunday dinners are a big deal in the Walker household. The whole family gathers for the best southern cooking, which is usually prepared by Mom and our in-house cook, Martha. It's the only time during the week where everyone gets under the same roof to eat, drink, and meddle in each other's business.

Trust me. I didn't miss out on anything by ditching dinner. I've had twenty-two years of my share of Walker drama. If I missed last night's performance, then I'm sure I'll get the highlights next week, even though each dinner feels more like the same rerun to me.

I stuff another forkful in my mouth, hoping she will get the hint. But even if she does, she isn't going to drop it.

"Finn, sweetheart, slow down. Tell me, how was your night?"

"It was fine," I retort with a lukewarm smile.

"Just fine? I'm sure you can do better than that. I mean, it isn't every day that my youngest starts courting a girl."

"I'm not courting anyone. And by the way, who says courting nowadays? This isn't a reenactment of Gone with the Wind, Momma. So don't go all Scarlet O'Hara on me now. And besides, I thought you said you couldn't remember what I was up to last night. It's a sin to lie, Mom," I tease, pointing my fork toward her.

She rolls her eyes at me in such a way that I'm oddly impressed they didn't pop out of their sockets. My mother might be in her mid-fifties, but she can give an eye roll that would rival any teenage girl. Setting down the jar of baby food, she turns and gives me her undivided attention, all because of my lip. I slump in my chair, knowing I'm not going to get off so easily.

Way to play it cool, Finn. You moron.

"Boy, you might be twice my size, but don't think for a minute I won't jump across this table just so I can give you an ear pulling," she threatens. "Now tell your momma what she wants to hear. How was your date last night?"

"It was okay."

"Just okay?"

"Yes, Momma. We went to dinner and had a nice time. Then I drove her back to her dorm. Like I said, it was okay."

"If it was okay, then why do you look like someone kicked your puppy?"

"Puppy!" Noah yells ecstatically, looking at the floor in search of one. "Puppy! Puppy!"

"Jesus, Charlene! Quiet that baby down. Can't a man have one peaceful morning in his own house?" my father blurts out, snapping his precious newspaper closed and slamming it on the table. "And if the boy doesn't want to give all the sordid details of his date to his momma, respect his privacy and leave it be. Finn has more important things to worry about than girls anyway. Football season has begun, and he has to keep his head in the game. The only thing he should be concerned about chasing is a championship, not girls."

"Not everything should revolve around football, Hank. Finn deserves a life, too."

"He'll get a life once he's drafted, not before," my father deadpans, looking directly at me, making sure I have my head on straight.

I look over at my mother, her head bowed down into a coffee mug, unable to look me in the eye. Even baby Noah has his little chubby fist in his mouth, somehow sensing the tense mood. Breakfast continues on in this awkward and strained atmosphere, until my father finally excuses himself, leaving the room to go about his business elsewhere.

The minute he leaves, I place my elbows on the table and shove my hands into the sides of my head, feeling a migraine coming on.

"Don't pay any mind to your father, Finn," my mother tries to console, ensuring that he can't hear the disobedient remark.

"Pretty hard to do when his voice is permanently ringing in my ears," I confess, shaking my head, wishing his words would somehow slip out of it and stop tormenting me so.

"I know. He's a difficult man, your father, but he loves you, Finn. All he wants is for you to be happy."

"No, Momma. All he wants is bragging rights for his friends. My needs don't factor into the equation."

Her lips thin as she takes stock of my every sunken and defeated feature, but she doesn't deny my statement either. She knows, as well as I do, that all Hank Walker really wants is for his sons to be football gods like he was in his heyday. He wants to bask in their glory, hoping it will satisfy his nostalgia of the times he used to run onto the field while everyone cheered the Walker name.

Beau was an utter disappointment to him when he ditched football to become a high school gym teacher. We all saw how that shitshow went down. Calvin got off a little bit easier when he wrecked his knee in his freshman year of college, destroying any chance he had of going Pro. Unlike Beau, Momma didn't have to come up with an alternative that would please my father because Calvin switched his major to broadcast journalism that same year. Now he's the face that every home in North Carolina waits to see on the evening news, for player interviews and daily sports highlights. Being a sports newscaster is enough to appease my father, so Calvin doesn't get any flak from him, but it also means that all his eggs were put in one basket—mine.

I have to go Pro, so deviating from that plan is not an option. If I told my father that I would rather become an astronomer, then I'd have to kiss my family goodbye and never see any of them again. They can be pains in the asses at times, meddling where they shouldn't, but they are still my family.

I look at baby Noah as my mother starts to clean him up and think of all my nieces and nephews. I begin to imagine what it would be like not seeing them grow up, not being a part of their lives, and something inside me just cracks. I would give nearly anything to follow my dreams, but I can't see my life without my family in it. It's inconceivable to me.

So I have no other choice but to go Pro. I'll throw a ball for a few years and make the old man proud. Once I've outgrown the league, which will probably be in my early thirties if I'm lucky, then I can do what I've always wanted to, and no one will give me a hard time about it. I'm looking at ten years max. I've already given him my last twenty-two, so what's ten more?

"This girl you've been seeing, what's her name again?" my mother asks, trying hard to move the conversation along to a more favorable topic.

Little does she know that talking about Stone is just as sore of a subject for me as it is following my father's demands of playing ball.

"Her name is Stone, Momma. I told you that already."

"So you did. Odd name for a girl, don't you think?"

"Not for her," I huff out. "When you meet her, you'll see just how perfect the name suits her."

"And when will that be?" she questions further with an excited sparkle in her blue eyes, one that I really wish wasn't there.

"Huh?"

"I asked, when will I get to meet this girl? And don't you dare play dumb with me, young man. I know she's important to you. If she weren't, you wouldn't have made a fuss at getting me to book you a table at Alphonso's. Did she like it? She must have been ecstatic when she learned you were taking her to the fanciest restaurant in town."

I just nod repeatedly because no way can I tell my mom that Stone preferred a food truck to the fancy dinner my mother set up for us. The last-minute change was actually nice, though. I hate those uptight places. They have so much cutlery that you don't know which one you're supposed to use. Six forks, WTF? They all do the same shit. Give me a meaty hamburger out of a greasy kitchen on the side of the road any day. Even though the night ended the way it did, I really had a good time. But then again, I always do when I'm with her.

"I think you should bring Stone to your father's sixtieth birthday Saturday night. I'd love to meet the girl who is able to put such a goofy look on my boy's face." My mother giggles cheerfully.

I can't help it, but the minute those words fly from my mom's lips, I begin to choke on my own saliva. My mom immediately places the baby back in the high chair, walking her way over to me to slap my back just so I don't suffocate on my own stupidity.

"Martha, be a dear and get us more orange juice, please?" my mom asks our cook, who is elbows deep in preparations for today's meals, trying hard not to laugh at my mishap.

"Yes, Ma'am," she singsongs with a pep in her step.

Martha brings over the juice, filling my cup up and giving me a stare that reads, 'You sure have gone and done it now, you fool,' along with an all-knowing, teasing smirk that needs no translation.

Even Martha knows I just fucked myself into a corner. Bringing a girl to a Walker event is overkill in any relationship. It's like pulling up a large billboard announcing to all of Asheville's population that I'm taken, and the girl in my arms is the *one*.

Beau and Calvin made sure not to bring their girlfriends to one of Mom and Dad's parties until they had already bought their engagement rings. That's how serious this shit is. And Mom asking me to bring Stone along to my father's birthday party as if it weren't a big deal, is all sorts of messed up.

Shit! How the fuck will I get out of this?

"I'll think about it. Stone and I are still getting to know each other, so I'm not sure we are really *there yet*. You know, for the whole meet-the-parents thing."

"Have you met hers?"

"Her momma," I answer truthfully.

"See? If Stone isn't worried about you meeting her family, then why are you concerned about her meeting yours? You're not embarrassed by us, are you?"

"I don't think giving you an honest answer will win me any favors, Momma."

Martha's loud snickering from the other side of the kitchen can be heard from way over here. Even baby Noah cackles, happily drooling down his chin.

Traitors.

My momma just slaps me upside the head instead of using her words. Lord knows it's always been her go-to move when we give her sass that she doesn't appreciate. She walks back to Noah and picks him up, nestling him at her hip.

"I can't force you to bring your girlfriend to your father's birthday party, but sooner or later, I do want to meet this girl."

"Momma, don't label us, please. She's not my girlfriend. We're just friends," I reply, hating the 'friends' word with the passion of a thousand suns.

"Friends? Is that right? Fine. If that's all you are, then you won't hear a peep out of me."

"I doubt it," I mumble under my breath.

"What?"

"Nothing," I reply, showcasing my most charming smile.

She starts making her way out of the kitchen with Noah in hand, and I think that will be the end of that. But again, like with everything in my fucking life, I'm wrong.

"But Finn," she starts, turning around just enough for me to see her face, and continues, "if by any chance you change your mind and discover that you're more than just *friends*, and I have a feeling that you will, my invitation still stands."

I don't say anything in reply. Why bother? I'd just be fueling my mother's curiosity. When that woman gets something into her head, she will go to great lengths to get it. I won't be the least bit surprised if, by the end of the day, she somehow has Stone's number on speed dial.

I push my plate away and thump my head repeatedly on the kitchen table while Martha is on the other side of the room, laughing her face off. I get up from my seat, bringing the plate to the sink and give her my least threatening scowl.

"You were a real help back there. Thanks," I mumble.

"You're a grown-ass man. You should know how to handle your momma by now."

"Hello?! Obviously, I can't!"

But instead of sympathy, all I get is more laughter.

"Traitor."

"Go on, boy. Get your ass to school!" She laughs, ushering me out the door.

The thing is, attending Philosophy class isn't really high on my priorities list at the moment. So when I arrive late, I don't even give Professor Donavan the polite 'sorry, I'm late' nod. I just walk in searching for Easton, knowing he would have saved a seat for me. When I find him at the far back of the class, I make my way there, slumping in the chair next to him.

I'm not really sure why I'm doing this dog and pony show of coming to class. It's not like I'm going to be able to retain any piece of knowledge from this lecture, or any of the ones that follow. But if I stayed home, then I would just raise my mother's suspicions. Right now, she thinks I've been a little bit more secretive because of a girl. And even though she's not completely wrong, it would benefit me immensely if my mother continues to think all my problems only revolve around Stone.

But I guess they kind of do, don't they?

East is also surprisingly quiet today, diligently taking notes, which is mind-boggling, to say the least. But upon closer inspection, I see what he's really doing is sketching the profile of some girl's head on his notebook.

Wait. I know that ponytail.

I look around the classroom and, lo and behold, just a few rows down is the girl he gave shit to a few weeks back. I'm about to tease the fucker, going for the notebook, but he's too quick for me and stashes it in his book bag before I can reach it.

"Ah, come on now, Picasso. Don't go shy on me. Show me what you were drawing," I tease him.

"Stop giving me shit," he rebukes coldly.

"Woke up on the wrong side of the bed this morning, did you?"

"Worse. Didn't even make it to bed," he laments, tapping his pencil on his knee.

"What were you doing all night? On second thought, I don't want to know."

"It's not like that. I spent the whole weekend up at Lincoln's trying to find out something about *you-know-who,*" he explains bitterly with a scowl deeply ingrained on his face.

"Any luck?" I ask hopefully, but the sentiment quickly disappears when East shakes his head.

"Motherfuckers are goddamn ghosts. We couldn't find a trace of them anywhere."

My face slumps, feeling the metaphorical noose tightening around my neck.

"Finn, we'll find these assholes. Okay, brother?" He nudges his knee with mine, trying to uplift my spirits. "How about you, though? How are things with Stone? Is she still giving you the silent treatment?"

"We went out yesterday," I explain with a dismal taint to each word.

"You did?" he asks, surprised.

"Kind of. Yeah." I nod.

"So, everything is good with you guys then?" he asks skeptically. "Because you don't look like a guy who got some last night," he adds with a forced chuckle.

"That's none of your business, asshole."

"So touchy this early in the morning. But it's cool. I'll back off as long your head is still in the game."

"I really wish people would stop telling me that," I mumble under my breath, letting out a long exhale.

"Sorry, brother," East begins, giving me a light squeeze on the shoulder. "It is what it is. Just be thankful that hanging around Stone is enough to placate, for now, whatever nefarious plan The Society is up to. Pretty soon, they'll ask for more. You just watch."

I start to open my mouth, ready to tell him about the box I received last night, but then shut it closed. If I tell Easton or any of the guys, they'll pressure me into fulfilling The Society's command. The only one who would probably have my back would be Lincoln, but I can't be sure.

I can't fuck this up. There are too many lives at stake, but there's only one that I'm really worried about. And no one needs a crystal ball to know I'm not talking about my own.

CHAPTER 20

FINN

After four days of wracking my brain, trying to come to terms with what to do, it's my heart that ends up making the decision. I give in to its wants and text the Southie who has plagued my mind and soul non-stop since the minute I landed eyes on her.

I look at my phone, thinking of any excuse in the book to get her to see me, but in the end, my lame ass just texts her with the douchiest one-liner that can come up with.

Me: *Want to hang out or something?*

Brat: *Are you for real?*

Me: *Hmm, yeah.*

Brat: *I'm too busy for 'or something', quarterback.*

Me: *Aren't Thursday's your night off, though?*

Me: *And no one is too busy for 'or something'. *winky emoji**

Brat: *Yep, I'm not working tonight, but that doesn't mean I'm not busy.*

Brat: *We are talking about sex, right? I never know with you. 'Or something' could be geek code for some meteor shower you want to take me to watch.*

Me: *Busy doing what?*

Me: *Just so we're clear 'or something' always involves you sitting on my face.*

Brat: *I'm studying. Some of us do that shit in college.*

Brat: *Good to know. And as much as I'd love to ride that pretty face of yours, I'm still busy.*

Me: *Need some company?*

Brat: *…*

Me: *I mean, I've got a paper to work on, too.*

Me: *Stone?*

Brat: *…*

Me: *Fine. Promise, no 'or something'.*

Me: *Stone?*

Me: *I'll bring pizza.*

Brat: *You should have led with that. No pineapple, quarterback. Be here in an hour.*

Me: *Always the brat.*

Brat: *And don't you forget it.*

Forty minutes later, I'm at her dorm room door with two large pepperoni pizzas and a six-pack of Cokes. Stone flings it open after my third knock, wearing nothing but boy shorts and some indie band T-shirt, snug enough for me to notice the missing bra.

Great! That won't make this hard at all!

"I see you've come prepared," she teases me, taking the pizza boxes out of my hand.

"I got food and plenty of caffeine. If we have to study, we might as well do it right." I force out a chuckle.

"I couldn't agree more with you. Come on in, quarterback. Make yourself comfortable," she adds, taking a slice out of the box, but immediately dropping it back down to blow over her fingers, realizing that they just came out of the oven.

"I see I've come just in time," I joke, as she tries to wolf down the slice while I take in the cramped space around us.

Stone's dorm room is just big enough for a single bed and a desk, but its loud posters and bold décor has the same vibrant savagery as its owner. Just like her—small in stature but packing a mean punch nonetheless.

"You can have the desk if you want. I prefer studying on the bed anyway."

I give her a little nod and set up shop on her desk. After I have everything in order, I turn my head over my shoulder and see that Stone is already deep in concentration. She's sitting on her bed with her back resting against the wall and her laptop on a pillow over her lap, while an opened pizza box lies next to her, a spot from where I can easily grab a slice, too.

Not wanting to ruin her mojo, I actually end up working on my paper for Professor Donavan's class. Sure, the paper isn't due for another two weeks, but somehow, just being in this room with her while she's doing her hustle inspires my own. I only realize how much time has passed when Stone lets out a loud yawn, stretching her arms over her head, announcing the late hour.

"I'm exhausted," she half-yawns, half-laughs.

"Shit. It's late. I should be heading out." I wince upon checking my phone and see it's well past one in the morning.

How the hell did that happen?

My mind is usually aware of every minute passing by, but I completely lost track of time. More laughable is the fact that it happened while doing actual school work. Will wonders never cease? Being able to zone out of every fucked-up thing happening in my life is elating, but more so is realizing the reason behind my sudden inner peace—Stone.

Just her presence calms my hectic brain.

Fuck.

"Not going to happen, pretty boy," she says adamantly, interrupting the small freak-out I'm inwardly having. "There is a strict no-boy rule after midnight, and if someone sees you leave, I'm screwed. The residence hall director is an utter bitch and would just love to catch me on a technicality to throw me out of the dorm. No way is that happening."

"Let me guess. Your dorm supervisor is Miss Pigtails and Bubble Gum?" I ask, remembering the annoying girl.

"You know it." Stone scoffs. "Which means you aren't going anywhere tonight. You'll just rest for a few hours here, and when everyone is asleep, you can sneak off. Unless, of course, you have somewhere else to be at this hour?" she adds, turning her back to me and moving the endless clutter of textbooks off her bed and onto the floor.

"If I didn't know any better, I'd swear you were fishing for something," I tease half-heartedly.

She straightens her spine, turning around to face me, with her hands on her hips and an aloof expression marring her stunning features.

"What would I be fishing for?"

"Hmm, I don't know. Maybe you want to know if I have any jersey chasers waiting for me the minute I leave your side."

"And do you?" she cocks a defiant brow at me.

"Does it matter if I did? Would you really care?" I ask, putting on a more serious tone.

Instead of giving me an answer, she pulls the covers back from her bed and sneaks in, leaving me a small opening to crawl behind her. My eager and prideless cock is already telling me to get my ass in there, but my heart is saying otherwise.

"Hmm."

"Are you afraid of sharing a bed with me, pretty boy?" she taunts.

"No."

"Then come on. Get in," she insists, a little more playfully.

"I don't think I should, Stone," I reply, shifting from one foot to the other.

"Why not?"

My stare falls to the floor while my foot shyly kicks the air, unwilling to explain how my heart is bruised and mangled from her rejection. Sensing my discomfort, Stone gets up to her knees and grabs my hands, commanding my full attention to her gorgeous face instead of listening to the forlorn thoughts playing around in my head.

"I won't take advantage of you. We'll just sleep, Finn. I promise," she explains patiently, with a sweetness I doubt many have ever witnessed.

"Okay," I concede softly, still unable to look directly into her eyes, but also powerless in denying whatever she asks of me.

I take off my Jordans and then my T-shirt. Thank fuck I changed into these comfortable sweat pants before I came over. If I was still in the same jeans I had worn today, I'd have to take them off. Trying to sleep in those would be pretty unbearable. Not to mention that I wouldn't be able to sleep in the same bed as Stone in only boxer briefs. But then again, lying next to her will be excruciating either way. Once she's made sure I'm settled in, she asks me to turn off the lamp on her desk, and even though the bed is tiny, I manage to keep enough space between us to avoid touching each other.

The only light that comes into her room is from a small window on the opposite wall. The beams of moonlight cast enough of a shadow to make me very aware of everything around me, especially the immobile figure lying at my side.

When we were both so focused on studying, the silence in the room calmed my racing mind, but now it's running at a fast pace. I hear my heart beat erratically with every little shuffle she makes under the pale-blue bedsheet, but when she finally turns toward me and places her hand over my bare chest, I swear the fucker actually skips a beat.

"I'm glad you called. To study, I mean," she says softly.

"Hmm."

Another pregnant pause ensues, but the awkward silence doesn't even affect me now since all my focus is on her dainty fingers running up and down my feverish skin.

"I remembered something the other night," she begins, coaxing out my curiosity.

"Remembered what?"

"When we were up at the gazebo last time, playing our little game. You told me two secrets, but I only gave you one."

"That's okay," I mumble, not really thrilled she's bringing up that soul-crushing night.

"I would still like you to know, though," she continues, inching her warm body closer to mine, her emerald eyes intent on the left side of my face.

I turn my body on its side to face her because I'm a lovesick fool who can't help wanting to be close to her. My body instantly burns hotter when she bridges the small gap between us, leaving us a hair's breadth away from each other. Stone's usually fierce features are soft, yet hesitant. There is a speck of fear swimming in her green rivulets, making me wish I could dive in deep and extinguish whatever she's so afraid of.

"You met my mom, Finn. You can imagine what type of childhood I had, but you should know it wasn't all bad. Not all of it, anyway," she explains, swallowing dryly.

Stone's eyes lower from my face, latching onto my chest, where her fingers continue to play around in circles. Whatever she wants to tell me is draining all her bravery, turning me utterly speechless. She is the most fearless person I have ever met, so seeing this smidge of vulnerability is gripping my heart in an almighty fist, squeezing the life out of it.

My protective instincts speak louder than my sense of self-preservation, and before I'm able to stop myself, my hand is already cradling her cheek comfortingly. Stone instantly covers my hand with her palm, holding me there and causing my breath to hitch with her gentle touch.

"You don't have to tell me anything you don't want to," I hush, caressing her soft skin with the pad of my thumb.

"But I do. I want to," she replies emotionally, before placing a kiss on my open palm.

I place my forehead on hers, and with our breathing in sync, I silently tell her that she can share with me whatever she wants. As long as I have her in my arms, she will always be safe.

Will she, though?

God, I hope so.

"We used to be happy once," she mutters. "When my dad lived with us, I mean. Momma had her spells, but Dad always knew exactly how to handle her. How to keep me from seeing the worst of it. He did everything for us. He took me to school, helped me with my homework. He took care of me, but most importantly, he took care of her. When he was put away, all of that changed."

"Put away?"

"My father is in jail, Finn. Living on the Southside doesn't come easy, you know? My father had to do a lot of shady things to keep a roof over our heads. Sometimes that meant he had to do some illegal dealings for us to get by. Unfortunately, he got caught up with the wrong crew—a bunch of scary assholes who didn't like to leave witnesses of their criminal ways.

"On one particular truck heist, the driver pulled through and gave the police a description of one of his assailants, which fit my dad to a T. Since he was a known associate of a crew that was already under investigation, the cops didn't hesitate in pinning it on him, regardless of the fact that he wasn't even there when it all went down."

"Shit, Stone," I interrupt gruffly, feeling her pain and anger roll through her body in waves as she recalls that troubling time in her life.

"And since our judicial system is a goddamn joke, my father took a plea bargain just so he wouldn't have to serve a full sentence. He knew for a fact that no jury would believe him since his track record wasn't the greatest. He was only supposed to do fifteen years, ten with good behavior.

"While he was inside, some of his old crew members thought he'd rat them out. At the end of the day, they knew that my father was a family man and would do just about anything to get back to us sooner. So the assholes went after him inside. My father had to defend himself in any way he could, which resulted in him killing for real this time, adding more time to his already steep sentence. He'll most likely never see the light of day again," she explains distraught.

Her eyelids shut closed while her hand keeps its hold on mine against her cheek, comforted by the solace it offers.

"He drew up divorce papers once he knew he'd never get out, hoping my mom would sign them so she could start her life over without being chained to him. She couldn't, of course. To this day, Momma refuses to move on. Sure, she has a boyfriend here and there to fill up her lonely time, but she'll never give up my father. Even if she never sees him again, she'll never let him go."

"When did this happen, Stone? When was your father put away?"

"Almost thirteen years ago. I was just eight when my world fell apart. When my father was put behind bars for a crime he didn't commit, my mother dove head-first into a downward spiral. I had just started third grade when I officially became the adult of the house—the one who needed to pick up my mother's shattered heart from the floor and ensure she'd always be taken care of."

"That's a lot of pressure to put on a little girl's shoulders, Stone."

"I was never a little girl, Finn. That's a luxury I never had."

"Is that why you're taking law? You want to be a defense lawyer?"

"Something like that. I want to be in a position where I can have a voice to shape this country's laws. I want to help better our judicial system to ensure innocent men don't feel that accepting a plea deal is their only option."

I move an errant strand of hair away from her face, my heart filling with her drive and passion to better such a flawed world. Stone is defined by her past. While others would cower facing such adversity and take the punches that fate hands out, Stone just swings her left hook right back at it. She's never been one to back down from anything, not even at the tender age of eight.

"If anyone can do it, it's you, Stone. I'm as certain of it as I am that the stars light up the night sky."

"I don't need your flattery, Finn. That's not the reason why I'm telling you this."

"Why are you telling me this, then?"

Her eyes slowly open, her light jewels sparkling with a teary-eyed emotion that leaves me, yet again, tongue-tied.

"My mom was never the same after my dad was put away, Finn. A love like that might be rare, but it's also devastating to watch it fall apart. To love someone so deeply that their mere presence is your oxygen terrifies me to my very core."

"I get that, Stone. It's okay," I hush, trying to console her anxious state. "We don't have to talk about your parents anymore."

"That's just the thing. It's not them who I'm talking about. Please, Finn, just let me say this before I lose my courage," she explains restlessly.

"Okay." I nod.

She swallows dryly three more times before she's able to say a word, all the while making my foolish heart beat frantically for her.

"I never understood how one person could have that much power over someone else. How falling in love could hurt as easily as it could mend. It was always something I never wanted to experience, and all my life I've made sure to keep everyone at arm's length, ensuring no one could make me feel that powerless. I like being in control, Finn. I like to be the one who has the last say."

"I know you do." I smile tenderly.

Her big eyes go wide, her cheeks flushing as she grabs my hand with both of hers, holding it close to her bosom while staring into my eyes.

"I think I might have fucked up along the way, though. I don't think I'm in control anymore. Last Sunday night, when you left, I felt like you took a piece of me with you. I was scared you'd never bring it back. And then I didn't hear back from you for almost four days, and I was slowly losing my mind."

"You were?"

"Yes. And I have to be honest. I hated you all the while you kept your distance. I mean, I really fucking hated you. Don't do that shit again, pretty boy," she adds with a pissed-off tone that her teary eyes don't reflect.

"What are you saying, Stone?"

"Honestly? I don't know. All I know is that I don't want to go about my days without seeing you. Without being with you. Does that make sense?"

The little smile on my face grows wider as I say, "Yeah, it makes sense. I feel the same way too, you know?"

She holds onto my hands tighter, her lids shutting once again, letting out a long relieved exhale.

"Does that scare you?" I ask, leaning a little bit closer to her.

"Yes."

"I didn't think it would be possible to scare Stone Bennet." I try and tease her, hoping to lighten up the heavy atmosphere.

Her eyes open, the green emeralds still twinkling with unshed tears, and my heart leaps into my throat, unprepared to face this open vulnerability in her.

"But I am. You scare me, Finn. So fucking much."

I grab her by the nape of her neck, her head softly nestling itself on my shoulder.

"I'm scared too, Stone," I confess hoarsely, holding her tightly in my arms.

"You are?" she mutters into the hollow of my neck.

"Petrified." I chuckle nervously.

She raises her head to look deep into my eyes and asks, "So what are we going to do?"

I give her a little smile, running my thumb on her luscious, full lower lip and reply, "Be scared together. Because being scared with you is the most alive I have ever felt."

The little smile that crests her lips is my undoing. I can't hold it in any longer, so I take what I've been craving the moment she opened the door—a kiss. One that shows just how much she terrifies me, and how much I yearn for that fucking feeling to be in my life for all my days.

She opens her pouty mouth, letting me in to taste all of her, as her hands find their way into my hair. I keep tasting her as my hands travel down her luscious body but all too soon does our kiss become a volcano of need, turning my light touch into a brutish craving.

It's always like this with Stone. It's consuming and unparalleled to anything else.

Her leg throws itself around my thigh, and I know she's seconds away from being on top of me, making me mad with desire along the process. But tonight, I want to do this differently. I want us to touch what frightens us most and let it burn through us. I pin her on her back, leaving me on top, her eyes widening of their own accord.

I don't say a word as I peel her T-shirt off, and crawl down to savor every last inch of her body. I kiss and nibble on her breasts while pulling down her boy shorts. With her trembling hands, she tugs at the seam of my sweatpants until I oblige her and kick them off, along with my boxer briefs. Before I can even cover her body with my own, my mouth takes over, forcing me on my knees and between her thighs. She thrashes the minute my tongue touches her wet core, extracting the whole of her desire onto my greedy tongue.

"Finn," she mewls, unable to keep still.

"Let me have this. Let me have all of you," I plea, thrusting my tongue into her center, my fingers hardening on her thighs wrapped around my neck.

Not two minutes go by when her body lifts off the bed, arching her back, unable to contain the orgasm ripping her in two. She rides it out as I lap all her arousal, savoring all of her dripping nectar.

She came far too quick for my liking, so I make a mental note of going down on her again before this night is through. Only this time, I'll prolong my assault on her pussy, making sure it only cums when I've had my fill and not a minute before.

When I slither up her body, licking her sweet juices from my lips, the look in her eyes spears straight into my chest, splitting it wide open. It's almost as if she were intent on creating a breach inside me, so she can sneak her way in there and brand me as hers forever. Her stellar eyes have become two deep pools I yearn to drown in, wishing her clear green waters could purify me and wash away my sins.

I loom over her post-orgasmic body, her legs immediately latching themselves around my waist, ready for me to do my worst. I push my aching, hard cock inside her, and the sweet symphony that leaves our lips is like an angels' song brought down from heaven.

"This is where I always want to be. Inside you. Always with you, Stone," I grunt, thrusting into her soaking pussy.

She moans out as I take my time getting deep inside her, her nails racking over my back, digging deep into my flesh with my every merciless push. My mouth latches onto her neck as I slow down our tempo, maddening us both.

"I dream of doing this every night before I fall asleep. But when I wake up, all I yearn for is to hear your voice. Just your voice, Stone," I profess.

"Finn," she exclaims on a tormented howl.

"I think of excuses to see you. Excuses just to touch you. To smell you. You've made a mess out of me."

"Oh, God," she purrs, her ankles pushing my ass to give her more. And fuck it, do I ever.

I pound her greedy pussy hard and relentless, speeding my tempo into such a frantic state that I'm not even sure what universe we're in anymore.

"It's when I'm inside you—when you let me make love to you like this—that all my fears go away. I'm no longer scared of anything. I'm whole, Stone."

The tears that track down her cheeks are just as beautiful as the wails of want and desire that fall from her lips.

"Be scared with me, Stone. Be whole with me. Just fucking be mine," I beg as I pound into her with such intensity that her core clenches just as mercilessly around my rock-hard cock, completely dominating it.

"Yes. Oh, God! Yes, Finn!"

I plunge into her, demanding even more of her body, and she responds to mine in kind. Her desire is always so willing to follow me. But just how far is her heart willing to?

"Tell me you want this, Stone. Tell me what I want to hear," I order, beads of sweat falling from my temple as I bend down to lick her tears that have reached down to her neck.

"I want you. I want you so much," she admits on a ragged wail, the sensations of her body and soul becoming too much for her to keep denying them.

"And," I provoke insistently, pushing her to knock down all the walls she has built up around her heart, torching them until they are nothing but ash around us.

"I need you. Please, baby. I need you so much," she continues to beg, slicing at my back, branding me with her nails.

"And?"

"I'm yours. I'm yours! Just keep loving me, Finn. Please!"

"I will, Stone. God, I will," I promise, knowing that's exactly what I'm doing, and will do for as long as she'll have me.

"Baby, I'm cumming!" she yells.

No longer able to keep the earth shattering from under her, Stone reaches the peak of her orgasm. Allowing me to share the euphoria, I follow right after her, spilling her name from my lips as ecstasy wraps its warm embrace around us.

I collapse on the bed beside her, rolling onto my back and cradling her soft, sated body to my side. We're both drained, physically, and emotionally, but along with the fear that comes from baring our souls, a certain calm washes over us both.

"So we're doing this?" she asks after a long pause, her fingers once again drawing patterns across my chest.

"Yes," I state plainly, not wanting any miscommunication to happen between us.

"Okay," she replies with another soft smile that rips my heart to shreds.

I grab her chin softly and press another tender kiss to her plump lips.

"Sleep now, Stone. I'll be waking you up in an hour to do that all over again."

She lets out a little giggle and nestles herself closer to me. Within minutes, her breathing evens out, and her heartbeat becomes steady while my own heart feels as if it were about to burst with happiness.

But no sooner do I think that nothing could beat this feeling, a little ping from my phone alerts me of an incoming message. Without waking her, I pick it up from the top of her desk and see a text from an unknown number.

Do it now or face the consequences.

My body instantly turns cold, facing the one thing that could ruin us—The Society.

They don't have to leave their trademark emblem for me to know this threat is theirs, which means they know where I am.

Fuck.

Just like Lincoln and Colt warned, these fuckers really do have eyes on my every move. Otherwise, how would they know that I'm over at Stone's?

Shit!

After what Stone confided in me about her father, I'm more torn than I was before setting foot inside this room.

Stone couldn't live a life loving someone just to have him be put away in a cage like the system did to her father. She's strong and fearless, but I don't think she could overcome something like that happening to her twice.

I only have two options, and neither of them is good.

I could go to the cops and come clean on what happened that awful night, betraying my best friends and ending their freedom in the hopes I could get a plea deal. But who's to say that what happened to Stone's dad wouldn't happen to me? I'm not the calmest of guys, and if anyone came after me in the big house, I'd probably end up taking a life, too. By going to the cops, not only would I condemn my friends, the brothers I have vowed my loyalty to, but I would end up losing my freedom as well as Stone.

The second option is to follow The Society's orders and let the chips fall as they may. But who knows what other horrors may come if I do what they want. I still don't know why Stone is their target, why she's gained their wrath. From what I've been able to verify, she doesn't even know they have set their sights on her. After tonight, she would have told me if she sensed any kind of danger.

Stone is clueless to The Society's very presence in her life. I'm positive of that.

If I do what they want and replace her phone with theirs, she will remain clueless. However, the repercussions of such an action will only cause trouble in her already screwed-up life. That's the only certainty I have.

My anger, more than discern, is what fuels my next step—delete their damn text from the phone and make no move to take hers away.

I'll protect Stone. I'll keep her safe somehow.

By not following their demands, they'll come for me, but I won't allow them to come after her.

I can't.

Stone has become more important to me than I could have ever imagined.

Maybe even more important than my freedom.

CHAPTER 21

STONE

"A party?" I stutter, wide-eyed.

"Uh-huh." Finn nods, absentmindedly playing with my hair.

I place my chin on his chest, looking at him as if he's completely lost his mind.

"At your house? Tomorrow? You want me to come to your house for your dad's birthday party tomorrow?" I repeat his moronic invite, word for word, hoping my tone will knock some sense into his head.

"You make it sound like you've never attended a birthday party before," he jokes, his warm body chuckling with amusement under me.

"Not one on the Northside, that's for sure," I mutter into his chest.

"It's no big deal. My mom throws one for my dad every year. There will be so many people attending that no one will even notice I brought a date."

"I bet." I scoff. "No doubt all of Asheville's high society will be making an appearance."

"So? Who cares who will be there?" he asks playfully, pushing me flat on the bed to be on top.

"I care," I exclaim, playing with my tongue ring nervously.

"You're going to have to do better than that, brat," he taunts, crawling down to one breast and giving my sensitive nipple a little tug with his teeth.

I pull his head up with both hands, unwilling to be distracted by his sexy ways when this conversation hasn't met its end.

"First of all, won't your parents be pissed that I'm crashing their party?"

Finn lets out a little chuckle that, I swear, never fails to annoy the hell out of me just as much as it warms my insides. Or maybe it's because the sound leaves me a gooey mush, that it irritates me so.

"You won't be crashing. You'll be my date. A guy can bring his girlfriend to his parents' party, can't he?"

I try not to give too much thought to how easily pretty boy just latched the 'girlfriend' title on me, especially when there is a bigger issue at hand.

"Finn, I'm serious. Don't you think they'll be just a little bit upset you're bringing me?" I insist cautiously, leaving out the fact that his parents may not be thrilled with the idea of him showing up with a Southie on his arm.

"I don't see why."

"Really? You don't see any problem at all? They don't even know who I am, Finn."

"So? What better way for them to get to know you. You'll come and dazzle them with your sassy ass. Besides, my mom is on pins and needles waiting to meet you." He chuckles, kissing the inside of both my wrists.

"She is?"

"Yep," he explains excitedly. "But I didn't invite you for her benefit. It's time I show off my girl to my friends and family," he coos, slowly slithering his body down mine so his mouth can once again latch onto my nipple. "And anyway, I met your mom, and I didn't feel all this resistance when you brought me home."

"That was different."

"I don't see how," he counters, looking up at me with a new frown edged on his lips. "Why are you fighting this so hard, Stone? What's the real reason why you don't want to come?"

I maul my lower lip and look up at the ceiling instead of his stellar, baby-blue eyes. They always seem to stare right into my soul, trying their damnedest to disarm me of every weapon I might have against them. Thankfully, my cautious heart always keeps some ammunition stored away, precisely for protecting myself from situations like these.

I let out a long exhale, turning my gaze back to him, knowing I'm about to cause some serious damage to his fragile heart.

"I don't think it's time to meet the family, that's all. Or your friends."

He gives a stiff nod, instant sadness coating every feature of his beautiful face.

"Message received," he quips back harshly.

He pulls his hard body off mine and gets out of the bed in one quick jump. Taking just a few seconds to search for his clothes, he grabs them from the floor and begins to get dressed.

"You're angry," I utter, sitting upright on the bed and leaning against the headboard.

I pull the sheets to cover my naked form as I watch him pull up his sweat pants and yank his T-shirt over his head in record time.

"I'm not angry, Stone. I'm disappointed. There's a difference," he snaps back, looking for his sneakers.

"It kind of looks the same from where I'm sitting."

He lets out another scoff, and my chest begins to feel heavy with his reaction to my unwillingness to go to a stupid party.

"Where are you going? It's not even daylight yet."

"Didn't you say you didn't want to be caught with a boy in your room? Now is the perfect time for me to leave. Besides, I can't be here right now."

"You mean you can't be here with me," I quip back, getting pissed at his little tantrum.

He throws his hands in the air and looks over at me, his soft, blue eyes now holding a harsher shade.

"You're right, I can't. Because if I stay in this room, I'll just end up making love to you again. And honestly, I want more from you, Stone. I want to feel like I'm not just another notch on your bedpost, and that you actually give a shit about me."

"You're being ridiculous and a bit of a drama queen. You know you mean more to me than just a quick fuck, Finn."

"Oh, do I? Tell me, how am I supposed to know that? Tell me, how I'm supposed to believe you care for me at all? It's like I push us to take one step forward in our relationship, only for you to pull us two steps back. And maybe that's exactly how you want it," he croaks, looking lost and confused, making my own eyes begin to burn, witnessing how he's hurting.

"Finn," I choke out, my heart not able to keep up with all these new feelings bombarding me so mercilessly.

I watch him shake his head, finally locating his Jordans, so he puts them on. Completely dressed now, Finn picks up his book bag and walks toward the door, stopping in front of it, but never once turning back to look at me.

"Figure out what you want, Stone. When you do, come and find me," he utters. But before he has time to leave me to my sorrow, I jump out of bed and latch onto his back, holding him as if my life depended on it.

"Don't go," I rasp in panic. "Just don't."

He bows his head, and I feel his body trembling as hard as my own.

"I don't know how to do this, Stone."

"I don't either," I admit.

He turns around in my arms, holding my naked body tightly with his clothed one, his face lost inside the crook of my neck.

"Why does this have to be so hard?"

"I don't know," I hush, holding onto his rigid frame, praying I can say something, *anything*, to make him stay.

I wasn't lying yesterday when I told Finn how much I missed him this past week. Somehow, without my consent or approval, he weaved his way into my heart and just won't let go. Like the North Carolina sun on my face, I've come to be dependent on his presence. Crave it even.

The mere idea of him leaving while hurting is excruciating to me, only proving his theory right—we are both well past playing games, but somehow stumbled into the biggest one there is. We've fallen for each other, and I'm not sure either of us is equipped to deal with the rules that love has set out for us.

"Finn," I stutter, the words burning inside my throat, demanding to see the light of day.

"Yeah?" he asks, breathing me in.

"Are we in love?"

He lets out another deep exhale and pulls his head back, allowing me to get lost in his sky blue eyes once again.

"I know I am. I'm just not sure you are, Stone. And it's fucking killing me," he confesses, his eyes crinkling at the sides so that I don't see them start to water.

I take his head into my open palms, softly cradling his cheeks.

"I've never been in love."

"I know," he replies, his eyes dropping to the floor in disappointment.

"I don't know if I'll be any good at it, either."

He lets out another long exhale, his eyes still not able to look directly at mine.

"I'll go to the party, Finn. If it's that important to you, I'll go."

"No, it's okay. If you're not ready for it, then I just have to give you time," he replies in defeat.

"I want to go. I want to meet your family and your friends," I state assertively, tightening my grip on his face.

"Why?"

"Because they're important to you, and you are important to me," I admit with such certainty that his somber features begin to soften if only just a little bit.

"Okay." He nods, but I still feel him miles away.

Damn it all to hell!

Why can't I say it?

Why can't I tell him I'm in love with him, too? Because I am. As much as it frightens me, I know that this gut-wrenching feeling can only spring from falling in love. So why can't I just give him what he so desperately wants? Why?

Because the minute I do, he'll have all the power, that's why.

I won't be in control anymore, and that means he'll be able to hurt me more than anyone ever has. I might act brave and courageous, but when it comes to my heart, I'm a coward, and I know it. I've seen what love can do. How it can break a person and leave them in ragged fragments that no glue could ever repair. Love is a deadly virus that kills the best of us, destroys our dreams and our inspirations if we let it. It's a gun aimed at our chests, and we're the ones with the itchy trigger finger. Love is a game of Russian roulette, and I, for one, never thought I'd be pulled into play.

That is until Finn Walker showed up at Big Jim's that night, with bedroom eyes and a crass tongue, making it impossible not to fall like a ton of bricks.

He deserves better, and when he realizes it, he'll end up leaving, and I'll be a shattered mess. I can't let that happen. As much as his pain is drowning me in my own, admitting he has my heart will be the real beginning of my demise.

It's better to cause pain than feel it.

Maybe the kindest thing would be to end this now. It would be a less cruel alternative, but my selfish heart won't let go of him. Not when I just found him. One day he'll leave, either by his own volition or by me doing the pushing for him.

All I can do now is enjoy the time we have together, because the minute he admitted he loved me, he switched on the timer. The countdown has begun and who knows what time is left in store for us.

A week? A month? A year?

Whatever we get, it will never be enough. All I can do is make the precious time we do have, count. Even if that means attending a fancy soiree on the north end of town with all of Asheville's elite.

I'm pacing back and forth on the paved sidewalk, aggravated I let Finn have his way yet again, and convince me to go shopping after class. I only caved because, if I'm supposed to go to this damn party, the least I can do is look semi-presentable. Like hell I'll let those entitled Northside pricks make Finn embarrassed for having me at his side. I couldn't give two shits about any of them, but I won't make tomorrow night any harder on Finn than it needs to be.

I look at my phone again and realize that he's late by fifteen minutes. Very unlike him since Finn usually shows up well before the agreed time. He's always so eager to spend time with me. I'm about to text him, but a soft poke on my shoulder interrupts me. When I spin around, I come face to face with one of Northside's finest and Asheville's most prized debutant—Kennedy Ryland.

"You're Stone, right? Stone Bennett?" she asks with a wide, old-Hollywood smile.

Kennedy's long, light-blonde curls cascade down her slim shoulders, accentuating her heart-shaped face. All of her screams out privilege and grace—two things I have none of.

"I am," I reply, cocking my brow up as to why she, of all people, is suddenly talking to me.

Her smile widens even more as she looks me up and down appreciatively, not even being discreet about it, either.

"Hi, I'm Kennedy," she introduces herself, her hand reaching out to me.

As if I needed an introduction on who Montgomery Ryland's only daughter is. I think everyone at Richfield knows the dean's children.

"I know who you are," I quip back, crossing my arms over my chest, looking every which way around the street instead of giving her the time of day.

However, from my peripheral, I can see that not even my cold greeting has her bright smile wavering in the slightest, which gives Kennedy a Stepford-wives aura about her.

I heard the Ryland twins were sharp as tacks, but maybe her twin, Jefferson, got more in the brains department than her. So far, Kennedy hasn't been able to sense my not-so-subtle cues that I'm not interested in idle chit-chat with a total stranger off the street. This leads me to believe that maybe the rumors of the twins' stellar intelligence are completely unfounded or, more likely, fabricated by their father. We can't have people believing that the dean of a prestigious university, such as Richfield, has kids that are total duds, now can we?

"Finn said you were a knockout. He also said you were naturally suspicious. I really can't blame you for that. I would be, too, if I were in your shoes." She winks at me.

"You know Finn?" I ask, my arms dislodging themselves from their guarded pose with the mere mention of pretty boy's name.

"All my life. We grew up together, and I have to say, I never thought I'd see that boy be so enamored with someone. Now that I've met you, I can see why he's fallen so hard."

I try to keep my blush at bay, but the little smirk she throws at me tells me I'm doing a terrible job at it.

"I was waiting for him, actually," I state, completely deflecting her comment about how Finn feels about me, but her eyes continue to twinkle in approval as if I just confessed to something.

"Actually, you're here to meet *me*, not Finn. Consider me as your own personal shopper for the day. We're going to pick something that will leave Finn even more of a drooling fool than you've already made him," she teases, opening the door to the fancy shop and ushering me in.

Hesitantly, I step inside the extravagant boutique, instantly noting how the store clerks bombard Kennedy even before she's made her way inside. I also don't miss how the same eager clerks look at me sideways but keep their plastic smiles on their faces while Kennedy tells them what she's looking for. As they leave to retrieve the items, Kennedy pulls me to her side, her arms latched onto mine as if she has known me her whole life. My knee-jerk reaction is to pull away, considering we just met five minutes ago, but blondie has one mighty grip that keeps me locked to her side.

"I'm going to make a little confession here," she begins to susurrate in my ear, my hackles rising in preparation for whatever she's going to lay on me.

She begins to giggle, her head falling all the way back, the sound of her laughter not as annoying as I would have expected. A remarkable feat since this whole situation is irritating the fuck out of me. I make a mental note to castrate Finn when I see him. Okay, maybe not snip his junk since I've got good use for it, but definitely a good tongue lashing.

"Don't look so worried, Stone. I'm not going to tell you I'm after your man or anything." She continues to laugh, pulling me toward the dressing rooms where two clerks are already standing with various dresses in their hands.

"I just wanted to thank you," she adds, her genuine tone taking me even more off-guard.

"Thank me? For what?"

"Isn't it obvious? For Finn," she beams, but the confused scowl on my face hints that she'll have to clarify her statement. "Okay, so you might not know this, but our little group has gone through some hurdles these past few months. Not all of us are dealing with it so well. I guess I'm just glad that Finn, at least, has been able to find happiness throughout all the chaos. One of us deserves some joy in their lives."

Kennedy's blue eyes darken with the same sadness her words are tainted with.

"What type of hurdles?" I question, my curiosity piquing at the details of Finn's life that I'm not aware of.

"One of our best friends tragically lost both of his parents earlier this year, and we haven't quite moved on from the shock. When one of us hurts, all of us feel the pinch," she explains.

"The Hamilton murders? I read about it in the paper. I didn't realize Finn was so close to Asheville's founding family," I murmur.

No wonder he was so insistent about me attending his parents' party tomorrow. It's pretty boy's desperate attempt to merge his two worlds together. I just wish this union was going to happen on my turf rather than his.

"Yes. Our families are very close. Lincoln is like a brother to Finn. I'm surprised he hasn't talked about him," she states, her brows deepening in disappointment.

"Finn talks about his friends all the time. It hasn't been a huge topic of discussion, though. The murders, I mean."

"Right. Of course not. I mean, who wants to talk about such depressing issues when you can spend time making out, right?" she teases, nudging my shoulder, trying to lighten up the mood.

"Right," I grumble, uncomfortable with the discussion of my sex life with a total stranger, no matter how good of a friend she might be to Finn.

"Are you happy?" she asks all of a sudden, halting our step inside the vast dressing room, her eyes drilling holes into my head.

"What do you mean?"

"I mean, I know Finn is happy. That *you* are making him happy. But is he doing the same for you?" she continues to interrogate me.

I unlatch her arm from mine and face her head-on, wanting to make it completely clear to her that we are definitely not going to have a heart-to-heart. We're not BFFs, and this isn't some teenage rom-com where we are about to do a montage of the popular girl giving the town's reject a makeover to impress the jock.

Fuck that!

Kennedy turns around and closes the door, asking the clerks to give us some privacy so that I can try on the first dress. However, when she turns my way again, the look on her face is dead-serious.

"So? Is he?"

"I don't see why my happiness is any of your business."

The minute the words fall from my lips, a predatory, feline gaze begins to simmer in her eyes, and a sick sense of déjà vu slaps me across the face—I've seen this same vulturous look somewhere before, and it had left me just as unnerved then as I am now.

What the hell is going on?

Have I met Kennedy before today? I mean, I could have. We are attending the same university, so I'm sure I've bumped into her before.

But that stare.

The unsettling prick on the nape of my neck is somehow familiar to me. It's reminiscent of something that, for the life of me, I can't recall. Or maybe I don't want to.

I school my face as best I can, trying to look unaffected, so the Barbie doesn't realize she's getting to me. But instead of toning down her nefarious gaze, she just amplifies it, twisting her stunning features into something lethal. So much so, I take a step back from her to gain enough room in case I need to throw a bitch down.

"I know coming into our world may be a little overwhelming for you, so I understand you putting up your defenses. Finn, however, is a typical guy. I doubt he has a total grasp on what a big deal it is bringing you as a date to his father's birthday party. But you and I aren't that clueless, are we?" I roll my tongue over my teeth, her domineering gaze never faltering as she continues with her rant, "By him bringing you along, he's telling all of Asheville that you are the woman he wants to be with. All I'm asking is are you ready for such a commitment? Because, honey, I have to be honest with you. If you do this, you can't be of two minds about it. You're either all in, or not. And if you're not, maybe you should reconsider your choices."

"Tell me something, Kennedy. Did Finn ask you to help me pick out a dress this afternoon, or did you offer to do it?" I ask suspiciously, thinking this chick has an agenda all of her own.

"I offered, of course." The corner of her lip tugs into a mischievous smile.

"And did you do that because you like shopping so much, or because you wanted to size me up? Or perhaps you wanted to tell me where my place is at?" I ask her, point-blank.

Her snicker becomes a full-blown, carefree laugh once again, the devious glare no longer governing her face.

"He said you were super smart, too. I'm glad to see he wasn't just blowing smoke," she replies with a giggle, not denying my suspicions.

"So that's it. You wanted to check me out and see if I'm good enough for your little group," I sneer, pissed as hell that this debutant wanted to vet me for their rich club.

Her former grin dissipates from her face, making the serious glower that was previously embedded in her eyes return at full force.

"Not at all. I just wanted to make sure Finn is giving his heart to someone who deserves it. Yes, his family and friends will be in your life, but I'm not worried about them. You can take us or leave us. That will be your prerogative. I just want to be certain, if push comes to shove and we're too much for you, will you break my friend's heart? Finn may have the strength of a giant, but he's frail and sensitive. I don't want some girl to take advantage of that, no matter who she is."

"I thought you said you weren't after my man? It sounds to me like maybe you are. If that's the case, then you're in for a rude awakening. Finn isn't yours to stake claim to. He's mine," I growl with more confidence than I actually have.

In reality, my heart is shriveling up inside, thinking of Kennedy Ryland as my rival for Finn's love. If that's the case, then how the fuck can I keep him? I couldn't compete, and she knows it. Being born and bred in the wrong part of town will make it difficult for most people in Finn's life to accept me as his girlfriend. Which means our relationship is already set up to fail. Add Kennedy to the mix, as the girl gunning for his affections, then I might as well give up now.

Too bad for her, I'm not a quitter.

I'm a fighter.

Always have been. Always will be.

Sure, Kennedy might have turned the tables on me for a second, but like hell will I let her back me into a corner and try to take what's mine. I'm not giving up pretty boy so easily. Not without one hell of a fight, anyway.

My hands are already curled up in fists, imagining how I'm going to claw her pretty eyes out if she says one more thing that pisses me off, when I realize that the intimidating, no-nonsense Barbie is nowhere in sight.

Nothing about the Kennedy that is standing in my presence now is threatening. Actually, she kind of looks like someone just took her inheritance away and told her she will have to work at a fast-food joint in my neck of the woods to make ends meet.

"Yes, I love Finn, but like a brother. Nothing more. That torment lies with someone else, unfortunately," she confesses, her blue eyes taking a somber shade.

"That bad, huh?" I retort, taking stock of how defeated she looks.

"The worst," she half-chuckles, half-laments, rubbing the engagement ring on her finger.

"Let me guess. He's not the same guy who gave you that rock, is he?"

"Like Finn said, beautiful and smart. I think I'm going to like you in our little group."

"It didn't sound that way a minute ago."

"What can I say?" She unapologetically shrugs with a wide grin to her lips. "I believe that someone will only show their true nature when they are put under pressure. I just had to make sure Finn wasn't getting conned by you."

"He's not," I bite back.

"Oh, I know," she beams. "It's written all over your face how you love him just as much as he loves you." She snickers amused.

"I didn't say that."

"You didn't have to. You were about two seconds away from punching my teeth in."

"I still might," I grunt.

She continues to giggle as she opens the dressing-room door to grab the dresses from one of the clerk's hands, who apparently had nothing better to do than stand post outside until Kennedy made her next request.

Rich people. I don't think I'll ever understand them.

Well, maybe I'm starting to understand a little bit of Kennedy, at least. If she went through all this trouble just to make sure Finn's feelings were protected, then I guess she can't be all bad. Not many people would have put in the effort or the time to look out for a friend. Sure, she's still a

Northsider, but then again, so is Finn—the sweetest, most intense man I know.

Maybe that's just how they are bred on the Northside—sweet as apple pie one minute, and put the fear of God in you the next. Who fucking knows? There's only one of them I care about anyway. I won't waste my time on the others.

"Try this dark-red one. I think it will bring out your best features," Kennedy singsongs, shoving a silk dress up against my breasts.

"My boobs?" I joke, relaxing a little.

"No, your eyes. It's one of the things your boy gushed over the most."

I laugh at the idea of Finn gushing while I put the dress on. The minute the silky fabric touches my skin, it's hard not to stand straight facing the mirror to admire it.

"Wow. I think we found a winner on the first try," Kennedy exclaims excitedly, her eyes trailing all over my body.

"Yeah? Do you think Finn will like it?"

"I think after he's lifted his chin off the floor, he will love it."

"So my eyes pop in this, is that what you're saying?"

"Honey, everything pops! You have killer curves, and that dress is shouting them all out. If I didn't have my boy troubles, you might get me batting for the other team," she goads, and I can't help but laugh at that.

Who would have guessed that the dean's daughter was such a flirt?

I let my eyes focus on the mirror's reflection one more time and tell her, "This isn't me, you know?"

"Looks like it is to me."

"But it's not. It's just a fancy dress on a girl from the wrong side of the tracks."

"Does that even matter? Who cares where you were born. It's the destination ahead of you that counts."

"Is it? Sometimes I feel like I'll never outrun where I came from," I mutter, looking at the lie reflecting in front of me.

Kennedy comes up behind me, placing her chin on my shoulder like a long lost friend would. My eyes fix on hers, and I see genuine understanding in them.

"We're all trying to run from our past, Stone. Finn included. The only thing we can do is make sure the place we are running to is better than the one we left. Do you understand?"

I give her a tight nod, perfectly understanding what she is trying to tell me. It doesn't matter if you're born dirt poor or filthy rich. That shouldn't define us. Only the choices we make in life should.

And it dawns on me that I've already made my choice.

I choose Finn, just as he has chosen me.

CHAPTER 22

FINN

I should have gone to her dorm and picked her up.

Why did I have to listen to Stone and agree to let her come in a damn Uber all the way from campus? If I hadn't caved to her demands, then she would be wrapped around my arm this very minute. Instead, I have to wait anxiously for her arrival, making each second without her presence more excruciating than the last.

"Are you really going to have that ugly-ass scowl stitched on your face the whole night? Because I have to tell you, brother, it's not a pretty look," Easton taunts, taking a full gulp of his champagne.

"Leave him alone, East. Can't you see he's nervous enough?" Kennedy comes to my aid, throwing me a comforting little wink. "She'll be here soon. Don't worry, Finn. Okay?" she adds sweetly, bumping me on the shoulder in an attempt to relax my impatient mind.

I nod, giving her my own thin smile, but deep down, I'm worried as hell.

What if Stone is second-guessing her decision, and has fallen head-first into her doubts? She didn't exactly jump at the chance when I asked her to come. What if this is just too much for her, too soon? What if she doesn't show because of it?

Fuck! I should have picked her up myself. But the brat batted those fucking gorgeous, green eyes at me, and before I knew it, I was buried deep inside her, making my dad's birthday party the last thing on my mind.

"Damn it, Finn. You're going to give yourself a coronary. Your girl will show up eventually. She probably just had some mishap with her dress or her makeup. Girls are frilly like that," Colt chastises, making fun of my pain.

"Not Finn's girl," Kennedy explains boastfully. "She's special. Different."

"Sure, she is. They're *all* special," Colt replies sarcastically, stopping one of the waiters passing by to grab his own champagne flute.

"Jesus, Colt. You are one insufferable bastard when you want to be. Just because you don't know how to treat a woman, doesn't mean Finn hasn't learned how."

"I'm sorry, are we in an upside-down world all of a sudden?" Colt says after he's gathered his wits about him, almost having to spit out his first sip of champagne because of Kennedy's remark. "I treat the ladies just fine, Ken. They fucking love my ass, and you know it," he adds smugly.

"Oh, dear lord! You're one vain asshole, Colt Turner. Seriously! I don't know why we even put up with you."

"Because life without me would be boring as fuck, Ken." He deviously winks at her, to which Kennedy responds by jerking her hand as if jacking off an invisible dick.

None of us are surprised by her comeback gesture. Sure, the outside world believes Kennedy Ryland to be the very definition of southern propriety, but when she's huddled with us like she is now, her decorum is just as bad and crass as *The Hangover's* Mr. Chow.

"Bite me, Colt."

"No can do, Ken. Don't even offer. Someone called dibs on that years ago, and it wasn't me."

Kennedy's cheeks start to flush, making East and I look at Colt like he's got a death wish or something. I mean, Tommyboy is somewhere in the room, smooching up to his father's constituents. And although Lincoln has been cornered by the current governor on the other side of the room, he wouldn't appreciate his cousin insinuating such things, especially where other people could easily eavesdrop on us.

"And since when has Finn turned into an expert of the female gender?" Colt adds, trying to move past his epic fail and direct everyone's attention back on me. "We all know chicks aren't the big guy's forte. No shame in that, either. We should just stick to what we're good at."

Colt chuckles and slaps his hand on my shoulder, making my frown only deepen with his goading.

"You're wrong. Finn's done just fine by landing himself a hottie with more brains in her pinky than you have in your whole head," Kennedy defends, throwing me a conspiring smile.

I can't help but return the same grin back at her. I knew Stone would capture Kennedy's heart and affection in just one afternoon. And Kennedy, being the great judge of character that she is, probably saw through the whole bravado right into her gooey center.

"She really is incredible, isn't she?" I whisper under my breath.

"Yes, Finn. She is. You did good, honey. She's one in a million."

"I know," I state proudly, my chest puffing out, warmed at the idea of being the lucky bastard who got the Southie's affection.

Stone might not want to love me yet, but I'll wear her down. Once all her defenses have plummeted to the ground, she'll come to understand how her feelings for me aren't just carnal or lustful. They might have started that way, but they grew into something immeasurable from then on. It may take me some time to get her to the same place I'm at, but sooner or later, Stone will just have to face the fact that what we have is bigger than she realizes. And when she does, she'll either be scared as fuck or beyond joyful. With Stone, it could go either way.

"Finn?" Kennedy adds softly beside me, her face looking a bit more serious than a minute ago.

"Yeah?"

"Don't fuck this up. You'll regret it if you do."

"I won't," I promise wholeheartedly, even though there is a nagging feeling in the pit of my stomach telling me otherwise.

"That's good." She grins, her eyes leaving me for a minute. "Especially now that Stone just walked through the door."

Without a second to waste, my eyes are directed at the entrance of the ballroom, taking in the girl who has captured my mind, body, and soul.

I can't picture my life without her anymore.

"Fuck! Is that her?" Colt exclaims as Stone waves over at me.

I must look like a madman with my wide smile, but damn, she looks incredible. In a long, red dress, resembling something you'd see in those old black-and-white movies, she looks like the epitome of grace and sophistication.

"I've never wanted to ignore the bro code so hard until tonight," Colt snickers, making me throw him a sinister growl along with a scathing look to make sure he rethinks his statement.

"Don't be a dick, Colt. Besides, you couldn't handle all of that," Kennedy teases. "Go on, Finn. Go get her."

I don't have to be told twice.

I slice through the crowd, making my way to the wet dream walking toward me in five-inch heels. The minute she's within arm's length, I grab her by the nape of her neck and kiss her. Stone lets out a little whimper and moves her hands to my chest, feeling my erratic heartbeat under her open palms. Since we're in my parents' house with too many people already eyeing us, I try to keep our kiss as PG as possible, but it's an almost impossible effort. I reluctantly pull away, ending our kiss sooner than I'd like, to avoid providing these old farts any more spank bank material. I tug a loose strand of hair back in its place, getting lost in her green meadows.

"Hi," I finally rasp, my voice gravelly and deep, demonstrating my desperation for taking her to a more intimate setting.

"Hi, yourself, pretty boy," she taunts, her sexy-ass smile tugging on her lips.

"That's some dress."

"I'm glad you like it."

"I'm going to like it much more when I rip it off your body later tonight."

She pulls on my chin and shakes her head playfully.

"Don't you dare. It's too pretty to destroy."

"So are you, but it doesn't weaken my desire to ravish and ruin you."

"Aren't you a sweet-talker tonight?" She laughs, making the organ inside my chest rattle its cage, demanding to leap into her arms.

"I'm serious, though. You look beautiful, Stone. But to me, you always do."

"You don't look half-bad yourself," she answers, appreciative of the monkey suit I'm wearing.

The little blush that rises on her cheeks makes it impossible for me not to want to lean down and kiss her again. But this time, I want to do it in a place where I can surrender to it, which is not in the middle of a ballroom full of people. So I grab Stone's hand, pulling her with me in search of a secluded spot to finally greet her the way I wanted to.

"Finn." She giggles. "Where are we going?"

"You'll see," I reply, my feet wanting to rush their way out, but taking great pains to keep a slower pace because of Stone's high heels.

My eyes wander through the house, contemplating the guests. As I foresaw, every inch of this place is filled to the brim. Calling defeat and pulling the most cliché move ever, I take her to the only place that will ensure us some form of privacy.

"You have got to be joking?" she exclaims the minute I lock the bathroom door behind us. "Don't you even think about having sex in here, Finn Walker. I haven't even met your parents yet, for crying out loud. No way will I be known as the girl who locked herself in a bathroom with their son for a quickie before introducing myself to them," she snaps, crossing her arms under her breasts, making those puppies even more mouthwatering.

Fuck, but this dress really is something.

The dark-red silk perfectly hugs all of her curves like a second skin, the backless cut giving a little hint on the sides of the swell of her breasts. Her hair is up to showcase her long neck, just begging for my hands to clasp around it. The whole ensemble could quickly be on the tile floor with just a tug of the bow at the back of her neck. I'm positive I won't be able to think of doing anything else for the whole night.

"We've fucked in worse places, Stone," I tease, licking my lips as my eyes continue to travel up and down her body.

"That was different," she bites back, unamused.

"Why?"

"Because," she mumbles out in exasperation, walking backward as I keep my predatory gaze on her.

"Because why?"

She squints her eyes at me, her anger starting to shine, and her little fist getting ready to do some damage.

Shit.

Abort! Abort!

This is not how I wanted to start this night out.

"Stone, I'm kidding. I'm not going to fuck you the minute you waltz through my front door. I do have some restraint, you know? This dress really isn't making it easy on me, but I'm not a total caveman. I brought you here because I wanted to talk to you in private before everyone else wants a piece of you. That's all."

She bows her head toward the floor, which hurts my heart just by looking at her.

"Hey. I swear, I just wanted to talk," I vow, caressing her cheek with my hand.

"Then talk," she quips back, still pissed and not entirely convinced of my motives.

"Okay, maybe not talk, but more like I wanted to give you something," I stutter, my nerves starting to make an appearance.

"If the next words out of your mouth are about your cock, I swear to Almighty God I'll bite the thing off." She snarls, and I can't help but chuckle as the jitters of my initial intention evaporate completely.

"No, you wouldn't. You need it just as much as I do. But rest assured, this isn't dick-related."

"Hmm," she mumbles suspiciously with her defined eyebrow still up in the air.

I swallow dryly, pulling out a velvet box from inside my tuxedo pocket and placing it in her palms.

"What's this?" she asks, looking at the small box in her hands as if it were a foreign object to her.

"Open it and find out."

Stone hesitates for a moment but then gives in to her curiosity. When she opens the lid and sees the two diamond-studded earrings inside, all she can do is stare with her mouth agape.

While she and Kennedy went on their little shopping spree yesterday afternoon, I went on one of my own. The minute I saw them at the jewelers, I knew they could only belong to my girl. Just like Stone, they are beautifully breathtaking in their loud savagery and compact size.

"Finn," she begins to hush.

"Do you like them?"

"Of course, I do. They're magnificent. But I can't accept this," she laments, placing the box on the vanity sink. "I already accepted the dress you bought me, so I can't accept this. It's just too much."

I bridge the gap between us and raise her chin with my knuckles.

"No, it's not. Nothing is too much for you. These are just rocks that turned into something beautiful under extreme pressure, just like you. You thrive, even when the world is set against you. I think they suit you perfectly. Do this for me, please. Keep them. You don't have to wear them if you don't want to, but I would really love it if you did."

"Why?" she probes, her brows pinched together in both suspicion and curiosity.

"Because I want to know that every time you look in the mirror, you'll see a little bit of me there too," I admit shyly, feeling my face warm at the confession.

"I see you just fine, Finn. I see you even when my eyes are closed," she admits softly, grasping the hand under her chin and placing a tender kiss onto my open palm.

"You do?" I stutter, my foolish heart doing laps all around my chest.

"Yes, you fool. I do." She laughs. "I'll wear them tonight if it's so important to you."

"The only thing important to me is you."

A small blush colors her cheeks, and it takes everything in me not to grab her and kiss her how I want. Stone grabs the velvet box again and places it in my hands.

"Put them on me, will you? You look like you need the distraction," she jokes, tilting her head down at my swollen cock.

I shift the fucker to the side, to which he only complains. He wants to play while there are over five hundred guests prowling just on the other side of this door. My mind might tell me that a quickie right now is not very prudent, but my cock is not on the same page.

I carefully take the earrings out of the box and place one in each of her lobes. Thankfully, tonight Stone decided to have them free of all the usual hardware. Even the piercing on her brow is a no show.

A sudden frown crests its way onto my lips, and sensing my discomfort, she questions, "What's wrong?"

"You know you don't have to change a thing for me, right? I'd never ask you to do that."

"Jesus, quarterback, what's going on inside that chaotic mind of yours now?" She chuckles, pretending to knock on the side of my head.

"You look beautiful tonight, Stone. You do, but I don't want you to think that this version of you is what I want. The real Stone Bennett is just perfect the way she is."

She rolls her eyes and turns around to look at herself in the mirror, the sparkle in her emeralds even more breathtaking than the diamonds on her ears.

"It's just a dress, pretty boy. I am the same girl, regardless of what I'm wearing. Don't get your panties in a bunch."

"Always the brat," I joke, feeling myself relax.

I stand behind her and hold my arms around her waist, admiring the reflection in the mirror while she appreciates her gift. As I look at both of us, one thing is very clear to me— we are nothing but two opposites of the same coin. As unlikely a pair as we might be, somehow, we still fit perfectly.

I lean in closer to plant a kiss on her neck, the scent of her perfume wreaking havoc on my senses. The minute my lips touch her skin, goosebumps runs all throughout her shoulders. With one hand placed softly on her stomach and the other slowly grabbing one ass cheek, my swollen cock begins to make its presence known, acknowledging the cruelty for tempting his strained composure.

"I know that look, pretty boy. Don't you fucking dare," Stone threatens at my reflection, the very one who can't take its eyes off her.

"I'm not going to fuck you," I rasp, rubbing my hard length through the small crack of her butt cheeks.

"I hear the words, but your body is telling me something entirely different," she whispers, and the damn Southie bends slightly over the sink, pressing her ass harder on my dick, just to aggravate me further.

"Judging by your body's reaction, I can't say yours isn't having a similar conversation with mine."

"My coochie is a total slut when it comes to you, pretty boy. You should know that by now," she purrs, her eyes already at half-mast, her arm coming behind my head to encourage the soft peppering kisses on her neck.

"Is she now? Is your pussy already drenched for me, Stone?"

"Only one way for you to find out," she taunts, throwing me a mischievous wink.

"I thought you said that fucking in the bathroom was off the table?"

"It is, but that doesn't mean I can't tease you." She lets out a soft giggle.

"Brat," I growl, slapping one tempting ass cheek, and spin her around so fast that she slams into my chest. "You're going to pay for that later."

"Then you're in luck, pretty boy, because I always pay my debts," she quips back, cupping my hard junk in her soft hands.

"I'm going to kiss you now, Stone. Just a kiss, and then I want to introduce you to my family and friends. After that shit's done, this ass is mine," I vow, grabbing her ass cheeks in both palms, making her ample breasts rub against my chest.

"We'll see." She smirks before going on her tiptoes and latching her arms around my neck, only to deliver a kiss that has both our asses staying locked in this little cocoon of ours for the next ten minutes.

If I had it my way, we'd never leave.

CHAPTER 23

FINN

"Mom, this is my girlfriend, Stone Bennett. Stone, this is my mother, Charlene Walker," I introduce them proudly, my grin spread wide at both.

"How do you do, Mrs. Walker?" Stone adds confidently, extending her hand to my mother.

Mom's eyes sparkle as she takes stock of the fearless brat at my side, and when she smiles approvingly, I can't help the swell of happiness in my chest growing larger.

"Now, young girl, no need for such ceremony here," my mother singsongs, wrapping Stone in her arms.

I fake a cough, trying to keep my chuckling at bay as my mom holds Stone just a little bit tighter than expected. She throws me a 'help me out here' stare, uncomfortable with such familiar affection.

Thankfully, Mom releases Stone from her death grip and pulls away, but only enough to continue taking inventory of Stone's every feature.

"Finn didn't tell me how beautiful you were. Not that I'm surprised. My son has always had impeccable taste. However, I do wish he wasn't so secretive. I feel like I know so very little about you."

Stone keeps her facial features as placid as she can, but I know that, underneath the cool exterior, she's uncomfortable as hell with my mom's prying eye.

"You'll have plenty of time to get to know each other, Mom."

"Will I? Does this mean you'll bring Stone to our next Sunday dinner?" my mom asks hopefully, her blue eyes widening on her face.

Before I'm able to say anything, Stone interjects, "Unfortunately, I work on Sunday nights."

"Really? Where?"

"Big Jim's. The biker bar on the Southside," she explains without batting an eye.

If I didn't know any better, I'd think Stone dropped that little nugget of information just to see my mother's reaction. Hell, who am I kidding? I'm positive she did it to test the woman.

But Stone doesn't know my mother. It's very difficult to stun Charlene Walker with anything. The woman grew up in the seventies and has raised three sons, for fuck's sake. She's seen it all by now. The small, infectious grin on my mother's lips, added with the twinkling in her eyes while patting Stone's hand in hers, says as much.

"Well then, we will just have to do a family brunch instead. I want to get to know the girl who has my Finn so infatuated."

Stone just nods, discreetly releasing her hand from my mother's grip to grab onto mine.

I give her hand a little squeeze, silently telling her there is no need to be nervous. But when my mom suddenly calls for my dad to come over to meet Stone, I become just as agitated. With each step he takes in our direction, my apprehension increases. I know that disapproving glower. It's the same one he uses when my throw isn't on target, or if I take a sack. It's the one that tells me that nothing from this encounter will please him. Not by a long shot.

"Hank, dear. This is Stone Bennett, Finn's girlfriend. Isn't she lovely?"

"Quite," he mumbles as he gives Stone a quick scan, looking over my mother's shoulder once he's finished.

"I was just talking about how we should have Stone over for dinner or brunch one Sunday."

"If you think that's necessary," he replies with no emotion whatsoever in his tone, while scanning the room for better company, obviously bored with this encounter.

"Hank," my mother begins to say with a reprimanding stare for his rudeness, but my father pays her no mind.

"Excuse me, but I need to go have a word with Owen Turner about his beloved Redskins. Fool is in for one hell of an uphill battle with his team this season," my father gloats and waltzes off.

He doesn't even have the decency to give Stone more than a moment's thought, preferring to just give Colt's father a hard time about his team's performance.

"I'm sorry about my father, Stone. Only football can grab his attention."

She shrugs not one bit affected by his callous ways.

"No worries. Maybe next time I'll wear a dress made of pigskin to get his attention."

"Beautiful and funny. I'm going to like you," my mother says with a laugh.

"Don't forget smart. Stone here is going to change our judicial system into something that is fair for all. Not just for the rich and powerful."

"Is that so?" my mother questions with a more serious tone.

"Yes, Ma'am. At least I'll strive to do my best."

"I'd love to hear more about what you aim to accomplish, dear. Maybe the two of us could have tea one of these days, and you can tell me all about your future aspirations," my mother adds, but her enquiring, somber tone confuses me a bit.

I need to move this conversation along, not really thrilled by my mom wanting a one-on-one with Stone, especially because she's a definite flight risk if our relationship gets too real for her. But before I can move to a safer topic, someone insistently pulls at my arm, ordering me to turn around.

"About fucking time! I've been looking all over for you," East interrupts sternly, completely oblivious to the fact this is Stone's first meeting with my mom.

"Kind of busy here, East," I reply through gritted teeth, trying to shake his hold on my arm.

"Sorry, this can't wait. Hey, Mrs. W. How you doing, Stone? Sorry but I gotta steal Finn away from you for just a couple of minutes."

"Is everything alright?" Mom questions with concern while Stone just gives Easton her evil eye.

What's that all about?

"Everything is fine, Mrs. W. Just saw Colt go upstairs with Betty Lee, Ma'am. I'm not sure the sheriff will appreciate Colt giving his lovely young bride a private tour of the house."

"Oh, for crying out loud. Can't that boy keep it in his pants for just one night?" my mother whisper-yells in aggravation. "You boys do damage control before that fool ruins my whole party. Scoot! Go on, now!" my mother insists, but my feet are still frozen to the floor, not ready to leave Stone alone with my mother just yet.

"Come on, asshole. You heard, your ma," East growls at me, pulling on my arm again, but I still don't move an inch.

"You'll be alright on your own for a few minutes, brat?"

"I'll be fine, pretty boy. Go on before someone gets shot." She snickers.

"Remind me never to introduce you to Colt," I kid lightheartedly, bending down to give her a quick peck on the cheek.

"Jesus, Romeo. Get on with it," East hollers, pulling my lips away from hers.

"You're a real jerk, you know that, East?"

"Yeah, yeah, yeah. Tell me something I don't know, sweetheart," he snaps back at Stone, succeeding in pulling me away from her once and for all.

"What the fuck was that about," I bark at him.

"I'll explain later. We got bigger shit to worry about."

Not from where I'm standing. I couldn't give two flying fucks who Colt sticks his dick into. Serves him right if he got a beat down from the sheriff for messing with his woman. Although, if she were mine, I'd send her packing just as fast as I'd rearrange Colt's handsome face.

A woman who is so easily seduced, means she wasn't his to begin with. A wedding ring means fucking nothing if the heart is that fickle. Even though Stone might not be one hundred percent in love with me, I know for a fact she would never two-time me. My girl has more integrity and dignity than most of these southern belles profess to have.

As we both rush out of the room, my attention is grabbed by Kennedy's blonde curls as she stands near one of the floor-to-ceiling windows. I sway off course for a second to make sure that Stone is ok in my absence.

"Ken, do me a solid. I left Stone with my mom. Rescue her for me, will you?"

"On it," Kennedy replies steadfastly, already heading toward the two women on the other side of the room.

Knowing Stone is in good hands, I run after East, who is dashing madly up the foyer to the second floor.

"You're making a mountain out of a molehill, East. Colt knows how to cover his ass. I'm sure Sheriff Travis is already falling down drunk on compliments and champagne, none the wiser to his wife's infidelities."

But instead of Easton slowing his step, he continues to haul ass as if someone set fire on his butt.

"East!"

"East!"

He doesn't waver and only stops when he's reached my bedroom door.

"That fucker better not be screwing on my bed!" I growl, pushing East away from the door, ready to kick Colt's ass.

But when I get inside my room, there is no live-action porn happening on my duvet. I let out a long, relieved breath, only to hear hushed voices coming out of the bathroom. I walk over to it with Easton on my heel, and when I open the door, Lincoln and a half-dressed Colt are staring at my mirror with worried faces.

I walk in closer, my feet suddenly sluggish, and when I lock eyes on the message written in black ink on the vanity mirror, my heart stops.

We warned you.

All four of us stare at those horrific words like a bad omen of what's about to come.

"They're getting more restless," Lincoln states gravely.

"You mean, dangerous," Easton interjects behind me. "Did anyone besides us see this shit?"

Colt shakes his head profusely, tucking his white collared shirt back into his tuxedo pants.

"No. I came into the bathroom to get a condom when I stumbled on it. I sent Betty packing after that, but I don't think she caught my sudden mood swing. Just gave her the runaround that there were too many people in the house, so I think she bought it."

I'm too fucked in the head to even give Colt a hard time for wanting to screw the sheriff's wife in my room.

"There has to be a reason why they have upped the ante. Why would they leave such a message for anyone to see?" Lincoln continues, trying to decipher The Society's inner workings.

"All I know is they're here, probably mingling with the guests downstairs as we speak. Who knows what they'll do next?!" East hollers, throwing his arms behind his head, grabbing at the short ends of his hair in frustration.

"Settle the fuck down, East. We don't know if they're downstairs or not. They could have just easily slipped in and out, leaving this little threat without being noticed."

East shakes his head, unconvinced with Lincoln's explanation, and retorts, "These assholes are a big deal. You said so yourself, Lincoln. They are the elite of the fucking elite. Of course those fuckers are downstairs. Probably gorging on caviar and champagne, laughing themselves into a frenzy about how they've got us over a barrel."

"Just give me a minute, East, before you do something stupid like go downstairs searching for the boogieman. They have been cautious up until now. They value discretion, so what changed?"

"Not when it came to Finn's car. When they painted it with pig's blood, right in the middle of our school's parking lot, they didn't seem to be worried about discretion."

"True," Lincoln agrees, rubbing his chin in thought. "They did go off the rails there, too. There has to be a connection, though. Why were those two messages so in your face, while the other three were discreet?"

My stomach starts to twist and turn, making me nauseous.

Fuck.

I know exactly why these fuckers went all DEFCON five on us.

"I know what the connection is," I huff out, returning to my room, immediately sitting on the edge of my bed to keep my bearings.

"What is it, Finn?" Lincoln questions, taking a seat next to me on the bed.

I struggle to get the words out as Lincoln patiently waits for a reply.

"I fucked up," I tell him truthfully. "I did this. It's because of me they went all psycho on us."

"The fuck did you do, Walker?!" Colt barks, towering over me.

Lincoln gives him such a scathing glare that it's enough to shut him up, making him take a few steps back away from me.

"When they fucked my Porsche, I wasn't exactly making progress with Stone. They must be following me or some shit because they know my every move. When they saw I wasn't making any leeway, they got creative to persuade me into getting my shit together."

"Okay, but that was weeks ago. Since you started spending time with Stone, we haven't heard from them," East interjects, his face pinched with confusion.

"Yeah, we have. I just didn't tell you guys. Last week, I received a package from them. It was a small box with a brand-new phone and one of their letters inside. They said I only had to replace Stone's phone with theirs, and that would be it. If I followed through, it would be my last order."

"And let me guess. You didn't do it?" East laments, running his fingers through his dark hair.

"Did you give her the phone, Finn?" Lincoln repeats, his tone more tolerant.

"I couldn't do it, Linc. I'm sorry."

The little, saddened smile that appears on my best friend's face guts me. That look says it all—I let him down, and yet he doesn't fault me for it.

"Hold up! Hold up! You mean to tell me you are putting all our lives in danger because of pussy?!" Colt belts in outrage, instantly making me jump to my feet, ready to slam my fist in his face.

However, Linc is already on me, putting himself in the line of fire between his cousin and me.

"Don't you ever talk about Stone like that again, asshole, or I swear to God, getting caught will feel like a vacation compared to the pain I'll inflict on you!"

"Colt is not going to say anything like that again, Finn. I promise you," Lincoln says, trying to calm me down. He then looks over to Colt with a death glare in his eyes and demands, "Apologize."

"The fuck? He's the one fucking this whole shit up, and I'm the one who has to apologize to this asshole?"

"Did I fucking stutter, Colt?" Lincoln deadpans. "I won't ask you again. Apologize. Now!" he orders.

Pissed beyond rage, Colt grits out the most pathetic apology known to man, only to appease his cousin. Looking at the way he's contorting his face, I'm pretty sure he never apologized for anything in his life. Like I give a shit. I couldn't give two fucks for his apology, either. I won't allow him to talk about Stone that way. Not him or any other fucker.

"Don't mind my cousin any, Finn. The bastard has never been in love before, so he has no idea what you're feeling,"

Lincoln adds as he pulls me away from Colt, forcing me to take a seat back on the bed.

"So it's true, huh? You love her. Fuck. I knew it. Jesus, Finn," Easton retorts as if Lincoln just announced I have cancer or something.

"I haven't been handed out a death sentence, moron. I just fell in love."

"Is there a difference?" he asks, pulling out a pack of cigarettes from his pocket. "Because from where I'm standing, you falling for Stone has put all our lives in a pretty dicey situation," he explains nonchalantly, lighting one up. "But hey, aside from that, congrats man. She's a catch," he adds, blowing thick smoke into the air, his fumes choking me less than his lukewarm compliment.

"Have you told her?" Lincoln questions at my side, paying no mind to Easton's sarcastic tone.

"In so many words," I tell him truthfully.

"That's not good enough," he states adamantly. "When you love someone, you need to tell them. Don't let a day go by without making it clear in their heads. Trust me, you'll regret it if you don't," he continues, his dark-blond brows joining together.

"Talking from experience there, Linc?" I ask him outright, to which he gives me a forlorn nod.

"I waited too long. Learn from my mistakes, Finn. Loving someone from afar is worse than rejection. Trust me," he laments, the regret burdening his shoulders. "Does she love you?"

"I think so. Even if she doesn't want to admit it yet, I think she does."

His smile cracks a little wider, and it hurts to see that someone this compassionate has to have such a shitty past.

"Okay, can we all focus on what's important here? This doesn't change anything. I'm happy for numbskull here finding himself a girlfriend. Still, it doesn't change the fact that we're all screwed because he decided to grow a heart," Colt interjects, fuming.

"You know what, Colt? You're a real prick sometimes, you know that?" Easton reprimands, blowing smoke in Colt's direction.

"Takes one to know one, asshole. It doesn't change the fact that I'm right. What are we going to do, now that Finn here grew an extra pussy and is bailing on us?" Colt demands, crossing his arms over his puffed-up chest, looking like a fancy peacock on acid.

Lincoln lets out a huff while I try to keep myself in check to avoid hitting my best friend in the mouth.

"We face the consequences," Linc finally says, stealing the air out of my lungs.

"You have got to be shitting me!" Colt yells out.

In all fairness, I do get where Colt's coming from since I'm just as stunned as he is by Linc's statement.

"Listen to me, Colt. We've been searching for weeks and haven't found anything on The Society. Nothing that helped us, anyway. Maybe we've come as far as we can. I won't jeopardize any lives just so we can go unpunished."

"Unpunished?! Look at you, Lincoln! Look at us! We've all been punished one way or another. If we break now, then all of this is for nothing!" Colt belts, bridging the gap between us, going to his haunches to face me head-on. "Finn, our lives are in your hands. You get that, right? I understand you like this girl, or love, or whatever, but this is our freedom we're talking about. What could they possibly do to her that would be worse than us going to jail? Tell me!"

"That isn't fair, Colt," Easton mumbles behind him, but his tone lets me know that he's not happy with my decision either.

"None of this is fair! None of it! I fucking wish we'd never gone to the house that night. If we hadn't, none of this shit would be happening to us."

"But we did, Colt," Lincoln interrupts patiently. "However, the police don't have to know you all were involved. It's my fault anyway, so I'll hand myself in and end this for good."

"Are you insane?! No, you won't!"

"Yes, Colt, I will. This is enough. We are all losing our minds, waiting for the shoe to drop. Let me do this and end our suffering," Lincoln explains, hinting that he may have been thinking about this shit for a while now.

None of us have the martyr complex, but Lincoln always had a bit of the savior gene in him. He has always been the one to throw himself into the deep end and get us out if we found ourselves in a shitty mess. However, the repercussion of his parents' murder isn't quite the same as breaking the neighbor's window with a football.

"Finn! Finn, look at me!" Colt commands anxiously, grabbing my shoulders and shaking them for all their worth. "You see what will happen, don't you? Your best friend… You know what? No! Your fucking *brother*—the one who has been by your side your whole goddamned life—is going to turn himself in for us! For us, Finn! And you won't even do one measly thing for The Society because you don't want to make your girlfriend cry? Is that it?! Are you that fucking selfish?!" he shouts from the top of his lungs.

I slump my shoulders, my head bowed to the ground so that I don't have to face Colt's disapproving glare. Shame, guilt, and an array of feelings start to drown me, making it hard to keep them all straight in my head.

"You know what? Fuck you, Finn Walker!" Colt yells, straightening up and taking two steps away from me. "If you do this, I'll never fucking forgive you," he vows, turning around and walking toward the door. He stops at its threshold, and as his hand reaches the knob, he turns his head over his shoulder to look at his cousin one more time and affirms, "I always looked up to you, Linc. You've always had my back. I just wish you trusted us enough to have yours. But I guess with friends like Finn, I can't blame you for quitting on us."

And with those words falling from his lips, he gives us all a scathing look and leaves us to stew in our misery.

"Don't listen to him," Easton says, knowing that Linc is the only one willing to place his head on the butcher block.

"It's okay, East. Colt's angry. He's been angry for a while now. I understand, and I don't blame him for it."

"Are you serious, though? About handing yourself to the cops, I mean?"

"That depends on you, Finn. Is that what you want me to do?" he questions, his expression sincere and without an ounce of hesitation in it.

I read everything in his ocean blue eyes. I could tell him I can't do this, and he will go to the cops, no questions asked. That's just the kind of man he is.

But Colt is right. I am being selfish. Why should Linc go down for all of it? Why should I live my life knowing he'll be rotting in some jail cell while the rest of us go scot-free? We're just as guilty as he is. We've all got blood on our hands. I won't be able to live with myself, and worse, Stone will see right through my lies eventually. I'd change into something bitter and cruel if I let my best friend take the fall for something I, too, had a hand in doing. That's not the man I want her to be in love with. It's not the man I want to become.

And as I stare into Lincoln's eyes, I know exactly who my role model has always been.

"I'll do whatever they want, Linc. You won't go down for this."

I hear Easton let out long exhale, relief filling the air around us. It's obvious he was just as pent-up as Colt, even if hid it better.

"I don't want you to do anything you don't want to," Lincoln counters sincerely, making sure I'm good with my decision.

"I won't. Colt is right. We are family, and family protects one another."

"What about Stone?"

"I'll protect her the best way I can. Even if it's dealing with the aftermath of whatever The Society has in store for her."

"Are you sure?"

"I'm positive," I deadpan, firm in my decision.

"Okay, then. Where's this box The Society sent you?" East questions as he goes to the bathroom to flush his cigarette butt.

"I'll grab it. It's in my closet," I explain, getting up from the bed to go fetch the damn thing.

I need to find a way of giving this to Stone tonight without looking conspicuous or fucking desperate. I already gave her a pair of diamond earrings, so perhaps giving her a new phone won't seem too far-fetched. I'm just not sure how Stone will react to another surprise gift.

"I've been thinking, maybe we've been looking for dirt on The Society in the wrong places." I hear Easton say from behind me.

"What do you mean?" Linc asks.

"Well, no offense to you or Colt, but maybe you two aren't looking in the right places. I can get down in the dirt if I need to. We've all seen how The Society likes to play dirty, so they must resort to some unsavory characters from time to time, if you get my drift."

"I never thought of it that way," Linc mumbles in deep thought.

"Of course you wouldn't know the first thing about being sleazy and underhanded. That's because you're the good guy in our quartet," East tries to joke, hoping to lighten the tense atmosphere.

"Oh, I think these past months have taught me a few things," Linc laments.

I don't hear any more of their conversation because I'm too busy looking for a box that seems to have gone missing. My head begins to get dizzy, my stomach churning on end with each passing second that I can't locate it. I'm deep in my freak-out, throwing stuff over my shoulder while trying to find the damn thing, when Easton and Lincoln join me in my meltdown.

"It's not here! It's not fucking here!" I shout, losing my goddamn mind.

"Are you sure this is where you stashed it?" Easton interrogates harshly as he joins in throwing things left and right, looking for The Society's time bomb.

"Yes, I'm sure! It's gone. It's fucking gone!"

"Easy, Finn. Just breathe, brother," Lincoln pulls me back out of the closet and onto my feet.

He grabs my trembling shoulders, trying to calm me down, but his composed voice and steady touch aren't enough.

"They must have taken it when they left me that fucking message in the bathroom. Fuck! What does this mean, Linc? What's does this fucking mean?!" I spit out, clinging to Lincoln's shirt to prevent me from falling to the floor.

"It means we're shit out of luck, Finn. The ball is in their court now. We just have to sit back and wait for their next move," Easton explains beside us, looking way too cool, considering we are all royally fucked.

"East is right," Lincoln agrees stoically. "If they took the box, it means they know you had no intention of giving it to Stone. We just have to wait and see how they'll react. There's nothing we can do now, Finn. No sense in you getting all worked up. Whatever they end up doing, we'll figure a way out of it. Together."

I stare at my two best friends with my mouth agape, as they both pretend to act prepared—just so they can ease my anxious, frantic state—for the shitstorm that is about to come. Even as they try their best to comfort me without losing their own shit, it still does nothing to lighten my weary heart. I feel the walls continue to close in on me, making me realize that my time has run out.

'We warned you.'

I recollect the words written in black lettering on my bathroom mirror, left there for all to see. And it's true. They did warn me. I simply didn't follow through as they expected, which means they are now coming for us.

But most terrifyingly, it also means they are going after Stone themselves, which is the real reason why I feel my world is suddenly coming undone.

What are those fuckers going to do with you?

And how can I fucking stop it?

CHAPTER 24

STONE

"You've been more in your head than usual, quarterback. Want to talk about it?" I ask, running my fingers through his silky blond hair as he clings to my hips.

Something has been on his mind for the past few weeks now, and whatever it is, it's consuming Finn from the inside. Ever since I went to his father's birthday party, there has been a dark cloud cast over him, and as much as he tries to shake it off, the looming presence just won't give him a moment's peace. I'm not sure what happened, but I'm positive it's something to do with that night. He was fine and happy one minute, and the next he looked as if his whole world was falling apart.

I didn't want to pry at the time, but if I were a betting woman, my money would be on his father. I don't think Hank Walker appreciated my presence in his house, nor the fact that Finn introduced me as his girlfriend. I'm sure he must have accosted him at some point in the evening and told him just as much, while I wasn't looking. If that's what has the Finn so upset and worried, then there really is no need to probe further.

The old man doesn't like his star-athlete son dating a girl from the south side of town. So what? Like I care what he thinks of me. I'm sure he believes I'm just another gold-digger from the wrong side of the tracks, wanting to latch myself onto his son as a meal ticket out of the filth I was born into. As if I haven't busted my ass to do that on my own. As long as Finn knows the truth, then I couldn't care one way or the other about his father's opinion.

As far as I'm concerned, there are only two people in this relationship—me and pretty boy. Everyone else can go fuck themselves, and I'm not afraid of saying those exact words right to the old man's face, either.

"You know you can say anything to me, right?" I continue to probe patiently.

I'm hoping Finn will just come out and say whatever is troubling him. But instead of fessing up to his old man's grief, he just tightens his hold on me, his head nestling on my chest to seek the comfort only I can give him.

"Nothing's wrong, Stone."

"You're lying. And if it's to spare my feelings, you really don't have to. I'm a big girl, pretty boy. I can take the hit."

"But maybe I can't," he mumbles, not wanting to look me in the eye. "I don't want to lose you." He breathes out hoarsely, making my stupid heart ache for him.

"Pretty deep conversation to have in the school's parking lot, don't you think?" I try to tease, but his grip on me increases, revealing the intensity of his worries.

Damn it.

His old man must have really done a number on him. I know Finn is doing everything in his power to please his father, even going as far as giving up his dream of being an astronomer. He does everything not to disappoint the old prick. And I get it. From what Finn has confided in me, I understand his father is a real tyrant who wouldn't lose any sleep disowning his own flesh and blood.

But if Finn thinks his father can scare me away, then he has another thing coming. I'm not going anywhere. I don't care who Hank Walker thinks he is. The only person who can push me away is pretty boy himself, and by the way he's desperately clinging onto me so tightly, I don't see that happening.

"Hey, look at me," I command softly, pulling the short ends of his hair, forcing him to crane his head back to look me in the eye.

"You have me, Finn. Nothing and no one will change that."

His eyes turn a melancholic shade of blue, the deep-seated frown lines on his brow just as profound as the desolate look on his beautiful face.

"I wish that was true," he mutters, pain and misery tainting each word.

What did that old man do to you, baby? I swear, if he were here, I'd punch him in the nards.

"If I didn't have class in a few minutes, I'd show you just exactly how true that is."

I wiggle my butt on his lap, his cock instantly coming alive. I can always count on the little devil in his pants to be ready to play. It's the chaos swimming in Finn's head that gets in the way sometimes, much like now.

"Stone?"

"What, baby?"

"Just kiss me, okay? Kiss me like you love me. Can you do that?" he asks anxiously, and the pinch of suffocating guilt wraps its ugly claws around my heart, telling me I'm just as pigheaded and cruel as his father, if not more.

How much of a bitch am I, that I can't at least erase this doubt from his mind? His father plays with his head while I toy with his heart. How fucked up is that? No wonder Finn is unraveling. Everyone wants a piece of him, and no one is willing to soothe his vulnerable soul.

Instead of telling him how I love him with all my Southie-born heart, I do as he asks and kiss him. I let my lips ease his doubts, my tongue erase his worries, and my heart silently whisper to his that it belongs to him only. When Finn pulls away, his eyes beam brightly, acknowledging the words I've been too much of a coward to confess out loud. His warm hands gently caress my face as he takes me in, almost as if trying to memorize this moment. There is so much adoration and worship in his steel-blue eyes that my heart begins to tick frantically like an overwound clock, making my lips dry, my throat tighten, and my chest heave.

Say it.

Say it.

Just say you love him for, fuck's sake!

"Finn," I stutter, but the pad of his thumb begins to play with my lower lip, halting my words from spilling over.

I stare back into his bright blue eyes, unable to stop the love I feel for him emanate out from me. Just like the ink permanently tattooed on my skin, so is the love for him imprinted on my very soul. Its warm glow burns even brighter when I see a genuine smile begin to tug on his lips.

"Life is funny, Stone. Sometimes, it's in the bleakest of situations that you find yourself. I had no idea I'd find the other half of my heart serving drinks in the world's shittiest bar. But I did. I found you. And no matter what happens, I want you to know that everything I ever told you is real. I love you, Stone. I've never loved anyone as much as I love you. Please remember that."

"You sound like you're going to be shipped off to war."

His eyes crinkle at the sides as he continues to caress my face with all his tenderness.

"Some wars are fought right at home. Just promise me you'll remember what I said."

Even as confusing and cryptic as his statement is, I nod just the same, knowing it will settle his anguish. I'd do just about anything to keep his smile on his face at this point.

"Just one more kiss, then you've got to jump off my lap and get to class. Otherwise, I'm going to fuck you right in this car, and I don't like the idea of having an audience," he tries to joke, sounding more like the Finn I adore.

I look behind my shoulder to the dashboard and see that I still have fifteen minutes before my next class. It's not ideal, but I guess it'll have to do. I look around the parking lot and make sure we're out of sight. At this hour, mostly everyone is already on campus, so I doubt we'll have many peeping toms for what I have in mind. My fingers begin to travel down his chest, ever so slowly, until it reaches the hard shaft between his thighs.

"Stone," he warns, not liking where my head is at.

His cock, though, is twitching away in his jeans, plenty happy to have my hand rub against it.

"Stay still, quarterback, and just enjoy the ride." I wink at him.

"Don't you fucking dare, brat," he continues to threaten, his eyes scanning around, worried someone will see me take his swollen shaft out of its cage.

"Shh, baby. I know what I'm doing. We're just two college kids making out in a car. That's all. Totally innocent."

"Jerking my cock in your hands is far from just an innocent make-out session."

"As if you didn't enjoy it," I tease, wiggling my skirt up and shifting his hard length to where I need him most.

I slip my thong to the side, and the instant his cock crowns my center, he echoes my hiss, gripping my hips with a strength that will undoubtedly leave bruises on my skin.

"Fuck, but you're already wet. Jesus!" he stutters, the rasped words sounding strangled in his throat.

I love it when he loses all coherent thought the minute he's inside me. There is only one thing on his mind when we're connected—loving me.

Only me. Always me.

My pussy clenches around him as I bounce up and down on his long, hard cock. I grab his hair with the same ferocity as the hold he keeps on me, while he whispers filthy words in my ear, describing in detail the lengths he'll go to ruin my pussy. It's already ruined beyond measure, as is my heart.

It will only ever want him. Only him. Always him.

I maintain my frantic tempo, his hands helping to keep me steady, no longer concerned with the lack of privacy. Finn keeps thrusting inside me, satiating my body, while the words of love he utters have the same effect on my soul.

"This. I'll never get over this."

"You are so fucking beautiful while riding me."

"Fuck, I could live inside this pussy."

"God, I love you, Stone."

"I fucking love you so much that it physically hurts not to be inside you."

"I love you."

"I love you."

And with his words and promises singing in my ear, his mouth eating up my cries, I cum with my heart leaping out of my chest, begging refuge next to his. As I fall off the precipice, Finn follows me over, never wanting to leave my side.

Inside the scented mist of sex and sweet surrender, our hearts begin to slow down their erratic pace, giving me the energy to go for one more kiss.

'I love you,' my heart resonates.

Finn kisses me back, his smile ten miles wide, hugging me to him as if I'm the most precious thing he has in this world.

'I know,' his broad smile echoes.

However, his desperate kiss says something entirely different, making my cautious heart leap back into my chest, whispering that it isn't safe.

I realize that his kiss is an apology. For what, I do not know.

"Miss Bennett, can I speak with you for a moment?" Professor Harper requests as the class ends and everyone begins packing up their book bags.

Damn it.

She's probably going to give me a hard time for coming in late again. Harper is a stickler for the rules, and she doesn't bend them for anyone. I sure as shit can't tell her the reason for my lateness, now can I?

I take the stairs down to the auditorium floor, mentally preparing my speech.

"I'm sorry I was late, professor. It won't happen again," I promise before she has time to reprimand me for it.

"This doesn't have anything to do with your tardiness, Miss Bennett. Although, I would appreciate it if you refrained from coming late to my class."

"Promise," I vow, crossing a finger over my heart in a playful manner, leaving her utterly unamused by my gesture.

In fact, her usually stunning features are tarnished and have been replaced by a strict and severe look, which is rather unsettling. She's been nothing but kind to me, which is saying a lot since she usually keeps a cold barrier between her and the students.

However, Professor Harper's precaution is understandable since she's considered to be one of the hottest teachers on campus. With her leather skirts and dark, black-framed glasses, she's a mixture of naughty librarian and dominatrix. It's no surprise most of Richfield has a hard-on for the professor, and if I batted for the other team, I'd probably want to take a swing at her, too.

So, to keep assholes at bay, she usually has a no-nonsense demeanor about her, leaving very little leeway for any of her students to get any funny ideas. And believe me, they do. I've seen plenty of male students trying to seduce her, and not because they want her to up their grade. Sharing her bed is reward enough for the horndogs.

Despite her cold front, she has never been that way with me. In fact, since my freshman year at this university, she's been more like a counselor, always ready to help me with my academic endeavors. So her looking at me with an accusing and disappointed stare is making me nervous.

"Professor Harper, what's wrong?"

"You tell me?" she quips back, just as harshly as she looks.

My face must show puzzlement because she leans against her desk, letting out a long exhale.

"You didn't tell me you changed your mind about New York, Stone. Frankly, I'm disappointed you made the decision without coming to me to hash out your doubts about leaving Asheville."

The hell?

"Ms. Harper, don't take this the wrong way, but what the hell are you talking about?"

She raises her brow and crosses her arms over her chest, disapprovingly.

"No need to be coy with me, Stone. My friend at Watkins & Ellis already called me and told me you turned down the job."

"I did what?!" I shout, almost spitting in her pretty, framed, cat-like glasses.

"You turned down the job in New York, so I assume pulled your candidacy for the scholarship at Columbia University as well," she states, her confusion just as fierce as my own.

"Professor Harper, I don't know who you are getting your intel from, but I did no such thing!" I choke out, but as

I witness her unwavering confidence to the ludicrous statement, I begin to feel like my insides are about to explode.

The air around me starts to get heavy, leaving me struggling to get oxygen into my burning lungs. I start to hyperventilate, placing my hands on the edge of the desk to keep my head from spinning.

What the fuck is happening?

"Do you need some water? Are you alright, Stone?" I seem to hear her faint voice ask, but I'm unsure since her last words are still a jumbled mess in my head.

As I feel her gentle hand rub my back with no immediate relief, I slowly start losing my mind.

"Stone, tell me what you need?"

I take a deep breath, forcing myself to get my shit together and prevent a total freak-out in front of my teacher.

"I need answers, Professor Harper. That's what I need." I seethe through gritted teeth, my anger already taking hold of me. I straighten my back and looking the troubled professor in the eye, I say, "I have to go and make this right."

"If there is anything I can do for you—"

"I got myself into this mess somehow, I'll get myself out," I snap, taking my fury out on the messenger.

"Do what you must. Remember, I'll always be here if you need me," Professor Harper adds, not one bit upset for me being seconds away from biting her head off.

Despite the respect and admiration I have for the woman before me, I'm not sure my stubborn anger won't lash out at her again, so I just offer a stern nod and walk away without saying another word.

I have no recollection of how I got to my dorm room, nor do I remember dialing human resources at Watkins & Ellis. The only thing that snaps me out of my fevered haze is the pissed-off woman on the other line, repeating word for word what Professor Harper had told me in her classroom earlier.

"There must be some mistake," I plea with the representative.

"I'm sorry, Miss Bennett, but there isn't. In fact, your candidacy has already been filled. We sent you a few emails requesting you to reconsider. However, you were adamant that your engagement was your main focus at this stage, and you wanted to put your law degree on-hold," the woman continues with her rant, sounding more annoyed with each word she has to explain to me.

I fall to the floor in my room, my legs no longer able to support my trembling knees.

"No, you don't understand. This is a mistake! I never rescinded my candidacy for the internship. Why would I? This is all I've ever wanted," I stutter, clasping my hand over my mouth, unwilling to let the representative hear me crying.

She takes a beat, letting me draw some composure, which only intensifies my humiliation for falling apart with a stranger as my witness.

"Again, Miss Bennett, *you* were the one who contacted us, advising us that you were no longer interested. We even called you, and your fiancé told us the same thing over the phone."

"My fiancé?!"

"Yes. Just give me a minute. I think I still have the email here. Ah. Here it is. His name is Finn Walker, am I correct?"

"Finn? You talked to Finn?"

She huffs out, her patience dwindling down at rapid speed.

"Yes. We did. A week ago, if I recall correctly. We tried to reach you, of course, but he was the one who talked with us. Aside from your email, we haven't been able to reach you until today. I have to say, I find it quite disappointing we are only having this conversation now."

This can't be happening. She's wrong. She must be. There must be some sort of mistake.

But how do they know Finn's name?

"Can I ask you to forward a copy of my email?"

"Just a minute," she replies, aggravated. "There, I've forwarded it back to you. Is there anything else you require from us, Miss Bennett?" she retorts bitterly, her tone leaving no room for miscommunication—Watkins & Ellis are through with me.

"No. Thank you. That's all, I guess."

"Apparently it is. Congratulations again on your nuptials. Some women aren't made to lead successful careers anyway," she adds, the little bitchy reprimand serving as her parting words before hanging up on me, only adding salt to my already open wound.

I rush to my laptop to check my email box and, lo and behold, in black and white, there it is—the fucking email that crushed all my dreams and aspirations. In its contents, I explain in detail to Watkins & Ellis that I've become engaged to a football star, no longer wishing to pursue law in favor of supporting his athletic endeavors.

Aside from my laptop, everything ends up on the floor, thrown by my maddening rage.

I wish I had never laid eyes on Finn Walker—the destroyer of dreams and my goddamn future.

I'll kill him!

I'll fucking kill him!

Since I don't want Finn to hear my anger over the phone, or give him time to get his story straight, I run out of my room with the sole intent of finding him to get some answers face to face. If I haul ass, I can make it before he gets to his next class.

Ten minutes later, I stand outside Finn's Philosophy classroom, drenched to the bone, and getting angrier by the second. Even the typically sunny Asheville weather suddenly turned to match my wretched mood. However, I was too furious to go back to my room for an umbrella. I shift from one foot to another, my wet clothes unable to dampen my boiling rage.

As I watch the students beginning to leave the classroom, my eyes first land on a bored Easton. But following behind him, looking chipper and right as rain, is the bane of my existence—the man who somehow made his way into my heart, only to trample on it. Finn is talking Easton's ear off until he finally sees me standing there, waiting for him in a dripping pool of water.

"Stone? What's wrong? Why are you all wet, brat?" he bombards worriedly, looking concerned.

However, I'm the one who needs answers, so I promptly ask, "Why did you do it?"

"What?" he asks in confusion, trying to wrap his jacket over my shoulders.

I grab the damn thing, throwing it to the wet floor, and yell, "WHY, FINN?! Just fucking tell me why?!"

My little outburst grabs the attention of everyone around us, leaving a thunderous expression on his face. He grabs my elbow and pulls me away to prevent me from continuing to make a scene. He is shit out of luck if he thinks I give a rat's ass about what other people think. I never have, and right now, other people's perception of me is the last thing on my mind.

I just want him to answer why he did it. How could he claim to love me and rip my world apart so callously?

"Answer me, Finn! Why did you do it?!" I yell out once he's stopped behind a pillar, which is big enough to keep us both hidden from curious, prying eyes.

"I'll answer you when I understand what the fucking question is about, Stone! Why did I do what, exactly?"

"God, you are such a fucking liar! How can you lie so well? Was everything you said to me a lie, too?"

"Stone, I have never lied to you."

"Oh, no? Then how about lying by omission. Have you ever omitted something from me? Something that would change my life forever?" His stark, pale face is all the answer I need. "How could you, Finn? I trusted you! I fucking trusted you, and you took everything away from me!" I yell, throwing my fists into his chest and beating it as hard as I can, wanting to hurt him the same way he hurt me.

"Stone," he croaks, the sound of his pain finally coming through. "What happened? Tell me."

"What happened is that I fell in love with a liar. A liar who made sure all I had in life was him and nothing else. Well, congratulations. You succeeded."

"Stone," he begins to plea, grabbing my wrists in his strong, warm hands.

"Was it because it was in New York? Did you think I was going to forget about you if I went? Tell me. Explain it to me. Just make me understand how you could do something like this," I wail, snatching my wrists away from his hold, unwilling to let him touch me. "All my life, I dreamed about doing something good with my life, and become someone who would change the world for the better. Working for Watkins & Ellis would get my foot in the door and guarantee my place in Columbia for law school. But after the email you fabricated, and the call you answered in my stead, they want nothing to do with me. I doubt any respectful law firm ever will, once news gets out of why I turned their offer down. I'll be branded as the girl who preferred to cheer in the stands, watching her boyfriend get beat up by Neanderthals fighting over a damn ball, rather than advocate for justice and save innocent lives."

"Stone, it's not like that," he tries to interject, attempting to get me back in his arms, but I keep my distance, refusing to be played for a fool again.

"Nice touch on the fiancé part, by the way. You really fucking sold it. Kudos for the creativity, quarterback. I didn't think you had it in you," I snap, my nose flaring in disgust.

"Stone, just let me get a word in, will you?" he rasps, his voice struggling for sound.

"You want to talk? Okay, then talk! Tell me, how could you have done this to me? No, not how. I already fucking know *how* you did it. It's right here in my inbox, reminding me of what an idiot I was," I bark, pointing at the email on my phone screen.

"Stone, where did you get that phone?"

"Are you fucking kidding me? You gave me the damn thing! Don't try to change the subject. Just tell me why? Why would you take my dreams away from me?" I cry, my trembling body wanting to cave and melt against him, craving to feel his warmth and consoling touch despite him being the one who ripped me to shreds.

"Why, Finn?" I ask him again after a long pause of silence.

I take a step back, my spine straightening as much as it can while looking up into his tear-filled eyes.

"I never wanted to hurt you."

"But you did. You did more than hurt me, Finn. You broke something in me that you'll never be able to fix. I'll never be able to trust you again."

"Stone." He chokes, a rebellious tear falling down his cheek.

"You wanted to know if I loved you, well, now you know. Because a betrayal like this can only hurt this much when it's done by someone you gave your heart to. I loved you, Finn. I did. But now I can't stand the sight of you." I seethe, backing away from him, one step at a time.

His tears mean nothing to me.

His false words and promises even less.

"Don't call me. Don't come looking for me. Just forget me. Trust me, if I could, I'd sell my own soul to the damn devil himself to forget you. We're over," I spit out, throwing him one last cold look as if he were a total stranger to me.

And he is. The Finn I fell in love with was a mirage, a figment of my imagination.

I turn around, making my way through the rain. With razor-sharp scissors, I cut the ribbon of the deceitful love that had me tethered to such a beautiful lie. If there is a lesson in love that must be learned, let this one be mine—never trust my heart again. Its foolish desires just ruined my entire future.

CHAPTER 25

FINN

"I want you out! I mean it! I can't even look at your face!" my father yells the minute we walk through the door.

"Hank," my mother pleas anxiously, looking at my father and then back at me, not knowing who to console first.

"Don't 'Hank' me, Charlene. This is your fault as much as his. You coddled him all his life, and this is how he repays us," he roars, walking into the living room and heading straight to the bar, obviously thinking alcohol will calm his nerves.

It won't. At this moment, there's nothing that can be said or done to temper my father's angry disposition. But I guess it's to be expected since all the dreams he had for me were ripped from his clutches so mercilessly.

I keep my mouth shut, knowing nothing I say will make him believe me. The damning results on the lab's conclusive report are all the proof my father and the dean will take into account. Professing my innocence is just a wasted effort, and frankly, I'm too tired and distraught to give a fuck. The dean and my father, however, are acting as if the four horsemen just stampeded through Richfield's gates, storming their way onto campus to unleash hell on earth. To them, this is the apocalypse. To me, it's just another fucked-up day, and not the worst one I had this week by a long shot.

This whole afternoon they locked themselves in the dean's office to do damage control while I stewed in my seat in the same room, ordered to remain silent like an errant child caught with his hand in the cookie jar. No matter how innocent I am, pretty words will never restore their faith in me. The funny thing is, I'm too broken and weary to even try.

"What are you still doing here? I told you, I want you out of my house, boy! You are no longer a member of this family. The disgrace you've brought, this blemish you've made on our family name, can never be undone," my father bellows, chugging his bourbon in one go and looking at me with daggers in his eyes.

At least my mother is not siding with him. But she's not making any attempts to side with me, either. Switzerland, that's what she's like. Maybe that's what she's always been like, and I just never noticed. My mother is a neutral force in this family, who only implements her rule when she sees fit. My father kicking me out of my childhood home doesn't merit her intervention, apparently.

Unwilling to hear another bitter word from my father, I turn around, knowing that the next time we see each other we will be strangers. But I guess we already were. If he knew me at all, he'd believe me the first time I told him the lab results are bullshit.

"Finn, don't take another step," my mother suddenly interjects. Unsure if she is going to be kind or hammer me to the cross like my father, I sway my body to face her as she continues, "Hank, I know what happened today was a shock. A shock that none of us saw coming, but I don't want you to make rash decisions. This is our son. This is his home. No matter what he's done, this will always be his home."

My father sucks in his teeth, his scowl wrinkling his forehead, making him look older than his sixty years of age.

"This home is for people of integrity. Not cheaters."

"I have never cheated a day in my life," I growl, my sudden outrage making it clear that his condemning words hit their intended mark.

My father's head falls back, unleashing a contemptuous cackle, making my anger increase tenfold. I'm his son. How can he believe I was capable of doing such a thing? Doesn't he know me at all? Guess not.

"Oh, you're not a cheater, huh? Then what do you call this?!" he shouts from the top of his lungs, throwing my failed dope tests on the ground.

Hmm.

What can I call a piece of paper that proves my steroid use? Do I call it my penance for being a manipulative bastard in trying to right a wrong? Or do I define it as my own karma kicking my ass for being an unfeeling asshole all these years?

Perhaps neither.

After all the lives I've ruined, I think I can only call this scathing, false document The Society's way of reminding me exactly what I deserve.

And maybe they are right. By all accounts, I should be behind bars for all the criminal things I've done. My freedom should be ripped from me, and my reputation tarnished beyond repair. I sure as shit don't feel like I deserve any better. Not when the woman I love hates my guts, thinking I jeopardized her chances for the future she always envisioned. Not when she spends her days hating me while I wallow in my misery, loving her.

Missing her.

"You haven't let the boy even explain himself," my mother pleas again on my behalf. However, at this point, I really wish she wouldn't.

"What is there to explain? He got lazy and thought he could cheat his way into the NFL. You should be down on your knees, thanking Ryland and me for convincing the lab to destroy your results—for a price, I might add. If word got out that my son needed to shoot up to win a game, I'd never hear the end of it. But you're still a liability, and Ryland is too astute to let you embarrass the school by keeping you on the team. I can't fault the man for protecting his interests. I'm just ashamed you were so careless to not do the same to yours."

"Hank, you are blowing things out of proportion. Montgomery said that Finn could play ball as long as we did a private test each week to prove he's clean. Benching him for a few games is not the end of the world," my mother defends, trying hard to settle my father's concerns.

"I'm not doing the tests," I mumble. "I'm quitting the team."

"What did he just say?" my father asks my mother in outrage, only to snap his head back in my direction. "What did you just say to me, boy?!"

403

"You heard me. I said I'm quitting the team. I never wanted to go Pro. That was always your dream, not mine."

With those words still piercing through his eardrum, he throws the tumbler of bourbon against the wall, making my mother jump back, clasping her trembling hands over her mouth to keep her horrified shriek at bay.

I, however, keep my footing steady, not one bit intimidated by his fury. I'm done with his bullshit. I'm done with football and every expectation he ever had for me. But most importantly, I'm done being The Society's butt boy.

They thought *this* would break me? Did they really believe that my father kicking me out or disowning me would be the thing that would cripple me? Or that making me look like another steroid-filled jock would ruin me? Is that what they thought?

Idiots, the lot of them.

They had already succeeded in breaking me. This extra bit of hell doesn't compare to the one I've been living in since they went after Stone. I couldn't give two flying fucks that they threatened my place on the team, or made me gain my father's wrath.

I was already a mess of a man when the one person who knew me—really *knew me*—gave up on me. When Stone told me she loved me, with hate seeped deep in her gorgeous eyes, I died that day. There is no pain greater than seeing the person you love in such tremendous agony, thinking you are the cause of their suffering.

This little sideshow act of theirs does nothing for me. The first shot already pierced a bullet through my heart. Why waste extra ammunition when they got the job done in their first go of it?

"Charlene, by all that is holy, get this boy out of my house before I strangle him."

"But, Hank—"

"Now!" he yells, his face turning an ugly shade of red.

"Don't bother. I can show myself out," I quip, turning my back to him and heading toward the front door.

"Finn." I hear my mother beg, but I don't turn around.

Instead, I just walk out, leaving everything I've known behind. I don't even have the will to go up to my room and grab some of my things. This house holds nothing I want to take with me anyway. If I'm no longer a Walker as my father declared, then he can keep all my shit. I even leave my car in the driveway for the asshole to do whatever he pleases.

It was never the material stuff that made me obedient. It was the threat of being disowned from my family that kept me loyal. Being able to see my nephews and nieces grow up, or spend time with my older brothers and their wives were the only reasons why I worked so hard and sacrificed so much.

If my father is adamant in giving me my walking papers, I just hope Beau and Calvin can at least find forgiveness in their hearts, and not deny my presence in their children's lives. They both felt my father's tyranny long before me, so all I can do is have faith that my brothers won't be as merciless as him. At least I hope they won't. Unless, of course, they are more scared of my father's retaliation than I am. However, I doubt Hank Walker will disown all his children. Not that he cares, but he'll want to save face around Asheville. If news were to spread that he'd disinherited all three of his sons, it would stain his reputation, which would be by his own making, not ours.

Mom, though... I'm not sure how she'll react to all of this. She's the pacifist in our home, and I saw how conflicted she was in trying desperately to dampen my father's temper. She's never hid how much she loves all three of her sons, and I know her first priority is to keep this family whole. It always has been. Hopefully, she'll make the old man see sense, but if not, I'm positive she will never turn her back on her children, no matter what her stubborn, ass-of-a-husband says.

As I walk to the house that's been a second home most of my life, all these thoughts run through my head. So when I get to Lincoln's after a full hour's walk, I'm not surprised, not only to be drenched in sweat but also filled with the desire to right my wrongs. Just not in the way my family would expect.

I wasn't lying when I said I was quitting football. If anything, this little revenge from The Society has taught me is that there are too many people pulling my strings. I want to be my own man, free of anyone's dominance and authority. I want to be Finn—the man Stone fell in love with.

She didn't want me because I was a star quarterback. She didn't love me because of my family or social standing. And she sure as shit didn't care about my money. If what Stone said was true, that she loved me before all this shitstorm went down, then I have to find some way to show her that version of Finn is the only one that exists. It's probably too late to win her love back, but like hell will I let her remember me as the man who stole her dreams away.

Fuck that!

If The Society has a problem with what I'm about to do, then they are shit out of luck. Aside from locking my ass up in jail, I don't think there is much more they can do to me. Sure, outing me to the police is still a likely possibility, but my gut tells me they are done playing with me. They gave out their last assignment, and I blew it big time. Because of it, they went ahead and did the task themselves, only to punish me later for not submitting to their demands.

It's public knowledge that Hank Walker only cares about football, so of course people would assume I was just as fanatical as him. I'm sure The Society thought that falsifying a drug test would be my demise—not only for getting me kicked off the team and losing my shot at the draft, but also for being disowned by my father. Too bad they had no way of knowing my true inner desires, because I never told anyone, only Stone.

I was only real when I was with her.

As I knock on Lincoln's front door, I feel the burdens on my shoulders being ten pounds lighter than before. It's almost as if The Society did me a fucking favor in throwing me under the bus the way they did. My smile is just as wide and manic as Heath Ledger's version of Joker. When Linc opens his front door, I rush in, wanting to set my plans in action as fast as possible.

"Finn, don't take this the wrong way, but you look like a lunatic who just escaped from an asylum."

The most unhinged laugh leaves me as I place both hands on his shoulders and say, "In a way, I kind of did. My father kicked me out."

"Shit! What the hell happened?"

"It's a long story. I'll tell you everything about it, but first I need to ask you for a couple of favors."

"Anything, brother. Whatever you need," Linc answers sincerely, just as I knew he would.

"Can I crash here for a few days? Just until I get my life in order."

"You don't even have to ask. My house is your house, Finn. Stay as long as you need."

"Good, because I might overstay my welcome." I chuckle.

"Never. You and the guys are the only true family I have left. It's the least I can do."

I pull him into a hug because I know Linc means that shit. He's had a hard life, made even harder after what we did last May, yet he would never abandon us. Never forsake us. And I'm counting on his friendship more than ever to do what needs to be done.

"What else do you need, Finn? Whatever it is, I'll make sure you get it."

"I was hoping you'd say that. I've ruined enough lives as it is Linc. It's time I start saving some, and I need your help to do it."

CHAPTER 26

STONE

"You look upset, baby girl," my mom says at my side as we walk over to my truck after leaving the doctor's office.

"Huh?" I mumble absentmindedly.

"I said you look upset, Stone. Didn't you like the new doctor?" my mom asks suspiciously as she opens the truck door.

"I liked him just fine, Momma," I reply, throwing her a lukewarm smile in the hopes that it's enough to dissuade her from continuing this conversation.

However, once I jump in the truck and fasten my seat belt, my mother grasps onto my hand before I'm able to put the key into the ignition.

"What's wrong? I know something is troubling you. You should be over the moon, and yet you look sad. Why, baby? Tell me what's wrong. Maybe I can help?"

I let out a long exhale and lean my head against the headrest.

"I just don't like charity, that's all."

"Charity?" my mom repeats, confused.

"Yes, Momma. Charity. You know as well as I do that we can't afford this fancy new doctor and all the treatments he's planning for you."

"Ah, I see. You don't want me to go back, then? If it upsets you this much, I won't set foot in this practice again."

Shit on a stick! I'm such an asshole.

"No, Mom. Don't you even think about it. If the Richfield Foundation is willing to pay for your treatment, then we are not going to look a gift horse in the mouth. Pride will not be the reason that will keep you from getting better."

"And don't forget the help they are offering your father, too," she beams brightly.

How could I forget?

It sickens me how people with flushed bank accounts can suddenly get the justice system to work in their favor, while we have been trying in vain for years. But this thought, I keep to myself.

I watch my mother hug her midsection to keep the joy from spilling forth like a busted dam, so utterly happy that she has a hard time keeping her elation in check.

"These last few days, I've had to pinch myself non-stop to make sure I'm not dreaming. Your father's new attorney is confident the appeal for his case will go forward without a hitch, since the last appointed lawyer botched it all up. He should have never forced your dad into that awful plea deal when there was no real evidence to support his conviction. This new fancy attorney even said that if all goes well, your father will be home by Christmas. Isn't that wonderful?" she sings, her eyes watering with happiness.

I take her hands in mine and kiss her knuckles. It's been years since I've seen true joy in my mother's eyes. The sight of it warms my broken heart.

"Yes, Mom. We are very fortunate."

"Baby, this is the miracle we have always dreamed of, and you don't look one bit happy about it. Please talk to me."

I bite my lower lip, unwilling to be the one raining on her parade, but I'm still incapable of keeping my trap shut.

"Don't you find it odd that our family has become Richfield Foundation's top priority all of a sudden? That they know of our existence and want to help us, just out of the blue?"

"No, not really," she retorts with her brows drawn together. "I just assumed your boyfriend was behind this generosity."

"Finn's not my boyfriend," I clip, pulling away from her touch, upset that I just uttered the name that has been haunting me for the last few weeks.

"Are you sure? Because the boy sure is acting like one. I mean, a man who tries to improve every part of a woman's life in any way he can, must be looking for more than friendship. Love can be his only incentive, sweetheart. Don't you think?"

"Or he's motivated by guilt."

"What do you mean? Did that boy hurt you, baby?"

Did Finn hurt me?

He ruined me. I gave him my heart, and he stole my future in an effort to keep it.

Hurt doesn't even measure up to what Finn did to me. Obviously, I can't explain that to my mother as it will only worry her. Since we got word that all her medical expenses, as well as my father's legal fees, were going to be handled by the Richfield Foundation from now on, she's been in high spirits—and not the manic ones that I've grown accustomed to.

"No, Momma. I'm hard as a rock, remember? No one can hurt me." I try to play off with a wink, but the worried glare in her eyes shows me that I'm doing a piss-poor job at easing her concern.

"Stone? Just tell me what's wrong. Please."

I let out another exaggerated sigh and confess, "I didn't get the New York job that I wanted. That's what I'm upset about."

"Oh, is that all?" She smiles, her shoulders visibly relaxing at my admission.

"Is that all?! Momma, are you serious? That job would have opened a million doors for me. It would have enabled me financially to stay in New York and take that partial scholarship at Columbia. This means, without that job, there's no Ivy League school either. So, excuse me if I'm a little upset about it," I explain, the wave of rage and resentment hitting me hard.

I try to swallow down the bitter taste of my anger and disappointment, but as I watch my mother look even more cheery-eyed than she was a minute ago, my wrath plummets over. I'm on the verge of calling my mom out for being so apathetic to my pain, but she holds her hand up, stopping my wicked tongue from lashing out.

"I know how much you wanted that job, baby girl. I understand your frustration, but I can't say I'm unhappy that you won't be moving states away from me, to a place where I wouldn't be able to see you so often. And anyway, it's not like Columbia was your only option. Richfield University is an amazing school, one that has already offered you a full ride. Therefore, I never understood why you wanted to leave your whole life behind to go up North in the first place."

"Maybe I wanted a new start, Momma. Go to a place where people don't see me as Southside trash."

"Oh, Stone. People will always see you in the way they want, and there isn't anything you can do about it. A new location won't change that. You can move to the other side of the world, and people will still have their opinions and prejudices. Your daddy and I raised you to be stronger than that. Or at least I thought we did."

"You did, Momma. I don't care what anybody thinks of me."

"If that's true, then what's all this talk about a new start in a different city?"

"I just wanted a better life, Momma. Can't you understand that?" I spew in frustration, only to have my mother's eyes soften.

"Asheville is your home, baby. You want a better life? Then work to get one right here in your home town. Dreams are nothing if you don't work hard to achieve them. You know that, as well as I do. But the wonderful thing about a dream is that it can change, adapt, and grow into something even more spectacular than you thought. I think it's a blessing in disguise that you didn't get that job. This way, you can carve out your future right here, where your talents will make the most difference."

My eyes lower to my feet on the pedals, my mother's words sinking in, despite my reluctance to accept them.

"Or do you think New York is the only place you can do some good in the world?"

"I didn't say that," I grumble.

"No, you didn't, but your refusal to stay says as much. Look at your father's situation, baby. How many men and women, right here in Asheville, have been condemned for a crime they haven't committed, just because of their poor circumstances? You want to be the force of change? Then start by cleaning up the mess in your own backyard. Asheville needs you, Stone. Just as much as I do," she insists passionately, her eyes filled with love and admiration for the hopes of what I can accomplish in the future.

My throat starts to clog with emotion as I lean in to hug my mother. She's a fragile woman whose hidden strength and belief in me have never wavered, even when fighting her own demons and battles.

"I love you, Momma. You know that, don't know?" I whisper in her ear, hugging her tightly.

She lets out a melodic giggle, her joyful tears falling down her face.

"I do, sweet girl," she murmurs, running her fingers through my hair. She then pulls me away, her smile still ten feet wide—even though her cheeks are stained with tears—and asks, "Now, are you going to wallow in what could have been? Or are you going to fight to achieve your goals, regardless of this little mishap?"

"Fight. Like I always do."

"That's my girl," she hushes, palming my face in her hands, leaning in to place a tender kiss on each cheek.

I give her one more hug and then turn to start the engine, but my mother halts me, yet again, by placing her hand on my shoulder and says, "Stone, just one more thing. And this is important."

"Okay," I reply, confused as to what more she has to say.

"Whatever that boy did to you, he's trying to make amends. Don't let your heart grow cold when love is begging to be let in. Believe me when I tell you, life is too short to hold on to resentments. Take it from a woman who has lived most of her life clinging to her memories of love because the real thing was too far from her grasp."

"I never said I loved him."

"You didn't need to. It's written all over your face. Only love can hurt so much. I should know. It's like looking in a mirror."

"That's different. Daddy never hurt you intentionally."

"Oh, baby girl. Does it matter if it was intentional or not? Pain is pain. It's finding the strength to forgive and allowing yourself to be happy that is challenging."

"Are you done, Momma? I really have to get back to the dorm and study," I lie, not wanting to talk about Finn any longer.

She finally lets me start the damn car and take her home, all the while letting me stew in my seat with her nuggets of heartfelt wisdom. She might be right on some accounts, but not all. Changing the vision I had for my future might not be that far-fetched, but forgiving Finn is something my mind won't allow, even if my heart begs me to.

I thrash from one side of the bed to the other, unable to get a wink of sleep. Since I took my mother to her doctor's appointment last Thursday, I've been more agitated than ever. Somehow, her words seeped into my subconscious, tormenting me even in my dreams.

The minute my weary heart and exhausted body allow sleep to take over, not only do I dream of stars just out of my reach, but also of a warm body hugging me to his side, begging me to love him. Knowing this is the misery that awaits me in my slumber, my brain wrestles with exhaustion, doing everything in its power to keep me awake. My bed has become a battle zone, the duvet and sheets all entwined at my feet, as I roll from one position to another, ordering my restless spirit to give me a moment's peace.

To my mind's dismay, the only comfort I find solace in is the pillow that still holds Finn's lingering, woodsy scent. I've vowed to wash the pillowcase a thousand times or throw it away for good, yet I've never had the courage to part with it. I inhale sharply, hoping its scent can soothe my aching heart, but all it does is remind me that, sooner or later, even this small piece of him will fade, leaving me with nothing.

I hate him. I hate him so much.

Why would he do this to me?

To us?

I'm still wallowing in my grief when my phone starts vibrating madly on the desk beside me. I reach my arm over to pick it up, answering without even looking at the screen to see who is calling me so early on a Sunday morning.

"Hello?"

"Good morning, Stone. So happy I caught you. It's Charlene," Finn's mom announces with a jovial disposition.

My back instantly lifts off the bed, thinking I must be hallucinating from my lack of sleep.

"Mrs. Walker?" I choke out, unable to prevent the perplexed tone in my voice from coming through.

"Yes, dear. I was wondering if we could do our brunch today. Say, around eleven at Magnolia?"

"I, uh… actually, it's not a good time for me right now."

"I'm sure you can spare an hour or two from your busy schedule to meet me. I look forward to spending some time with you, dear. See you there, Stone. Goodbye," she says before hanging up the phone, not allowing me to get a word in edgewise.

I throw the phone on my duvet and slump back down onto the bed, my arms covering my eyes.

Great!

Now I have a date with Finn's mom for brunch of all things. I've been doing everything in my power to forget and move on, avoiding all things Finn, but apparently, Mrs. Walker didn't get the memo.

Fuck my life!

At least her son has taken the hint. For the past two weeks, Finn has stayed clear of me. He hasn't come by Big Jim's, nor has he come to my side of campus to see me. Just as suddenly as he disrupted my life with his imposing presence and stalkerish ways, he disappeared with a snap of a finger. He pulled a total Houdini on me. But then again, isn't that what I wanted? For him to stay away and leave me to pick up the pieces of the shattered life he left behind?

Snap out of it, Stone!

Enough of this pity party of one.

Mom is right. I need to get my shit together and stop wallowing in what could have been. This is my life now, and it's about time I suck it up and do something about it. New York is no longer an option. So what? I can kick ass here at Richfield, just as I have done for the past three years. I'll get my law degree, and during that time, I'll look for other opportunities where I can do some good. But none of this is going to happen if I'm stuck in this room reminiscing about star-filled nights and strong arms holding me tight, vowing to love me.

That was then.

This is now.

With a new resolve in place, I jump out of bed. I pick up my pillow, throwing it against the door, as a reminder to toss it in the dumpster on my way out. I'll just go to this stupid brunch and tell Mrs. Walker that this little get together of hers is going to have to be a one-off type of thing. Finn and I are no more, so there really is no need for her civil pleasantries.

Out of sight, out of mind, right?

That's exactly what I need to do from now on. No more Finn or anything that reminds me of him. I'm sure that my heart will forget him, too, sooner or later.

For my sanity's sake, I hope it does.

It has to.

CHAPTER 27

STONE

"I'm so glad you could come," Charlene coos, wrapping me up in her arms for an awkward hug before letting me take a seat.

"You didn't leave me much choice," I say overly sweet, as a way of hinting my displeasure for being here.

If she was offended by my rebuke, she has hidden it quite well with her poised smile.

"Ah, yes. I forgot how frank you are. It will make this conversation go a lot smoother," she retorts, ordering us some mimosas from the waiter passing by.

"I figured it wasn't just an invite to eat cucumber sandwiches."

"Now, Stone, you're a clever girl. You must assumed that my invitation had an underlying agenda."

"Yes, Ma'am. I just didn't think you'd be so open about it," I reply, surprised with her candor.

"What can I say? I hate beating around the bush if I can avoid it. I think we have that in common," she beams, self-assured.

"I guess we do. So, what I can I do you for, Mrs. Walker?"

"Please, it's Charlene," she insists as the waiter hands us our drinks.

"Okay, *Charlene*. Why did you invite me to brunch today?"

"Isn't it obvious? I need your help. My son is being quite unreasonable of late, and I need someone to persuade him to see sense."

"And you think I can help how, exactly?" I ask, more out of curiosity than anything else.

"Oh, you'd be surprised what a loving word here, or a gentle push there, can do when it comes from the woman a man loves. Trust me, gentle persuasion goes a long way," she singsongs, taking a sip of her spiked orange juice.

"That sounds awfully like manipulation to me," I clip back, unimpressed with her cunning tactics.

"We women use all the talents God afforded us, in any manner possible. A girl like you, who has worked so hard all her life to achieve her goals, should know that by now."

"I'm sorry to disappoint you, Charlene, but I think you've got the wrong girl. I'm not a fan of manipulation of any kind."

"But are you a fan of my son?" She cocks her manicured brow at me, making my lips thin at the question.

"Not at the moment, no."

"Hmm. So the rumors are true. You have broken up. Can I ask why?" she asks, looking saddened with the idea of her son and I no longer being together.

"I'd rather keep my personal life to myself if you don't mind. And if Finn hasn't said anything to you by now, then I think he shares the same opinion about privacy."

"I do see why he is so infatuated with you." She grins yet again, her forlorn frown no longer in place. "You know, most women would take this opportunity of having an intimate brunch to win me over."

"I guess I'm not most women."

"No, you're not," she deadpans.

I suck in my teeth to prevent myself from asking just exactly what she meant with that underhanded comment, but then she surprises me with her next statement, leaving me even more baffled.

"I think you're better. You are just the type of partner my son needs in his life."

Feeling my cheeks starting to blush at the unexpected compliment, I take a sip of the tainted champagne. Before I know it, I drink the whole flute in an instant, without leaving even a measly drop to keep me occupied. I place the glass back on the table and look around for the waiter, anxiously waiting for a refill to get me through this heart-to-heart with Finn's mom.

"I am curious, though, how my son pushed you away. Why did you end it?"

"What makes you think I was the one who ended it? Finn could have easily done it."

"Stone, if we are going to have a relationship based on respect, please don't offend my intelligence. My son would have never ended the courtship, and please, no more nonsense of keeping your personal life to yourself. I have no patience for it. Rest assured, I'll find out one way or the other. Believe me, there isn't a thing I don't know if I'm so inclined to look."

"I believe you."

"As you should. Now out with it. What did my foolish boy do that deserved you breaking his heart for?"

"You really want to know? Fine. Your precious Finn sabotaged my opportunity to get the job of a lifetime in New York, destroying all my hopes of getting a law degree from Columbia. That's what he did. Satisfied?" I snap at her, angry for having to list all the ways her son has wronged me.

"My Finn did that?" Her eyebrows pinch together, obviously not believing a single word.

"Yes, he did," I repeat, rudely snapping my fingers at the waiter for that damn mimosa, hoping that liquor will get me through this conversation.

"Hmm. Tell me something, Stone, with everything you know about my son, does that seem like something he would do?" she probes further, clearly not satisfied with my reason.

"I didn't think so, no. But I have proof he did everything that I just told you."

"Ah, yes, proof. There's that pesky word again. I've been hearing it a lot lately." She seethes, running the pad of her finger around the rim of her flute.

Now it's my turn for my forehead to wrinkle in confusion, so I counter, "What do you mean by that?"

"You don't know?" she questions, surprised.

"Know what?" I demand a little too loudly, gaining the other patron's eyes on me. I inwardly slap myself for being so reckless with my outcry, and sit quietly until their prying curiosity is focused elsewhere before I repeat, "Know *what?*"

"Of course you don't know. If you are bitter with Finn for ruining your chances of moving to the big city, then it's obvious you'd stay clear of my boy and any news pertaining to him."

"Charlene, I thought you weren't one for idle chit-chat."

"Quite so." She chuckles, but there is no humor behind her laugh. "Finn quit football."

"He did?" I stutter my eyes beginning to bug out of their sockets.

"Yes. I know my son never wished to pursue it anyway, but the way it all came to an end was unfortunate, at best. You see, Richfield University makes sure to test all its players on occasion to prevent any scandal, should one of them test positive before a big game. After all, it's the university's reputation on the line."

"What does that have to do with Finn quitting?"

"Everything, darling girl. Finn tested positive for steroid use."

"That's impossible! Finn wouldn't do that," I holler again in outrage, this time not caring about the audience around me.

"My thoughts exactly. I know my Finn. My son may live on another plane of existence with his mind constantly focused on the stars, but he has always been responsible in fulfilling his duties. Football being one of them."

"He's not a cheater," I add with all the conviction in the world. "I know Finn's heart wasn't set on going Pro, but he would never cheat."

"Unfortunately, Dean Ryland and my husband believe more in a piece of paper than the word of my own son."

"But you don't believe it."

"Do you?" she asks, her eye narrowing on me to gauge my response.

"No, I don't."

"Good. Neither do I," she replies with a relieved smile on her lips. "So tell me Stone, if you think my son is incapable of committing such an act, would it also be possible he didn't do what you are accusing him of?"

I play with my tongue ring, deep in thought, putting together all the sinister pieces of a game I didn't even realize I was playing.

"Someone is trying to hurt him. But who?" I conclude at last.

"Such a clever girl." She smiles broadly. "The minute I met you, I knew you'd be good for him. Finn needs someone who is grounded and can think clearly within the fog. But I think the better question is not who, dear, but why?"

I give her a curt nod, thinking if we find out the 'who,' then the 'why' will reveal itself sure enough.

"What do you need me to do?"

"Honestly, I just want to make sure Finn is alright and being looked after, more than anything else."

"What do you mean? Aren't you looking out for him?"

"My quick-tempered husband kicked Finn out of our home a couple of weeks ago."

"Let me guess? Because of football," I quip, my nose flaring in disgust.

"Yes."

"Don't take this the wrong way, Charlene, but your husband is an asshole."

"None taken, dear," she says with a light chuckle. "I know exactly the kind of man I married. But I also know, despite his faults, Hank loves his boys, even if he has a funny way of expressing it. Not three days after Finn had left our home, my husband began brooding all over the house, latched onto photo albums of when Finn was a child. My husband will never admit it because of his pride, but he knows he's wrong. However, their relationship is for them to repair. My only concern is my son. Anytime I try to bring up the subject of him coming back home, he dismisses me."

"Finn's a grown man, Charlene. He can handle being on his own."

"Not if someone is toying with his life. I'd rather have him under my roof than at the Hamilton Estate," she adds, sounding distressed at the idea of her son being at the deceased governor's home.

"He's with Lincoln Hamilton?"

"He is. Lincoln has always been like a brother to my Finn, so I understand why my son took refuge with him. Although I love Lincoln dearly, I don't want Finn to be in that house for longer than necessary."

"Why? If they're friends, close to brothers as you say, then Finn is as safe as he can be."

"No one's safe in that house."

I swallow dryly, my skin beginning to crawl from the look of dread in her eyes and the cryptic statement that fell from her quivering lips.

"What do you mean by that?" I question, but she still seems locked away in the thought that is troubling her. "Charlene?" I probe further, but when she looks up, her bright mask is suddenly in place once again as she orders fresh fruit and a quiche for us.

"So, can I count on you to have a word with my son? To bring him home?" she asks, completely disregarding my previous question.

I give her a tight nod, my apprehension still heavy on my shoulders.

There's more to this story than she's willing to tell me. I just know it. If I want answers or any kind of enlightenment, I guess there is only one place where I can get them—the Hamilton Estate. The very place Charlene Walker is so adamant in keeping Finn away from.

The minute I leave Magnolia, I drive through town with Finn's mother's words still loudly ringing in my ear, trying desperately to make sense of it all. I pull at the jumbled strings, a ball of baffling chaos, but with each thread I stretch, there are only a few certainties laid out for me—the most flagrant of them being that Finn would never take any illegal substances to improve his game.

Finn's love for football was limited, so if he wasn't any good on the field, it would give him the perfect excuse to not go Pro. Sure he was willing to postpone his dreams of being an astronomer just to appease his father, but to take performance enhancing drugs is just not something Finn would do. That is the action of someone who *wants* to have a big NFL life, and he didn't. I know that much.

So, could his mother be right in all her conclusions?

If someone fabricated his guilt just to ruin his chances of going pro, could that same person try to sabotage his love life, too? I've been so focused on blaming Finn—thinking he intentionally ruined my plans of going to New York just to keep me here, afraid that somehow he would lose me if I left Asheville—that I never considered an outside force being responsible for it. But what if there has been someone out there all along, intent on making sure Finn loses everything in his life that is important to him?

His football career.

His home and family.

And me—the girl he was falling in love with.

Some things are still not adding up, though. If someone is making Finn's life miserable, and if he wasn't the one communicating with Watkins & Ellis on my behalf, then why not tell me? Why didn't he defend himself when I blew up in his face? I saw the look in his eyes when I accused him of it. The guilt embedded in those stellar, crystal blue eyes was clear as daylight. If Finn wasn't the one behind it all, then his guilt tells me he knows exactly who is. And if I want to find out, then there is only one person who can give me the truth, and that's pretty boy himself.

I quickly go to my dorm room and pick up all the things necessary for my interrogation. After I have everything in my book bag, I haul ass out of there, pushing my truck to the limit, to get me to Linc's mansion, which is now known in most of Asheville as 'The House of Horrors' after all the deaths that occurred there.

When I enter the grounds of the lush estate, the facade doesn't honor the macabre history behind it. I guess you can't judge a book by its cover. With my bag in hand, I walk up to the door and ring the bell. My heart starts beating profusely in my chest, my hands clammy and trembling with anticipation of seeing the boy who stole my heart, praying he won't stomp on it further by lying to me.

When the door opens, though, it's not Finn who stands under its threshold, but the owner of the impressive home, Lincoln Hamilton, who is displaying a broad smile on his face. He stands at about six foot two, towering over me, in designer jeans and T-shirt, which to me looks far too clean-cut for just bumming around at home all day.

There is one thing that I notice right away—Lincoln's eyes. He might have the same light-blue tone as Finn, but while pretty boy's baby-blues remind me of a clear summer sky, Lincoln's look like the abyss of a deep ocean, so profound that you fear to drown in them.

However, that is just one of the many differences between the two men. Finn is as tall as an oak tree and thickly built, reminiscent of everything solid and secure. He's earth, dirt, and real. Lincoln, however, reminds me more of the inconsistencies of a body of water. Yes, it can look clear and innocent if contained, but left unchecked, it can quickly transform into to a fierce, crashing wave, demolishing everything in its path. Lincoln is the very definition of contained refinement, even with his ruffled sandy beach hair and ocean-blue eyes, while my Finn is crude, massive, and perfect.

"Stone," he greets me, before I'm able to remind him of who I am.

His memory is impressive since he only saw me briefly at Finn's father birthday party. It seemed like everyone wanted a piece of him that night, so he hardly had much time to be with his friends, much less chit-chat with their girlfriends.

"Hi, Lincoln. Is Finn here?"

"He is. I'll go and get him. He'll be very happy to see you."

His smile is genuine, at least.

"We'll see," I mumble beneath my breath. I then re-think my manners, and before he's able to take another step into the foyer, I grab on to his elbow and say, "I just want to thank you for all the help you are offering my mother and my father. I guess I should have said that first, huh?"

His eyes widen as does his sincere smile.

"I'm not the one doing anything. I'm sure you figured that was all Finn's doing."

"Yes, but you're the one stuck with the bill."

"What's money if you don't have happiness? If it can help you, then I know it will make Finn happy."

"Is that why you did it? To make Finn happy?" I ask suspiciously, knowing there are no free lunches in life.

"Loyalty and friendship are why I'm helping. I'd do anything for any one of my friends. Just as I know they would do anything for me."

The words should be nice to hear, but somehow, I get an awful cringe in the pit of my stomach, wondering just how far their loyalty to one another would go.

I'm about to say as much when I hear footsteps approach behind Lincoln.

"Who's at the door?" I hear Finn ask, his throaty voice reminding me how much I've missed it whispering in my ear.

"Look for yourself." Lincoln chuckles, opening the door wider so that I'm no longer hidden from Finn's view.

"Stone," he croaks, his beautiful eyes bulging from their sockets.

"Hey, quarterback. We need to talk," I tell him point-blank, grabbing his hand and pulling him away from his rooted spot.

"Talk?" he asks, confused, yet keeps his hold on me, unwilling to let me go.

"Yep, and you're going to tell me everything I want to know. You can count on it."

CHAPTER 28

FINN

Stone remains dead silent as she leads me by the hand into the Oakley woods. With every leisured step she takes, my heart thumps madly in my chest, remembering the last time I took a walk down this path. But last time, it was under the light of a full moon with my best friend guiding me through the vast area, not beneath the sun's beaming rays accompanied by the girl I was ordered to ruin.

I have no idea why Stone came over to Linc's this afternoon, but I'm too fucking grateful for having her this close to even care that she's leading me into the last place I want to be.

I entwine my fingers in hers, never wanting to let go, as she walks us further into the wooded area. We walk deeper and deeper, until the mansion behind us is far from view, ensuring we are surrounded only by large oak trees and the clear blue sky above us.

"Stone?" I mutter behind her, hoping she doesn't take us too far in.

Who knows what she'll find if she keeps going farther. I sure as hell haven't been back to check if we did a proper job that night. Perhaps one of the guys paid a visit to the macabre place since then, just to be sure we didn't fuck up and leave clues of our guilt. If I had to wager on it, my money is on Easton. He's never been one to leave loose ends.

"Stone?" I repeat again when all I get is radio silence from her.

"I don't want to hear another peep out of you, quarterback. Not until I say so," she orders, her voice cold as steel and just as punishing.

I keep my head down like a scolded child but do as she says. It's clear that, even though Stone has come to see me, she's still pissed as all hell. The only thing that comforts me is the way she keeps hold of my hand, squeezing it from time to time, letting me run my thumb lightly over hers. I'm still focusing on the little patch of skin she's allowing me to touch, almost crashing into her when she begins to slow her steps. She takes one long look around before giving me a curt nod to confirm she's found her spot.

"This will do nicely," she says, letting go of my hand to take the book bag off her shoulders.

My frown deepens as I shove my hands into my pockets, trying to hide the fact that my hand feels naked without hers. I keep rooted in place as she goes to her haunches and begins to take some stuff out of her bag.

"Stone?"

"I said zip it."

I look up at the heavens to give me the fortitude to keep silent, but my confusion only heightens as I watch her throw an old blanket over the cold grass.

"Sit," she orders, her head tilting up at me, commanding me to do as she says.

I'm tempted to call her out on her bossy behavior, but I doubt my playful teasing will change her stern disposition. So instead, I sit down on the edge of the blanket, the spiky, hard grass biting into my butt cheeks, even through the blanket and my thin, gray sweat pants. If I knew we were going to have a tête-à-tête in the woods, I would have worn jeans and spared my ass some grief.

Stone sits cross-legged just a few inches in front of me, placing her bag in between the hollow of her bare thighs. While she has her head bent down, rummaging through it, I take the opportunity to just look at her. She's not in her usual in-your-face gear today. Actually, if I didn't know any better, it looks like she just came from church, which is silly since I know everything there is to know about Stone, and going to Sunday Mass isn't on her weekly to-do list.

She still looks good, though. More than good. In a simple, sleeveless, white turtleneck, and knee-length, black skirt and boots, Stone continues to be the sexiest woman I have ever laid eyes on.

Some people say that you don't know what you have until it's gone. This couldn't be truer for me when it comes to Stone.

Funny thing is, in my case, I always knew that she was one of a kind. In my very soul, I felt that the Southie was someone I would be a fool to let go of, regardless of the reason. To me, she will always be Stone—beautiful on the outside as she is on the inside.

I'm probably the only lucky bastard who can say I know all her facets. The world may know the fierce brat who doesn't take shit from anyone, but I saw the vulnerable, scared girl who didn't want to give her heart away. I held her in my embrace, where I would have kept her if The Society hadn't fucked everything up.

After me, I wonder who will earn the privilege to hold her. To dry her eyes. To kiss her lips. Whoever he is, I'll surely hate him with every fiber of my being. I will hate the man who wins her heart when I lost it so ruthlessly.

Stone's jet-black hair is all over her face as she continues to ransack through her bag. I'm about to take advantage of her absentmindedness and touch a fallen strand, when she finally pulls out a small bottle of tequila, tilting her head back up to face me once more.

The minute my eyes see her beloved Jose Cuervo in her hands, a chill runs through my bones. My sudden apprehension begins to yell at me to get myself up and haul ass out of here as fast as I can. Even though I might miss the hell out of Stone, I know all too well what that bottle signifies.

As they say, loose lips sink ships, and with the state of my mournful heart, I'm not sure I won't blabber everything out and tell her what she wants to know. Not the best circumstances to be in, considering it's not only my frail heart in jeopardy but hers, too, if I tell her the truth.

She might hate me now for thinking I stole her only shot at leaving Asheville, but if she knew the real reason behind her downfall, I doubt her hate would be the only thing I'd get in return for such a confession. I'm thinking some steel cuffs and iron bars would be part of my immediate future.

"No," I state, already pushing myself up from the ground.

But Stone is having none of it, so she grabs one of my wrists to keep me still while shaking her head disapprovingly, and retorts, "Yes. You are going to sit down and do exactly as I say, quarterback. You're not in a position to negotiate."

"Nuh-uh. Not happening. I don't want to play this game with you." I shake my head profusely.

"Yes, you do. If you want me here, you'll play. And if you leave, I won't be coming back. Ever."

I crack my knuckles and press my tongue to the side of my cheek, conflicted with the fact that the damn brat is playing hardball. I do want her here, and the idea of not ever seeing her again just breaks my heart further.

These past two weeks without her have been hell—total and utter hell. It's been the little things that have been driving me up the wall the most. Unable to see her glorious face up close, or smell her perfume. Unable to caress her cheek, or hear her voice. She must know that the distance has been killing me, and now she wants to play one of her games just to torture me further. I'm not sure who's squeezing my balls tighter—The Society or Stone.

"Same rules as before," she begins after making sure that I'm not going anywhere. "I'll ask a question, and you'll tell me the truth. If not, then you either drink or strip."

"I don't want to play by your rules anymore, Stone. I'm tired of playing games."

"Okay, then I'll do you one better. For every truth you tell me, then I'll be the one who strips."

My cock immediately claps and nods madly, confirming that he definitely wants to play. The fucker doesn't even see the trap she's setting for him. All he heard was Stone getting naked in front of him, and fuck the consequences.

"That's not fair."

"Life's not fair. Now get with the program, quarterback. We haven't got all day."

"I could just get up and go back into the house," I threaten half-heartedly, not moving a muscle to follow through on my threat.

"You could, but then you would have to live with the fact that you could have seen the twins once again and passed at the chance."

"That's playing dirty, and you know it," I grumble, almost pouting like a three-year-old because, apparently, I like to be pussy-whipped like a motherfucker by the tattooed she-devil.

God, help me.

"We're well past playing nice," she pinpoints with an all-knowing stare.

"Whatever," I quip and grab the tequila from her hands, taking a long gulp until I feel the warm liquid burn my insides.

If I'm going to watch Stone take off her clothes without being allowed to touch her, then I might as well do it drunk to numb the pain.

"I'll go first," she sings, pleased.

"Of course you will." I sigh, taking another long-ass sip.

"First things first, why did you quit football?"

"You heard about that? Keeping tabs on me, brat?" I try to play it off, but the endearment just falls flat on the ground, with her no-nonsense glare. I let out a long exhale, and give her what she wants. "I quit because I was tired of doing something I didn't love and for the wrong fucking reasons. There. Question answered, so pay up."

There is a little smirk beginning to surface on her pretty red lips as she begins to take off the diamond studs I gave her, one at a time. My stupid heart latches onto the thin thread of hope as I watch Stone carefully place them in her bag, making sure nothing happens to them.

"You're going to have to do a lot better than that," she retorts, her brow up in the air.

"If you want better answers, then you're going to have to show me more than your bare lobes," I rebuke, wetting my lips, yet again, with her liquor of choice.

Before I'm able to take another sip, she snatches the bottle from me, denying my need to self-medicate, and turning my near pout into a full-blown sulk.

"My turn," I announce when she takes her own little sip. "Why are you here, Stone?"

"To play a game with you, pretty boy. See how annoying it is to only get half an answer? That one should get me to see your toes, at least." She winks teasingly.

"Cute," I grumble, taking off my T-shirt instead.

She eyes me below her long, dark lashes, taking a swig of tequila, even though the game didn't call for it. I'm about to ask if my bare chest is to her liking, since she's sporting a cute little blush on her cheeks, when she stops me dead cold with her next question.

"Why did your dad kick you out?"

"You know about that, too, huh?"

"Yep. Now answer the question."

"You already know the answer, Stone. He kicked me out because he's an asshole who wants to live his past youth vicariously through me, and he can't." I shrug, frustrated with her line of questioning, pulling a few strands of grass beside me.

Stone leans in and covers her hand over mine, making my chest expand, and my throat dry up with the innocent touch.

"I'm sorry he did that to you, Finn. You deserve to live your life how you want to," she whispers tenderly, making the beating organ inside me thrash out in violence, demanding I tell her that the life I want is with her at my side.

"How's your mom?" I ask, instead of laying out my bleeding heart at her feet.

Stone's green eyes soften at the mention of her mother, making me tuck my hands under my legs just to keep them from reaching out to her.

"She's good. In high spirits because of you." She smiles genuinely, the first true smile I've seen on her pretty face since she arrived.

"I didn't do much."

She lets out a long sigh, looking up at the sky for a minute before her eyes land on mine again.

"This game has always been about us telling each other the truth. Don't lie to me now, Finn. We both have to recognize that your friend Lincoln wouldn't even know of my mother's existence, nor my father's situation, if you hadn't had a word with him."

"I would have paid for it myself, but my father cut me off. That's why I went to Linc," I confess, ashamed.

"I'm sorry," she replies saddened.

Such words feel awfully wrong coming from her lips. She shouldn't be speaking them, even if only to console me. I should be the one showering her with a million apologies, but I know none of them will make right what I've done.

"Going against your father's wishes like that was a brave thing to do, Finn. I'm proud of you."

Fuck! She's killing me.

"Stone, please don't say shit like that. Don't be proud of me. I've done so many things not worthy of it. Especially from you."

"Like being tested positive for steroids, you mean?" she asks without a single hint of disapproval in her sweet voice.

441

"I never did that. I'm not a cheat," I reply steadfastly.

"I know."

"You do?"

"Yes. You may have many faults, Finn Walker, but you are not a cheater," she adds, and there is such tenderness in her green eyes, such unconditional belief that it makes me want to be the man she sees in me.

"Stone," I choke, my hand already finding its home against her cheek.

She leans in and cups my hand in hers, closing her eyes to take in the warmth of my palm, everything around me suddenly seeming to play in slow motion. I hear birds singing above us as the heat of her skin scorches mine. The racing of my heart, threatening to leap out of my throat, is too poignant to ignore, and yet I do. Let it explode inside me if it has to. As long as I can stay like this forever, just cupping her cheek in my palm, feeling her skin next to mine, then nothing else matters.

"Stone—"

"You're not a cheater. But you are a liar, aren't you, pretty boy?" she asks, no judgment in her words.

"Yes," I admit, forlorn.

She grips my hand and pulls it away from her cheek just to kiss my open palm. The erratic beating of my heart only increases when her lids open, and those green jewels stare into my eyes as if coaxing my soul to kneel in submission.

"Have you ever lied to me?"

"Yes."

"Because you wanted to?"

"No," I confess, struggling to find my voice as her gaze on me remains tender and true.

She kisses my wrist this time, and my own eyes shut of their own accord, treasuring her soft graze.

"You didn't send those emails to Watkins & Ellis, did you?" Unable to speak, I just shake my head from side to side and keep listening. "But someone went through a whole lot of trouble to make it seem like you did."

I don't say anything to that either. Stone has always been clever. I was a fool in thinking she wouldn't see through The Society's ploys.

"The first night you came into Big Jim's, it was because that same person sent you there, wasn't it?" Even without uttering a word, she sees my guilt plastered all over my face. With her confidence wavering, she hushes, "Was all of it a lie?"

I open my eyes and look at the woman who has turned my life upside down more than The Society ever could. Stone came out of nowhere, and hit me like a freight train, changing the man I used to be. Before her, I was just going through the motions, detached and keeping an apathetic wall around me, holding everyone at arm's length. I didn't allow anyone to truly witness my chaotic mind, because I thought the version the world demanded of me was better than reality. Aside from the guys, Stone was the only one that didn't fall for my pretenses and accepted me just as I am. That was never a lie.

"No."

"Tell me, Finn. Which part was real?" she insists.

"The part where I fell in love with you, Stone. That was real."

A small, meek smile crests her lips before she presses them on my knuckles, leaving one gentle kiss on each one.

"Stone," I croak on ragged breath, begging her to either leave me to my misery or end it entirely.

"Do you still love me?"

"With all my fucking heart," I vow.

Another soft smile rises from her lips as she wraps my hand around her neck. My thumb instantly caresses that soft hollow of her throat as she leans in and places her hands over my broken heart.

"So, this is mine?" she asks, stroking my bare chest where my heart beats.

"Yes. Then, now, and always."

She sweeps her tongue over her lower lip, as she continues to stare into my eyes.

"If that's true, then it can't lie to me. Not if you want mine in return."

"Fuck, Stone, that's all I want," I reply in earnest, cupping her cheeks with both my hands, cradling her gorgeous face in them.

"Then prove it."

"How?"

"By telling me the truth. All of it, Finn."

I bow my head and shake it from left to right, knowing if I do as she says, then there is no turning back.

"I can't."

"I believe you." She shrugs with a sad smile. "But you're going to do it just the same."

"Stone," I try to beg, but she stops me by leaning in and pressing a soft kiss to my hungry lips.

My fingers instantly weave through her hair as hers remain perched on my chest, keeping me from diving into the kiss and losing myself in it. She breaks away and lowers her head to leave one small kiss where my heart resides.

"No more games, Finn. This is the only chance you have to tell me the truth. If you love me like you say you do, then you will fight whatever is keeping us apart." My eyes go wide as she pulls my chin down, and as we are just a hair's breadth away from each other, she whispers, "Don't lose me, Finn."

"I don't want to."

"Good. Then you won't."

"You say that now, but once you know the whole story, you'll never look at me the same way."

"Try me. Maybe I'll surprise you."

I grab the back of her head and kiss her one last time without letting her stop me. I plunge into her hot mouth, taking out everything I need to give me courage. When I finally find the bravery she seeks from me, I pull apart from her and stand up to my feet.

If I'm going to do this, then my mind can't be clouded by her closeness.

"Before I say a word, just know that I'm still me—the man who will always love you, even when you can no longer look at me."

"That won't happen," she replies assuredly, unaware of the atomic bomb I'm about to drop.

"Yes, it will. No one can love a murderer, Stone. Not even you."

CHAPTER 29

FINN

I shift from one foot to the other, biting my thumb nail as I watch Stone take it all in.

I mean, all of it.

I told her every sordid detail, not leaving anything out. She wanted the truth, and she got it.

At least she hasn't run away screaming.

Not yet, anyway.

I begin to pace the earth, looking every once in a while at the woman I love, deep in thought. It's been ten minutes now since I confessed to all my sins, and she still hasn't said a single word.

"Stone?" I stutter, my anxiety getting the better of me.

"Give me a minute, Finn. It's a lot to absorb all at once."

"I know," I mumble in defeat.

"I mean, it's not every day you are told that the man you love was involved in a double homicide. Triple, if what Governor Hamilton said was true."

"It is. Linc made sure of determining the truth. Afterward, I mean."

"Of course he did. Damn. I don't even know how he is walking about, acting as if that night never happened."

"It's been challenging. For all of us."

"I can see that. Okay. Let's recap, pretty boy. So, this so-called society knows your dirty little secret, but do you think they have any proof?"

My brows pinch together, realizing I never once thought of that.

"They must have. I mean, does it even really matter if they don't? As long as they know what happened to Lincoln's parents that night, they can snitch on us to the cops anytime they want. If The Society is as high-up and connected as we think they are, I doubt they need proof to get the police sniffing around us."

"Hmm. That's true," she replies, playing with her tongue ring, considering all our options.

I pause in place and look down at her, trying to sort all of our shit out. I've played this scenario a million times in my head, and not once did I think Stone would react like this. Trying to solve the puzzle we've been working at for months on end, with no success.

I mean, she just said...

Hold up!

What did she just say?

"Wait. Did you just say the man you love?" I almost shout, gaining a huge eye roll from the love of my life.

"Good thing you're pretty to look at, quarterback. Took you a while to pick up on that, huh?" she teases, with a huge fucking grin on her succulent mouth.

"Always the brat." I purse my lips to feign irritation, but I'm incapable of keeping my scowl in place with such a fucking awesome revelation.

"So, what does that mean? Do you forgive me?" I ask anxiously, wanting to hear those words come out of her mouth again.

"You didn't do anything that warrants my forgiveness, Finn. Sure, I'm not thrilled you chased me only because you were being blackmailed. But if The Society led you to me, then I guess I can't be too angry about that, now can I?" She winks, getting up to her feet and walking toward me.

I let out a long, stuttered exhale, my body beginning to tremble. I run my fingers through my hair, my eyes starting to prick at their side.

"Finn," she whispers as she comes closer to me.

"I thought I'd lost you," I croak out, emotion tainting each word as I pull at my shorthairs.

"I did, too."

"But I didn't, did I, Stone? You're still mine, right?" I ask on a quivered breath, desperate for her to take away my suffering.

"Yeah, baby. I'm still yours. I've only ever been yours, Finn."

"Fuck," I growl, picking her up in one fast move, her legs clamping on my hips and hooking around my thighs.

"Even after what I just told you?"

"You told me the truth. I didn't expect it to be pretty."

"Stone," I mumble, holding her tightly. "How can you forgive what I did?"

She pulls at my hair, so I have no choice but to gaze into her eyes.

"Guess loving someone means you take the good, along with the bad. We might suck at everything else, Finn, but not where it counts."

I break my restraint, pushing her against a tree to balance her with just one hand while the other holds her pretty face.

"I've been lost these past few weeks, Stone. It felt like hell, being without you."

"For me too," she admits. "As much as I tried to deny it, you're a part of me now."

"And you're everything to me," I profess, caressing her cheek with the pad of my thumb, memorizing her flawless face, and thinking to myself how I ever got so lucky in finding such a wondrous creature.

"Finn?" she susurrates.

"Yes."

"Just kiss me already, will you?"

"Always the brat." I chuckle, but the laughter quickly subsides when my lips finally press against hers.

My heart leaps to my throat, urging me to never stop kissing this woman. This fierce, beautiful girl, who loves and accepts me for who I am, and not what the world expects me to be. She's the other half of my soul who, despite seeing how black and tarnished it is, still wants to cast her bright light on it and heal it from within.

Our kiss deepens until all we are is unyielding tongues, bruising lips, and clashing teeth.

"I need you," she mewls, the desperation in her voice mimicking my own.

"Not as much as I need you, Stone. Not half as much."

"I love you, too," she cries on a moan, rubbing up against me, eviscerating what remains of my control.

Shit.

Unable to hold back from taking what's mine, I push my sweats down just enough to liberate my hard cock. I raise her skirt, pushing her panties to the side, and her wet core instantly coats my fingers with her arousal.

"Say that again, Stone. Moan out that you love me while I'm deep inside you," I growl, thrusting into her hot core, making us both gasp out at the connection.

"Ahh," she cries out.

But that's not what I want to hear, so I pull her hair to crane her head back, forcing her to look at me as I fuck her against the oak tree.

"Say you love me, Stone. Say it," I beg, as I pummel through all of her walls with my hard length.

"I love you."

"Again," I growl, keeping up my merciless tempo.

If I don't slow down, this is going to be far too quick for my liking, but I desperately need to cum inside her. Stone withers against me, her chest heaving up and down as she moans out her pleasure. She sweetly clenches around my cock with each hard thrust, leaving me mere seconds away from cumming, whether I slow down or not.

"Tell me. Make me believe that you're mine. Because I'm so fucking yours, Stone. I'm yours," I swear, my own voice rough with an emotion not many will ever feel in their lifetime.

I fuck her with brutish force, all the while giving her my heart, praying she will never leave it again. I can never go back to a life without her in it. It would be as if someone stole all my senses, leaving me blind to the beauty of the world. The stars would lose their glow, food and drink would have no taste. Without her, my whole existence would be a waste because all I've ever done right is love her. She is, and always will be, my everything. Nothing else matters, as long as she is mine and I am hers.

Stone wraps her arms around me, kissing me madly, and as she promises herself to me, I cry out with the same devotion and worship that pumps through my veins.

"I love you, Finn. I'll always love you. No one will take me from you again."

And with that beautiful promise kissing my lips, scorching them with her love, I give all I have left until her vows are heavenly cries, succumbing to her nirvana, and compelling me to follow her and together embark on a journey to the stars.

It takes us a while to return to reality, but neither one of us is in too much of a hurry. In the same woods where I once promised my loyalty, I now promise—with my body, heart, and soul—my never-ending love to her.

I place Stone back on the ground and keep my firm hold on her.

"Are you sure you want me? After everything you've learned, I won't hold it against you if you want to walk away," I whisper in her ear, running my fingers through her dark mane, loving the feel of her silky strands.

She places her chin on my chest, her loving gaze never wavering, and says, "I told you, I don't scare easily."

"I know."

"Then you also know that I've always been a fighter. I've got your back, pretty boy, don't worry about mine."

"I'll always worry."

"I know, baby. But the only ones that should be worried are those blackmailing assholes who are playing with our lives. They're the ones who need to be on their toes."

"Stone, I don't want you involved in all this mess. I want you as far away from their radar as possible," I reply, terrified by the idea The Society might come for her again.

"Too late for that," she mumbles as the gears inside her head start spinning.

"What are you thinking about?"

She throws me a mischievous smile, one that does nothing to ease my nerves.

"Stone?"

She pushes up to the balls of her feet and silences me with, yet another, earth-shattering kiss.

"Don't you worry that pretty little head of yours, quarterback. We have more important things to talk about," she coos, pulling my hand and taking me back to the blanket on the ground.

Once we are right at the very center of it, she unlatches her hand from mine, taking two steps away from me. With a sly smirk on her lips, she pulls her turtleneck over her head, and sashays out of her pencil skirt, leaving nothing on but her black lace lingerie, high-heel boots, and her red-and-black phoenix tattoo, proudly on display.

My mouth waters as she crooks her finger with a come-hither look, and like the lovesick fool that I am, I go to her instantly.

"And we are not done talking." She winks, licking her lips as she unsnaps her bra, leaving the twins in plain view.

'I fucking love this girl,' my cock says, weeping in elation as he watches Stone bending down, taking her panties off, her pretty ass just begging for my teeth to latch onto it.

Get in line, fucker.

I smile inwardly, thankful that my cock, mind, and heart have found the one thing they can agree on. They all love the foul-mouthed Southie who wormed her way into my life and captivated all of me with just one look.

Tattoos, thick thighs, and pretty eyes. I never stood a chance.

She bends over again to unzip her boots, but I tsk at that and retort, "Keep them on, brat. I want to hold onto them while you sit on my face."

"Aren't you the romantic," she teases as I go to my knees, my tongue ready and starving to eat her sweet pussy out.

"Fuck romance. What we have is better."

She lets out a giggle, the sound warming my heart more than any other melody.

"Come here," I order, grabbing onto her naked thighs, leaving my mark on her perfect, unblemished skin.

"Here I am," she taunts, her dripping core inches away from my lips. "Now put that mouth to good use, pretty boy. I've missed it being on me."

Like the obedient, enamored fool that her love tamed me into, I do exactly as she orders, only stopping when she's too hoarse from crying out my name. And after she thinks she can't climb any higher, I make love to her, showing her there is no such limit.

With my body, heart, and soul, I tell her the only universal truth that seeps through me as I worship every patch of her skin with my mouth, lips, and tongue.

There is no cap on our happiness.

And I dare every last motherfucker to try and prove me wrong.

CHAPTER 30

STONE

"Whose cars are those?" I ask as we emerge from the Oakley woods.

"Easton and Colt's," Finn grumbles under his breath, squeezing my hand while throwing me a meek smile.

"Were you expecting them?"

He gives me a forlorn nod, hesitating to take a further step back toward the mansion.

"Well, let's not keep your friends waiting, quarterback," I exclaim, rushing my step and pulling him along to match my pace before he has a chance to change his mind.

"Stone," he begins to protest but stops when Lincoln opens his front door, apparently expecting our arrival.

The smile stitched on his face is just as wide and genuine as when I first showed up on his doorstep. It troubles me that I can't pinpoint if Lincoln is as trustworthy as his smile indicates. Especially after everything Finn confided in me this afternoon, I'm more than torn in regards to the Richfield heir.

"All caught up with, I see," he taunts, eyeing Finn up and down.

When I see the traces of grass in pretty boy's golden locks, I know his friend has a good idea of what we've been up to for the last few hours. Not that I care. What happens between Finn and me is our business. I'm not embarrassed by one minute spent in his arms. Unlike Lincoln, who has plenty to be ashamed of.

Finn opens his mouth, yet again, but Lincoln's sunny expression suddenly changes and shakes his head while pressing a finger on his lips, indicating Finn to keep his mouth shut. Lincoln then shifts his sights from Finn to me, making my unease with his eagle-eyed scrutiny that much more intense.

"Do you mind if I borrow your phone for a minute, Stone?" he asks out of the blue, polite as ever, even if his expression is as stern as steel.

I look up at Finn, his features just as stoic as his friend's, as he nods for me to do as Lincoln requests. I take my bag off my shoulders in search of my phone, and once I find it, Lincoln silently extends his open palm, waiting for me to hand it over. But when I finally relinquish the damn thing to him, I'm surprised to see Lincoln throw the gadget back over to Finn. As I'm about to ask what the hell is going on, my boyfriend cracks the device in two, but not before taking the SIM card out to do the same.

"I'll get you a new one, brat," Finn says sweetly, pressing his lips on my temple. "Like I told you back in the woods, that one was compromised. Better safe than sorry, right?"

"Okay, now that that's done, Stone, please come in. We have plenty to discuss."

Lincoln's smile returns to his face as if ordering Finn to annihilate my phone with his bare hands was second nature to him. I get where he's coming from, though. The fear of The Society using it to keep tabs on us or listen to our conversation is real.

"Oh, trust me, I know," I scold, walking into the lavish home, ready to get down to business.

I'm pissed as all hell that Finn so obediently followed his general's orders without missing a beat. His unconditional loyalty is what got him in this mess in the first place—a factor that doesn't sit well with me, and one that Lincoln seems to exploit without remorse.

"Linc," Finn stammers behind me, but his friend just squeezes his shoulder, fondness swimming in his blue eyes.

"Don't even sweat it, Finn. The minute your girl showed up, I knew you were going to tell her everything."

"She's my heart, Linc. I can't lie to my heart." Finn tries to defend, but Lincoln doesn't even look one bit upset about it.

"I never expected you to." He smiles genuinely, and I witness the weight on Finn's shoulders evaporate.

"If you two are done with the bromance, we have a lot to talk about," I snap, still trying to come to terms with the influence that Lincoln has over Finn.

Lincoln chuckles at my sass, the small laugh making his whole face light up. I can definitely see why everyone in both

Carolinas wants a piece of him. After all, he is Asheville's golden boy, and it doesn't hurt that, along with all his wealth, he isn't hard on the eyes either. If they only knew what I know now, maybe people wouldn't be so eager to be a part of his life. I sure as hell can't say I'm thrilled about it.

"Where are the guys at?" Finn asks, looking around the large foyer.

"They're both in the kitchen having dinner. We've been waiting on you for a while now."

Finn rubs the back of his head, embarrassed that his best friends have been twiddling their thumbs while we were fooling around.

"Come on." Lincoln chuckles again. "You guys must be starving."

"I could eat," Finn admits shyly, but I'm not surprised.

Even my stomach grumbles with just the mention of food, considering the workout pretty boy laid on me this afternoon. Then again, there is still plenty of lost time we need to catch up on, so we'll need to refuel if we don't want to wither away.

Lincoln's wide grin is still on his lips as he guides us to the left wing of the house, passing each room, one more luxurious and ostentatious than the last. Some people might get the green-eyed monster just by strolling through such opulence.

Me, however? Not so much.

What's the point of having such wealth and riches when your life has been filled with nothing but despair, sadness, and tragedy. Whoever envies Lincoln Hamilton is a fool in my book. I wouldn't want to trade lives with him for all the money in the world, that's for damn sure.

I'm still forming my own conclusion on our host when we walk into a large kitchen, where two familiar sets of eyes lock with mine. Easton's all-knowing smirk irks me to no end, while Colt's cold demeanor makes my skin crawl.

"Why the fuck is she here?" Colt reprimands, the deep-rooted scowl making his handsome features look ten times more menacing than attractive.

"Just breathe, asshole. This is Finn's girl," Easton announces, sliding a pizza box our way. "Sorry, kids, but the pie is cold. You two sure do take a long-ass time to fuck each other's brains out," he mocks, pulling out one of his trusty cigarettes.

"If you don't, then I pity the girl who falls for your charms," I reply overtly sweet, batting my eyelashes at him in sarcasm and ignoring the other asshole at his side.

"Always with a comeback. I knew I liked you."

"Yeah? Sure didn't act like you did when you came to Big Jim's warning me to stay away from your best friend," I bark out bitterly, still sore that he acted as if I were no good for Finn.

"You did what, now?" Finn hollers as he lunges at Easton's throat, but his dark-haired friend just chuckles, swiftly running to the other side of the large island to keep his distance from my pissed-off boyfriend.

"Hold on, big guy. Don't get your panties in a twist. You had been sulking for days because she wouldn't go on a date with you, so I figured a push was in order. A little reverse psychology and poof—you got your girl. You're welcome." Easton has the audacity to wink at me.

"You played me?" I retort in amusement, oddly impressed by his scheming ways.

"Kind of, yeah. It worked, didn't it?" Easton wiggles his brows as he lights up a cigarette.

"I don't know if I should slug you or kiss you." Finn laughs.

Finn's heartwarming smile is plastered all over his face, as he pulls me closer to him, wrapping his arms around my waist and putting his chin on my head, clearly happy that his friend's interference in our love life paid off.

I can't say I'm mad either. If it wasn't for Easton's meddling, I probably would have stuck to my guns, hoping Finn would abandon his ultimatum. I'd be missing out if that had happened.

"Keep your lips for your girl, asshole. I'm just happy you're not moping about anymore," he adds with a cocky smirk, sending small rings of smoke up into the air.

"Guess you're not as much of a jerk as I thought you were. That's good. Otherwise, hanging out with you was going to be tricky."

"Oh, you're not out of the woods yet. That title has been taken by this motherfucker beside me. Ain't that right, Colt?"

"Blow me, you dick," rebukes the foreboding friend, standing at his side with his arms crossed over his chest.

"Sorry. You're not my type," Easton mocks, making Colt look even more sinister.

If I were him, I wouldn't poke the bear. Colt might look like he should be on the cover of Vogue or something, but so did Ted Bundy at one time or another.

"Finn, take your girl home. We've got to talk," he announces hauntingly, and if we weren't indoors, I would have sworn a dark-gray cloud loomed above us just from the chill of his voice alone.

"Stone is staying," Lincoln deadpans, leaving no room for misinterpretation.

"Then I'm leaving," his cousin retorts, grabbing his car keys off the island countertop as he walks toward the door, throwing a distasteful glare my way.

Easton was right. Colt is a major dick.

"No, you're not, Colt. You're staying," Lincoln orders, sidestepping in front of him and putting himself in the line of fire.

"Linc, step aside." Colt seethes through gritted teeth.

"I can't do that, brother," his cousin replies, his expression just as serious.

Colt sneers but stops when Lincoln takes something from his back pocket, tossing it to the middle of the marble countertop. All eyes fall onto a black envelope, and before anyone can tell me what it is, I ask, "Is that one of The Society's letter?"

"The fuck?!" Colt snaps his head accusingly over to Finn. "How the fuck does she know about The Society?"

"I told her," Finn explains point-blank, not one bit intimidated by his dark, brooding friend.

If I wasn't completely sated from our venture into the woods, I'd climb him like a tree trunk just with the confidence he's displaying now. Colt is the very definition of an elitist bastard that thinks he can order people around. I'm glad Finn is immune to his temper.

"You dumb motherfu—"

"Enough!" Lincoln belts out, gaining the attention of all of us. "She's here to stay, Colt. Stone is Finn's, and therefore family. Deal with it."

I watch the two cousins, stare each other down, and I know who I'd give my allegiance to. Lincoln has all the traits of a fallen angel, while Colt's are of the rising devil. One is beaming light, even if tormented, while the other is pure vengeance, ready to bring destruction to the world. If their features weren't so identical, I would have never thought them to be related.

Finn's hold on me tightens, and I wonder who he's more fearful of—the devil with the handsome face or the angel that, somehow, has his hooks set in every person in this room.

"Fuck this," Easton states, sounding aloof to the confrontation between the cousins.

With his cigarette dangling at the corner of his mouth, he reaches for the envelope and opens it with a kitchen knife, before spreading the black stationery wide on the smooth countertop.

With the real threat staring us all in the face, all five of us sit around the kitchen island to read The Society's latest correspondence. As my eyes read each sentence, a shiver runs down my back that not even Finn's warmth can subdue.

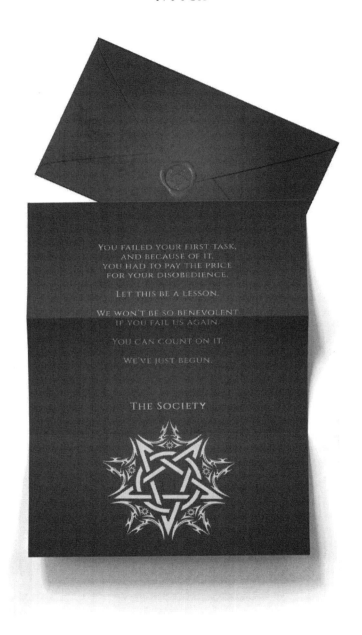

You failed your first task,
and because of it,
you had to pay the price
for your disobedience.

Let this be a lesson.

We won't be so benevolent
if you fail us again.

You can count on it.

We've just begun.

THE SOCIETY

I clasp my hands over my mouth, the gravity of this fucked-up situation hitting me like a ton of bricks.

"Shit," Colt exclaims bitterly, no longer looking so threatening compared to the real villains at hand. "These fuckers will only be done once they've ruined all of us."

"Take it easy, Colt," Lincoln tries to console him, squeezing his cousin's shoulder, when not two minutes ago they looked like they were going to tear each other limb from limb.

"How can you be so calm, Linc? They just told us that they aren't done with us?!"

"And did you really expect they would stop with Finn?" He raises his brows, patting his cousin on the back.

"Fuck, you're right. We're all going to play their twisted game, aren't we?" Colt looks for confirmation in Lincoln's blue eyes and bows his head when he gets it.

"Not if we can find them first," Lincoln says reassuringly, but I don't hear the same conviction he had a few minutes ago.

"Do you have anything on them yet? Anything concrete that can help us out of this?" I ask, looking at each of the four men in the eye, getting a response from Easton, who seems to be the only one keeping his cool together.

"We got nothing. Nada. Zip. Zilch. For the past two months, we have come up with squat. These fuckers leave nothing to chance. Not one measly clue for us to follow on," Easton admits in frustration.

I slap my forehead, astounded by the fact that these fools have lasted so long.

"No wonder you guys are in this mess. Hello?! *I'm* your clue!" I exclaim like they should know better.

"What do you mean, Stone?" Lincoln asks curiously, his full focus on me.

"Isn't it obvious? I mean, have any of you guys followed up on why The Society went after *me* of all people?" All I get are blank stares, infuriating me further. "Oh my God! Are you serious right now? Guys, I'm no one of importance. That's your first clue. Why would such an elitist, secret society waste their time on me, when I'm no threat to them. It doesn't make sense."

I throw my arms up, amazed that they didn't follow up on such a flagrant clue. All three men look at Lincoln, his placating smile not offering me the same solace as it seems to offer the rest of them.

"There's your answer right there, Stone. They are the elite. Maybe someone up in the ranks didn't like seeing a girl from the other side of the tracks being successful, making something out of herself," Lincoln concludes assuredly. "I'd say it's enough for them to have you on their radar."

"That's just one possibility, but what if you're wrong?"

Lincoln's eyes soften, and I hate that he's not giving my insight a second thought.

"Thank you for not turning your back on Finn after he told you the truth. Not every woman would stand by her man's side when faced with such adversity. But leave The

Society to us, Stone. Don't get involved more than you already are. For Finn's sake."

At the mention of his name, Finn holds onto my waist even tighter, afraid The Society will waltz into Lincoln's kitchen and take me away from him.

"I'll protect her."

"Oh, yeah? And who protects you? That's my job, Finn. So excuse me if I want to make sure you guys are doing everything in your power to eradicate these fuckers," I holler adamantly, unimpressed anyone in this room could ever deem me to be a helpless damsel in distress in need of sheltering.

"Now I see why you two get along. She's got some mouth on her," Colt taunts, leaning against the counter.

I point my finger at him, ready to rip him a new one, but Finn just pushes me away before I have a chance to have my say.

"I think this is enough for one night. I'm going to take my girl out for some real food and come back later."

I'm about to protest, but I then remember why I came over in the first place, so I turn around in Finn's embrace to get him on board.

"Wait. Your mom wants you to move back home."

"You talked to my mom?" Finn asks, surprised.

I nod and take another look around the large house. Sure, it may look like a trillion dollars, but somehow even my mom's trailer feels much safer in comparison.

"I did. I think she's right, Finn."

Pretty boy's face saddens as he shakes his head, refusing to move out.

"I can't go back. And before you say anything, it has nothing to do with my father. If I go back, The Society will think they didn't succeed in their pesky punishment, and they might retaliate. I can't risk it. We shouldn't even be seen together, brat. Just in case they're watching us."

Now it's my turn to shake my head.

"That's not happening. You don't want to move back home, fine. But like hell, are we going to hide from them. It's you and me from here on out, quarterback. Got it?"

He bends down and presses a sweet, tender kiss on my lips, keeping it PG since we got three pairs of eyes on us. "I got it, brat," he breathes into my mouth, his smile splitting his face in two.

I take a step back and tilt my head just enough to look at the other men in the room, but mainly at the one who owns it.

"If Finn is staying here, then expect to see much more of me."

"Wouldn't have it any other way," Lincoln replies in earnest. "As I said, you're family now, Stone."

"Well, I guess every family has skeletons in their closet, right? I guess it's better to know what ours are up front. Come on, pretty boy. It's time you feed me."

I give them all a curt nod before taking Finn's hand and rushing us out of the mansion. The instant the cool autumn breeze hits my face, I feel like I can breathe again. There was too much tension inside, something they have all been living with long before The Society paid a visit to them.

I know Lincoln thinks he can get to the bottom of who their blackmailers are, but I think he isn't looking in the right places. It wouldn't bother me so much if it were only his life on the line, but it's Finn's, too. Unlike Finn, I have no unconditional bond to any one of them, so my view on their predicament is clearer as an outsider. My only concern is pretty boy. Nothing, and no one else, matters to me.

"Was that too much for you in there?" Finn asks as we walk over to my truck. "You look stressed and unusually quiet."

"No. I'm fine," I mumble, playing with my tongue ring as I continue to contemplate what I should do.

Finn stops halfway to my car and pulls me into his arms, raising my chin gently with his knuckles.

"Then why do I see the gears turning inside that beautiful head of yours?"

"Do you think Lincoln is right? That The Society just picked me by chance?"

"Hmm. Honestly, I don't know." He shrugs.

"Don't you want to find out?"

"And put you through more hell? No. That will be a hard pass for me."

"But they are still blackmailing you. This is not over for them."

"So let them. As long as you aren't anywhere in their crosshairs, then I don't care what happens next."

"Finn, they tried to ruin your life," I counter, wanting him to see reason.

"And they failed. They didn't take away what I value most. So, nothing they can do will hurt me," he says, trying to console me.

However comforting his words may sound, they could well turn out to be empty promises if The Society manages to take away his freedom. I can't let that happen.

"Stone, don't. I see that beautiful mind of yours already at work. I don't want you to do something we will both regret, just to protect me. I mean it, Stone. You are too damn important."

"And you're important to me. Your life isn't less valuable than mine."

Finn bends down, cupping my face in his hands, love and devotion painted beautifully in his sapphire eyes.

"Yes it is, brat. I'd give my life a million times over if it could keep yours safe. Promise me you'll leave The Society alone. Please, for me?" he pleads imploringly, playing with my heartstrings, displaying true fear in his eyes.

"I promise," I whisper lovingly, and he leans in to seal the vow with a kiss, unaware of the crossed fingers behind my back.

Finn is mine, and like hell will I let The Society have him.

They have no idea who they fucked with, but they will.

I guarantee it.

EPILOGUE

I turn off the ignition and just stay in my seat, admiring the pitiful view between two familiar cars a few rows in front of me in the school parking lot. I lean into the steering wheel, hugging it to my chest, my chin rubbing against the black vinyl as I smile at the wondrous, pathetic sight.

Look at them.

All huddled up together, whispering amongst themselves in hushed tones and fearful intonations. I watch in delight how one of them looks over his shoulder every once in a while, afraid of unknown lurkers. It's a true testament of how they've become scared of their own fucking shadows.

The tug of my smile only broadens as I watch Finn frantically pace back and forth, the little Southie whore next to him, unable to keep his temper in check.

How the mighty have fallen.

For someone who acted as if he were above it all, untouchable and remorseless, he sure doesn't seem so confident now. Just goes to show, anyone can be brought down. Even a God—as he proclaimed himself to be—can fall from grace if you pull at him hard enough.

Finn fumes and curses, only increasing his irate state with each word he utters, while his sidekick beside him just keeps chain-smoking, one cancer stick at a time, pretending he's unaffected by their little intimate convo. Easton tries to keep the facade of looking cool and collected for his friends' benefit, but the way he pinches the end of his cigarette butt and throws it to the ground, demolishing it with the heel of his boot, tells me all I need to know—he's just as anxious and rattled as his simple-minded friend.

But he's not the only one. There's another brittle spirit begging to be broken.

Right beside them stands Colt, wearing his cold, sinister mask—the one he likes to proudly flaunt to show his superiority. His soul is covered in filth and carnage, and yet he acts as if all that ugliness doesn't touch the crown on his head. The sneer of his pursed lips alludes to an inner aloofness he does not possess. Even his friend's meltdown seems to be a nuisance to him. Or at least that's what he wants them to believe.

My sinister smile broadens, watching his fake elaborate pretense.

Colt's icy exterior doesn't fool me for a minute. I've spent years deciphering such expressions, so I know when they aren't genuine. The way his eyes slant and his nose flares may look like signs of annoyance to the untrained eye, however I know they are nothing but schooled features he's perfected over time to mask his true inner turmoil.

What better camouflage is there than to act superior to a threat? Most enemies would bow out when confronted by such a fearless foe.

But it's just a smokescreen, one I can see right through. Just as I can see through all of their wretched souls.

The only one who still looks like he has it together is fucking Lincoln. I suck in my teeth as I watch him console his friends, offering hope when there is none. He's the beacon of light in their infested, grimy, black hole, and I, for one, cannot wait to extinguish it once and for all.

But not yet.

If I want to make him bleed, break his spirit as he broke mine, I have to be patient. Asheville's golden boy will get his turn soon enough.

Your time will come, Linc. I promise you that.

I need to hurt everyone that he loves, and make sure their pain keeps him up at night, consuming him with guilt and shame. His friends are his weakness, and therefore, mine to exploit. By the time I finally come for him, Lincoln will have very little hope to hold onto, much less offer to anyone else. I'll reveal his true colors to everyone who looked at him as the second coming and the pride of the Richfield name.

He's not. He's the blemish that ruined such an iconic legacy, the last one standing when he should have been the first to fall. I'll make sure to rectify fate's macabre plan into something of my doing, something of my liking. Saving the best for last has never tasted so sweeter.

My eyes fall once again onto the twisted group and take joy in seeing them cringe in despair.

They are all running scared.

Good.

Let them be worried. What I have destroyed in Finn's life is just a little taste of what they have coming.

As I watch the fucking Southie take center stage, giving her own opinion in their little get together, my jaw locks in place. I can't help but feel the pinch of disappointment that my carefully thought out plans didn't play out as well as I'd expected. It never crossed my mind the Southie slut would have gotten her claws into Finn the way she did. I knew he was a gullible idiot, but I always assumed he had some sense.

Guess not.

Finn is more of a fool than I gave him credit for, considering his intention of keeping that skank at his side. Oh well. It suits me just fine. She's nothing but Southside trailer trash, and she will never be accepted as anything more. Let's see Hank Walker trying to spin this shit into gold to save face. As I see it, Finn carrying on with Stone Bennett will just make his life harder, and until I put them all out of their wretched misery, his hardship is well-deserved. Judging by his erratic troubled state, I know he's just one push away from unraveling completely.

I bite into my inner cheek, hard and unyielding, to keep the bubbling laughter of victory confined within me. It's still early on in my grand plan, and as much as their visible desolation pleases me, there is still plenty more in store for them. Only after I have demolished every dream they've ever had, have every hope and want eliminated, and their lives and reputations ruined beyond repair, will I allow myself to bask in my triumph. Until then, there is work to be done.

One down.

Three to go.

I open the glove compartment, and as I retrieve one of the many black envelopes destined for the sham of a dark prince, an instant noxious thrill races through my veins. Gripping the rich, rectangular stationery in my hand, my eyes find the next target—Easton Price. He'll be my next little plaything to toy with in my merciless game of revenge and retribution. It pleases me how easy it will be to destroy him.

Easton is nothing but a big mama's boy with daddy issues, so it can't get any easier than that. I'll go for his heart, using his insecurities against him. Before he knows what hit him, I'll steal the life he so imprudently spits on now. I'll take it all away from him, leaving him grasping at straws, disgraced and humiliated. I'll make it my mission to return the dark prince from where he should have never left—in the gutter, penniless, and without worth of any kind.

But like Finn, I'll first have Easton take care of another pesky nuisance of mine. Killing two birds with one stone, so to speak. I have just the person in mind who will make sure Easton loses his. I'll tug at his heartstrings, make them shrivel to ash, ensuring he truly becomes the black soul he proclaims himself to be.

I'll leave him with nothing.

No life. No future. No heart.

He will rue the day he and his friends tried to do the same to me.

Ready or not, Easton, your time has come.

TO BE CONTINUED IN

HEAR NO EVIL.

Thank you so much for reading See No Evil.

If you enjoyed it, please consider leaving an honest review.

It may only take you a minute to write, but reviews are what get books noticed by other readers.

By writing a small review, you are opening the door for my love stories to be enjoyed by so many others.

If you liked the suspense, twists, and turns of See No Evil, then check out another book baby of mine with just as much angst-filled love written in its pages:

Heartless — The Privileged of Pembroke High

Hope you give this baby a go.

I'd also love it if you would check out my author page:
https://www.facebook.com/IvyFoxAuthor

And I invite you to join my Facebook group, Ivy's Sassy Foxes:
https://www.facebook.com/groups/188438678547691

Much Love,

Ivy
XOXO

Ivy Fox Novels

The Society
See No Evil

The Privileged of Pembroke High
Heartless
Soulless
Faithless

Rotten Love Duet
Rotten Girl
Rotten Men
Rotten Love Boxset

Bad Influence Series
Her Secret
Archangels MC

After Hours Series
The King

Standalone
Breathe Me

ACKNOWLEDGMENTS

It's amazing how I can write a four hundred page book, and this is the part I struggle with. Whatever words I write here, will never measure up to the true gratitude I feel for everyone involved in the making of the See No Evil book and helping me through my author journey.

But I'm going to try.

To the two men in my life, my kiddo and my husband—thank you for always believing in me and loving me unconditionally. Even when I'm a hot mess, wearing three-day-old pajamas and my hair hasn't seen a brush in days, just because I was on a roll writing a sexy-ass scene. I know it's not easy sharing me with all the voices in my head, but I'm so thankful you boys nurture my craziness instead of resenting how it takes time away from you. I love you both so much, and I thank God every day for having you in my life.

A huge thank you goes out to my editor, Heather Clark, who kicked butt trying to meet my deadlines even under quarantine conditions. Thank you, sweetheart, for all the hard work you do in all my book babies. You make my words shine.

To my lovely and patient-as-hell PA, Courtney Dunham—thank you for putting up with my wacky ways and disorganization. You make my life run smoothly when I desperately need it to.

I also want to send out a huge hug to Michelle Lancaster for the beautiful photo of Lochie Carey used in the cover, which was ultimately my muse for Finn. I'm in awe of your talented eye. Thank you for entrusting me with this beauty.

To my betas—Marjolein Van Laere, Laura Marrero, and Jenny Dicks, thank you for your input and enthusiasm while reading See No Evil in its first draft. It made all the difference.

A huge freaking hug goes out to Ashlee Little and Laura Frazier for your edits and teasers while I was still writing Stone and Finn's story. They gave me LIFE! You were able to capture the feel of this book perfectly, and whenever the words weren't flowing, all I had to do was to see one of these babies to inspire me.

To all the bloggers that had shared their love for this book, even when it wasn't out yet. Thank you so much for spreading the word. You have no idea how thankful I am for having your support.

My last thank you goes out to my Sassy Foxes, my ride-or-die tribe. Your love, loyalty, and unconditional support is every writer's dream. Thank you for always being by my side, and I hope you stay with me as we continue on this adventure together. I know I couldn't do this without you.

With lots of love and gratitude,

Ivy
XOXO

ABOUT THE AUTHOR

Lover of books, coffee, and chocolate ice cream!

Ivy lives a blessed life, surrounded by her two most important men—her husband, and son—and also the fictional characters in her head that can't seem to shut up.

Books and romance are her passion.

A strong believer in happy endings and that love will always prevail in the end.

Both in life and in fiction.

Printed in Great Britain
by Amazon